I0662533

Private
Lines

Emma Gates

Wells Street Press

Private Lines

PART ONE

France 2003

One

TYLER HARDING WAS TIRED.
More than tired, he realized as he dressed this morning in Paris. He actually felt weak, debilitated by eyelid-scraping, memory-erasing, cheer-sucking exhaustion.

But this was usual.

Nine cities in fourteen days. Bland conference rooms, strong coffee, hasty meals, his best suits. He'd expensed more dry cleaning than food. By now, nearly every piece carried a patina of sturdy guest-worker handprints as his clothing was pressed in Amsterdam, Budapest, Copenhagen and so on. Finally he had worked his way to Paris—his last and most important destination.

He straightened his tie in the hotel mirror. Tilted Systane into his jet-lagged eyes, used to the chill. Tried to wake up his reflection with a big white smile.

Here I am! Birth of a salesman.

If I can close FranceFon—especially that woman delaying my deal.

He halved his smile and lowered his eyelids, to project chilly composure.

She was new to a team he had already sold. He had to persuade her, as he'd persuaded the rest of her group, that his company—GlobeAll—was best suited to increase FranceFon's share of the lucrative U.S. telecoms market.

FranceFon was the biggest fish on his line: a conglomerate controlling thousands of miles of fiber around the globe, the monopoly carrier in France, now in serious financial trouble—at least, trouble that would seem serious to any company *not* subsidized by its government. "*Trance*Fon," his U.S. co-workers joked, of what they saw as the company's laissez-faire attitude regarding their fiscal straits. But he knew how dearly telecom workers in Europe valued their lifelong employment and how treacherous any attempt to disturb the status quo could be. Not my problem right now, he reminded himself. For once. His deal would increase FranceFon's profitability in North America. No negative impact to local French workers.

He went down for breakfast. On most trips, it was his only real meal of the day, unless he was entertaining prospects.

"Café, Monsieur?" asked the pretty young server who came to his table.

"Au lait, merci."

She smiled as she poured hot milk from one pitcher, coffee from another, into a wide cup. He was used to women's smiles, but he could not muster even a nod for her.

He rubbed his aching eyelids. *Three more days and I'll be home free.*

Ha!

Home free? His un-lived-in, undecorated Manhattan apartment, where mail would be piled into yet another unwanted task, did not feel like home.

Home meant his office, with the pent-up crises his team could not or would not solve without him, according to the hundreds of e-mails they sent him daily.

Home meant wrestling with a missed deadline for a renewal with TeleOne, a Canadian telco whose contract had him on edge: he needed more time to scrutinize its commercial terms. The original dealmaker had been a close friend—GlobeAll Canada's manager Nick Fournier. He hated remembering Nick's death at Tower Two, but he would always regret not having returned Nick's last call wherein Tyler heard 'TeleOne' mentioned. Forget following up on that now, a year and a half later.

Home meant prepping for the upcoming annual Global Traffic Meeting where the world's next subsea cables would be planned.

In spite of worldwide recession, business scandals, and terrorism, global bandwidth demand was greater than he'd known in ten years in the industry. And it felt like his company held him responsible for supplying all of it.

He forced himself to sit up straight and sip coffee.

A young couple sat down nearby. He watched them over the rim of his cup as they leaned into each other. Their body language spoke of new love, that all-encompassing, almost aromatic arousal.

How long since he'd experienced that? He couldn't remember. He barely had time to say hello to women anymore, let alone date them. Tomorrow was February 14th. Valentine's Day. Years since it meant anything to him.

The French girl's long blonde hair reminded him of Julee, his ex-wife: a fellow international MBA student at Thunderbird; he'd tutored her in intermediate Arabic. He'd admired her looks, her smarts, her ambition.

He'd married in haste, anointed by parental and societal approval, with only one skeptic—his old buddy Nick—advising patience.

He'd repented without leisure: he and Julee worked nonstop. What they'd shared in sunny Arizona hadn't lasted in serious New York City. They didn't reconnect on the rushed, errand/laundry/latest-new-restaurant weekends. They barely had time to make love. They hardly even pissed each other off.

"You don't *let* yourself get pissed off, Tyler," she'd snapped at him during one of their few arguments. "You just get all superior. Then you shut down."

"So?" He'd been annoyed that she wanted to waste time with inanities.

"See?" she challenged, one hand on her hip, the other flapping a dishcloth at him: they'd been squabbling about doing the damn dishes.

EMMA GATES

"There you go!" she shouted as he left the room. "You're a friggin robot!"

They divorced in less than ten months.

In the six years since, he'd hardly thought of his failed marriage, in spite of Julee's advice about considering his 'intimacy skills.' He had short-termers with women who understood he had no cycles to burn on maintenance.

Soul-searching wasn't on his very long, very pressing customer-driven list.

Back in fiscal 99-00—when GlobeAll, like many companies, could not keep enough good workers— Corporate Communications had issued a number of touchy-feely platitudes about work-life balance.

He'd told his direct reports, then, to ignore that and focus on business.

But when he tried to get a dog, it occurred to him, one typically lonely Saturday—he hated weekends, hated the word 'lonely'—how off-kilter his life was: he did not qualify at the local animal shelter. Some prim volunteer told him, when he called to inquire, his travel schedule wouldn't allow an animal to 'appropriately bond,' whatever the hell that meant. He'd been forced to recognize his limitations: he could not give emotional support even to a dog! But every Monday his wish—and its ache—were buried quickly.

The funny thing was, he *liked* his work, when he freed himself from micro crises long enough to care about the macro picture. He got a huge kick out of seeing hidebound executives, U.S. and 'foreign,' open up and approach each other to reach common ground. He picked up new words in each new country. When he wasn't feeling harassed, every encounter was a delight.

If only he weren't so fucking tired.

And it would be great to have a big friendly dog to welcome him home and romp around in Central Park.

Tyler became aware of the couple opposite him once more, of the boy's cold stare. He'd been letting his gaze rest on the girl, not realizing it. He swallowed the last of

4

his coffee, stepped out onto the rainy street, and flagged a taxi to take him to FranceFon's headquarters.

He studied the driver's name and photo and made eye contact through the rearview mirror. Hamid Bouchir. Must be North African. Tyler chatted in Arabic, enough to elicit a friendly smile and learn that Hamid had been a student, briefly, in Louisiana, but had settled in Paris where his wife's family lived: not a U.S. fan anymore.

Tyler's habit of checking drivers had become a reflex since he'd been cab-napped last year in South Africa. He'd escaped by giving up his mobile and briefcase, refusing his laptop but letting the driver keep his shoes. It was just money. He now kept a decent amount of local currency in his pocket, just in case. He figured his life was worth it.

Two

INSIDE THE FRANCEFON conference room, Tyler stood in front of Didier Terrell, Duc Nguyen, Youssef Hamzi, and Octavio Novoa, managers responsible for alliances in Europe, Asia, the Middle East and Latin America.

Although the men had developed rapport during the weeks of conference calls, Tyler's agreement closure depended on the unknown North American manager—and her lateness created a bubble of tension in the room.

Duc and Youssef, young men, were checking their handheld devices. Didier and Octavio, older, lit cigarettes. He'd lose them in another minute. Where *was* she?

His back was to the door, so he did not see their final participant enter, but the rich scent of her perfume preceded her.

He turned, put on a slight smile, and held out his hand. "Tyler Harding, GlobeAll Alliance Management. Bonjour."

"Bonjour. Welcome to FranceFon. Delphine de la Plante." Her lightly accented voice was softer than her severe expression and suit. She was a rounded woman, medium height; he'd guess late thirties, with dark hair and eyes. Her plump little hand filled his, warm as a live bird, and as their eyes met, he felt a jolt of awareness. He ignored it.

He launched into his presentation. Since the room was stuffy with smoke now, and they were fifteen minutes into their allotted hour, he kept it brief, only showing the maps of GlobeAll's worldwide network and expansion plans.

"We've engineered our network to be bulletproof," he concluded. "We've deployed lightwave division multiplexing in our fiber, and we've extended our Tier One internet backbone into major markets worldwide."

He looked at each one, studying body language and facial expressions, and concluding he'd better make this quick. "But you know this. The analysts, strategic planners, and legal departments of both our companies know this alliance makes good business sense. They agree we're a perfect complement to each other."

He turned off the projector and sat down on their side of the table. "The only thing standing in the way of lucrative new markets for both of us is our companies' inability—since they're waiting for the confirmation of *this* group—to finalize the geographic terms of the agreement."

He smiled, showing his teeth for the first time. "Let's do what's best for our companies and close this deal." He leaned back and folded his hands on the table. He looked around at each of them. He waited.

Ms. De la Plante was the first to speak. "You must know we don't like to tie ourselves to only one U.S. carrier. We have agreements with several."

"Of course we'll allow you to honor those that are outstanding. We can work out reciprocity in terms of market share."

"We'd like to know how could we lease some of your Turkish capacity," said Youssef Hamzi, the Middle East manager. "We need dark fiber right now. Could we accommodate that in a new market arrangement?"

Dark fiber in Turkey was hot right now, with war in Iraq on the horizon.

"Probably," Tyler said. He knew why FranceFon needed it. He figured he could afford to sell them some, in the spirit of cooperation.

"We wondered about your Latin America network," said Octavio Novoa. "We didn't light our facility in Caracas yet."

"Ours has been up since last year," Tyler told them. "We just engineered disaster recovery so the labor strikes couldn't affect us."

Novoa nodded slowly.

"Buenos Aires is a different story," Tyler went on. "We didn't hedge our investments against the devaluation, so we're pushing that launch out three more quarters." And he wouldn't give them even a kilobit: Latin America was off limits.

"We have heard that your debt rating has worsened recently," de la Plante said in a cool voice, surveying him with her large dark eyes.

"We've *restructured* our debt," he corrected. "We're forecasting a cash flow positive state by the end of the first half." He kept his expression just as cool as he looked at her. "Not many U.S. carriers could do the same right now, as you know."

He'd done his homework on her. Her former employer was United Telecom and Telephone, known as UTT; a major U.S. telco and a huge competitor to GlobeAll. But UTT had suffered financial setbacks in its Canadian and Mexican ventures and had posted larger than expected losses last year.

"You invested too heavily, perhaps, in your domestic wireless sectors," she mused.

This was a sore point for Tyler. He didn't have any reach into GlobeAll's wireless segment, and so could not express his frustration at their choice of CDMA technology, which was currently limited to the States and a handful of other countries. GlobeAll had, essentially, no global wireless play. He saw it as a huge competitive disadvantage. So, obviously, did Ms. De la Plante.

"It's our fastest growing segment," he countered. "The ROI proved out beyond analyst expectations."

"It is a gap in your global portfolio."

"Our core competency is unaffected."

"But your core competency is limited to fiber optics."

"Not limited to. Focused on. Specialized in." He was getting a little annoyed. If she was going to stand in the way of this agreement, he'd have to go beyond her to push it through. That was more time wasted. He'd allotted only two days here to wrap this up.

He let some warmth into his eyes as he looked at her. "But, given your concerns, we can have both our legal departments draw up an intellectual property agreement, allowing our R&D divisions to develop a joint wireless project."

Which would take a millennium: intellectual property was the most hotly contested component of any strategic alliance, on which the French were notorious for dragging their feet. He counted on her knowing that any new legal discussion was pointless. It would further bog down the already-stalled negotiations, and she would be blamed if her caveats caused that to happen. He let his smile grow.

"Legal," she sighed. She shrugged, a small movement of her neatly suited shoulders, and the gold pendant on her necklace winked at her throat. He couldn't see what the pendant was, but he wasn't going to risk a closer peek. She smiled back at him, for the first time, generating sparkles in the depth of her eyes. He ignored, again, the unexpected jolt she gave him. He would not let himself be distracted, not here, and certainly not by this woman.

Hamzi's pager beeped and he looked at his watch.

"I must go," he murmured. "Thank you for coming, Tyler, it's good to meet you in person. I'll follow up with you on this Turkish matter."

"Sure, we'll be in touch." Tyler rose to shake hands. His hour was over.

Ms. De la Plante was the last to leave. "You have been meeting this group for some time?" she asked.

"Several weeks of conference calls."

"But this is your first time ... to come to our office?"

Was she going to hold that against him? "For this project, yes, but our corporate execs have met often, here at FranceFon and at our own Paris office." He kept his smile casual but chilled his tone. "We've all been under the impression that my meeting here is just a formality, to work out geographic details."

"Perhaps you will want to spend more time with us."

"I'm sure none of us have that time, Ms. De la Plante. I'd asked everyone to lunch, when we arranged this meeting, but they weren't free." He wasn't going to ask her if she was free. He wasn't going to give her a chance to waylay the proceedings by asking for an extension.

"Call me Delphine." She studied him for a moment. "We are having a customer event tonight. Perhaps you will like to attend."

Meet their customers before the alliance was even announced?

"We do not have to refer to the proposed partnership," she added quickly.

"Will any other carriers be there?"

"No, it is for our local customers in the financial community. To show them our gratitude for their loyalty, during this last difficult year." FranceFon's service in-country had suffered due to strikes following the announcement of telecom privatization. French telecom workers thought of themselves as civil servants, guaranteed lifelong jobs, and they protested violently when this was challenged. Their opposition to FranceFon's IPO had actually forced a delay in the country's general election.

"What kind of event?" He had to get out of this gracefully.

"It is a showing, at Versailles, one of the wings is open for us." She smiled again. "It will be a nice evening, but short, just two hours. Not a dinner."

The last thing he wanted to do was drag himself all the way out to Versailles on a rainy night to stand around with FranceFon's domestic base, useless to GlobeAll, and this difficult woman. "That sounds … interesting, Delphine."

"It is a chance for you to know us a little better, Mr. Harding."

"Call me Tyler, please. It's gracious of you to invite me."

"We will have a minibus, to take us from here, we leave about six o'clock. I will have a badge made for you. Tell me your mobile number, just in case?"

He came around the table to hand her his card, watched as she took it. Her pendant was a quarter moon, resting above what looked like deep cleavage covered by her modest cream-colored blouse. He snapped his gaze to her face.

"I will see you out, Tyler."

"Thank you, Delphine."

She waited while he unplugged his laptop and packed it in its case. As she led the way out to the elevators he watched her walk—her hips' solid flow was too intriguing not to admire—and he heard a swishing noise he could only conclude was her stockinged thighs rubbing against each other.

He suddenly felt wide awake.

Three

ALTHOUGH IT WAS NOT FAR AWAY, he took another cab (Salem Aboud, Lebanese, claimed to be pro-U.S.) to GlobeAll's Paris office, half a floor in a small office building in the Right Bank, 14th Arrondissemont. The lingering impression of Delphine's scent, smile and walk was immediately eclipsed by the pressing business of checking with the local staff for the latest GlobeAll network updates, and the current performance of their partner networks.

There had been a major outage at GlobeAll's internet node in Singapore and he attended a long phone meeting to dissect the problem with the Singapore team. He finally let them go when it was past 9 pm, Singapore time.

He called the U.S. network headquarters to reiterate the Asian fixes needed. Although he wasn't responsible for Network, he always re-confirmed what was discussed on international conference calls. Often, Stateside engineers were too proud to admit they didn't understand accents across the globe.

He grabbed a Coke from the office vending machine and walked around the floor for a few minutes, gulping it and clearing his head. He rolled his shoulders and stretched.

Then he checked his e-mail, racing through as fast as possible by answering quickly, delegating, or deleting, but that was only good for about two hundred of them. The other sixty were thornier problems or issues, requiring more careful research, query or thought. He'd plowed through the top forty by four o'clock.

Jack Rigby, one of the best engineers GlobeAll had in Europe, stopped by the cube where Tyler was parked. He dropped a bag of pretzels onto Tyler's laptop.

"Didn't see you leaving for lunch, Ty, figured you could use something."

"Thanks Jack. As usual, I didn't have time for lunch."

"As usual, you're welcome for dinner." Jack's wife, Marie, was a fabulous cook. Tyler usually tried to dine with them on his twice-yearly Paris visits.

"I'm really tempted, Jack, but I have a biz thing with FF."

"Big biz thing?"

"Big enough."

"A closer for the final agreement?"

"It better be."

"You sound grim, Ty, you running into road blocks at this late stage?"

"You have no idea."

"Tell me." Jack perched on the edge of the cube.

"The new North American manager's biased. UTT background."

Unlike many engineers, Jack understood sales. "You figure that's why they brought him in? Trying for balance?"

"She. Maybe they brought her in to shake things up, but UTT's financials are a lot less stable than ours. We make a better partner and they know it."

"So she's what, putting the brakes on?"

"Going over old ground." Tyler grimaced, recalling his morning meeting. "Rest of the team's heard it already. They were on board before she showed up."

"But she gets the final say?"

"She's North America's manager, our HQ is North America, it's her deal."

"So why don'cha take her to dinner, do some sweet talking?"

"I don't have time to fuck around," Tyler snapped.

Jack's brows lowered. He stood. "Jeez, Ty, it was just a thought."

"Yeah, I know, Jack." Tyler heaved a sigh. "Sorry. It's not you. It's this damn alliance!" He made the effort to grin up at Jack.

"You need a little R&R, dude. You're testy." Jack checked his watch. "I'll buy you a drink. Give you some juice to deal with the bitch tonight."

"You're on."

Tyler followed Jack out of the office. The rain had tapered into a light mist that gave the darkening streets a nostalgic glisten, making it look like the Paris of old black and white movies.

Tyler noticed a few flower sellers, pitching bouquets with hearts attached to them: Valentine's Day in the city of romance.

In a bar nearby, Tyler's vodka burned relief clear through him. "Jack, you're right. I *am* testy."

"You need to take some time off. How long's it been?"

Tyler had gone home to see his parents in Colorado for a rushed three-day Christmas trip. It hadn't seemed like vacation, in spite of one good day on the slopes with his dad. "Can't. Too much going on."

"But if you wrap up this deal—"

"Yeah, maybe."

"You owe it to yourself, man. I'm sorry to say, you look like shit."

"Thanks."

"I mean, you look like you haven't slept in a year."

"That's about right."

"So you can't function that way." Jack signaled the bartender for two more. "Tell you what. Marie's uncle has a cottage in the country that he lets us use. Stay the weekend instead of flying back tomorrow. You can borrow his place to unwind for a couple days. No phone, no friggin e-mail. Hiking trails nearby. Sound good?"

It sounded like heaven. He shook his head with real regret.

"At least think about it, if you close this deal."

They finished their shots. "Good luck with the UTT-planted bitch," Jack said as he dropped some Euros onto the bar.

"She's not a bitch," Tyler said slowly, remembering Delphine more charitably now he had some vodka in him. "She's hot, tell you the truth."

"So make her come around for you, they always do."

"I'm not the player I used to be. I'm too old for that now."

"Yeah, an old man of what, thirty five?"

"Thirty-four. Going on seventy."

"You look it. I'm tellin ya, slow down."

"I'll slow down when I'm dead."

They walked out into the cold humid evening. The streetlamps made the wet pavement gleam. More flower sellers were out, catching the rush hour.

Tyler took a white rose, with a little red foil heart attached.

"Whad'ya think Jack, too corny? Too suggestive?"

"Yeah," said Jack, and he bought one too. "American tradition."

"I can't give this to her in front of anyone, it'd look stupid."

"Here." Jack reached into his briefcase for a GlobeAll France envelope. "The perfect disguise."

"Ha." Tyler tucked the envelope, with rose, into his inside coat pocket. "I'll say it's an addendum to the agreement. Tell her she's got 24 hours to respond."

"Giving you exclusive rights to ... her territory." Jack smirked.

"Thanks, Jack. For the drinks and the advice."

"Anytime, pal."

Tyler walked to the FranceFon office, enjoying the freshness of the damp air and the bustle of pedestrians, who stopped in the lighted small shops lining the sidewalk for wine, fruits, pastries, meat and cheese pies. He was hungry. Delphine said tonight wasn't a dinner, and it would be a long round trip to Versailles. He bought a meat pie and walked along, eating it on the street like an ugly American, wiping his hands and mouth on its doily. Delicious.

Four

His MOOD WAS MUCH BETTER on entering FranceFon's building the second time. *Maybe I should drink more often,* he thought, looking around the lobby for the alliance group. He spotted Novoa and Hamzi and went over to say hello.

He and Hamzi were just finishing their greetings when Delphine arrived.

"You speak Arabic?" she asked Tyler, sounding surprised.

"Just enough to get into trouble." He turned his attention to her, pouring charm into his smile. "You're kind to include me tonight, Delphine."

"You're welcome. I thought it's the least we can do, since we did not offer you even a lunch."

"I don't need lunch." He kept smiling. "I just need a final agreement."

She looked down into her briefcase, pulled out a FranceFon badge with his name on it, and clipped it to his lapel. He felt the light pressure of her fingertips and smelled, once again, her faint perfume. She gave his shoulder the lightest pat after fixing the badge, a pat that made him take a quick surprised breath.

Didier Terrell and Duc Nguyen joined them, bringing a number of local business owners and domestic FranceFon executives. About twenty people settled in for the forty-five minute ride through the Paris suburbs. Tyler sat behind Novoa, who was chatting with a client. Delphine, after minutes with a customer in front, came to sit next to Tyler.

17

He nodded hello. He hadn't decided what approach to take. He wanted an inkling of how she was leaning, so that he could either consider the agreement closed or strategize his next moves beyond her. It was the only reason he was doing this time-wasting little field trip. But he didn't know her well enough, yet, to choose either subtlety or directness.

She crossed her legs. He glimpsed her skirt rising on her knee.

"So, Tyler, are you in Paris often?"

"Couple of times a year. Do you come to the States a lot?"

"Not as much as I used to. But I don't mind less travel. It can be very tiring."

"Tell me about it." He smiled. "This is my ninth city in two weeks."

"Then I am even more grateful that you come out with us tonight."

"I wouldn't miss the opportunity to talk to you. You're the only one I didn't meet before, on our calls. I want to make sure you're comfortable with every aspect of this agreement."

She glanced away, then up at him again. "And have you been successful, in the other cities?"

"Yes." He smiled more broadly, raising his brows in a slight challenge.

"So, the other carriers you make alliances with, they are accommodating to you? I mean, to GlobeAll?"

"Yes they are." He kept his tone light, but gave each word emphasis. "They know our network, and our market reach."

"Mmm."

He decided to be direct. "Can you tell me why you're not in favor of the agreement?"

She drew back. "What gives you this idea?"

"What can I do to convince you? If there's anything you need from me to make your decision easier, just let me know. Research, references, independent analysis." He leaned against the window, angling himself to face her. He brought his hands out, palms up, in the universal gesture of defeat. "I'm all yours, Delphine, but you have to give me some indication here."

"I thought you're in strategic alliances, not in sales." She laughed a little.

"Delphine. We're *all* in sales."

But he knew enough about his former-monopoly global counterparts to know they did not, in fact, see themselves as salespeople. Sales was ... crass. *They* were global telecom experts, they were cross-border negotiators, they were carrier-relations brokers. They were not "salespeople." Different culture. He could work around that attitude.

"Tell me about this event."

"It is to show one of our native treasures, of course, to busy people who might not otherwise take the time to appreciate art."

Art?

And the expected ROI? He put on an encouraging look.

"We know these customers experienced a lot of ... difficulty with us this year, with privatization, so we want to say thank you for those who are able to come. We would like to do this every three months."

Thank you? Every quarter? To customers who had no choice but to use FranceFon local services? He would never okay budget for some zero-return project like this. But he didn't allow a muscle of his face to reflect his critique. "Nice idea," he lied. "So why is the alliance group involved?"

"We want to show these local banks the reach of our strategic plan. Some of them may eventually grow, they might need international connectivity one day."

"Just think, Delphine," he said softly, leaning toward her. "They might need access to the best network in the United States one fine day, and *you* can take credit for FranceFon's ability to supply them."

"You *are* in sales, Tyler." Her laugh lit the sparkles in her eyes. She reached over and patted his arm.

Touch me again and I'll come up with another kind of sales pitch, he told her in his mind. Was she always this demonstrative?

"What's your background, Delphine?"

"I was with UTT International for the last fifteen years."

"And before that?"

"It was my first job in the industry."

A lifer: her UTT allegiance would be rock solid. "And you enjoyed it?"

"I did, but I did not like to be away from my son so much."

"Mmm." Her son! Married, children: automatic turnoff. But she wasn't wearing a wedding ring. "So this is a smaller territory for you, Delphine, less geographic range." FranceFon had less money than UTT for travel, of course. "All the more reason to expand with GlobeAll. You won't have to come to us. We'll come to you."

She pursed her mouth, in the unique Gallic way, showing a lush lower lip. "I know you are trying hard, Tyler, I appreciate this. But I feel too new to make up my mind so quickly, about this idea. I am with FranceFon just three weeks."

He stared out the window at the lights of Versailles approaching in the distance. Its outline was unmistakable. "I'm available whenever you need me, Delphine. I'll do anything I can to help you make the right decision." He wanted to say, I assume you're enough of a professional to be unbiased, but no one, in his experience, was that professional.

"Thank you," she said finally.

He sensed her scrutiny, but kept his gaze on the view outside.

Five

VERSAILLES WAS THE BEAUTIFUL monstrosity he remembered from previous visits. His favorite part was its extensive series of gardens. He thought he could slip away for a quick walk, once he'd made polite chat with the FranceFon execs.

The reception was held in a wing used by a long line of French princesses. A docent was on hand to describe the various art works. Tyler found himself impressed by the tour, the excellence of the Champagne brand, and the elegance of the light hors d'oeuvres buffet. Too bad his policy was not to eat or drink at short customer events. He wandered over to the nearest group of FranceFon people, whom Hamzi pointed out, and spent ten minutes with them praising the venue and hinting that GlobeAll would make an able co-host for similar events, once their partnership was finalized.

Duty completed, he ambled out of the wing, stopping to look at paintings so his escape would not be apparent. He remembered, from here, how to reach the nearest garden. He took a few turns through the grand ancient hallways, frowned on by portraits of French royalty, and was soon outside.

The sky had shed its cloudiness and the moon shone on the grounds before him. It was so rare for him to be outside that the rush of freedom was intoxicating. He strode the winding path, relishing the movement in his worn-out body. If he stayed away from the maze he should be back in plenty of time to finish the evening sociably.

He'd laid the groundwork for this alliance months ago and conducted every move. The sudden departure of Georges Deauville, the FranceFon broker for North America he'd been working with, was an unexpected blow to his plan—but nobody could argue with a heart attack. Deauville was recovering, but had retired.

Delphine de la Plante. What was she doing at UTT International for fifteen years, that he'd never heard of her? Fifteen years at one company signified either astronomical career leaps, the way his own trajectory had been at GlobeAll, or stuck-in-a-rut undesirability. She must be in her forties, older than he'd thought. She hadn't been in UTT's alliance group; he knew them all. Product management? Marketing? Not sales, that was clear from her manner.

He should have just asked her, instead of immediately trying to sell her.

He touched the GlobeAll envelope inside his pocket, outlining the rose with one finger. Would she think it was charming or calculated? He didn't want to make a wrong move. Still, she was a Frenchwoman: she would know she was appealing. This simple gesture wouldn't be misconstrued in France.

He wondered how she'd react if he went above her. He needed to uncover her mentor and their bias against his agreement. He needed to secure the right kind of pressure above her to force compliance—if he couldn't force her himself.

Maybe it'd be a good idea to query Youssef Hamzi on the bus ride into town, get the lay of the land. He felt closer to Youssef than to the others; they'd hit it off after discovering they were alums from Thunderbird, the international MBA school.

He glanced at his watch. Time to head back. He was warm enough, after his light exertion, to take off his navy trenchcoat and loop it over his shoulder on one finger. He strode through the topiary, not minding the dampness he could feel beginning to seep into his dress Ferragamos. The garden smelled sweet enough to drink. He missed so much in Manhattan; Central Park could never compare to his native Colorado where he so loved hiking, skiing, and rafting. But he'd resigned himself years ago to the trade-off entailed by success in corporate America: he could not even manage short getaways anymore. An evening walk like this was a gift.

To his surprise, Delphine was standing on the terrace he'd left, arms wrapped around her sides as if trying to keep warm. He bounded up the steps.

"Enjoying the fresh air? You look cold." Without thinking, he put his coat around her. The solidity of her shoulders felt good, but he didn't let his hands linger.

"I saw you leaving. I thought I should see you did not lose yourself."

Oops. She'd caught his hasty departure. "I know my way around here. The gardens are my favorite spot." He smiled down at her. "I hope it was okay for me to wander off."

"I am glad you liked your visit. You must have been here often."

"Often enough to remember the magnificence of this landscaping. I'm glad it stopped raining."

They stood side by side for a moment, looking out at the partly moonlit hillside. Statues gleamed, white sentinels recalling ages past, in the shadows.

"Beautiful, isn't it? Excuse me, Delphine, I need something from this pocket." He reached for the side of his coat, still draped around her shoulders, and plucked the envelope smoothly out. He handed it to her.

"This is a token of our American holiday tomorrow."

She took the envelope, with a dubious little frown, and another purse of that luscious lower lip. She slowly removed the rose, and stared at it as if she'd never seen one before. The shiny red foil heart attached to it twisted, spangling.

"This is for me?" She seemed to be reluctant to look at him. He saw a darkening in her cheeks. Uh-oh. She was embarrassed.

"We say, Happy Valentine's Day." He spoke quickly, to put her at ease. "We give out flowers, candy, cards. It's just for fun, a break in the long winter."

"I know about that." Finally she raised her eyes. They looked black in the moonlight, moving over his face with a caution even more watchful than she'd shown before. "You were thinking of me, when you bought this?"

Sometimes honesty was an okay policy. "Yes." He let his admiration show in a slow smile.

Her expression relaxed as he held her gaze; her mouth loosened into a tiny answering smile. "You are candid."

He nodded.

"You are not afraid, of how I might think about this?"

"Should I be afraid?"

"You are not, I think, the kind of salesman who uses tricks like this on a woman."

He laughed. "I don't need tricks."

"Not in sales?"

"And not on women."

She stroked the rose on the palm of one hand, studying him. Then she laughed a little too. "I believe you, but I am not sure that I should." She tapped his chest lightly with the flower. "Thank you. This is a sweet gift." She tucked it back into the envelope, back into his pocket. "Don't imagine that you can influence my decision in this way about our alliance, Tyler. But thank you, anyway."

She'd said 'our' alliance. Progress. "You're very welcome, Delphine."

"And now I think we need to go in?" She slipped off his coat and handed it back to him.

"You're the hostess." He refused to allow disappointment to color his tone as he followed her back inside. So she didn't want the rose. Didn't quite trust him. In the end, none of that mattered, did it? All that was supposed to matter was that she get on board with his agreement.

Six

H E SAT NEXT TO HAMZI when the bus boarded. "Nice event, Youssef."

Youssef nodded, yawning. Tyler was used to this. Out of management's or the customer's eye, or away from the immediate task at hand, everyone was usually only a couple of blinks from comatose.

"Think it'll produce a good return?" He didn't keep the smirk out of his question.

Youssef laughed shortly. *"Insha'allah."* "God willing" did not invariably signify hope.

"So who dreams up these time-wasters?"

"Not the alliance team, you know that. There's nothing in this for us."

"Then why do you have to show up?"

"We're putting on our international face."

"Why do local bankers care?"

Youssef eyed him. "Some of them have international operations. Not that we can sell, Tyler, don't give me that look."

"So who's selling them?"

Youssef sighed. "I might as well tell you, there's talk of a possible alliance with UTT." He held up one hand at Tyler's expression. "Not to the extent of the GlobeAll agreement, no co-marketing or co-distribution. More an expansion of our existing bilateral arrangements."

Tyler stared at Youssef, hiding his fury. He needed to hear this.

"You know they have the strongest private line portfolio." Private lines were dedicated bandwidth connections between two points. They were the favored link, because of their security, in the financial industry. Youssef continued, "They've really invested in end-to-end capabilities. They built out to 23 foreign cities last year."

"And that's why you're wooing the financial community here? Because of UTT?"

"We have to expand our reach to wherever the customer is going. Paris is a world financial center."

"So Delphine's the UTT voice." As he'd suspected.

Youssef nodded.

"Who brought her in?'

Youssef named one of FranceFon's VPs. "They were on some board together, some arts council in Paris. She's the one who helped organize these Versailles outings."

"*Arts* council?"

"She doesn't have a telecom background," Youssef went on. "She was in the UTT International Foundation, like a kind of marketing rep for France."

A marketing rep for the UTT do-gooders' foundation?

He laughed.

He could blow her house down with one little puff.

"What's she doing in your group?"

Youssef shrugged. "I guess there wasn't any other place to put her. She might not stay with us long. I don't think she's qualified."

"She knows telecom, Youssef. She asked sharp questions today."

"She's intelligent. But she doesn't know carrier relations."

Another weakness he could exploit. But how, exactly, with whom?

"Youssef, are you in favor of the FF-GA alliance?"

"You know I am, Tyler. It makes sound business and technical sense."

"How can I push this past her?"

Youssef's black eyes were pensive. "I think you can't push past her. I think you need to try to convince her before you go above her. She seems like a nice lady, even if we're all afraid she tells everything to the VP."

"What could she tell?"

"That we smoke during meetings, tell jokes, drink too much? We've been a group of guys for so long, Tyler, you know how it is when a lady joins in."

"Uh-huh." He knew. The glass ceiling in telecom was thick. The industry was engineering-driven, and network engineers were overwhelmingly male. Women were few in R&D and international divisions and even less visible in sales right now, like other minorities, during these stringent economic times they were traversing.

"We just don't know her, Tyler. None of us feel close to her yet."

Not that Youssef probably ever would. He probably saw a woman like Delphine and thought she should be home in the kitchen, or driving kids to school. Same for Novoa, a courtly older Argentine, and Duc, whose parents had emigrated to France from Vietnam. Those cultures kept their distance from women in the workplace as effectively as any data guru did.

Tyler felt a sudden flash of empathy for Delphine, stuck in the middle of a standoffish, clubby group, with no background in their field and perhaps uncertain of her future with them. It wasn't easy to be brought in by a highly-placed mentor. He'd experienced it himself. The rank and file, men and women alike, would be afraid to befriend her because of her perceived power over them.

Youssef was right: the best way around this obstacle was to go right through it. If he became her champion, or even a strong ally, within her own group, she'd certainly benefit. She'd owe him. But he'd need more time.

"Youssef, you think we could get the group together while I'm still here?"

"I thought you're leaving tomorrow night?"

"I've decided to extend my stay. Finalizing this agreement has just become my number one priority."

"You weren't expecting this last-minute detour. We weren't either."

"It must be frustrating, not knowing what to tell your international customers about your alliances," Tyler said, leaking commiseration into his tone. "Makes it seem like FranceFon's unsure of itself."

"The French don't like change, you know, they're not into whiplash like you Americans." Youssef, a bright young Kuwaiti, had spent years in the States. Tyler'd actually been thinking about recruiting him for GlobeAll. He hadn't mentioned this to Youssef, though; it would be poor form to steal him before the agreement was signed. "Sure, Tyler, we can get together before you leave."

The bus stopped in front of FranceFon's building. The crowd mingled for a short time on the sidewalk and then dispersed. Tyler found Delphine, standing alone and looking tired, fishing for something in her briefcase.

"You made this a lovely evening, Delphine, I'm sure FranceFon earned some points tonight with the bankers. I appreciate your including me."

"Thank you for coming. I am sorry we did not have more time as a small group, to discuss your plan."

"I suggested to Youssef that I take you all to lunch when you're free."

"That is kind," she said, a little frown of surprise wrinkling her forehead. "But I thought your time was very limited?"

"I cleared my schedule for you."

She looked at him for a moment. He saw, clearly, exhaustion under her eyes and in the lines around them. He read, as loudly as if she'd said it, how uneasy she felt with his glibness, his insistence, his American-ness, even his height.

He stepped back, looking at the pavement. He yawned and tugged at his tie, loosening it. He slouched.

He felt her relax slightly.

"Delphine." What a musical name she had. "I'm very tired, but very hungry. I wonder if you'd join me for a quick meal? If you're not expected at home right away?"

"I am expected, but I could call—"

"No, no. Another time. I'll let you get back to your family dinner."

"I am sure my son ate already. He's probably playing the video games and e-mailing his friends and listening to music, all at the same time."

"A teenager, right? I bet I know the music he likes."

"That doesn't surprise me," she said. "You seem not much older than him."

Whoa! Was this intended as the insult she made it sound?

He backed away from her further, not hiding his frown.

"Tyler, excuse me. I am not thinking very smart right now." She fumbled in her bag and brought out her mobile. "I'll just call him, and we can go to dinner."

Why bother? "No, don't do that—"

But she was already speaking on her phone. He turned, to give her privacy, jamming his hands into his pockets. This was turning out to be one fucked-up day. His early exhaustion returned to him full force. He'd better go back to his hotel and pass out. She'd made her feelings clear, about the alliance and about him, and he didn't want to be around her anymore. He was afraid he'd be rude.

She finished her call, and smiled at him, hesitantly. "It's early, Tyler, only eight thirty, we have our choice of restaurants nearby. What food do you like?"

"Happy Meals." It was out, with a sarcastic smile, before he could catch it.

The laughter that exploded from her released his discomfort. Laughing, her mouth opened wide and her whole body seemed to shake. She suddenly seemed too big for her elegant, but stiff, navy suit: a pleasure to watch. He had to laugh a little too.

"Will you forgive me?" she asked, wiping mirth from her eyes.

"Hell no," he retorted. "I need all the leverage with you I can get."

She chuckled again. "Don't get ideas."

"I'm in alliances. I'm all about ideas."

They walked along then companionably, looking into restaurant windows where the menus were posted. As if they'd discussed it, they stayed away from the stuffy and the touristic, and chose a little bistro where a fire was lit in a corner.

Seven

THEY SETTLED INTO A BOOTH near the fire. Tyler ordered a bottle of red.

He loosened his tie further, stretched his legs out, and draped both arms along the back of the booth. He leaned his head back too, closing his eyes for a luxurious moment. His sigh was almost unconscious, almost a groan.

"You work very hard."

"We all do." He touched his glass to hers. "Here's to an evening off."

"You don't want to sell me any more GlobeAll?" Her watchful little smile reappeared.

"Of course I want to. Just not right now."

She looked at him, eyes still narrow, mouth pursed again. The red of her lips contrasted with the paleness of her skin. There was a softness to the contour of her jaw, a certain yielding, easy to sink into. He had to look away.

He took a sip of wine. Its rich flavor coated his tongue and throat. He saw her glance drop to his mouth, when his tongue touched wine from his lips, just enough to confirm that she was certainly as aware of him, physically, as he was of her. He smiled, as warmed by her awareness as by the wine.

She looked down quickly. "Then what shall we discuss?"

He decided to go for disarming. "Tell me more about your son. What's his name? How old is he?"

She sipped her own wine. "Guillaume. He's fifteen."

"What's he interested in?"

"He loves history, and computer games, and music of course, and climbing."

"Climbing mountains?"

"In the summer, yes, there is a camp where I send him for outdoor sport. In the Pyrenee."

"I grew up in Colorado, in the Rockies. I know mountains."

"Where do you live now? When you are not in a hotel?"

"Manhattan. It's a wonderful city. But no mountains."

"Just the skyscrapers."

He looked into his glass. He was used to this new little silence, during conversations about New York City architecture, the silence where the cloud-piercing iconic towers had been. Tyler had lost Nick in Tower Two, where he'd been on a sales visit. There were times Tyler wanted to stop everything, to think about Nick and mourn him properly; and fighting that impulse just made him feel more tired.

He thought the terrorists had chosen the wrong place as a symbol of mainstream America. New York City was not like the rest of the country: it was the world's city, the world's launching pad, the world's dream. The towers' destruction was the world's loss.

She was studying his face. "Did you lose many friends, Tyler, in the towers?"

"Everyone did. The May subsea cable meeting last year just wasn't the same. We all walked around noticing who wasn't there. It was ... very sad. So many PTTs had their U.S. headquarters there." PTT stood for Post, Telephone and Telegraph. It was the old name still used for monopoly telecom companies outside the U.S. "This year, of course, there'll be even fewer of us. I predict GlobeAll will be the last intact U.S. telecom company. Everyone else is in jail or bankrupt."

She leaned back, rolling her shoulders and stretching her legs out. He liked watching her lower her guard some. "You really believe that, I can tell."

"Even UTT's in trouble, Delphine, you know that. The Canada venture's bust, the Mexico venture's going south, no pun intended, the European strategy fell apart, the U.S. core is imploding. Not a lot of stability in a partnership there."

"I thought we weren't discussing business."

"We're discussing current events."

She smiled a little. "You like your work very much."

"Like Guillaume, I'm a history fan. We're making history right now in global telecom. I think it's fascinating. Don't you? I wouldn't choose any other industry."

"You always wanted to be in business?"

"I wanted to be an explorer," he remembered. "I was a language major in college, went to Mexico junior year, got hooked on the adventure. One of my professors suggested Thunderbird—the grad school?"

She nodded. Everyone in international business knew Thunderbird.

"So I became a T-bird, spent a semester at the campus here in Paris, actually. I was lucky enough to be recruited by a great GlobeAll guy—Nick Fournier. It was a good choice for me. I wanted a job that would let me see the world."

"And you got one."

"And the sightseeing!" He laughed. "Airports, hotels, conference rooms. Same four walls, different countries. I don't have to tell you, Delphine, you know the glamour of international travel."

"I know, yes, I try sometimes to explain to friends, but still, their envy does not subside."

"They don't get it unless they've lived it."

"I don't have any friends who have lived this."

That sounded lonely. "You'll make new friends in the carrier relations community. We only meet in person once a year, at the Global Traffic Meeting in May, where we do cable planning. But we all understand the complexity of the job, and we can be supportive, even amongst

33

competitors." He touched her shoulder with a light hand. "You're in good company, Delphine."

Once their food was served they ate in the concentrated way of people who were too busy to eat particularly well or particularly often.

"I can perhaps tell you, Tyler, I don't have a lot of experience in this area of alliances." Her smile was more trusting now.

"It's not rocket science," he said. "You assess what FranceFon needs to offer its customers, outside of your own footprint, and go after whoever has it. Commercially, geographically, technically."

"You make it sound simple."

"It is simple." He smiled. "That doesn't mean it's easy." He poured the last of the wine for her. "Tell you what. We'll consider our alliance as a kind of case study for you. I'll teach you everything you need to know, as we go along, give you pointers. Then you can look like an expert at all the next ones you do."

"And then I will be as clever as you?"

Her glass, tilted up, hid most of her expression, but he heard judgment in her voice, and her keen gaze was wary again. She'd seen right through his offer of guidance: his clumsiness must be the fatigue of the last weeks catching up with him. "I'm not clever, Delphine, just single-minded. I never give up."

"Never?"

"No."

"And do you always win?"

"So far, yes."

"Do you ... fight fair, as they say?"

He shook his head, grinning, trying for charm. "I get as dirty as I need to. As they say."

"Then I am right to be careful with you."

"But I'm on your side."

"Not if I don't give you what you are looking for with me."

He pushed his plate aside and rested his forearms on the table. The long day was starting to collapse. He

34

fiddled with the bubble of glass, in the middle of the table, that held a fat red candle. Its color reminded him of the red foil heart attached to the white rose, surely smashed flat in the pocket of his coat, thrown carelessly beside him. He glanced at his coat and then over at her. She was composed, guarded, watching him without a smile. Back to square one. Fuck it.

He signaled for the bill and put it on his corporate card. He didn't even look at Delphine when she tried to protest. He did, however, help her with her coat, patting her shoulders briskly.

Once outside, he flagged down a cab.

"Take the lady where she needs to go," he told the driver, whose name was Achmed Houari. He greeted Achmed in Arabic and handed him some Euros.

"I am used to *le metro*." She sounded cross. "I live one stop from here."

"At this hour, please, I insist."

"You go to a lot of trouble for me. It isn't necessary."

He bit back an irritated reply. "I would do *anything* for you."

"*Merde*." She scowled.

The late hour, the good meal, the nice wine, the shyly smiling driver, her pout, his frustration—all conspired to make him reckless.

He took her soft hands firmly in his, and brought them to his lips, in the old-fashioned European gesture. He kissed them both, quickly enough for courtesy, emphatically enough to leave no doubt as to his interest. He held onto them tighter, longer, than was appropriate, even in France, enjoying the color that rose slowly in her face as he stared at her. Then he let go, abruptly, to reach into his pocket. He brought out the now-drooping rose and handed it to her with a little flourish. "Happy Valentine's Day, Delphine. This will revive in water."

"If I keep it," she snapped. But she took it.

"*Bon nuit*." He handed her into the cab and shut the door on her disdain.

Eight

THE LOOK ON HER FACE was amusing enough to buoy him into deciding to meander slowly back to his hotel. He had to stay awake to talk to Singapore at midnight anyway. He might as well keep active until then.

At least he didn't have meetings tomorrow—he could actually sleep eight hours! He'd get over to the office in the morning to arrange his stay for several more days in Paris; maybe he'd even take Jack up on the country weekend offer. He was determined not to leave until he had a signed FranceFon contract.

He wouldn't allow Delphine to stand in his way. Tonight he'd confirmed the weakest vulnerability he could exploit in her, one that would be pure pleasure to press to the limit. He grinned, remembering the instant where he'd caught her eyeing his mouth. He rubbed his chin reflectively, wished he'd gotten in a quick afternoon shave. But women seemed to like the swarthy look on him.

She'd touched his arm twice, tapped him with the flower. In his experience women did not touch men in a business setting, unless there was a level of physical comfort between them, like longtime colleagues could have; or a level of attraction. And he'd confirmed their attraction was mutual by kissing her hands. Such soft hands. He'd been tempted to set his teeth on the pad linking her thumb to her forefinger. How did she smell so sweet after working all day? Damned if he could ever manage that.

Was there any chance of their actually getting together?

Nah. Too many obstacles. The tangle of their work, their far-apart locations, her son—and she might be married. Lack of a ring was not proof.

What a shame.

Indulging himself, he let his mind's eye rove freely over the lush curves apparent under her proper clothes, the red lips, the creamy skin, the gleam in her eyes. His breath hitched as he imagined how good she would feel.

Then, frowning, he walked a little faster.

He had to banish the excitement she aroused, welcome though it was to his worn senses. He'd let it inspire their arguments during negotiations.

But he should keep a tight lid on any further acknowledgement—the rose and hand kissing were definitely over the top. Might work against him, in fact.

On the other hand, she might think she could exploit *his* attraction to *her* as a vulnerability too. He could play that just as well, maybe even better.

Either way, it should be more fun than the average settlement. As long as it was wrapped up soon.

His wanderings had taken him a little out of the way, he realized. The street he walked was dim, shops shuttered, bistros not as numerous as nearer the France Fon office. He stood under a streetlamp and took his hotel card out of his pocket to double-check the address. Yeah, he was several blocks from where he should be. He consulted his Paris guidebook.

A cab drew up and idled next to him. When he glanced over he realized it wasn't a cab. The driver was hidden, but a young girl leaned out the back window with an unmistakable leer on her face, thrusting her ample chest forward with all the slick salesmanship of a product display expert at a convention.

"You like companion?" She spoke in English—they always knew he was American. Her voice was a husky insinuation. Her face was pretty despite heavy makeup, her breasts voluptuous-looking even if fake. For a moment he was tempted to get the arousal of Delphine out of his system.

But he shook his head. He never used prostitutes. It was a measure of how strongly Delphine had affected him that he would even look at this girl.

The car kept pace with his hastened walk. Not good. He picked up his stride, every nerve alert now. The girl called out to him again, and he turned abruptly down a narrow side street and then sprinted to the opposite end, thinking he could lose them.

The boulevard he ran into was wider, better lit. He darted into the first bar.

He peeled off his coat, stripped off his tie, and stuffed it into a pocket. He needed to look more casual if he was going to stroll after dark in strange Paris neighborhoods. What had he been thinking, getting lost?

He ordered brandy and sipped it slowly. Its mellow flavor calmed his beating heart. Five years ago, hell, even two, he wouldn't have bolted like this. There was no way a pimp/hooker combo would risk kidnapping a visiting businessman; it would freeze sex sales for weeks and the gangs who ran things would react badly. He wasn't sure why he'd responded with fear, instead of realizing this obvious logic right away.

Ever since last year's Jo-burg cabnapping incident he'd been over-cautious. He could feel his age now in ways he'd never felt before. He wasn't even fit anymore—he was still breathing hard after that little hustle. Disgusting. He took a healthier swallow and checked his watch. Almost eleven. He'd take a cab from here, for sure, and be settled comfortably for his Singapore call at midnight.

His mobile rang. "Harding," he snapped.

"Tyler?" The soft voice was hesitant but instantly recognizable. He sat up straight. "Hello, it is Delphine."

"Hello." What was this?

"I hope it is not too late for you, I thought it probably isn't?"

"It's fine."

"I called to say, thank you again." He heard the smile in her voice. "For the dinner, and for the—other gift." If she'd been any other woman he'd say this was flirting. "I think I wasn't completely nice before," she continued. "I wanted to assure you that I appreciate your kindness to me tonight." He wondered if her husband or son were listening. He'd guess not.

"You're welcome," he said quietly. He wasn't up to flirting anymore. If she were next to him, it might be different. But she was, actually, a stranger on the phone. And he had to do some pretty tough business with her.

Her voice acknowledged his unresponsiveness. "I will let you go, Tyler, you sound tired."

"I am, yes. But I like hearing your voice." Oh, fatal. What was wrong with him? He closed his eyes and bent his head, tempted to hang up.

She waited a moment before answering, low, "Thank you for that, also."

He roused himself. "Hamzi and I want to get the group together for lunch."

"The group, yes. We will call you. How much longer are you here?"

"I'm staying over until next Tuesday or Wednesday." Might as well give her a deadline, but let her know he'd have spent almost an entire week on this project. He didn't have to say he'd decided to build in vacation. "I can't afford more days here."

"That is a lot of time for you, I am sure."

"This is important to me."

"Yes. I realize." She was a little cooler now. "I will say goodnight then."

"Goodnight, Delphine. Thanks for your call. See you soon."

What an ambiguous conversation. Were they starting something, in spite of all the obstacles? He must be tired beyond reason to imagine any such liaison. He'd have done better to go with that young hooker, clear his mind for nailing this fucking deal.

He yawned suddenly, hugely. He finished his drink and picked up his coat. He put some money on the bar and went out to get a cab.

Avi Shur, a rare Israeli cabdriver, took him to his hotel. Tyler tried out the few words of Hebrew he knew, enhanced by a Tel Aviv IT conference last year, and was rewarded by Avi's huge grin. These little exchanges always tickled him.

At midnight he called Asia. Singapore was live again, he was glad to hear, although the card insertion upgrade to the switch would cost GlobeAll a quarter of a million dollars a month. Ouch. They'd need to find five good mid-sized billers, ASAP, to fill that hole. The money wouldn't come out of Tyler's cost center, of course. He wasn't Network. He was just the liaison to their foreign partners. However, like a spider in the middle of the web, he was seen as a key link in international communication because of his mobility—network engineers were mostly kept chained in the basements of GlobeAll's secure data centers—and because of his relationships with all the PTTs.

"Hey, do me a favor, BK," he told the Singapore lead techie. "Send out an e-mail to the partners distribution list? Let em know we're live again now?"

"And why I have to do your job?"

"I had meetings tonight, so I locked my laptop in the office."

"So who's on your lap then?"

His colleagues liked to vicariously imagine that Tyler, single and presentable, had a raging love life on his frequent travels. He didn't enlighten them with the dismal reality. "Don't get cheeky. Do this one for me, and I'll owe you."

"Hmm, I wonder, what I can extract from you?"

"Don't hit me while I'm down." Tyler usually enjoyed Boon Kiat's lively, clipped British tone and argumentative manner, but right now it grated on his nerves.

"I like to haggle now, while you are at disadvantage."

"Easy for you to haggle, man, you just woke up."

"Not so. We never sleep."

"You're invincible, BK, okay? Just send the friggin e-mail."

"You take me, my wife, and her sister, to dinner. Raffles Hotel, next time you are in town. Maybe her mother too."

"That's serious money. They cute?"

BK's laughter was a staccato echo of his voice. "The mother, but not the sister."

"Deal. Next time I'm there."

Finally, he was free to collapse into the soft pillows that had been beckoning throughout the call. Free to give in to his exhaustion at last. Sleep was more seductive right now than what he remembered of sex.

Nine

H E SLEPT SO DEEPLY that when he finally woke he was disoriented. He lay looking up at the intricate crown moldings that wrapped the ceiling. As a child in Telluride, snowbound, he'd sometimes liked to lie on his back to look at ceilings and pretend they were floors—windows became doorways, furniture turned interestingly upside down.

The ribbons snaking around the corners here were like drapery winding around a Greek statue's feet. He wondered about the plaster workers, from decades back, who crafted this decor. Did they take pride in their art? Or were they cursing the builder, craving their lunch? A joy, or a waste of time?

Speaking of which. He rolled over to check his watch on the nightstand. Past ten o'clock! Fuck!

He staggered into the shower and scrubbed himself awake. He put on jeans and a GlobeAll sweater, not anticipating a need to meet the public today, and hurried out of the room. He was too late, of course, for the hotel breakfast, so he grabbed a giant coffee to-go at a nearby café, four espresso shots, earning him a raised eyebrow from the neatly ponytailed clerk. *Les Americaines*, he could hear the guy thinking.

The coffee and his walk in the cold air drove cobwebs from his brain. Once settled into his borrowed cube, he roared through his accumulated laptop messages like a ninja, beating them back as if his flying fingers were nunchucks on the keyboard, feeling, as always, that he was vanquishing an enemy that threatened to eradicate him with crises; but new enemies leaped out at him from every corner of the globe, every minute.

He monitored a revenue issue with Embratel, the Brazilian PTT; placated the Mumbai office director with promises of renewal of their agreement with VSNL, the dominant Indian telco; and considered again the major pending deal he had to approve, with the Canadian company TeleOne.

He stared at the screen for a moment, trying to see beyond the black and white, into the source of his unease about the TeleOne agreement. He'd looked over the financials on the flight from Budapest to Paris, wondering why the numbers didn't add up to him the way they'd apparently added up to his GlobeAll VP. It was the first time this agreement had been considered for renewal since Nick's death. Nick had been in charge of the Canadian deals that Tyler was now having to review.

Someone had made a mistake on the access piece of it. Access was the price paid to in-country local loop providers for allowing traffic to terminate on their switches. It was the most costly component of international telecom service, since local control was the last-gasp attempt of the monopolistic PTTs to hang onto their lucrative pre-privatization revenue streams. But in this Canadian deal, access was minimal.

That didn't make sense to him. TeleOne was a gouger of the worst kind, operating in areas where there was no competition and therefore no alternative. Ergo, he was obliged to sign off on using them, but he'd ask Finance to run this again. Maybe these nonsensical numbers were some kind of spreadsheet formula error.

If only he could just ask Nick. If only he'd returned that call from him about TeleOne. Nick had been in Canada meeting with them before going to New York. If Tyler had called him then, listened to Nick's airing of TeleOne issues, maybe Nick wouldn't have gone to Tower Two the next day, maybe he'd have waited until Tyler joined him to talk it out in person.

His hands retracted into fists on the keyboard. When he felt his nails scratching his palms, he straightened up and shook his hands, irritated. He thought he'd trained himself to stop thinking about the way Nick died.

Was there anyone else he could ask? He thought of Georges Deauville, the Canadian who'd been Delphine's predecessor at FranceFon. FranceFon had numerous dealings in Canada, and Deauville had known Nick. He quickly punched in some numbers on the desk phone.

"Novoa, FranceFon."

"Hola, Octavio, hablo Tyler. Le pido un favor, el numero de la casa de Deuville." He figured Novoa would have Deauville's home number.

Novoa produced the number, adding that he shouldn't call until evening.

Tyler would call tonight. He could query Deauville about Delphine's reluctance to sign, after he'd found out about Canada.

To distract himself from TeleOne, he scrolled down to the next bit of pressing business, and refused to approve a resale deal with a newbie ISP in Slovenia.

Slovenia, give me a break, he thought with annoyance as he hammered out his terse response. In spite of their stellar emergence from Soviet domination, their telco infrastructure wasn't nearly robust enough to support a resale agreement. These fly-by-night PTT offshoots must think he was born yesterday.

After three hours, the caffeine and the furious work drained him. He packed up his laptop, threw it over his shoulder, massaged his hands, and went to find Jack.

"Thank God it's Friday. Let's do lunch."

"Can this be the workaholic formerly known as Tyler Harding?" Jack unfolded himself from his workstation, unwinding his headset. "I didn't think lunch was in your vocabulary." He grinned when he saw what Tyler was wearing. "Didn't think jeans were either. You're slackin, man, I'm telling on ya."

"Tell away. I am officially on vacation."

"Get out."

"Yep. Took your advice. Gave myself two days."

"Counting Saturday and Sunday? We don't work then anyway, remember? Unless we're in the Middle East." Jack leaned into the next cube to drawl in French, "Eh, Jean, are we still in France? Tyler doesn't know where he is or what day it is. Again."

"I'm taking the rest of today, and Monday," Tyler said, used to the ribbing. He was a target for time-zone jokes whenever he traveled.

"Whoa. Tyler goes wild. Who's gonna prop up the modern world of global telecommunications in your extended absence?"

"Fuck if I care, Jack. Let's eat."

They wolfed the plat du jour at a nearby brasserie.

"So how'd it go with FF last night? Didja close her?"

"Not yet." Tyler mimicked BK's curt accent. "Outcome uncertain. Communication not clear. Mercury in retrograde."

Jack snorted. "Husband in town, more like."

"Jack. What d'you take me for?"

"A winner," Jack said bluntly. "She's making you take these extra days? For a deal that was essentially done weeks ago? What're you gonna do about this?"

Tyler sat back and took a deep breath. "Well, we're having a group lunch on Monday, she left me a voice-mail setting it up."

"So much for that vacation day. You're hiding out at your hotel till then?"

"Actually I thought I'd ask you if I can hide out at Marie's uncle's place. If you're still offering. I figured I'd rent a car, escape for the weekend."

"That's cool, but it won't close your deal, letting it alone for three days."

"Dammit, Jack, you're the one who told me to take time off. How'm I gonna change her mind over the weekend anyway?"

"You have to *change* her mind? She's not in favor at all?"

Tyler thought about Delphine. A good night's sleep had not made yesterday's interaction any clearer. He fiddled with his flatware.

"*Tyler.*" Jack snatched the cutlery away. "Wake up, man. This is serious. You have to call her, set up a meeting right away. You can't let this go a long weekend."

"Fuck. My pitch isn't working this time. With her, I need something else. And damned if I know what."

"What's her weakness?"

"She's a she, for one thing," Tyler said. "She's new to alliances. So she's unsure of herself in the group. They're not making it easy for her, either." He thought back to her body language with him, the late-night call. "And ... she might like me. But maybe not." Last night, he'd thought he could use that against her. Now he wasn't so sure.

"Yeah?" Jack leaned forward, grinning. "She like the rose then?"

Tyler winced at the memory of thrusting it into her hands, after he'd mauled them. He pushed a hand into his hair. "Not really. It made her suspicious."

"Bitch."

"No, she isn't. She's just ..."

"What?"

He shrugged. He thought of how tired she'd looked after the Versailles trip, how her face had brightened when speaking of her son, how worried she'd been when she thought he was offended by her age-ism, how hesitant her voice had sounded when she'd called him so late. "Human, I guess."

"Ty. There are no humans in telecom." Jack slapped Euros down on the table. "Snap out of it, man. Remember, this is war."

"I know that." Tyler lifted himself heavily out of the seat, sighing again. "But Christ I'm tired." His laptop felt like it was made of lead.

"The cottage is only an hour from here, traffic'll be light if you leave right away. Keys are under a rock in the front garden." Jack scrawled directions on a napkin. "Call your FF lady and then split. You can be there by four, snoozing by the fire."

"Thanks, Jack."

In the cab on the way to his hotel (Salem Asheer, Eritrean, in Paris just three months), he called the concierge to get a car. His next call was to Delphine.

"*Allo?*" She sounded much crisper than before.

"Delphine, Tyler Harding here."

"Oh, Tyler." The way her voice softened emboldened him.

"I'm going away for the weekend, but I need to see you before I leave."

"Do you mean this afternoon? I set the meeting for next week—"

"Sure, that's fine, but I want to see you today, not the group, if you can get away for half an hour. We can meet wherever you want."

She didn't answer right away. Then she said slowly, "Perhaps we can just discuss, over the phone? I am busy this afternoon."

"No. It's got to be in person."

"You are very sure, you must see me?" Now she sounded irked. "It is not convenient, Tyler, I have a big problem that I must solve."

"Did you take lunch yet?"

"No, I usually don't."

"This is lunch then. I'll be in your lobby in twenty minutes." He clicked off.

At his hotel, he threw a change of clothes into his overnight bag. He'd have to check out. GlobeAll wouldn't pay for an empty room, on a weekend, when he was taking vacation days. He was downstairs in five minutes. He didn't want to give her time to change her mind. He dealt with his storage luggage and the paperwork the concierge was holding for him. The rental, a tiny stickshift Peugeot, was already waiting.

He lucked into a parking space halfway on the sidewalk across from the FranceFon building. He leaped out just in time to see Delphine exit the elevator inside the glassed lobby.

Ten

HE STRODE UP, smiled, shook her hand. She wore slacks and a corporate logo sweater much like the GlobeAll one he wore, he was amused to see, and her dark hair was gleaming loose on her shoulders instead of pinned up like yesterday. Casual Fridays had become universal. But her bright scarf was neatly tied, her makeup perfectly set. She did not smile, did not let her hand linger in his, did not hold his gaze for long.

"There is a coffee shop here, Tyler, we can lunch inside." Her tone was as brisk as her walk across the lobby. They sat opposite each other in a bright plastic booth. She must have chosen this place deliberately; it was hardly conducive to the atmosphere he needed to create. She snapped a menu open. "They have sandwiches, only, but I am in a hurry. You don't mind."

"I'll just have coffee," he told the waiter. She ordered a *croque Monseiur*, the enigmatic French name for a ham and cheese sandwich.

She folded a napkin into little triangles as they waited for their order. Her nails were a wet-looking hot pink, the color of fantasy. "You must have something very important to say to me." She didn't look at him.

"I can't wait until Monday for your decision, Delphine. I need to get status on this to my HQ tonight. Close of business, Eastern U.S. time."

The little pout again; lips still lush in spite of the tension around her mouth. "I need more time. Your office has to wait."

49

"What do you need to make up your mind?" Tyler made his tone aggressive, even though all of a sudden he'd be content to sit for awhile, just watching her mouth. "I told you I'll produce any kind of backup docs you want. Anything. Just name it."

She frowned. "I need," she began, then shook her head.

"What do you need, Delphine?"

He took the napkin from her hand, and let his fingers brush against hers as he drew his hand back across the table. An unexpected sensual charge raced through him like a shudder. He quickly sat up straight.

She fixed dark eyes on him. "I need that you leave me alone." Her mouth was a thin line now, her voice cold. "I need that you give me the time I deserve to absorb the information associated with this proposal."

Shock chased away the potency of touching her hand.

"I am sorry, to be so blunt, but you must understand my position. I am just too new at this to make a mistake now, in my first big decision."

"Why would it be a *mistake?*" He welcomed the stirring of anger.

"I cannot know yet. It's very soon."

"Deauville had already made this decision for FranceFon, Delphine. He signed off on it before he took his early retirement, did you know that?"

"I know. But my name will be on this now."

"I could go above you. I know your management and they know me. I've waited on this out of respect to you, as the new North American negotiator. But I can escalate whenever I need to during this process, you know."

"That would not be fair to me, Tyler." She retrieved the napkin, tore at it.

Fair? What did she think this was, a game? His anger took sail. "You're asking me to put *my* reputation with *my* company on hold while you take your time reviewing an agreement that was all but approved before you even joined FranceFon? You know how many companies would jump at this chance? DT's just itching to do this with us."

Deutsche Telekom, the huge German PTT, had indeed been courting GlobeAll for months. But although their footprint dwarfed FranceFon's in size, their business model was even more flawed and their current financials even shakier. Their stock had dropped nearly 80% in the last year, following their IPO. He'd never do that partnership.

Her food came but she didn't touch it. "I understand."

"I'm not sure that you do. Maybe you're too new at this to realize the implications of your delay, for your top execs as well as mine. Alliance creation has its own timeline, and it can get old fast. My coming to meet with your team was just a courtesy." He fixed her with his hardest stare. "An extraordinary courtesy on my part, actually. I've got three bigger deals waiting for my attention right now."

He knew from her stricken expression that he'd scored a direct hit, but seeing her gaze drop didn't feel like victory. He resisted reaching for her hand. He sipped coffee. He tried to remember his next line.

Usually this was so easy. He'd engineered plenty of successful strategic alliances over the years for GlobeAll. Except he usually said he'd 'facilitated' them since it made him sound like more of a team player than the ruthless first-person shooter he usually ended up having to be in these scenarios.

But she was making this difficult! She wasn't behaving like a worthy adversary; she should be arguing and fighting and threatening to bring in Legal and, generally, giving him a hard time. That's what he was used to. They should end up, finally, coming to terms, laughing about what a bastard he was and going out for drinks. Their companies would thank them and give them bonuses based on percentage of booked ROI. That's how it was supposed to work. Furious but fun.

He sighed. "Delphine. Give yourself a break and sign the bloody thing. It isn't the end of the world, it's a good solid deal, for FranceFon and for you as your first agreement on the alliance team. Get it over with and you can go on to the next one."

"It isn't that easy to sign without looking at the small print."

"Small print?" He laughed, amazed. "Jesus, this one's as straightforward as they come. Some in-country co-marketing, co-branding, fiber leasing and a few customer list trades. Some Private Lines connecting us. Oh and by the way, some payments back and forth, and a boatload of money to be made for both our companies. What's not to like?"

"There are always—variables." Her voice was so uncomfortable, her avoidance of his eyes so obvious that he realized she was dissembling on purpose.

"Care to give me specifics?" he asked quietly.

She studied her folded hands.

"You haven't even read it."

Her silence confirmed this.

He unzipped his laptop case. "Delphine. Let's go over it together, line by line. I'll explain the whole thing to you." He restrained himself from saying 'in terms even you can understand.'

He pushed her sandwich toward her. "Eat, drink, and I'll go through it. We can finish this today. You can get it over with and get me out of your hair." He clarified, at her puzzled look, "I won't bother you anymore." Somehow he produced an intimate smile. "Unless you *want* me to."

Her eyes grew wide before she looked down. "It isn't that simple for me, Tyler."

"What isn't?"

"The agreement. You know I've been with UTT a very long time."

"And …"

"It isn't easy for me to just forget all that I learned there, about GlobeAll, about FranceFon, about WorldFon, everyone."

"Look, we all brainwash our own people about the competition. We all have to make our own company seem like the only good one. Otherwise how could we motivate the salespeople? Or anyone else? How would we ever keep customers, or get new ones?"

"It isn't all propaganda. Some of it is truth."

"Sure, some. And frankly, most of us are pretty good at what we do, but we all suck at other things, like billing, and we all tend to struggle with the same issues internationally. Ergo, alliances." He smiled again. "We fill in each other's gaps."

"But you, for example, wouldn't go to UTT to make an agreement like this."

"We're domestic carriers, Delphine. We're prohibited in the States from colluding. Remember when WorldFon wanted to buy Stint? Our Justice Department shut it down to keep enough competitors on the playing field. We call it anti-trust."

"Yes, the European Union was against that merger too."

"I didn't ask you out to talk deregulation. What in your UTT experience makes you hesitate to approve this agreement?"

Her gaze dropped again to her folded hands. "It is … awkward."

"This *conversation* is awkward."

"I can tell, just from knowing you one day, that you are an honorable person."

"I am. And I work for an honorable company. And you do too. And this is an honorable deal in front of us. It's all good."

Her silence made him lean forward in the confrontational way that he'd wanted to prevent but which now he couldn't help. "Look, if something's not right somewhere, just tell me and we can iron it out. That's my job. That's what I'm here for."

"I don't think you can iron out this thing."

What the hell?

"Try me."

She glanced around the deserted coffee shop. He repeated slowly, "try me."

"It is ... complicated."

"Start at the beginning and go slow. We'll break it down."

She looked down, shook her head.

"Then you leave me no choice but to go above you," he warned her quietly. "I have to status my boss in a few hours." This was not true—his VP was still in Hungary celebrating the alliance Tyler had signed there—but such claims always worked as a catalyst for reluctant partners, to move them toward progress.

"No, please don't do that yet. I need some time."

"Time for what?"

She stood suddenly. "It is my business only. I cannot discuss any further."

He stood too. "But I don't take no for an answer."

"This time you must." She turned on her heel and walked swiftly away, out of the shop and back across the lobby. He watched, frustrated, as she disappeared into an elevator while he snapped Euros out of his billfold to leave for the check.

Eleven

HE HURRIED OUT to the lobby, intending to follow her.

He was shocked by the impact of Delphine brushing past him, without even noticing who she bumped into, as she raced out of the lobby, coat on, briefcase slung over a shoulder. She was running to get outside, he realized, perhaps to get better reception, perhaps to get away from the prying ears of FranceFon employees. Her phone was clamped to her ear like a stethoscope and her face as she spoke into it was as grave as a doctor giving bad news.

He followed her outside and leaned against the wall a little way from her, to give her privacy. As she paced next to the building she saw him. She stopped, and stared, but apparently could not cut her conversation short. She continued in a furious whisper while glaring at him.

"Guy, you were forbidden to go," he heard her hiss in French. Sounded like a personal call. "I told you what the consequences would be. You leave me no choice."

She spun away from Tyler. He wasn't sure she'd hung up until he saw her drooping head, hair hanging down as if to hide, what, could that be a tear falling down her cheek? Yes, the building's shiny facade showed her crumpled face as clear as a mirror.

This was uncomfortable territory. Should he offer any acknowledgement or let her have some dignity? He ostentatiously opened his coat to fumble in the pocket, the same pocket where he'd stashed yesterday's rose. His rustling gave her a little cover to compose herself, enough so that when she turned back to him her face was clearer.

Clearer, but still very troubled, the strain around her eyes and mouth pronounced.

"Tyler. I told you to leave me alone."

He pulled his coat tight around him, searching her face, sorry to see her so upset. She looked down quickly and he saw the flush rise again in her cheeks.

"This isn't—this is only my business. It has nothing to do with you, so please, I am asking you again, leave me alone."

"I can't," he said simply. "I wish I could help you out with whatever problem you're having—" he gestured to her mobile phone "— but I can't let your crisis get in the way of my deadline."

She whirled away again. He heard a muttered French curse spit out as she clenched her hands into fists. She walked to the corner, her arm raised to flag a cab. Wasn't it just rotten luck for her, he thought, that for once none were passing? After several moments of watching her stand on the windy corner, he followed.

"Delphine, if you need a lift, let me drive. My car's right across the street."

She turned to stare at him. "Perhaps you *can* help me, since you seem to be so rudely determined to attach yourself to me."

Sensing opportunity, he ignored the fierce contempt, warring with desperation, in her voice. He smiled. "Anything."

"I have … a problem with my son. He went to a concert with friends against my wishes. The place is not safe and it is supposed to go on all weekend, and I told him he absolutely could not go. These friends of his, he has been forbidden to see them for weeks now. He is defying me because …" She stopped. He could see her fighting tears again. "I don't know why I am telling this to you. Of all people."

Why indeed? Why didn't she call her son's father? Or any close family friend with a car, which wasn't as simple as it sounded given that many Parisians didn't use cars in town. But here was a mystery, certainly, a gap he could drive a tank through. "Sure, let's go get him," he said easily. "I'll just ask you, as a small favor, bring along your copy of the agreement, and I'm at your disposal."

She rummaged in her briefcase, brought out a pristine document to wave at him. Untouched, as he'd known. He plucked it from her with a wry grin. "We can lock him in the trunk and review this at our leisure."

He enjoyed her shocked laugh. "I'm going away for the weekend, to the country, after we kidnap your boy." He smiled. "You're welcome to join me, both of you, if it would help to have a change of scene or you want to make sure he doesn't escape to these no-good friends."

"You sound as if you know him already." She produced a shaky smile. "And thank you, for your kind offer. But I can't impose on you that way."

"Think about it. It might be an option." Where the hell was her husband?

"Ready for an adventure?" He grinned as he gunned the engine. "Road trip, Delphine, come on, smile a little."

She gave him a wan lip-stretch. If they were lovers he'd know how to get a real smile out of her. This thought must have shown in his eyes, for she looked quickly away from him, sat up straighter and tightened her belt.

She gave him directions out of Paris on the old periphery road heading northwest, toward Rouen. The concert stadium was about half an hour's drive, she thought, and she got on her mobile to double-check its location, repeating directions for Tyler as he re-acquainted himself with shifting gears. He'd forgotten what a pain in the ass it was! He never drove in New York. Other drivers sped past, honking occasionally, while he maneuvered into third at last.

She held her phone for a moment, listening.

"A friend," he heard her say, 'man friend': in French, nouns were always male or female. Apparently the person she was talking to had something to say about this, for Delphine turned away so that she could speak quietly into the mouthpiece.

Gossiped about already—good. He was ready to push the relationship along. She, too, must have considered the implications of this little joint venture. She'd crossed the professional line by inviting him into a very personal realm. She couldn't expect him to back off now.

He'd propose the distraction of a brief weekend getaway from her domestic malaise, purely platonic of course, no strings attached, just so she could read the alliance docs in peace. Walks in the woods, quiet evenings by the fire, a friend who'd proved himself to be very reliable in need, who would be willing to listen to anything she might want to express, whether about her family or the discomfort she'd displayed over the agreement.

Was he this much of a cad? Yeah, he was capable, in the right circumstances. Once upon a time, he'd been an expert. If he had his eye on a woman and she gave off the right kind of signals, he always got what he wanted. He suddenly remembered Nick again. Funny how the pressure of the TeleOne deal was bringing his friend to mind. "Ya wanna close em, Ty, ya gotta love em," Nick had used to say.

It had been a long time since he'd done this, though. He glanced again over at her profile. She looked young and lost, chewing on a nail as she looked out the window for the right traffic signs. She looked soft enough to sleep on, in her loose cashmere sweater that his warm hands would slide under so easily. Her scarf would unroll by itself and fall off in a bright splash. Her head would loll, her hair would sweep back to reveal that soft underside of her chin. He kept his smile to himself. He didn't want her to see it, not yet, not until he knew the whereabouts and disposition of her errant son and mystery husband.

Twelve

He was surprised the stadium was open air—in February, in France? This was hard core music fandom indeed. The car park, far from the stadium itself, was a chaotic muddy shambles, the noise deafening, the tawdry youths passing in front of them as unsavory as he would have expected. The scrawled signs said "Antiwar Anti-Globalization Three Day Peace and Music Green Festival."

Right: this was the weekend scheduled for the biggest demonstrations throughout Europe in a quarter century. Everybody was protesting the U.S. incursion into Iraq.

Good time to get out of town.

There'd been an e-mail exhorting GlobeAll employees outside the States to take security precautions this weekend, to not look too 'American,' whatever the hell that was supposed to mean. He'd always been spotted, anyway, throughout his travels.

He looked at Delphine now, raising his brows, wondering what she wanted him to do. She was looking anxiously out at the crowds, as if she'd see her son just by serendipity. He said, "Call him."

She turned, quizzical.

"Doesn't he have a mobile? Call him. Tell him you're here to pick him up."

Her laugh was nervous. "He won't like it. He might not come."

"If he refuses, tell him we'll call security. Give them his description."

Leaving her to make the call, he got out and walked around a little, searching the surroundings for anything resembling a security post, or first aid tent, or even a ticket booth. Kids were pouring in and out of the crumbling old stone stadium—which was Roman, if he recalled his French history—as if oblivious to the music, to their environs, to each other. Half of them looked more drugged than drunk, he realized, understanding a little of Delphine's fear.

He got back into the car just in time to catch the tail end of what had obviously proved to be a fruitful conversation.

"He will meet us here," she said. Her relief was evident in the looser set of her shoulders. "He was very surprised that I came to him. Thank you, Tyler, so much, for helping me in this."

He nodded. "Do you want me to get closer to the entrance?"

"No, I told him where we are. He will come outside."

"I think it might be best if you have this—reunion—alone with him, and I'll come back after a few minutes. You need to look like his rescuer here, not me. I'm just your ride, you know?"

She considered him for a minute. "You are full of surprises, aren't you. You must know teenagers very well."

"I don't know many. But I like them. I have a nephew." His brother Gerard's seventeen year old, Jerry, lived in Connecticut and was as frequent a visitor to Tyler's apartment as could be arranged, the only visitor who did not cluck over Tyler's lack of nesting skills. Jerry and his friends were Tyler's entrée to current trends, and his favorite visitors. They were funny, full of ideas, crazy about music. They probably would have thought this concert was very cool. But Jerry wouldn't have been allowed to attend for three days either.

"So, I'll just wander around, until I see him with you here, and then I'll come back." He got out and added, "You can drive if you want to, show him who's boss."

He walked a little way into the meandering swarm, glad he'd dressed down today. He could just see doing this in his nice pinstripe. The kids were mostly pale and thin, and their metal piercings and ragged outfits seemed painful in this cold weather. They looked like they all needed a good bath, warm clothes and a hot meal. Bourgeois sensibilities, no doubt. He hoped they wouldn't spot him as an American businessman and set on him like the pack of hungry wolf cubs they resembled. But he had to laugh a little at the thought: if he was outed and torn apart, how would the Paris office explain to his cohorts around the world?

He glanced back at the car after about fifteen minutes, and saw two youngsters standing outside with Delphine. She was patting the longest-haired one on the shoulder. It was probably safe for him to mosey back.

The youth who turned at his approach had the distinctive stamp of his mother on his long, wary face, a face so striking that Tyler found it hard not to stare.

He let Delphine make introductions. Guillaume had a firm handshake, for all that he stood slumped over as if a good wind would blow him away.

"Hello, Guillaume, your mother has told me a little about you."

"Who are you?" Guillaume addressed him with the formal 'you' in French, suspicion coloring his tone. He didn't mean Tyler's name, which he'd just heard.

"Your mother and I work together." He held his gaze steady on the boy's.

"But why are you here?"

"Guy," began Delphine.

"I'm in France on business, and I just happened to have a car when your mother needed one. She didn't want to leave you here for another minute. That's how worried she was about you."

Guillaume's hard eyes seemed to assess Tyler as acceptable, finally, and he nodded once.

Monique, Guillaume's little blonde companion, was equally sullen, and her pale face was garish with too much eye makeup and overdone dark lips. Her top—it looked like a negligee, was that actually considered clothing?—did not cover her at all, and when she was introduced to Tyler she responded to the new male presence by lifting up her tiny chest. He briefly frowned his discouragement.

"Madame de la Plante, are you driving?" he asked Delphine.

"If you don't mind, I would prefer to sit with Guy so that we can talk."

"Sure." He opened the back door for them. Looked like he was stuck in front with Guillaume's Euro-trash girlfriend. Luckily, she solved the conversational dilemma by turning on the radio to an unmelodic French rap station and singing along in a whiny undertone, hollowed eyes closed, muddy-booted feet propped up on the dashboard.

Tyler didn't say a word until they reached the outskirts of Paris. "Where to, Madame?"

"Take the Periferique past La Defense, the apartment is just a short distance north of the Palais de Congres. Thank you."

Rush hour was picking up in the opposite direction, coming out of the city. The village where Marie's uncle had his retreat was southeast, near Fontainbleau. He'd have to drive all the way through Paris. He'd be stuck in traffic for hours.

The apartment building Delphine directed him to stop in front of was one of the grand old Parisian structures preserved at great cost through so much history, with back balconies that faced the Arc de Triomphe a couple of blocks away. It was a wonderful location, and he thought that her husband must be doing very well; FranceFon salaries alone couldn't support this lifestyle.

Delphine got out with Guillaume. Monique followed. The three of them had a short conversation on the sidewalk. Tyler was in a no-parking zone, of course, and he wondered what he was supposed to do now. Leaving the car idling, he got out to open the trunk where he'd put Delphine's laptop case. He brought it around in time to see the teenagers entering the building.

"Thank you, Tyler." Her smile was self-assured once more. "It was wonderful of you, to do this favor for me. Please, come in, you can park in the lot." She indicated a small driveway beyond the building. "I have a pass."

Come in? That could be … sticky. "Actually, I'm in kind of a hurry now. I was hoping to get out of town sooner, you see, so …"

She wasn't listening to him. "Here. It's number seven." She took her laptop case, opened a flap, handed him a keycard. "You'll find us on the fourth floor, de la Plante."

"But …" she was walking away, hurrying into the entryway after her son.

Okay. He could handle this. He drove carefully around, down into the underground lot, and managed to ease the Peugeot into the tiny space for number seven.

Then he took the stairs up, slowly, thinking about his upcoming presentation. He'd have to stifle his designs on Madame, since he knew he was incapable of a seduction in front of her family, but never mind, the agreement was the most important part of this act, the only real part that he needed to pay attention to.

The building was as elegant inside as out, and he admired the proportions of the hallway as he waited for his ring to be answered. He ran a hand through his hair, aware of looking less than corporate, and straightened his sweater.

Thirteen

"Bonjour?" The woman who opened the door was a stranger. But the name on the plate said 'de la Plante,' so he smiled encouragingly.

"Excuse me, I'm looking for Delphine de la Plante and her son, Guillaume."

"Ah, you must be Monsieur Harding, yes?" She opened the door wider. As she smiled he realized she looked like Delphine, but was younger, more slender, with a less formal bearing. And her hair was lighter, shorter. "Come in, please. I'm Juliette de la Plante, Delphine's sister. And Monique's mother. Thanks to you I may let her live for a few more days, at least."

Monique—that horrid little vampire was Delphine's niece?

"You're our new hero, we can't thank you enough for this brave rescue," she continued, laughing, talking in a very rapid French that he strained to understand. "Delphine and I were both frantic. Delphine's husband is out of town on business, but you knew that, hmm?" She shot him a disconcertingly knowing look. "We were desperate."

She led him down a formal hallway to a glassed-in back room that was a combination kitchen/family space, obviously a remodel from the apartment's original interior. He saw an open roof terrace beyond, showing a grayish white twilight studded by the Paris skyline, through glass doors in the exposed brick back wall. A mouth-watering scent of sautéing onions wafted toward him.

Monique, who'd been scrubbed free of makeup and covered in a huge sweatshirt so she now looked about twelve, was sitting with Guillaume at a round table, eating from a plate piled with fruit, cheese and crackers and watching Asterix cartoons on a TV in the corner. This was so much what he'd thought should happen that Tyler went right to them to say hello again. Guillaume shrugged; Monique giggled through a mouthful.

"That music festival," he said to Juliette, passing the teens to stand near her, "remember Les Miserables?" He was thinking of the starved children from the play.

Her back was to him as she put on a kettle at the stove, but her voice sounded amused. "That bad, eh? You weren't tempted to stay and hear the concert?"

"It wasn't Hives, or White Stripes," he said, naming a couple of the bands his nephew Jerry had turned him on to. He glanced over to see if Guy got the references. He knew most of the world's kids were tuned into the same music. "No Linkin Park."

Guy looked up briefly. "Hives couldn't make it to this one," he said in French. "But they're coming for the Mayday manifestation."

"I saw them in New York. They're good," Tyler answered, also in French.

One side of the boy's mouth lifted just a tiny bit as he turned back to the TV. Asterix the Gaul's sidekick, Obelix, had just appeared on the screen.

Juliette turned and looked at Tyler, one hand on hip, and a grin spread across her face. *"Formidable,"* she seemed to say to herself. She reached for a bottle of red from a wine rack on the wall, took a corkscrew from a nearby drawer and opened the wine. She hooked three glasses and poured. Holding two, she advanced on Tyler.

"To you, Monsieur Harding. Thank you for bringing them back to us so quickly."

He wondered how much this might delay his getting out of town. But, wanting to seem gracious, he took the glass, touched hers, sipped. Smooth. "Call me Tyler."

"I still can't believe you dropped everything just when Delphine asked you to," she went on, studying him over the rim of her glass. "You are an extraordinarily helpful business partner." Juliette must have been the person Delphine had phoned on the way to the concert, he realized. He gave her an amiable shrug, and took another swallow.

"You will stay, I hope, to have dinner with us." She lifted a lid on a large saucepan. The scent he'd noted earlier steamed out. "The chicken is nearly ready and I'm just doing the salad and fried potatoes."

Well, he *was* hungry, and it smelled so good. Who knew how long he'd have to be on the road later? "Let me help." He liked fooling around in the kitchen; he was a good cook when he had the time and the right ingredients. He took the silly daisy-splashed apron she handed him, tied it around his waist, and started peeling the bowl of potatoes she pushed his way.

He had just finished when Delphine appeared. She'd changed into worn jeans and a red V-neck sweater. Her face was younger-looking, more relaxed, with less makeup. She smiled at him and he raised his glass, then looked down at his colander before she caught him staring at the way her jeans hugged her.

He wondered again whose home this was. Delphine's clothing was here, obviously, but Juliette knew the kitchen intimately. He supposed it could be that way, with sisters. He hadn't a clue where anything might be in his brother Gerard's stately house, composed as if photographers would arrive momentarily to do a shoot for the Greenwich Sunday supplement. Ger was an attorney who made big bucks fighting white collar crime for major corporations, and his wife Natalie took pleasure in spending a lot of it on interior decoration. He knew Jerry chafed at the carefully arranged atmosphere and so was always happy to escape to Uncle Ty's bachelor pad.

Tyler had nothing much to arrange: a miniscule spotless-because-unused kitchen, some CD equipment, speakers standing around, a bed, a soft couch.

Julee had been scrupulous in neatly dividing their wedding presents according to taste and available space: she hadn't stayed in Manhattan. She'd given him the kitchen stuff. He thought he'd gotten the better deal, and had planned one day, when he found the time, to unearth it from the hall closet and equip his kitchen properly.

Now Delphine took the glass Juliette handed her, leaned against a counter, and looked at her son, her niece and Tyler, in turn, with an expression of wonder that grew as she took in each one.

"Mon Dieu," she said to Juliette, "is this a dream? Don't wake me up, please."

Tyler cut the potatoes into sticks, scooped them into the bowl Juliette had provided, rinsed his hands. He poured himself some more wine.

Delphine surveyed him, her lips twitching as she examined his flowered apron. "You look ... quite comfortable."

"I am, yes. Thanks for inviting me up."

"We can go over the documents after dinner, will it be enough time for you, for GlobeAll's New York headquarters?"

He'd forgotten he had invented this deadline to pressure her. "Sure. Anytime before midnight here." But what about the misgivings she'd expressed? Or had she been inventing too? He frowned slightly. "Is that enough time for *you*?"

Her mouth began its purse and her eyes narrowed a little. She drew herself up into a taller figure, folding her arms around her waist, her long glass dangling from negligent-seeming fingers. "It buys me some time, no? If you just status them on the progress of our discussion?"

Buy time for what? What was she still keeping from him? He wondered if he had the energy to hear it tonight. The small signals of awareness that he thought they'd been exchanging seemed not to exist in the ambiance of this homey apartment; in her renewed poise; under her sister's keen observation; in the noise of the TV cartoon;

even in the wistful city dusk that leaked into the warm kitchen.

She watched him watching her, waiting for his response. "I don't know," he mumbled. "I'll give them a call." He couldn't even use his GlobeAll mobile to call the States; he'd have to ask for a land line in another room here, and that would remind her again of his company's limited wireless range.

"You look hungry," Juliette broke in briskly. "The business talk can wait, no?" She handed out plates, platters, dished out salad, broke a baguette apart in her slim, capable hands. She put another bottle in Tyler's hand, with the corkscrew, and he quickly opened and poured. He remembered to tear off his apron before they sat down.

Much as he'd have liked to find out more about the sisters, and about Delphine's absent spouse in particular, he was outnumbered and they ended up eliciting information from him. They were quick eaters, eager questioners, efficient monitors of their children's intake and behavior at the table. His nephew Jerry would have loved it—they gave the teens a little wine.

He felt overwhelmed by their rapid French and by the determination with which they tried to extract his life story. Even Monique joined in, asking him pointedly about his girlfriends. Guy, at least, rolled his eyes and told them to leave the poor American alone and let him eat in peace. Tyler indicated his gratitude with a slight lift of his glass to the boy. He and the kids talked music while the mothers listened, bemused by the multitude of bands they referred to. Tyler told them about Jerry.

"I'll give you his e-mail address," he said. "You can IM. You'll have to use English, though, he doesn't speak French."

"We can't IM from here," Guy said glumly. "We don't have that kind of ISP."

"GlobeAll has a nice residential package. We have a lot of bandwidth in our Paris node, and our IP speed is the best in the industry. I can get you a special deal, probably." He looked at Delphine. "You'll have to get FranceFon local access, but as a residential customer you can minimize that cost if you don't already have an employee discount."

"You are such a good salesman, Tyler, I am surprised GlobeAll isn't using your talents in that capacity," Delphine said. The warmth was back in her eyes.

"They are, of course." He smiled. "It's all sales. All the time."

When the meal was finished, the teens went into another room to play a video game, and Delphine went to make a phone call. He and Juliette sat alone at the table. "Are you still thinking you'll drive to the country tonight?" Juliette asked, opening a bottle of brandy.

"I have to," he said. He shook his head at her offer of a glass. He didn't like the idea of driving to a strange place in the dark, navigating a little town that would probably be shut up for the night, trying to find a key in the garden. "I gave up my hotel room."

"But it is late now," she said, glancing out at the black night. Rain had begun to streak the windows. "And it is raining. Why don't you stay here tonight? That gives you the chance to finish your work with Delphine in the morning."

"That's nice of you, but it's really not necessary. Not—appropriate."

"I insist. After the kindness you have done for us? I'll prepare the sofa in the office."

"Who lives here? I mean, where does Delphine live?"

"This is Delphine's apartment, but we are all living here right now," she said, carefully. "Delphine's husband is away so often, we decided to share the expenses and the children. This is near their school, and close to everything else, her work."

He wanted to ask more, since this seemed an incomplete explanation for her sister's domestic circumstances, as well as her own, but he nodded. Juliette was already too perceptive. This wasn't supposed to be his business.

"Well, thank you for your offer. I'm very grateful."

"In that case, have some brandy. We can watch a video." She indicated the long couch in front of a fireplace on the opposite side of the room. "Are you good at building a fire? You can do that while I clear up here."

He got the fire going and joined Juliette in her cleanup. Then she shooed him away, reminding him he'd told them he had to status his New York office. He went to the little den, closed the door, and called Deauville.

"Allo."

Tyler smiled at the sound of the gruff voice. He'd enjoyed Deauville's feisty banter during their many alliance conference calls.

"Georges, it's Tyler Harding. The team told me your news. How are you doing?"

"Tyler Harding! The world-beater!" Deauville's rumbly laugh filled the line. "I am well, merci a Dieu, and I am not missing FranceFon. Or you!" He laughed again. "But thank you for asking. That is kind."

"Actually, I have an ulterior motive—"

"But of course you do! It would be so unlike you, otherwise!"

"—I'm wondering why Delphine de la Plante doesn't want to sign our agreement."

There was a pause. "This is strange," Deauville said slowly. "I do not know her at all, so I could not surmise for you what is the basis of her resistance. We had all of the team lined up in support, as you know."

"Too bad you're not still with us, Georges, I could have used that support now!"

"I am happy to be away from it, Tyler, there is so much more to life. If you ever get the opportunity to slow down you will realize this also."

This sounded more than trite. It rang truer than anything he'd heard in a long time. He stared at the desk, wondering how soon his long-overdue weekend getaway was supposed to begin. If only he were done with this fucking deal! *Why* was she stalling?

"Good luck, Tyler. Perhaps you should use your famous charm on her!"

Ha. She was charm-proof, at least so far. "Georges, I had another question. You know the Canadian telco TeleOne?"

"Thieves."

"Do you remember my colleague Nick Fournier?"

"I do. So sad. He was a good man."

"He'd been dealing with TeleOne right before 9/11." Tyler didn't like to say "before Nick died." "He'd just signed an alliance agreement for the far east provinces."

"That is unfortunate, but of course, he would have had no other choice of providers, in that region."

Tyler's unease increased. "You ever hear of a TeleOne guy named Levecque?"

"Levecque, yes, they finally got rid of him last year. He was a menace. Very unethical person."

"That's not good news. He's the one Nick made the deal with." Tyler sighed, feeling frustration mount. "The deal I'm supposed to have renewed, like, yesterday."

"How difficult for you. I would choose another carrier. There is more choice now than there was two years ago." The Canadian market had indeed diversified, responding to numerous call centers being established in Newfoundland, but solidifying another carrier meant a trip to Canada, as soon as he was finished with this one, as soon as his team in New York could due-diligence the choices. At least St. John was an overnight, not a three-weeker. Maybe he could even catch a show of Great Big Sea, the whimsical Newfie sea-shanty band.

"Thanks, Georges. I've heard all I need to."

"Adieu."

He returned to the couch and forced himself to relax, sitting back, waiting for the sisters to join him, sipping the brandy Juliette put in his hand. He told himself to go with the flow. The FranceFon agreement would have to wait until tomorrow. So would his Canadian arrangements.

Fourteen

A GENTLE WATERFALL of staccato piano music woke him. Minor key. Coldplay, "Clocks." He let his eyes stay closed as the song began, eerie and poignant:

Lights go out and I can't be saved, tides that I tried to swim against
have brought me down upon my knees, oh I beg I beg and plead
...
Troubles that can't be named, tigers waiting to be tamed ...

His dream had been hazy and erotic, suffused with soft skin, softer sighs, sliding hair, barely moving limbs, sly sideways looks out of dark eyes. He couldn't recall who he'd been with in the dream, though, Delphine or Juliette or Monique or even Guillaume, Jesus, maybe all of them? He rubbed his eyes.

They'd all ended up on the couch last night, brandy poured liberally, teens draped over each other and their mothers. He could not now remember one scene of the video they'd watched, some French comedy they'd found hilarious but that was mostly lost on him. He'd perched as far away as he could comfortably get from the slight pressure of Delphine's thigh in her worn jeans, her shoulder in that sensual red sweater, the scent wafting from her every time she moved or laughed.

He needed to get clear of this infatuation, either consummate it or kill it.

He rose, pulled on his clothes, went out to the empty kitchen. It was just eight thirty. He must be the only one awake. The song was stuck on repeat.

Beyond the music, he heard a bigger sound, something like a parade. Was it a holiday? He went onto the terrace, shivering in the cold morning, and looked toward the Champs Elysees. He could see a crowd of people gathered at the bottom of the Arc de Triomphe. The big antiwar demonstration! Better get out of the city before it became impassable.

He went back into the kitchen and poked around until he found a jar of Nescafe. In his many visits to French homes, he'd never once seen that American simpleton, Mr. Coffee. He filled the kettle. He was pouring hot water into a cup when he heard Delphine's voice.

"Good morning, Tyler. I hope you slept well."

He turned. She looked even softer today, in the same faded jeans with a flannel shirt. He took in the relaxed look on her face, the loose messiness of her hair, the way her shirt molded her breasts. "Delphine. Good morning."

"I can make you a proper coffee." She pulled a glass carafe out of the cupboard, put a filter into it, poured from a bag of coffee that she took from the refrigerator. He leaned against the counter, watching her. She gave him a tentative little smile.

"I was thinking that we could discuss the agreement today, Tyler. We should have time to talk about it in detail."

He took a breath. "Why don't you come with me where I'm going? We can work in peace there, without interruptions."

Her eyes flew to his. "In, in the countryside? With you?" she faltered.

"That way you can get a bit of a break." He nodded toward the hallway, indicating the rest of the family. "Gives us plenty of time to come to a final decision even before next week."

She stared at him, one eyebrow rising, her expression caught between shock and, yes, it was temptation there, he sensed it. She bit her lip. "I can't believe you are suggesting this thing."

He held up his hands. "No pressure, no implications, Delphine. Just a little getaway." He kept his face impassive. "It'll be quieter there than here." He tilted his head toward the terrace, where the sounds of people gathering grew by the moment.

"Oh, the manifestation," she murmured, going to the glass doors to peer outside. "Juliette and the children will march today." She glanced at her watch.

"Aren't they grounded?" he asked. She wrinkled her brow, uncomprehending. "Aren't you punishing them for going to that concert yesterday?"

"But we cannot keep them from this, it is their civic duty."

He refrained from expressing his opinion. He wasn't a parent, after all, or French. "And you? Were you planning to march?"

"Not when they do, in case there is trouble." She eyed him. "Would you?"

"Not here, where I'm a foreigner," he said. "What kind of trouble would there be, Delphine? For sure French police are on the side of the protesters in this cause."

"It isn't always that way. It depends on how the people behave. We don't like to see property destroyed, for example, and sometimes the crowd is very rough. I always advise Guy to stay away from the rough people, and from the police, just in case."

"He's been to demonstrations before?"

"He is very anti-globalization," she said, wry. "He is always telling me to quit my job with the bad multinational corporation."

"Sounds like my nephew. Unless it's his birthday, and then he's happy to enjoy some of the profits of evil capitalism." They shared a smile. "I tell him telecom's a clean industry, an aid to local economic development, and it's other industries that are evil. Our customers' industries, in other words." He grinned. "But you know teenagers."

"I am sorry we are bringing them to this brink of war," she murmured, her smile turning sad. "It does not seem fair, that their generation may have to pay for our failures."

"There's still a chance for diplomacy to work."

"But I think your leader is not interested in finding any solution."

Tyler didn't answer.

"I still wonder how he finally got his office," she mused.

"I voted for him. So did most of the people I know."

"Yes. That is what the UTT people did also. But apparently businessmen do not represent the majority of Americans, hmm? He did not win the popular vote."

Tyler remembered feeling relieved when the President had finally wrangled the number of electoral votes needed. During the month of uncertainty about the election's outcome he'd endured a barrage of e-mails from his contacts around the world. Most of them were humorous—everyone remembered the spoofed-British announcement that the U.S., if unable to control its internal affairs, should revert to English colonial rule— and he thought, now, that it was the last political humor the world had enjoyed. Some of the e-mails had been scathing, with pointed remarks about democracy versus aristocracy.

Defending his political choice, then, had been a curious sensation. It was one of the few times he disagreed with his international colleagues; usually the global teams were in agreement on politics since everyone supported free trade. Among his U.S. fellow workers there had been very little diversity of opinion regarding the 2000 election.

She must have thought his short silence indicated discomfiture. "We don't have to discuss, maybe this is a delicate subject for you."

"I'm okay with it." He shrugged. "I believe our President is a fundamentally decent man. I voted for him because I thought he would make a good leader."

"You are crazy!" Guillaume's voice, from the hallway, startled Tyler. He turned around. Guy advanced, glowering, his long hair swinging over his face as he stalked. "He is more dangerous than Osama or Saddam! He wants to start World War Three."

Tyler crossed his arms and considered the boy. "I guess it depends on your point of view."

"He has ten times their power, and he thinks he is like some kind of god." Guillaume poured himself some coffee and set the carafe down with a thump. "He is a thief of your so-called democracy. He and the wicked ones around him."

"Guy," Delphine warned, glancing nervously at Tyler.

"Your English is very good, Guy," Tyler said mildly.

The boy sipped coffee, eyes narrow. "You Americans—you think you are the masters of the universe."

Tyler didn't like the contempt in his voice. "No we don't."

"Guy, that's enough. Monsieur Harding is a guest in our home," Delphine said severely. "And he works in the international arena. He isn't like a typical American."

Tyler looked at her, wondering where this was going.

"He knows our language, our culture, and others as well. He even speaks Arabic."

He could have told her that was overkill; his Arabic wasn't that strong.

"Good, maybe he can translate the Al Jazeera news for me," Guy snapped, turning on the TV where, sure enough, the controversial Arabic station was covering the Paris demonstration getting underway outside.

Tyler stifled a laugh as Delphine frowned. The kid was a pain, but smart..

On the screen, the crowd was increasing by the second, it seemed, and the convivial atmosphere depicted was underscored by the noises from the street. The demonstrators so far seemed not so much angry as excited; gusts of laughter and bursts of rock music washed up in the crisp winter air to the open kitchen window.

It sounded like fun, actually, the kind of rowdy mass fun in which the French rarely indulged unless a World Cup was going their way, and for a moment Tyler considered joining the family in their "civic duty," just for the adventure. He sipped coffee, dissuading himself, enumerating the reasons why that would be impossible: he was on GlobeAll's time, even if he was taking a couple of days off; he was not sure that he supported the demonstrators' motivations; he was a foreigner here; and he had a timebound mission to accomplish.

Speaking of which. He looked up to find Delphine's dark eyes on him. He stared back, trying to decipher her look. He could tell by the solemnity of her gaze that she was thinking about his proposition, and he produced an intimate smile for her.

"It's the only way we'll get any work done," he said softly.

As he watched her quickly look away, blush creeping up her cheeks, certainty dawned, along with fierce arousal, so strong he had to readjust the way he was standing. She wanted him too; now he was sure of it in a way he hadn't been before.

"I have to get out of the city before it's too late," he told her, making his tone cool with regret, glancing at the television. "I can still use the side streets, but soon they'll be impassable."

She reached a hand up to massage her neck, fretfully. "But what could I say to my family?" she seemed to be asking herself.

"Tell them the truth." He shrugged. "I need your full concentration on this, and it probably won't happen here, and we have to come to terms by Monday."

"But—I don't intend for this to—imply anything, about our agreement," she began stiffly.

He smiled, innocently. "No strings, I told you, just peace and quiet." He put his cup down on the counter. He knew the value of timing. "I'll go get ready."

Guy chose that moment to look around at him.

"Tell me, Monsieur, will you come to the manifestation with us?"

Tyler knew he did not have to rise to this; in fact, he knew he should not, if he wanted to keep his momentum with Delphine. But something in Guy's face, something resigned behind his sneer as much as the sneer itself, made him want to meet the boy's challenge with a serious response.

"I can't. I'm not on my own time here in Paris, Guy, and even if I were, I don't believe I have the right to express myself in your country that way."

"And in New York? Would you then?"

"Probably not."

"You want to kill innocent Iraqis?"

"Absolutely not. I don't think we should invade their country. But, I'm sorry to say, demonstrations won't stop it. The people behind this aren't paying attention to world opinion. They have their own agenda, Guy, as you've probably figured out."

"Oil?"

"I doubt it." Tyler sighed. He didn't see any clean solution coming out of invading Iraq. Unilateralism was always bad for trade, and he envisioned negative business ramifications spreading out like ripples in a toxic pool. The current anti-Europe mania sweeping the States, for example, had created incredible tension in his recent European negotiations. People were more suspicious of Americans than ever before. "It's more complex than oil, it's the history of our relationships in the Middle East—"

"The Zionists use your country like a puppet!" Guy spat.

"It's *complex*," Tyler repeated, trying to hold onto his patience.

"Why don't you make war on *Saudi Arabia*? Saddam didn't fly into your towers."

"We're too closely tied up together, Americans and Saudis."

Guy frowned his incomprehension. "So what is this Iraq invasion?"

"I wish I knew exactly." Tyler confessed, "A lot of us are pretty confused right now. We're not quite sure what to fear, what to believe."

"Americans are so stupid, they believe whatever their media tells them," Guy said dismissively, turning back to the screen. Tyler glimpsed an intense Al Jazeera journalist interviewing an avid blond French youth, who wore a black-and-white checkered kafeeyeh wound around his pale neck, and an Osama photo button on his jean jacket. Mujahid chic.

"Oh, *we're* the only ones in the world who buy what the media portrays?" Tyler drawled, but his sarcasm was wasted on Guy and on Delphine, who was still eyeing him.

"You see, Tyler, it isn't easy for me to just drop everything to go with you." She sounded angry. He shouldn't have let Guy distract him from her, but he'd wanted to give the boy the honesty he deserved. Too bad Guy's conclusions were solidified; Tyler's remarks hadn't made a dent.

He stood still and let his full attention focus on Dephine. Her expression was so troubled that he doubted his earlier perception, wondering again whether they really were on the same wavelength. He took in her whole persona, anew, in the unforgiving light of morning, stripped of the artifice of makeup, of corporate camouflage or evening candlelight. She still got to him in a way he hadn't been gotten in a long time. And he was determined to turn around her reluctance concerning this agreement.

"I can't stay here," he told her quietly. "I want you to come with me, but I can't make that decision for you. We have important business to discuss. You're willing to put it off until next week, but I can't guarantee GlobeAll's ability to extend your company that kind of time." He shrugged. "You've been very hospitable, you and your family, but I can't impose on you any longer."

He walked down the hallway to the den where he'd slept, and stuffed his stray sweater and shaving kit into his backpack. He gave a perfunctory glance around the room to ensure he wasn't leaving anything behind, and his gaze caught a photo of a smiling, sandy-haired man whose arm was wrapped around a much younger Delphine and a little-boy Guy.

Damn. Here was the husband, after all, making his presence felt in the most subtle way, watching by night as the sleeping intruder dreamed about this attractive nuclear and extended family. Tyler supposed he should feel guiltier than he did.

He picked up the photo. The man looked as if he'd been a happy guy, ten or more years ago. Delphine looked harried in the picture, pulling Guy onto her lap, squinting into the camera. The tantalizing sexuality that emanated from her now was not at all apparent in this faded photograph.

He wondered suddenly if she'd had an affair, or maybe was still having one, if that was the reason for what he sensed was an estranged marriage. That would be very French. Perversely, the thought aroused him again. If she was already fooling around, his come-on wouldn't be the affront she seemed to pretend it was.

Of course, he mused, setting the photo down, he and Delphine had a clear conflict of interest standing between them, one which was serious enough to give any sensible person pause. But sensible people didn't make spectacular sales—that took imagination, and passion, and a kind of visionary belief that went beyond optimism into delusion. He embraced delusion. He'd never have the patience to create any alliances without it.

He thought of Nick again.

"Ya wanna close em, Ty, ya gotta love em," he used to say, pointing his cigarette at Tyler. He'd been a smoker when that was de rigueur international business, a source of common ground with "foreigners" that Nick used to his advantage, packing cartons of Winstons and Marlboros to sweeten the deal on every trip. He'd been accepting of the wilier aspects, like bribery, of global business. Had he been accepting of some TeleOne shenanigans?

"When you're overseas, boy, ya gotta play by their rules," was another of his favorite expressions. "Overseas" had sounded quaint, to Tyler. "Don't leave your good sense behind, though: remember, culture doesn't matter if you're buying." He'd tap a long ash and peer under bushy brows. "But it matters more than anything else when you're selling."

Tyler remembered being impressed by Nick's worldliness at their first meeting. He always came to Thunderbird to recruit, he said, it was a decent training ground for global commerce wanna-be's. He'd taken a liking to Tyler and had followed his career at GlobeAll, turning up to take Tyler out for dinner and proffering advice which rang even more true after Tyler started picking up the check and telling his own stories. Nick had been the lone voice of doubt when Tyler announced his plans to marry Julee.

"She's not enough for you, Ty, I see your eyes wandering," he'd insisted quietly. "She doesn't grab you. Ya wanna close em, Ty ..."

"Yeah I know, ya gotta love em, but Nick, she's perfect for me."

"Okay." Nick also understood delusion, apparently.

He had sent the newlyweds a handsome lighted globe for the study they'd planned on having. It was packed away in Tyler's apartment closet. Nick had taken on the Canadian market as country manager for GlobeAll in 1998. His death on 9/11 had not yet, Tyler knew, fully sunk in. He preferred to imagine his friend was on a long business trip, ever-seeking that perfect deal, ever closing.

He stood now in the De la Plante den, noting they didn't have a globe, wondering what Nick would have thought of Delphine. *Ya wanna close em, ya gotta love em.* He

stuffed Delphine's copy of the agreement into his jacket
pocket.

Fifteen

WHEN HE CAME BACK into the kitchen Juliette and Monique had joined Guy around the table, sipping coffee in thick café au lait cups, dipping croissants. Delphine was not with them.

"I need to leave before the traffic's blocked," Tyler told them, slinging his pack onto his shoulder. "I enjoyed meeting you all. Thanks for your kindness."

"Au revoir, Monsieur," cooed Monique, peering at him from under heavily made up lashes. She had her game face back on this morning, he was amused to see, geared up for the flirtation possibilities that might present themselves during the demonstration.

He reached to shake Guy's hand. "Thanks for sharing your opinions. Your good questions will make your life very interesting. Try to keep an open mind."

Guy shook firmly, eyes suddenly fixed on Tyler's face. "*Merci, aussi, por votre honetete,*" he said. Thanks for your honesty.

"You know how to get away from the city?" Juliette asked. "There's a route around the roadblocks for the manifestation, I can show you ..." She stood, took a map from a stack of papers next to the phone, and unfolded it on the countertop. "Delphine can help you to navigate, although she hasn't driven in years."

He took in this new information, keeping his face still as he leaned to look at the map. "So she's able to come along after all? She wasn't sure of her schedule," he murmured.

"I told her to go ahead, I don't have plans except to be with the children during the manifestation." She added carefully, "She didn't want to miss the conference you're attending." She glanced back at Guy and Monique.

So they were in cahoots. A conference, good excuse. Juliette acknowledged his little smile with a smaller one, with eyes that held a hint of warning.

"I can help her with FranceFon, Juliette. The agreement we're working on will be a solid achievement for her new group. It'll be positive for her."

"I hope so," Juliette muttered.

Delphine came in, wearing the red sweater from last night with a buttery leather jacket, and carrying a neat case. She put her hand on Guy's shoulder.

"Be careful. Stay away from the loud people, and remember to keep together."

"*Oui, Maman.*" Guy's tone said he'd heard it all before.

"I'll have my mobile on all the time, of course, if you need me for anything."

"We'll be fine," Juliette told her. "Go now, before you get stuck."

Delphine seemed to hover for a moment, as if she might change her mind, and she finally looked at Tyler. Her eyes were bright, and she'd put on makeup, but her mouth and back looked stiff with tension, or fear. He smiled easily, trying for reassurance, and something in his relaxed posture must have reached her, for she took a deep breath and dropped her shoulders.

"All right," she said, lightly. "*On y va.*" Let's go.

He tried not to grin too broadly as they left the apartment and went down into the car park. He threw their bags into the back seat, and allowed himself to touch her arm as he held open the passenger door for her. Her jacket was a smooth promise under his palm, but she flinched.

"I don't want you to have the idea that I do this kind of thing very much."

"I don't have any ideas except to get our agreement discussed."

He was relieved to see the crowds hadn't yet spilled into the side streets; in fact, they were empty of traffic. Probably everyone was avoiding the area. He used the route Juliette had pointed out, and soon they were on the pereferique again, speeding around Paris past the Bois de Boulogne, passing through the sprawl of grayish suburbs until they were heading southeast. Within an hour they reached open countryside.

What a great day for a drive. The sun, a rare sight in February France, gave the sky a hard, high blue, and the road wound through endless fields whose golden stubble pledged a flourishing spring. It felt so good to be out of the city he rolled his window down to let the crisp air rush in, heedless of its chill. He breathed in deeply, and turned to smile at her. She'd been studying him intermittently.

"Do you like the outdoors, Delphine?"

The question seemed to surprise her, as if she had to think about it. "Yes, sometimes."

"We should go hiking," he said. "My pal told me there are some beautiful woods near the village. We can take a picnic. Would you like that?"

She watched him, still, but gave a little nod.

"Relax." He turned on the radio and found a nice jazz station. "Nothing's going to happen between us that you don't want."

"I know that, Tyler, I would not be here with you otherwise." She finally looked away from him. He could see her chewing on her lip.

"Then, let's enjoy this, hmm? Since it's all about what you want?"

"Maybe that is the problem," she said in a voice so low he could hardly hear her. "I am not sure what I want with you, or for our work relationship. I am confused."

"That's why I'm here to advise you. You have only to ask." He gave her his most charming grin, eliciting a reluctant little laugh.

"Do you go to these extremes with every deal?"

"Different deals, different extremes," he shrugged. "But you are completely unique in my experience, Delphine. I don't mix business with my private life." This was not entirely accurate. His professional life was so intense that it had altogether replaced the personal; except for his brother's family he saw no-one regularly who wasn't somehow job-related. He was careful—he didn't date GlobeAll colleagues. But it occurred to him that he'd met all his women since Julee through work friends.

"So then ... why this?"

He couldn't give her the attention he wanted to in a stick shift on the narrow two-lane French "highway." "It's a mystery," he said simply. "We'll explore it later?"

She seemed content to let it go, and sat back more loosely in the seat, letting her head rest as she looked out at the passing bucolic scenery.

When shortly they came to Fontainbleau, Delphine told him its history. The grand chateau had been built originally as a hunting lodge by Francois I in the sixteenth century. It was surrounded by a vast forest, a favorite of Parisians needing a day trip into wilderness. They stopped in the small village to buy firewood, picnic supplies and other groceries. Tyler picked out several bottles of wine and an opener. They followed Jack's directions to the winding road past the village, up a hill, down a long driveway. The cottage sat in a copse of willow trees whose bare dry fronds stroked its wavy roof, thin caressing fingers Tyler imagined could be heard on a windy night, up under the eaves.

They sat in the car for a moment, both aware of the import of this arrival.

"We should be sure to tour Fontainbleau," Delphine said briskly. "It is the most magnificent example of Renaissance art outside of Versailles."

His expression must have reminded her that he had escaped Versailles as soon as possible the other night. "Of course," she added hastily, "the forest will be perfect for our picnic today, it is so dry." Anything, she seemed to imply, rather than go inside alone with him.

He hoped Marie's uncle had some old blankets for their picnic. Thinking of blankets made him smile at her. She looked delectable in her soft jacket, her hair shining on her shoulders, eyes wide as she met his gaze, hands clasped on her snug jeans. She opened her door and got out.

He found the hidden key, and wiggled it at the cottage door lock and pushed, as Jack had advised. The inside was more spacious and modern-looking than he expected—old walls had been taken down to create a great room whose gleaming wood floor was enhanced by thick carpets placed near comfortable pieces of furniture. They needn't have brought firewood—plenty was stacked neatly by the large fireplace. His fantasy of secluded rusticity was dashed by the sight of a large-screen TV and a galley kitchen shining with stainless steel.

Comfort was better than roughing it, he decided. He went up the short flight of stairs to a loft bedroom. There was only one big bed, piled with a luxurious leopard-print faux fur throw. It advertised such sleazy seduction that he thought he'd better offer to sleep on one of the couches down below. Marie's bachelor uncle must be quite the roué.

"This is a very interesting cottage," said Delphine, "I think the owner has less love for the outdoors than you do." She had come up right behind him, so close he could smell her perfume. She was looking at the bed with an amused expression, making him harden in arousal, and he walked away from her into the little bathroom. When he came out she was downstairs again, standing by the front door, car keys in hand. The bag of picnic food was at her feet, and a faded quilt: resourceful woman.

Jack, knowing Ty's love of climbing, had indicated in his map the hiking trails in the Fontainbleau forest. Mindful of Delphine's elegant short leather boots, Tyler chose one that didn't wind too steeply up the hills. Alone, he'd have tackled the most rigorous. Maybe tomorrow morning he'd come back out. Too bad he didn't have any rock equipment. If they weren't going to be intimate, he'd need a severe physical workout to take the edge off. He kept his mind resolutely on his feet as they walked.

There were a few other hikers and rock climbers out, but after they had hiked for about half an hour they found a quiet clearing to spread the quilt and sit down. Although the day was clouding up, there was still weak sunlight, and the wind was diminished by the surrounding pines. Tyler opened a bottle of red, and Delphine broke up a baguette and cut slices of Brie and pear.

They ate and drank in silence. The simple meal and fresh air dissipated his sexual tension and Tyler lay down, hands behind his head. He felt Delphine do the same, beside him, and he hoped it meant she was finally letting her guard down.

After some time, he heard her breathing slow and deepen. He leaned up on an elbow to look at her. Yes— she was asleep. Ha, he made fun of himself, so much for my stimulating effect. But it was a good sign, surely, that she trusted him enough to just fall asleep? He watched her face, younger in sleep, her lips parted. He could imagine outlining them with his tongue. He watched the rise and fall of her breasts. Her slick jacket was open, and her soft red sweater cupped them, tantalizing cashmere-covered hills with the most tempting peaks. He wanted to climb here too, sliding up the smooth leather to the fuzzy wool, letting his hand explore the velvet of her throat before following the V of her sweater into the valley underneath. Damn.

He sat up quietly, taking deep breaths until his excitement ebbed. This was nuts. He wasn't some horny teenager, and she wasn't some willing squeeze. Get a grip, he told himself, and not on her. He sighed, and as his chest rose he felt the crinkle of paper in his jacket pocket. The agreement.

The crackling must have woken her. "Oh, Tyler, did I fall asleep?" She sat up next to him. "I am sorry, how rude, it's just that I am always so tired, you see."

"Believe me, I know all about it." He smiled at her sideways. He didn't trust his body to face her just now. "You were talking in your sleep."

"Yes?" she asked, confused.

"You were saying 'Tyler, please, now.' " He eyed her, mischievous, pleased when he saw her blush.

"No, I did not say that."

"Uh huh, you did. You said, 'Please, *please* let me sign the agreement now.' "

Her laugh was the full one he'd seen at his Happy Meal crack, after their return from Versailles. Could that really have been just two nights ago? It seemed he'd known her much longer. She pushed his arm, playfully, and it took all his discipline not to nudge her back, not to start kindling the physical comfort level between them that would, he knew, flare into sex immediately, and it wouldn't be 'making love'—it would be a hot, fast fuck. And that wasn't how he wanted it. Not yet anyway.

When he didn't laugh, she quickly removed her hand. She smoothed her hair and started picking up the remains of their snack. Neither had eaten much. He twisted the cork back into the bottle and shook out the quilt. The sky was now gray.

He wasn't sure whether to be sorry or relieved that it started raining on their drive back to the cottage. He'd actually considered dropping her off and returning to the forest for a mind-drenching climb, to get clean the way he'd used to in his youth in the Rockies, when he'd hike beyond the timberline, with no more preparation than a canteen of water bumping against his leg and a slick of sunscreen on his nose. He'd cherished his solitude like his geologist father and gemologist mother, who loved the mountains.

Gerard had been the family's social animal, and Tyler had escaped his older brother's raucous gatherings in their Telluride ranch house with those long hikes. His dad was oblivious to teenage noise, typing away in his soundproofed office, but sometimes his mom had come along, both of them silent for hours, her long legs keeping perfect pace with his except when she stopped to collect crystals.

"Tyler?" Delphine's soft voice, hesitant, yanked him from memory. "What are you thinking of?"

People closest to him called him 'Ty.' He wondered if he should tell her that. He glanced at her, and was then surprised to realize they were past the village, nearly to their turnoff: he'd been driving blind. On this rainy road!

He tried to excuse himself: too many cities in too short a span.

Too much pressure to produce.

Too many deals juggled like knives that would slash him if he dropped even one. Too many goddamn millions at stake.

This unexpected interlude in time, in nature, in the sensual richness this woman exuded, was a disorienting distraction. He'd been running so fast, for so long, and she was making him want to stand still. Or lie down, actually, and lose himself in her until he felt rejuvenated.

"I'm tired all the time too, Delphine, and it makes me absent-minded."

"Then you should rest this weekend." At once she was cheerful, practical; comfortable in a nurturing role, apparently. "I will cook you a nice dinner, and you can go to sleep early. We can work tomorrow."

She probably used the same damn tone on Guy.

They were in the winding gravel drive already, the dripping trees darkening the way, dreary as fucking Manderley. *Rebecca* had been one of his mother's favorite novels, and he'd tried to read it one endless summer just to please her. Bor-ing! But its ominous setting came to him now. He snatched his mood back from the edge of gloom. He was just horny, dammit, it wasn't terminal. He mustered a smile. "Sounds good."

The clean space inside the cottage warmed him, as did the fire he built, and the glass of wine Delphine put in his hands, and the fragrance of sautéing mushrooms that emanated from the kitchen while he was stoking the fire. He went to lean against the thin counter, to watch her capable hands finding utensils in drawers he wouldn't have thought to look for; she was as skilled with a knife as with the grater, as with the whisk. He wondered what she'd do if he just flung them aside and grabbed her.

"Give me something to do."

"There is nothing. This is like vacation to me, Tyler. I love to cook, and I never seem to get the time."

"I like to cook too. Breakfast is mine, okay?"

"Okay."

"So, who does the cooking at home? Juliette? Guy?" He couldn't see Monique working the stove.

"Juliette, usually, but we have a lot of take-away, also." She sounded as if it was a shameful admission.

"Can I ask about your husband?"

She ducked her head in a neck roll. She took another sip of wine. Her shoulders rose as she inhaled, deeply. "You have that right, since I came here with you."

He waited.

"He is away almost all the time on business. I suppose you would say we are separated."

"By business trips or by design?"

"Would you think I am coward to say, we didn't really have the time to discuss?"

He sipped his own wine. "You didn't have the *time?*" he repeated.

"It's not an easy conversation, you know," she answered defensively.

"I do know. I'm divorced."

"But *you* don't have children." It sounded like an accusation.

"No."

"I didn't think so."

The bitterness in her tone made him pull back.

Heavy baggage.

He looked over at the fire crackling, the furniture easy enough to sink into, the gleaming floors. He summoned the energy to appreciate them, to remember that he was supposed to be on vacation, no matter the outcome of their being here together.

"My husband is with UTT." Her taut voice interrupted his meditation, said as if it should dispel his attempted peace.

It did. He gave himself a moment before answering.

"How did he feel about you leaving for FranceFon?"

"He ... wasn't very happy." She rolled her head around her neck again. "But it was a way for me to find independence."

"What does he do for them?"

"He's a Vice President, in Settlements."

"Settlements" referred to the traffic passed from one carrier to another, in mostly even trades between countries. UTT had been around forever; their settlement agreements went back to the beginning of telecom.

"That's bound to be a lucrative area." Now he knew who paid for the apartment near the Arc de Triomphe. Hell, he'd probably done business with the guy.

"It all depends, doesn't it, Tyler."

"On what?"

"On where the traffic is switched."

He looked at her, puzzled. Settlements were based on formally agreed-upon rates, or tariffs, which determined the cost of dedicated traffic that passed through fixed border crossings. Switched traffic took any available route and so its price was not as predictable.

"Where's the money in that?"

She shot him a narrow glance. "It depends on how the access is charged. Where traffic is switched," she repeated, and he had the feeling she didn't say it idly. But what was he missing here? And why was she bringing it up? Was this related to her husband's job? His hold on her?

"So ... there's money in it along the way, somehow?" he said slowly, thinking aloud. "If you take switched long distance traffic and drop it somewhere, let's say, make it look like a local call, and then route it out somewhere else? Without being charged by an access vendor?"

Long distance carriers, like GlobeAll and UTT, were always looking for ways to get around local access fees, but since those fees were mostly unavoidable they usually ended up passing them on to customers. If access fees were disguised, somehow, by switching traffic, a carrier could lower its costs dramatically, and make a boatload of money ... but that was strictly against FCC and International Telecom Union rules.

"You'd have to get collusion from inside the country. From whoever the access vendor is. Or you'd be cheating them. And the carrier who took it from there."

Her Gallic shrug said it all. "Just so."

"But—" but he couldn't imagine any carrier risking it. They'd be barred from doing business everywhere if the practice were discovered. "That would be stupid."

"Stupid but profitable," she said, eyeing him.

He laughed. "You're not trying to tell me UTT does anything like that."

"Maybe they do," she said, facing him. "Maybe we all do it. FranceFon, GlobeAll ... how would we know?"

"Come on, Delphine, we'd be the ones to arrange those deals, we, the alliance brokers. And there's just no way. It's illegal. Who could hide that kind of fraud? It would show up in the accounting statements."

"And the accounting statements—you always believe?"

He studied her. She was leading him on, but to where? "I believe *my* company's, absolutely. We have the cleanest record in the industry. I can't vouch for *yours*," he quipped, thinking he could draw her out with humor. "You don't have the SEC breathing down your neck here in France."

"And you want to make an agreement with us, not knowing for sure?"

Was *this* what was behind her reluctance to sign?

He set his glass down and stepped away from the counter. If FranceFon's accounting statements were suspect he'd have to rethink his entire strategy.

"You've lost me," he told her, cool.

"I don't want to spoil our dinner," she said quickly. "I wasn't meaning to start this conversation now."

"If not now, when? Obviously you know something I don't. That puts me at a disadvantage."

"Tyler." Her smile was more charming than she'd ever shown him. "Please give me some more wine?"

He knew a line when he heard one, but he poured for her, and filled his own again, thinking a little blur right now would be welcome. He wouldn't let this subject drop, certainly, but he was willing to reserve judgment until a more lucid time.

"Let's have a nice dinner together, and a ... good night of rest, and tomorrow we can talk about all of this," she said sweetly.

A good night of rest. Now there was a pleasant euphemism. He was sure, now, that his attraction to her was not returned. She had something else in mind for him, he just didn't know what yet. As he concluded this, she turned away from the stove and fixed him with a look of such fierce yearning that, startled, he took another step back.

"Tyler. I am so sorry that our time together would be spoiled this way."

"This way?"

She waved her spatula. "All this talk about telecom. All this—suspicion."

He sighed. "Delphine." He was reaching the end of his patience. "Telecom is who we *are*. I was never suspicious of you, or of your company, or of our planned alliance. But I'm not getting that same warm and fuzzy from you." She looked puzzled. He corrected himself. "I don't feel you have the same respect for my company, maybe not for me, it's just too hard to tell with you. I give up." He drank deeply, looking at her over the rim of his glass.

"Please, don't give up on me. Give me a chance."

"Maybe if I knew who you really are, I could consider it."

She seemed to deflate in front of him. Her head drooped, her hair slid forward to cover her cheeks. Her breasts rose and fell, distracting him anew; he wanted to reach for her. He resisted. She slowly lifted her face.

"I see you in so many ways," she said quietly. "I see a very attractive man who I want to be so close to. I didn't feel this in a long time, you don't know." She took a deep breath. "And I see a business adversary, trying to push me into something I'm not ready for—"she waved away his exclamation of protest—"and I see, too, a person who is open to the world, interested, able to talk to my family and make everyone like him so much."

"Maybe not Guy," he was compelled to interject.

"Especially Guy. Do you know how long it has been since his father talked to him about politics, or had any idea about the music he likes, or even really looked at him?"

He didn't know what to say. It seemed like a low blow. He figured *he'd* be a lousy father, given his travel schedule, so he wasn't going to judge the guy on that.

"I know, you travel also," she said, echoing his thoughts. "But you are still engaged with the people around you, all of them, even the taxi drivers." She smiled. "You aren't ... a robot."

She used the same word that Julee had flung at him. He thought of his chronic fatigue, of the animal shelter that had refused him, of his desolate apartment, of his unresolved mourning for Nick, of the melancholy stirred up in him by this, his first free weekend in months. "I don't know, Delphine, I'm damn near."

"Not yet, I think," she murmured, stepping toward him, so close there could be no mistaking her intention, and she was suddenly in his arms and he was kissing her finally, deeply, free to let his hands run through her hair, down her back, drawing her tightly against him as their tongues met and they pressed into each other. He had the presence of mind to reach behind her and turn off the stove burners before stumbling toward and sinking with her onto the thick carpet in front of the fireplace.

She was as abundant as he'd known she would be, as generously yielding, and greedier than he'd have guessed.

She enveloped him as he clutched her, as he pulled at her clothes to get closer; she bit his lips, wrapped his hair in rigid fists as he used his mouth all over her, too hungry to get enough, too excited to be gentle. As hard as he wanted to push, however, she met him in each frantic caress, urging him further, onto an agonizingly sharp precipice and then into an oblivion that was infinitely sweet.

He woke to find her stroking his hair back, threading her fingers lightly through it as he'd pictured the willow fronds on the roof outside. The fire was burning low in the grate and the lights were off. He was too stunned to move anything except his lips, in a lazy smile.

Sixteen

He heard the sound of rain pattering on the roof, not far from his head.

Good. The wetter the better. She could not put off their business with proposed tours of the chateau, and once it was concluded, they could use the cottage for its designed purpose all afternoon.

He grinned, stretching. What a night they'd made!

The sensuality he'd suspected in her matched his own. She had force in her opulent curves. He usually went for long, slim girls. She was deeper, darker, more abandoned; she threw herself into him with none of the careful athleticism he'd known with others. Her husband must be some kind of machine not to appreciate her heat.

They'd finally eaten around midnight and staggered up to the bed to keep on, all night long. He wanted her again, remembering.

He got out of bed, pulled on his jeans, padded downstairs. When she saw him she turned from the kitchen counter and enveloped him, wordlessly, so ardently that soon they were once more entwined, standing up right there in the kitchen.

Afterward he leaned into the refrigerator corner, laughing, panting, raking his sweaty hair back with a shaky hand.

"You're incredible, Delphine."

"You, you, you." She wound her arms around him and kissed him again, so deeply he lost his breath. "You are *formidable,* Tyler." She bit his stubbly cheek and then held him tight, rocking him to her with a strength he found surprising, clutching him so hard he had to push her away a little, laughing again.

"Let me breathe, honey."

She dropped her arms and looked at him from under her thick lashes. Her hair was as mussed as he knew his was, her cheeks flushed, her lips bruised by his mouth. Her eyes were black, burning, as she stared at him.

He felt pierced, deep, in some internal cranny previously untouched, as if she were a surgeon slicing him open without anesthesia. He shivered as he felt himself evaporating in the fire of her look.

She broke the intensity by pulling her robe closed, and turning back to the cooktop. "How do you like your coffee?"

He recovered immediately. "Au lait. I'll heat the milk." He reached behind him to get it out of the refrigerator, poured a little into a pan, stirred it.

"I'll be right back." He liked the way she walked across the great room, loose-limbed, as if she'd have trouble standing for long. Shortly he heard the shower running upstairs. He fixed his coffee and sank into one of the generous armchairs, stretching his legs out in front of him.

He smelled her on his hand holding the cup, closed his eyes to inhale. Mmm, she was wonderful. His moodiness was as erased as his exhaustion. He felt ready to charge back out into the world, and he grinned, figuring his work here could definitely be considered Mission Accomplished. Hell, he could get her to sign ten agreements now. Maybe he should figure out how much further their relationship could be expanded.

FranceFon's coverage in Africa and the Arabian Gulf was an area they hadn't outlined, since those countries were so highly regulated, but it was worth exploring. Demand for service in those regions was growing steadily for industries where the drumbeat of war meant drumming up business opportunities.

Too bad Dephine didn't handle the Middle East; they could have booked a week at one of Bahrain's luxe hotels at the privatization forum next month. He'd have liked to see the Arabian Gulf, one of the areas that intrigued him, through her eyes; to see how she responded to the hidden sensuality of that culture.

They'd have to plan frequent meetings. He'd clean up his apartment so she could stay with him when business took her to New York. She was just what he needed: healthy in her sexual expression, understanding of the stress of global telecom, and too sophisticated to make any unreasonable demands.

She came down, mesmerizing him by the way her hips swayed in their faded jeans. He should have told her not to bother dressing.

She stood close, stroking his hair. "What are you smiling about, mon cher?"

"How many deals we're going to do together." He pulled her in front of him, reaching for the buttons on her jeans, ready to yank them down.

"So, Tyler, you think it will be so easy?"

He slid her sweater up to plant a sucking kiss on her stomach. "I think it's going to be the easiest business we've ever done."

He moved his hands around her waist, to draw her onto his lap, but she pushed him away. It didn't feel like a playful push. He looked up, surprised. She wasn't smiling. "What?"

"I should have known all you will think about, now, is business." She was angry? What the fuck! "I suppose you think I will just happily sign your agreement, hmm?"

He leaned back and sipped his coffee, eyeing her, giving himself time. She ran her gaze over him and he watched, dismayed, as her features drew downward in what looked like despair. Oh no. She couldn't be a weeper, not his magnificent Delphine. Maybe she was just stunned by the same momentary bolt that had hit him earlier, a bolt of spooky intensity he had to think was lust-induced. He set his cup on the floor and stood to wrap his arms around her, tightly.

"Hey now, hey." He rocked her as she'd rocked him in the kitchenette. "Of course I'm not just thinking about business. I'm thinking about how we can stay close. How we can arrange our visits."

"You are? This isn't just ... once for you?"

"Once with you isn't nearly enough."

But her shoulders were shaking, and her sobs came freely, wetting his bare chest. He patted her head, feeling inadequate as he always did with crying women. "You don't know how hard this is for me," she sputtered. "This is not the first time I have an affair, but I didn't feel it like this, and I don't know this feeling. I am so afraid."

"Shh, shhh." He stroked her hair. He'd known, somehow, that she was a player, that he wasn't her first extra-marital venture. It eased his incipient guilt about her family. "You don't have to be afraid of me. I won't hurt you."

"How can I know that? Maybe this was a terrible mistake?" She was actually crying harder now. Jesus. "You are thinking one thing about us, but I know another, and you won't like it. You will hate me, Tyler."

Hate her? What was this? His scant experience with married women had him treading lightly. "Honey, no, I won't hate you. Hush. Let's have breakfast, and we can worry about this later, hmm?" He rocked her toward the couch and helped her to sit down. He smoothed her hair back and kissed the top of her head where it was springy and fragrant: what beauty. "Have your coffee, and I'll fix you something to eat, and you'll feel better. Unless you hate my cooking."

That made her laugh. He'd cheer her more, he hoped, once she was fed. He fetched a tissue from a box in the kitchenette. He left her mopping her face as he assembled omelette ingredients.

He brought breakfast to the low table in front of her and sat on the floor. She was composed now, he was relieved to see, and they ate companionably.

It would be easy, he knew, to lose himself in her today, to forget her family as well as the distance and business between them. But he wouldn't allow himself to do that. It was time to nudge the conversation along. He knew her well enough to gauge that sweet talk wouldn't work. Sincerity would. He moved around the table to lean back against the couch next to her, letting his head rest on her knee. He closed his eyes as he felt her hand stroke his hair, so sweetly he almost resented having to switch gears.

"This is a first for me, too."

She made a little noise of disbelief. "No."

"Oh, sure, I've had ... But not like this, like a— shock."

"You don't have to say this to me, Tyler, that isn't why I was upset— "

"I know I don't. I just want you to know, you're not alone. I'm as—surprised as you, that it's like this between us. I didn't expect it. I didn't expect anything."

"You expected an agreement to be the outcome, though, didn't you."

He shrugged as if it were the last thing on his mind. "In the scheme of things, does it matter that much?" He kept his eyes closed, savoring the smooth strokes of her fingers in his hair. Fully a minute passed before she spoke.

"Tyler. Look at me."

He turned.

Her face was sober, more serious even than in their first meeting in the conference room, which now seemed so long ago. He sat up straight.

"I can't sign the agreement." Her voice was low, as if she were confessing a crime, but her gaze was steady. "I need to explain why, and it isn't easy. Will you promise not to get too angry?" The last sentence came out in a little rush, and he saw now a shadow of fear in her eyes.

He couldn't speak. His expression made her hurry on, "It's complicated. It has to do with what we were discussing last night."

Last night? They hadn't said anything coherent after she came on to him.

"In the kitchen. Before." She swallowed, and reached again for a lock of his hair. He jerked back. "The settlement costs? The access fees?"

Access fees. "What about them?" He couldn't help sounding harsh.

"You remember, you asked, is UTT hiding them?"

"Or FranceFon?" He felt a rush of impending disaster.

"It's not FranceFon. Not UTT. It's GlobeAll."

He shook his head. He wasn't hearing this.

"It's GlobeAll, Tyler, switching traffic through Canada as if it's local, shifting it to UTT. So UTT has to pay the Canada access fees." When he still didn't speak she rushed on. "It has been systematic, for years, my husband thinks. GlobeAll chose small Canadian telcos in order to hide the deception. It's cost UTT millions."

Small Canadian telcos! Like TeleOne? Like Nick's deal with them? As he stared at her, her face seemed to grow suddenly tiny as if at the end of a long telescope, and he felt himself losing it.

"Bullshit." He wrenched away from her hand reaching for his shoulder.

"It's true, Tyler, but I am so relieved that you didn't know about it. I couldn't be sure, at first, you seem to be so much a very good salesman, I thought you were trying to be tricky with me."

"I'm not the tricky one here."

"Tyler, please, I asked you not to get angry. Isn't it better that you know the truth about your company? And I am telling you this before it becomes known, in the media, before the *Wall Street Journal* tells everyone. UTT has made its final investigations. Very soon, this will be the news."

"Some news, coming from a competitor, like anyone's going to believe this?"

She stared at him.

"We've weathered this kind of smear campaign before. This isn't news. This is slander." He stared back, feeling his pulse finally slow as he began to regain his equilibrium. "Access fees are something we all try to get out of, you know that, they're a leftover from the monopolies. Anything GlobeAll might have done to avoid them has been done by everyone else."

"Not this way. Not with this kind of deception."

"I don't believe you." He surveyed her for a moment, reviewing how her behavior had been such a strange mixture of aloofness and appeal toward him, seeing how guarded she'd been about the alliance from the beginning. "What I do believe is that you haven't been straight with me.

"You could have just said, directly, that UTT was going to do an expanded FranceFon alliance. That would have been honest, and I'd have accepted it." He amended, "I'd have been angry, but I'd have accepted it. I know you were brought to FranceFon for a reason. But you kept stringing me along, so I was thinking I had to do some special pitch, some kind of miracle persuasion—" he broke off as a worse, cynical thought occurred to him. "You knew all along you weren't going to sign." She nodded, miserably. "So why did you come here? What game are you playing?"

"I wanted to explain to you what we'd found out. So you would understand exactly why I wasn't going to sign. So that you could be warned, in advance, of what's going to happen." She leaned forward. "Someone like you, Tyler, so smart and skilled, you should be with a company that has your same integrity."

Jesus, she sounded like a recruiter.

"I thought you should know about GlobeAll because you won't want to stay there, once you know the truth. And I couldn't speak like this in some restaurant, or my office, or at my home. I wanted to take more care with you. Coming here was an opportunity to do that."

"And you thought you could only say all this once we had sex."

She reeled back. A flush bloomed on her cheeks. "That is not fair of you," she said, her voice trembling. "I

103

was afraid all the time of saying it. But you deserve it, this kind of honesty."

"You think I deserve this kind of intimacy too? Or wasn't that part of your plan? Just a happy accident?" He stood up, crossing his arms in front of him, trying to summon dignity that his bare chest and old jeans lacked. "Do you prep all your would-be jilted partners this way?" This was low, he knew, but he didn't care.

The anger that tightened her face made him think, for a moment, that she might rear upright to slap him. But she sat still, and spoke clearly, in spite of the tears he could hear behind her voice.

"What happened between us, you said this too, was not expected." She looked away from him. "I was not sure if I had a real chance with you, I didn't know even if you were really flirting with me. I wondered also if there was a game of yours. But I realized, last night, that you are a sincere person, that you truly did not know about GlobeAll. So then I allowed myself to express that tenderness I was feeling, about you."

Tenderness? She made it sound like some genteel nineteenth century novel, for Chrissakes, it was wild carnality. No tenderness involved.

"*Tendresse*," she corrected herself. In French, he knew, this would be a woman's expression of vulnerable passion. He could afford to cut her a break on this at least: she hadn't been faking her lust.

"Thank you for that."

"I am sorry, that I did not have the courage to speak with you sooner, about GlobeAll."

But this he would not let pass. "Then have the courage to admit there never was any deal after you came on board. Hamzi already told me about the expansion of the UTT-FF alliance, so you don't have to pretend about that."

Her face fell again. "But Tyler, that is not why—"

"That alliance isn't being expanded?"

"It is being modified, to take into consideration the new Private Line network UTT is building—"

"Uh huh. Those bankers from Versailles are gonna love it."

"It isn't what you are supposing!" She stood then too, and faced him angrily. "Your assumption is not right! I would never do business with GlobeAll after what my husband found when I was still with UTT. Nobody else will either, Tyler, after this. You should understand for the sake of your own career."

"What I understand is that all's fair in love and war, I think that's a French saying? So I'm not out of bounds here?" He smiled coldly. "I'm a gentleman, Delphine, I concede defeat in the alliance proceedings. I wish your company well with UTT."

He turned to the stairs. He needed a shower, a long obliterating one; he might need to stay under water until his plane left on Wednesday.

"Tyler, please," she said, in a voice that would have compelled him to turn around, under any other circumstances. But he didn't turn.

What a fucked up turn of events. She was unbelievable. The entire situation was unbelievable. Canada access. TeleOne. Nick! His mind couldn't even process what had occurred in an articulate sequence. His brain kept repeating fuck, fuck, fuck: an unproductive feedback loop.

As the water fell onto his aching head he began to formulate a plan. First, he had to get out of here. He'd deliver her back to her place. It wasn't a long drive and they didn't have to talk, beyond the kind of superficially regretful platitudes exchanged by those who had been very briefly intimate and would be no longer. He could flatter her into thinking he needed time to reflect, to process what had happened, and so on. Hell, he could tell her she'd hurt him, which was certainly true, and let her feel guilty about it.

What he could not admit to her—he gritted his teeth against the possibility that he might say this, since he was used to being frank with his lovers—was raw bleeding sensation: she was ripping something vital from him, something she had just awoken. It was making him blind with pain right now, as blind as he'd been before with lust.

He let the water run from hot to cold, turning his eyes open into the spray, trying to wash them into clarity.

He had to find Jack, to give back the key and sound him out as to whether this ominous rumor about GlobeAll dodging access fees was already common knowledge. He had to get to Canada to see who'd engineered that fucking TeleOne deal on their side, aside from the suspicious and long-gone Levesque. He might have to rip somebody's throat out, and it couldn't be Nick's, because Al Qaeda killed him a year and a half ago.

He shook his head vigorously against that thought.

If this was going to appear in the WSJ—and he wouldn't put UTT past that, it was routine for competitors to knock each other this way—Corporate Communications needed to know about it so a statement could be prepared. He had to get out an e-mail. It was Sunday, nobody at Corporate would be in the New York office—but he could call the VPs he knew at home. It might go some way toward salvaging his rep after his enormous intelligence failure here with FranceFon, the first in his career. He needed big-time damage control.

And he might as well move up his flight, there was no reason to stay in Paris. Hell, he could probably get out tonight. He knew the guys on the FranceFon alliance team would understand. Right now he didn't care if he ever spoke to any of them again. He would probably change his mind—he'd give it time and clench his teeth some more, since he wasn't one to burn professional bridges thoughtlessly—but at this moment he never wanted to come back here.

PART TWO

Milwaukee 2003

Seventeen

CARLY EMERALD MUTED HER PHONE and pressed her fingertips onto her eyelids to contain the tears that crowded for release. Deep breath, Carly, *deep* breath.

Damn Julian Trent, IT Director of StoneEdge, Inc, and major asshole.

His disdain was now bordering on verbal abuse. This was not the first time he'd humiliated her, but it was the worst.

"Honestly, Carly," he drawled in his sneering upper-class British way, "*really,* now, can you tell me there's any reason *not* to recommend our pulling the GlobeAll circuits altogether?"

She heard muffled laughter in the background as his London cohorts enjoyed what passed for him as a genteel tantrum. Of course, he had her on speakerphone there, her amplified discomfort providing entertainment for the StoneEdge IT team. "I mean, is there even a *ghost* of a chance our upgrades can be expected in time now?"

She unmuted her handset. She kept her voice even. "Our engineers have assured me they'll be at your facility this afternoon."

"D'you mean … *your* afternoon?" Another guffaw of laugher in the background. "Because it's nearly four thirty here, Carly, and nobody from GlobeAll's even called to say they might deign to pay us a visit before the weekend."

"Let me make a quick call, Julian, just to verify—"

"Best not use your GlobeAll wireless, darling, it won't work." The prick was really having fun with her. They couldn't see her grimace, at least.

"No worries, Julian, I'll make sure your tech is contacted as soon as I get off this call." Her fingers were already sending out a frantic e-mail cry for help. Was no-one still working in the GlobeAll UK office? Four thirty pm on a Friday, godammit, where was their work ethic?

"All right Carly, I'll give you one more chance then, shall I?" He was now into his benevolent mode. She could just picture the snide indulgence in his smile.

From what she'd seen on their infrequent videoconferences, Julian was handsome, blond, pink-cheeked, with a penchant for expensive-looking ties. He oozed sensuality, complacency and wealth, traits so unusual in IT Directors, and most especially missing in English ones, that she'd long suspected he must be a StoneEdge scion of sorts, someone's nephew or godson buying time by playing at business until his inheritance kicked in with a timely family death.

Most IT people Carly dealt with were thin, hollow-eyed, polo-shirted types who were so beaten down and busy they could barely keep eye contact with a vendor, let alone take the time for the kind of leisurely salesperson-baiting Julian specialized in. He was notorious at GlobeAll for his tirades. Only the strongest could deal with him and, as if he were a wild animal, it took numbers of them to subdue him. Carly had found herself in conversation alone with him one too many times, worse luck.

As soon as her call with Julian was over, she dialed the London office. She got tech support voice-mail the first three tries, but got live on the fourth. She made her voice cheery. "Nigel, Carly Emerald here, I'm glad you're answering."

"Allo Carly, what's up? Ow's that awful Julian treating you?"

"He's the reason I'm calling, actually, I need you or someone to get over there right away to configure some routers—"

"That wouldn't be me. I'm scheduled for a cutover at BP in an hour."

"But who was supposed to do StoneEdge?"

"Must've been Jeremy but he's out ill, let's see who else can 'elp you 'ere."

GlobeAll UK's music-on-hold filled her ears. White Stripes, Jesus, that was pushing the envelope: "I wanna hypnotize you baby on the telephone ..."

The UK office played an eclectic, funny string of on-hold songs about telephony, from Blondie's "Call Me" to Cake's "Never There" to Glenn Campbell's "Wichita Lineman."

She usually enjoyed the difference between GlobeAll's staid domestic corporate image and its jazzier international face, but this time she had only an hour, at best, to fix the StoneEdge upgrade, and she lifted the handset away from her aching temple. She wasn't into Jack White's teasing tenor right now. Where the hell was UK's tech management? She'd have their heads if Julian cancelled his orders.

"Sorry, Carly, it looks as if there might be a bit of a problem getting StoneEdge's upgrades done this weekend." Nigel's voice broke into the music, hesitant with apology. "I tried everyone, but no joy. I can ring Paris HQ for you and see if there's any kind of regional backup tech plan going—"

"Paris!" Carly exploded. "What the fuck good's that going to do me, excuse me Nigel, you know I'm not mad at you, but Paris is already an hour later—"

"Hang on, let me try, Jack Rigby's always on call on his mobile." The music came on again. Now it was the Grateful Dead's "Operator."

She calmed down a little. Jack Rigby was Technical Director for GlobeAll Europe. If anyone could fix this, he could. He'd always come through for Carly in the past, and he knew StoneEdge's network as well as their own engineers: a testimony to his expertise, since StoneEdge techs had tweaked their configs beyond recognition to accommodate their own incredibly complex virtual private networks.

"Yeah, all right Carly, e's on another call right now but he'll call you straightaway."

"Thank you Nigel. I really appreciate it."

"No worries."

As she sat huddled in her cube, massaging her forehead, her mobile vibrated in her lap. She snatched it, hoping for Jack Rigby, but the number was Francisco's. Her tense muscles tightened up even more. Okay. She might as well get this over with.

"Francisco, querido, listen—"

"*You* listen." A trill of fast-paced guitar music rolled from the receiver, a live version of one of their favorite songs by the Mexican band Mana. Francisco crooned in the background. "*Como quisiera poder vivir sin aire?*"

In Spanish, the words soared breathlessly lyrical, instead of the maudlin English whine, "how could I expect to live without air?" Carly clutched the phone. The echo of his husky voice struck at the core of her, and she felt the slight soreness from their last energetic sex ease into a moist welcoming as he sang. Her breath hitched.

"Francisco," she hissed over his singing, hoping her cubemates couldn't hear the desperation in her voice even though she knew they couldn't understand Spanish, "I can't meet you for lunch. I have to stay here and get something fixed."

The music stopped. After a moment she heard his annoyed breathing. "Again, Catty. Is too much. Is third time." He called her Caterina or Catty, after her given name of Catherine.

"I'm so sorry, querido— "

"*No me llames querido.*" Don't call me honey. He hung up.

She'd have to pay for this later with him, but at least he wasn't going to keep her on the phone now, arguing. As angry as she knew he was, she couldn't possibly leave until the StoneEdge upgrades were on track. She'd devote the whole day, if need be, to hunt down someone who could get into London to program their fucking routers—her desk phone rang. She snatched up the handset.

"Carly Emerald—"

"Jack Rigby here, Nigel said you're in a bind?" There were sounds of traffic in the background. It was nearly six o'clock in Paris. He was probably driving home.

"Thanks, Jack, I know it's after hours there. But StoneEdge was scheduled for an upgrade today. And it didn't happen. Julian Trent's livid." Everyone at GlobeAll knew who Julian was.

"Yeah, it was Jeremy's. He didn't make it in today. His backup got called out on another crisis, but I thought he'd get back in time. Okay, who's on deck ..."

She heard more city noise, and some kind of music, probably on his car radio. How curious that she could be listening to French rock'n'roll in a twilit Europe half a world away, when moments ago she'd been listening to a Spanish love song right here in her own Milwaukee morning, and before that the UK's on-hold playlist, at their teatime: the wonder of global telecommunications. Pulse-frequency modulation, or PFM, was the term used for a certain kind of analog signaling, but insiders used 'PFM' to mean Pure Fucking Magic: a tongue-in-cheek explanation of how telecom really worked. She grinned in spite of her dilemma.

"I can assign Ahmed Rasheed for you, he's supposed to come on at five UK time, will someone at StoneEdge be there to let him in if I send him over?"

"I'll make sure of it."

"Okay. I'll get Ahmed. Here's his mobile number."

She wrote it down. "Thanks Jack." She thought for a moment. "I don't suppose we have anyone higher up that could go pay a courtesy visit to Julian? Not right now, I mean like next week sometime? Is the VP around?" GlobeAll's International VP, Philippe Nouri, was a stuffed shirt—but smooth enough for most customers and, at least, enough of a big-wig title for Julian.

"He's in Hungary right now, celebrating a final agreement with Matav. We're opening call center capabilities there, might interest Julian."

"Nothing interests him right now except torturing me. I guess *you* wouldn't be able to go over and make amends somehow—"

"There *might* be someone," Jack broke in, thoughtfully, "but I won't be talking to him until Monday, probably, and I don't know his schedule."

"Who is it?"

"Guy named Tyler Harding. You may have heard of him. He's our alliance broker, director level, he could talk to Julian about our partnerships, that kind of thing—"

"Another corporate type, that's all I need, the last time one of those people visited Julian he threw them out of his office." Like he just threw me out electronically, she did not add. "I need someone *smart.*"

"Tyler knows network. He knows business drivers too. He engineered the Matav deal in Hungary, and right now he's wrapping up one with FranceFon."

"Would he really be able to go see Julian?"

"StoneEdge's one of our biggest European billers, so I think he'd consider making the trip, but let me ask him, okay? He's in Paris now, due to go back to New York next week."

"All right Jack. But I can't let him into StoneEdge unless I talk to him first. Have him call me before you book his time."

His laugh rang out across the ocean between them. "Nobody books Tyler. I'll ask him if he'll think about it, Carly."

Sighing, she hung up. She didn't hold out much hope for any in-person remedy as soon as she wanted one, but she trusted Jack to at least assess a fix. She called one of Julian's minions to alert him to let Ahmed into the StoneEdge data center for the upgrades.

Then she called the manager of StoneEdge's dedicated GlobeAll billing analyst, to go over the most recent erroneous bill and the analyst's glaring over-runs, which were unfortunately typical for GlobeAll but had not yet raised Julian's ire.

Her final StoneEdge discussion was with the GlobeAll wireless rep, who was supposed to have delivered new handsets to one of StoneEdge's subsidiaries last week and had missed the customer want date on it yet again.

She was so *sick* of StoneEdge.

Although it was the most impressive account in the Milwaukee office, and her only responsibility, their problems and demands seemed to be never-ending. As soon as she'd solved one issue another arose to take its place. And the few opportunities she actually found to sell them something new, and thereby actually get paid a higher commission, required such a marshalling of far-flung resources, such a concentrated effort of out-of-the-box solutioning, and consequently such a diplomatic twisting of GlobeAll's reluctant Finance arms, that it was akin to a war campaign.

Case in point was what she'd been trying to sell Julian before the upgrade snafu. He wanted GlobeAll to be able to manage StoneEdge's at-home workers' internet use by supplying, as an aggregator, their local DSL service throughout Europe. It was a neat idea, very 'productizable'—big GlobeAll buzzword—and she thought Julian's hopes for it quite reasonable, for him. He'd been a surprisingly good listener, asking smart questions as her engineers had explained their limitations in non-U.S. DSL provision.

That had been a week ago. She couldn't very well try to resurrect the subject given their just-concluded disastrous service review. Maybe next week, if the upgrades went okay and the wireless sets were delivered and the billing was cleared. Maybe.

She wished she could put her head down on her desk. She picked up her mobile instead and called Francisco.

"*Bueno,*" he answered curtly.

"Can we still meet, Franco?" she asked him in Spanish. "I can get out now, will you let me make it up to you? I really need to see you today."

Silence. He'd make her sweet-talk some more, but then he might relent. She lowered her voice. "*Angel. Corazon.* Please let me see you again." She tried to keep her voice steady, businesslike, just in case someone was listening: she could pretend she was talking to a representative from the Mexican phone company, TelMex. As far as the office knew, that's who Francisco was. "I'm addicted to you."

She felt someone hover behind her. She glanced back. Dave Seymour, one of the data guys. Just her luck; Dave was the only other GlobeAll person in Wisconsin who understood a little Spanish. He held a strange-looking object in his hand, holding it halfway out to her, but she was determined to solidify things with Francisco before she got off. She turned her back on Dave with a wait-a-sec wiggle of her hand.

She breathed into her handset, as quickly and quietly as she could, "Light of my life, you're my religion, if I don't see you today I'm going to die right here at the office and I'll tell everyone why—"

A little chuckle told her he was softening. "Okay. Half an hour, okay, I'm in my studio." He hung up.

Whee! She spun around in her chair. Dave was looking at her curiously. "Carly, I couldn't help hearing some of your conversation, that TelMex rep must be a pretty weird guy if you have to talk about religion to him."

She shrugged, smiling. "He's superstitious about telecom. Probably a wise approach, all things considered ... " She stopped as she saw what he was trying to hand her. A roll of duct tape.

"What the heck, Dave?"

"I'm our floor marshal, you know, I'm giving them out to everyone. The Administration's issued a bioterror alert, we're all being told to seal our windows."

"Here in the office?" She didn't have a window. Only management did.

"At home. Internal Comm's said we can leave early to prepare our homes."

Could that possibly be right?

She knew the company had spent millions so far just in these first two months of 2003 on IT security upgrades, scrambling to be in compliance with the Patriot Act so they could hang onto their lucrative government contracts. Was this part of it? She looked around him at the hallway, the other cubes, the bank of offices by the windows. Nobody seemed to be leaving. Rolls of duct tape sat unheeded on the floor by every workstation.

"It's a precaution." He handed her the roll. "Better safe than sorry, Carly."

"Thanks Dave, I might just take off now. I have a call with StoneEdge's Asia team this evening," she lied. "I was going to stay here, but I'll call from home."

"I'm sure Dudley would approve." Dudley was their branch manager, as humorless as Dave but about ten times more calculating. He'd probably already left. Dave smiled at her and went on to the next cube.

Carly packed up her laptop and hurried out of the office, duct tape stuffed into her voluminous tote.

Eighteen

Francisco's studio was in the newly renovated riverfront area, once home to sturdy warehouses and matter-of-fact shipping firms, now boasting bare-brick-walled restaurants and galleries whose wood floors emulated the district's muscular past. Franco worked on the third floor of one of these scoured structures.

Carly burst into the cavernous space and threw her things down on the clay-dust covered bare wood floor. She couldn't see him, but she knew he was here; she heard him talking on the phone in his bedroom. Mana music poured softly out of the speakers he'd attached in every corner. It was "Vivir Sin Aire," to live without air, the one he'd been singing to her earlier. She passed a forest of his sculptures, in her advance on the corner space he'd sheetrocked off to create a little bedroom.

He was sitting on the floor, phone headset on, speaking into it. As usual he was also leaning over a bowl between his bluejeaned legs, his hands smoothing its wet surface in rhythmic strokes. His long hair hid his face from her.

She watched him, struck as always by the graceful movements of his hands, the fluid curve of his body and the flow of his hair. He was a fascinating physical mixture: sleek skin and flat obsidian gaze of Meso-America; high cheekbones and curly hair of Europe. He wore more jewelry than Carly had ever seen on a man, more than a sculptor should; rings, necklaces, earrings, all beads and stones and leather, all spattered with flecks of clay.

"Make it two thousand and we have a deal. I can have it delivered by—" he broke off to squint into the distance, calculating, and saw her.

His black stare roamed slowly over her, but did not beckon her closer, as he finished his conversation—"next Wednesday at the latest. Okay, sure. Gracias." His thanks was typically offhand; he always sold his work as if he was doing a favor to his clients, a favor that was something of an imposition on his time. As a salesperson who sweated every transaction, she deeply envied his nonchalance.

With one nimble little finger he unhooked the headset from his ears. "So. Catty. *Now* you have time for me."

His full lips were straight, his narrow face still as he watched her. His hands did not miss a stroke on the lip of the bowl. Mana crooned their song again on repeat. A few dust motes floated between them.

There was a time, when they were beginning, when she'd have flung herself at him, bowl flattened, suit ruined, Franco's head thrown against the futon as he fell back laughing under her attack. That time had passed. Now she had to go slowly, ritualistically, as carefully as a cat slinking up on its prey, every move premeditated.

She started by sliding off her heavy down coat. Then she unbuttoned her formal suit jacket, keeping her stare on his as she delicately eased each button out of its separate notch. She unzipped her skirt, let it crumple at her feet. She didn't step out of it. She unfastened the clip on the back of her hair and let it foam out around her shoulders.

Franco had told her once he liked her because they had identical hair, curlicues which seemed to grow more out than down. Hers was shades lighter than his, streaked with salon highlights. She put the clip in her jacket pocket and stood, waiting, used to his appraisal by now, used to his deliberation.

It was not until the song ended and began again that he put the bowl aside.

He unfolded himself from the floor, splashed his hands clean in the corner sink, and walked over to stand in front of her. He put his hands on her jacketed breasts and rubbed his thumbs against her nipples. He looked into her eyes, still not smiling, as he moved his hands from outside the jacket to inside, to unfasten her bra, to pinch, and to then slide his clever fingers down her body. She leaned her head on his shoulder.

After a time, he took off the rest of her clothes and led her to the futon.

She woke later, dry-mouthed and dazed, caught once again between rue and amusement. He still slept beside her, motionless as his art, barely seeming to breathe, as if his life were so contained inside his substantial musculature that he didn't need to exhale. If he were her child she'd be constantly tiptoeing to his crib, holding up a tiny hand mirror in front of his nose to make sure he was still alive. She'd hook up a baby monitor to his chunky turquoise necklace. She'd sit vigil all night beside him, rocking, in the painted rocker she had ready for just such a sweet task back in her own apartment.

She rolled away, stood, and rummaged in his jumbled closet until she found a flannel bathrobe to put on. She went into the studio and perched on a stool by one of the enormous windows, watching the frozen river, wondering as she always did, here:

How could it go on? But how could she possibly end it? Did she even want to?

He was her only pleasure.

She had worked nonstop for years, putting up with Finance's rigidity and Product's obtuseness and Dudley's bullshit and Dave's creepiness and all the others' stultifying, smalltown smalltalk boredom, building up her successes at GlobeAll until she'd finally been given the most lucrative prize a salesperson could win—the biggest account in the region. Three times in a row she'd gone to Achievers' Club: an annual trip to an exotic locale to hang out with GlobeAll bigwigs, hoo-ah.

If she got any more successful she'd have to move to Corporate, in New York City. She liked the way it made her pulse race just to walk around there, the times she'd visited HQ.

But she didn't relish the idea of living there. She was used to Milwaukee's lower profile and human pace. She couldn't move far from her Mom, anyway, it was out of the question until the cancer either went into some kind of permanent remission ... or else.

She shifted restlessly on the stool. That was another thing. Franco understood perfectly how it was with her Mom. She never even had to use words when things were bad. He read her physically, always, as if they were animals.

She spun around, went to get a bottle of water from his little refrigerator, drained it. She opened her bag to check messages on her mobile. None. Was that a good sign or a deadly one? She dropped it back inside and spied the duct tape. She looked at it for a moment. Then, smiling, she found his big shears.

Slicing off a piece took a lot more effort than she'd have imagined. It was *really* sticky. She wrenched it away from the roll, cut through it and detached it on her fingers. She always managed to get messy over here, one way or another.

Where should she put it? Was it supposed to criss-cross the window like during a tornado or seal the openings like weather stripping? She supposed the Department of Homeland Security had an entire committee to ponder that. She decided the duct tape warning must be some kind of hoax, and Dave's insistence on it ridiculous. Like Osama would target Milwaukee, of all places, as the perfect smallpox-launching pad.

She plastered it onto the blank front page of Franco's flipchart in the rough, corny shape of a heart. She would have liked to make a more permanent mark, cause him some trouble to remove it, but that impulse was just her frustration with him, with their affair. She took her seat by the window again.

"Corazon," he whispered behind her. "Come back to bed. I didn't finish with you." He came around in front, cupped his hands under her and lifted her easily off the stool. "You have to give me a Valentine present."

"It's only an American holiday," she said weakly, slumping over his broad back.

He always wanted more and she always acquiesced. The sense of surrender he elicited in her was surprising: she'd been, before him, a more resilient, assertive lover. But he left her feeling so limp that she never had any strength to resist what he wanted. In fact, when she was with him, she wished for nothing more than to curl up in one of his shirt pockets and rest close to him, outside world forgotten.

"We're in America, *hijita mia.*"

"*Tan lejos de Dios*—" she began one of his favorite sayings, about his native Mexico, 'so far from God ...'

"*Tan cerca a Estados Unidos,*" he finished, laughing. So close to the United States. They usually spoke in Spanish. It was part of the excitement.

When he hurt her later, in the intensity of his exploration, she scratched her discomfort onto the top of his hands, which were clamped on the back of her collarbone, pushing her down. She tried to turn her head, in the pillow, to bite his fingers, but his grip was so strong that she couldn't move. At least this time, for once, he hadn't cuffed her. She could move her hands.

"*No me marques, nena,*" he gasped harshly over her shoulder, moving deep within her. Don't mark me, baby. She dug her nails in; she wanted to mark him, to scar him for life as she felt him scarring her. And she knew very well why he didn't want her 'marks' on him, dammit. Later, when they were clothed and he was again removed from her, in his separate space once more, watching her coolly, he repeated his reason.

"*Mi mujer viene pronto de Veracruz.*"

His mujer was always supposed to be arriving soon from Veracruz. Carly didn't know if she was real or not, if she was his wife or not. The convenient threat of her was another way of his conducting their involvement solely on his terms. Another thing for her to feel ashamed of, along with the way she let him do anything he wanted to her.

Nineteen

MUCH LATER THAT NIGHT, she went over to her friend Sara's house. Sara was her oldest friend and only confidant. To her credit, she still listened in sympathy when Carly bemoaned yet again her fatal-feeling relationship.

"Everyone has a sex life, or wishes they did," Sara chided. "You don't need to feel ashamed. If you'd let those stuffy women officemates of yours ever see him, they'd fall all over themselves trying to get a bite."

Carly recalled the bites she'd left on him in spite of his protests. He deserved to be bitten, to be punished somehow for the way he made her feel. She ached from him, inside and out, in ways she feared were not healthy. She could not confess that to Sara. But maybe she could bring herself to address something else.

"He keeps referring to his mujer in Veracruz," she said, stirring her drink.

"Which means?"

"He's got another woman." Well, that was right, *mujer* meant woman. Not necessarily wife. "In Veracruz."

"So let her stay there." Sara giggled. She was on her third margarita. They were celebrating Valentine's Day as they had a tradition of doing, when they weren't otherwise occupied: drinks at the end of the evening at one another's place, in pajamas. This was a Friday, after all.

"I think it might mean ... he might be married."

Sara put her glass down. "Aw." Her mouth twisted in sympathy. "Carly, really?"

"I don't know."

"Did you ask him?" Carly nodded. "So what'd he say?"

"He said yes. But I don't know if it's true."

"Carly." Now she sounded disapproving.

Carly puffed out a half-hearted little chuckle. "Yeah, it sucks." She felt her shoulders sag. "I guess either he really is, or it's his way of keeping me at bay. Whichever."

"When did you find out?"

"Oh, he's been chillier for awhile now. Several weeks, really."

They'd met during last year's Summerfest, a lakeside extravaganza of food and live music. Sara had been there too, and other friends; Carly had insisted they hear this fabulous Latin band, Mana. Carly'd been amazed that they'd come to Milwaukee, of all places; they usually played Los Angeles or Buenos Aires or Madrid. But there they'd been, gracias a Dios, at Summerfest. Milwaukee had a significant Hispanic population, but in spite of all of her hints of this to Dudley, GlobeAll had none on staff.

Francisco and Carly had spotted each other during one of the band's sing-along sets. He hadn't asked her the conventional questions—how a gringa like her knew Spanish, how she'd come to be a Mana fan, what she did, who she was—he'd just sidled up to her and sung with her for the rest of the show, looking at her whenever there was a particularly sexy verse.

Mana's repertoire was an irresistible mix of romantic and political passion. They sang fervently, jumping around the stage as they seduced the willing crowd. Carly had never seen such a symbiotic love between musicians and their audience. She'd sung her loudest, swaying to every chord. Francisco's vibrant hair had tickled her cheek and his smooth skin had brushed against hers as their bare arms met. He'd smelled like pine. She later learned it was the soap he used to take off clay slip.

The chemistry between them had erased caution, and she'd willingly gone back to his studio that same night for a glass of wine that lasted as they talked until morning.

She'd learned he was twenty-six, a gifted modern sculptor, with a visiting-artist grant from the Milwaukee School of Design and passionate ideas about life.

He'd learned she'd studied Spanish in college and had spent three years teaching ESL in Mexico City, loving it, but that she'd regretfully realized that for all her fluency, she'd always be a gringa there. She didn't let on she was thirty-two. He'd solidified his charm, and heightened her hunger, by not touching her once except for a chaste, soft pressing of his warm lips against her cheek, after taking her home in a cab.

Their subsequent affair, or whatever it was called, had flamed hotter than anything she'd known, peaking just before Christmas. He'd gone back to Mexico for his family holiday. He'd hinted he was married; actually, he'd alluded to it the first night, if she was honest in her recollection.

His return last month had brought an edge to him, a more demanding side that roused her unease and excitement in equal measure. She was following him, willingly, into uncharted sexual territory, with strange equipment, and games which made her laugh and which he took seriously. She wanted to be able to abandon herself to his darkness, just to see if it was a kind of freedom; but she was afraid they were heading toward an abyss that she could not admit to anyone.

"I don't know why I don't quite believe him," she told Sara now. She sipped her margarita. "I guess it's because if he were my husband, really mine, I'd make sure I was close by." She'd never let him out of her sight. Would she actually marry him though, given the chance? "But he mentioned it again tonight. He's miffed because I have to work so hard."

"He works hard too."

"But he's the man." Carly smiled. "He gets to work. I'm supposed to worship at his feet and do his laundry, or something."

Sara snickered. She'd seen his clay-spotted clothing. "For sure he has a boatload."

"I wouldn't know," Carly admitted. "I've never slept overnight at his studio. And when he stays with me, we … don't do anything domestic."

"So, all you really have in common is sex?"

"And Mana," she said, grinning. "At first that seemed like enough. It was—overwhelming. It still is. I'm still dazzled. But he's pulling away, I can tell."

Sara curled her long legs under her and gave Carly the same shrewd look she'd given her since tenth grade. "I can't understand why you don't just find some nice guy at work. Some ordinary, decent guy who'll want a family."

Carly leaned back on the floor cushions and gave Sara the same mocking look she'd given her since tenth grade. "Because they're BORING, Sara, dull as *drains*, dry, uninteresting, sexless, non-erotic, bland, banal, workaholic—"

"Aha!" Sara pounced, "so's Francisco! He works like a corporate tycoon! Like a construction guy! He's always working!"

This was true. Francisco had no social life. He had to be begged to go to restaurants or movies, dragged away from his studio. His attendance at Summerfest last year had been at the behest of his Design School sponsor. He'd thought it was mandatory and had been as surprised as Carly by Mana's appearance.

"He's full of creative fire. The men I meet at GlobeAll are drones. Anyway, they don't want us to date each other in the same office. Thank God." Sara knew all about Dave and Dudley. "Besides," she went on, "it feels like he knows me. He knows the essential things, anyway: my Mom's dying of lung cancer, and I'm a slave to StoneEdge." She poured herself another glass of margarita. "That's all there is to me right now, Sara. I have no room for anything else."

"So … he's a *comfort?*" Sara said this as if willing to give the possibly-married Francisco the benefit of the doubt, for Carly's sake, if he served some immediate useful purpose, but she did not hide the sarcasm in her voice.

"In my time of need," Carly agreed. "I'm glad I have you too, Sara."

"Yeah, you're lucky. Otherwise it'd be the psychic hotline, and I can just hear *that* conversation—'I'm choosing to be obsessed by Francisco so I don't have to deal with the fact I really have no life'."

"Ouch!" Carly interrupted, laughing.

" 'But I think he's probably married, which suits me fine since I can't make an emotional commitment anyway right now.' Then the psychic says, 'I see another in your future, he has a very sexy English accent,' and you go 'Oh no! Not Julian Trent!' and she's like 'He loves you yeah, yeah, yeah'. "

"Maybe it's Nigel," Carly offered, laughing.

"What kind of a funky name is NIjell?"

"One of our UK guys."

When Carly's mobile rang she stuffed down her giggles. It was an international number; she had to sound straight, even though it was past one in the morning on a weekend for her: StoneEdge global business never slept.

"Carly Emerald."

"Carly, hi, Jack Rigby here, sorry to call you in the middle of the night. I have some—not great news." It was past eight the next morning, French time.

"No."

"Yeah. When Ahmed Rasheed went to do the StoneEdge upgrades yesterday the customer contact wasn't in the building, and the lobby manager wouldn't let him into the data center. Everyone's paranoid these days, you know, and I gather Ahmed's an Arab. So no upgrades as of yesterday afternoon, sorry.

"You need to get ahold of Julian and tell him we'll do it on a Saturday, this once, just for him. I mean, *I* could call Julian, but it's your butt on the line with these upgrades, right, you'll make yourself look good if you tell him directly."

She listened in dismay, unable to respond.

"Call me back when you get Julian's okay so I can send Ahmed back out there. He'll only work a few more hours, they're shutting London down for the big demo. Paris too, I won't be available later. So we need to do this right away."

"Fucking *hell!*" Carly clapped her hand over her mouth as she realized she'd shouted this at him. Engineers thought most salespeople were flakes; she didn't want to earn that impression with the head engineer of GlobeAll Europe. "Jack," she added quickly, "excuse my language."

"No problem, Carly, I said the same thing when I heard." He sounded distracted.

"Uh, Jack, what demo are you talking about?"

"Antiwar."

Antiwar? She'd thought he was talking about some new product demo. AntiWAR, of course, the pending Iraq invasion. Dave and his duct tape. "So, is it uncomfortable over there for you right now? As an American?"

"Not uncomfortable, exactly, just—a waste."

"A waste?"

"It's a waste, good business relationships deteriorating because of our unilateral stance." Jack went on, "it might be one of the reasons Julian's getting so difficult. GlobeAll's his only U.S.-based carrier. We've seen a number of customers cooling off toward us here. So FranceFon, Deutsche Telekom, the others—they're looking like compatriots now to European-based companies. We're looking like imperialists."

In spite of the war fever sweeping the country, Carly hadn't given this particular aspect a thought: what a foolish oversight. "Thank you for that information," she said slowly. "I'll let folks here know, it's important."

"Oh, before I forget, Carly. If you have a StoneEdge executive briefing I'll send it to our Alliance Director, see if he can call on Julian, unless he needs an accent."

"An accent?"

"Yeah, my guy's American, so if Julian needs a European type we'll wait for Nouri, you know, the VP. Otherwise I'll line up the Director."

"No accent needed. Your guy sounds like he'll do." Carly tried to remember the Director's name. Taylor? Tyler? Something preppy. Executive briefings were incredibly tedious to assemble. Lucky for her, she'd just updated hers on StoneEdge. "Jack, I'll get the briefing to you as soon as I'm back online."

"Call me after you tell Julian about the tech visit today, so I can get out of here," Jack said.

As luck would have it, Julian answered right away on his mobile when Carly used Sara's land line to call him. She told him quickly what had happened.

"Right, Carly, I'll make sure we give him access this morning. What's the tech's name?" For once he sounded matter-of-fact, not sarcastic. A miracle.

"Ahmed Rasheed."

"*Ahmed Rasheed*," Julian repeated warily. "Make sure he has at least two IDs, could you then."

"Yes." She hesitated. "Julian, I regret this delay. I appreciate your taking my call on a Saturday. I hope everything's okay for you there, otherwise, in London, I mean with the demonstrations?"

"It's bloody amazing, the city's shut down, supposed to be a million people in the streets. Can't get out. Can't get anything done."

"That's ... inconvenient." This was the most they'd ever conversed about non-network issues. She wasn't sure how to proceed.

"Your President is on a mission." His laugh was brief, unamused. "Along with our Prime Minister." He sighed. "Course it's more business for us I suppose, lots of orders for the Stoney Fighting Machine." He added gloomily, "it's all good. Stock'll rise. Along with the body counts."

His grimness took her aback. She hadn't connected StoneEdge's product portfolio to the war, but of course Julian was right. Defense machinery was their core business. StoneEdge's armored tanks had the world's largest market share. But talking about politics was such a taboo with international customers, and this off-hours chat so unusual for her and Julian, she didn't immediately know how to answer him.

"Right then, Carly, thanks for letting me know."

"Julian," she blurted, belatedly, in a hurry to extend this little conversational bridge, "sorry about what you're having to go through over there."

"You'll be going through it as well this weekend, in your big cities, it's all over the news," he said, sounding almost friendly. "What time is it there anyway?"

"It's—"she checked her watch—"about two a.m."

"At the weekend! That's dedicated of you. I say, I'm impressed."

Now this was a Valentine indeed. "Anything for you, Julian," she told him lightly.

"*Anything?* Be careful what you promise, Carly. But thank you, anyway." He hung up, laughing.

Carly stared at Sara with a wide-open mouth and eyes, mimicking shock. "Call the psychic hotline, the sky has fallen. Julian Trent was finally nice to me!"

Twenty

CARLY WORRIED ABOUT THE STONEEDGE install all weekend, but as Jack had said, nobody in the London or Paris GlobeAll offices was answering, and Carly didn't want to bother Julian on his mobile again on the weekend. She knew he'd find her if he was livid.

She wondered if the demonstrations had blocked as much traffic and business as had occurred, as Julian predicted, in Chicago, New York, Los Angeles and other large U.S. cities. Even Milwaukee had seen an overnight peace vigil, in spite of the cold.

The coverage she'd watched of the worldwide demonstrations amazed her. She'd had no idea people were so opposed to the Iraq invasion, even though she herself had wondered why it was presented as such a necessity: it seemed to her that a few well-placed Special Ops guys could take out Saddam Hussein in an afternoon, if that was really the goal. As little as she knew about the Middle East, she didn't believe Hussein had anything to do with 9/11. But apparently she was out of touch—the news shows all said, portentously, that seventy-five per cent of Americans supported the invasion. She supposed that could be true; she rarely talked about current events with anyone at work, and only sparingly with her Mom's circle.

Francisco, predictably, was vociferous in his opinions. He'd laughed when he saw her duct tape Valentine.

"Now I feel protected, corazon. Thank you for thinking of my security."

"Better me than John Ashcroft."

"I am sure I am on his list. He is listening whenever I talk on the phone."

"What makes you think he understands Spanish?"

"He understand the *insultos* I use when I talk about gringo politics," he'd smirked.

At six thirty on Monday morning Carly called Jack, wanting to catch him before lunchtime in Paris.

"Rigby."

"Jack, hi, it's Carly Emerald. Just checking on StoneEdge's upgrades."

"StoneEdge, okay, that was in London, right?"

Carly reminded herself that he must have thousands of accounts and issues to track. She heard his keyboard clacking. "Yeah. Kinnaird House, dual entry, Colt's the local provider. Ahmed Rasheed turned it up at 10 am UK time, Saturday February 15th. Tested clean, circuit's running, no glitches. And Julian Trent was informed on, let's see ... this morning."

"Thanks so much, Jack, I worried all weekend."

"Mmm." He sounded even more exhausted than usual, and she wondered if that was due to the weekend they'd been through over there in Europe.

"Has the city calmed down now? I saw the street scenes on the news. Incredible."

"Yeah, it was."

She could tell he was about to hang up. "Listen, Jack, I sent you the Executive Briefing you'd asked me for, on StoneEdge, to engage director level attention for Julian."

"I recall our conversation."

"So ... will this guy get in touch with me about StoneEdge?"

A moment passed before he answered slowly, "actually, Carly, visiting StoneEdge *might* fit right into his schedule. He could swing by London on his way back to New York. I'd say, yeah, you can expect a call from Tyler Harding."

She clicked off. She looked up Harding's bio online. He had impressive credentials, but she'd seen high level types with stellar backgrounds turn into total bores in front of customers. They'd yammer on about their stupid golf handicap or congratulate themselves on what a 'winning team' they'd built. She'd had enough sports analogies to last several lifetimes. You'd think a Fortune 100 company could produce snappy yet serious speakers, but in her GlobeAll experience they were few and far between.

She had just stepped out of the shower when her cell phone rang. The French country code showed on the display. She snatched it up, along with a towel; it would have felt unprofessional to answer the phone naked.

"Carly Emerald speaking."

"Carly? Not Catherine?" the clipped male voice demanded.

"This is Catherine, yes. Carly is my nickname."

"Tyler Harding here. Jack Rigby said you want me to go to London for StoneEdge." He sounded testy, but that was normal; everyone in international telecom was chronically exhausted, on the edge of irritation—probably everyone in the international sector of any industry felt the same way.

"Yes. Thanks for calling so quickly. Julian Trent is my main London contact, he's the European Network Director, and he's a pretty high maintenance guy."

"How so?"

"Well, we kind of screwed up one of their installs recently, and it's just the last in a long string of problems. There was a billing glitch on their long distance invoice, and another when we switched their frame relay platform. We've been trying to get more executive involvement with him for some time, and—"

"What's your expectation of my role, if I see him?"

"I'm trying to give you some background, so you can understand the issues—"

"I picked up background from the database, and I got your Exec Brief. I know what we've done with StoneEdge. What do *you* want from a meeting between us?" He spoke rapidly, with an undertone of increasing impatience. "Why should I make this visit? I'm not in sales, you know, I'm in strategic alliances."

She clutched her towel around her, wanting to project dignity. "That's why you'd make a good impression. I want to reassure Julian that we're a full-service global carrier, with partnership arrangements in every region of the world, that our customer care is superior, that we have what it takes to keep StoneEdge's network running whenever, wherever, however—"

"We've already blown that image with him, if we just screwed up an install. What'll it take to keep him happy right now?"

"*Shmooze* him, Mr. Harding," she snapped, tired of his curtness. "Make much of him. Be fawning. But maybe that's not what you do." Uh-oh: once again, her mouth was working before her brain. Salespeople were not supposed to snap at senior directors.

To her surprise, he laughed, and it was a really appealing laugh. "I can fawn. What else?"

"Well," she stalled, trying to keep up with him, "uh, just make him feel important. Make him think you're really important, too, he likes high level attention."

There was a little pause.

"Of course," she rushed in to fill it, "I know you *are* important. And I really appreciate your time on this. I know what a busy schedule you must have."

"I like talking to customers," he said, cool again.

"Thanks, I'm grateful—"

"Don't thank me until I've produced results for you. What's your ultimate goal with them? Big-picture it for me."

Big-picture? She hated this kind of corporate-speak, and she drew a blank. She was usually too buried in daily crises to indulge in thoughts about ultimate goals for her customers. "I think ... to net it out, I'd like to ensure StoneEdge's *respect*," she decided. "To convince them that we're a company who can be a partner of integrity, for the life of our business relationship."

There was such a silence that she thought maybe he'd just hung up, having heard all he needed. He seemed brusque enough to do that.

"Mr. Harding?"

"Yes." He repeated, "Respect. Integrity," as if hearing the words for the first time. "I'll keep that in mind. Call me Tyler, by the way."

"Okay. I'll get ahold of Julian and see when he's free to meet with you—"

"I can do that. Jack has his number. I'll give you the credit for setting it up, of course. I assume you'll join us, you have videoconferencing in your office?"

This was gracious of him. On international visits most senior people preferred to meet with clients separate from live involvement with sales teams in the U.S., so they didn't have to take the time zones into account. "We do. I'd like to join, of course, but it depends on Julian's schedule."

"Let's just plan on it. I can be in London tomorrow. Expect a calendar message from me with our meeting time."

Apparently this was his way of saying goodbye. "Right-oh," Carly said to the dial tone.

At her office an hour later, she found an e-mail from him in her calendar, booking a videoconference for the following day at noon. Well, that was efficient. She went to reserve the video set-up with Dudley's admin.

"Suze, I'll need the small conference room for a meeting tomorrow. Is the Polycom working?" Otherwise she'd have to use the nearest Kinko's for videoconferencing, which seemed a bit ignominious when she'd be talking to two senior directors.

"Yep, it's doin fine." Suze Ralston, helmet-haired and older than sixty, which was unheard-of in telecom, had been with GlobeAll forever and was the office griot—she knew where all the bodies were buried and when the next murders would occur. She was the only one who knew that Carly's Francisco was not a TelMex rep. Whenever possible Carly slipped extra customer-designated sports

135

tickets to her—she was a rabid Green Bay Packers fan. She kept a cheesehead hat on top of her monitor.

"Hey, Carly, I couldn't help overhearing. You're meeting with StoneEdge tomorrow?" Dudley was suddenly standing beside her. He always listened in on Suze's conversations.

"Yes." Of course he knew; she had no other accounts. She dreaded what was coming.

"I need some more client appointments this month, so I'll join you. What time?"

She couldn't refuse him.

Suze gave her a sympathetic glance as he walked away.

"Maybe the machine'll break," she muttered to Carly.

Suze knew Dudley tended to take over an appointment, hogging the limelight, playing up his extensive contacts within StoneEdge—none of which had done Carly any good when she was on the hot seat with Julian, who had outright told Carly he thought Dudley was an ass.

"You know about life handing you lemons," she told Suze, shrugging.

"Yeah—some people should go suck one."

Carly laughed as she walked back to her cube. Even if the meeting was a bomb, at least the installs were on track. If she was diligent today she might even get the billing straightened out. Chance would be a fine thing, as her UK colleagues liked to say.

Twenty-One

CARLY DRESSED WITH CARE the next morning, recalling from her last videoconference how washed-out the medium made her look. She put on a royal blue suit and made up her face meticulously, bringing out the silver in her gray eyes and brightening her cheeks.

She twisted her light brown hair up and down; finally decided to keep it up, gelling it until it gleamed. Julian had seen her that way on video before and she'd learned it was better not to alter her appearance between customer visits—they noticed, and it took away focus. Julian caught every change in all the women around him, at StoneEdge UK or in her team in the States, even onscreen. He was the kind of man quick to compliment, which felt flattering until you saw the speculative gleam in his eyes.

She'd arranged for Jeanine, her billing rep, to join them on audioconference from Atlanta, figuring that since Dudley was already crashing this party it wouldn't make any difference. She was taking a risk—it was unorthodox to mix practical matters like billing along with the hyperbole that directors at Tyler Harding's level usually spouted. Billing was dear to every customer's heart; they cared deeply about teentsy percentages of cents; and it was anathema to GlobeAll execs, since GlobeAll's big weakness was fucked-up billing. But she knew Julian would genuinely appreciate a straightforward accounting of what had gone wrong and how it had been rectified.

She hoped she'd orchestrated a productive meeting. She'd already sent out an agenda detailing everyone's piece. She'd given Dudley five minutes at the end, so he could blab away about himself after Jeanine and Tyler had the time they needed. Tyler had e-mailed saying he was fine with her plan. That had been a relief—she'd been afraid he'd torpedo her agenda so that he could dominate the meeting; all she needed was another Dudley. But Tyler, to her amazed gratification, offered to take Julian out for drinks after the meeting, so he'd get plenty of StoneEdge face time.

Dudley had not been so accommodating. "Only *five minutes?*"

"Julian really wanted to give Jeanine the time." She'd shrugged prettily, knowing he'd never have the nerve to call Julian and check. "And of course Tyler Harding was booked with Julian before you, I'm so sorry."

"Tyler Harding," Dudley repeated. "It'll be good to meet him face to face. We've spoken, of course." Name-dropper extraordinaire. Carly had to pinch her lips together when she saw Suze rolling her eyes behind Dudley's back.

When the conference started, Carly saw that Julian was by himself in his office, clacking away on his PC.

"Julian, hello," she began. "You received my agenda?"

"Oh hallo, Carly. Yes. Tyler's just been called away at the moment, he'll be right back. Thanks for bringing on Jeanine, that's brilliant, I've asked some of the lads to listen in." He turned on a speaker phone in front of him. "Ian, Lannon, you on?"

Assent. Jeanine confirmed that she was on the call too. She and the 'lads' carried on a lively conversation about a spreadsheet that didn't show up on camera, and Carly studied her own copy during their discussion. Julian listened as his underlings confirmed that the new GlobeAll fix would alleviate their past billing difficulties.

Suze came in with another spreadsheet, and put it in front of Carly. On top of it was a note in Suze's handwriting: "Who's that gorgeous hunk of man?"

Carly kept her face straight. She was used to Suze's kidding, especially during videoconferences, which Suze regarded as a businessmen's' *Jerry Springer Show.* depending on the customer, this attitude was not always erroneous. She wrote back, "It's Julian Trent. Gorgeous is as gorgeous does, Suze, grow up."

"Not him, I know that snake," Suze scribbled. "The other one. Just walked in."

Carly looked at the screen. Sitting next to Julian was a sober-suited black-haired man who, according to his frown, was paying as close attention to the spreadsheet as Ian and Lannon, while Jeanine droned on about tollfree numbers in Europe.

"That's why this set of numbers hasn't been working, or billing correctly," Tyler Harding interrupted, in the clipped tone that Carly recognized from their phone call. "Vanity numbers have limited functionality outside the States."

"Vanity, what's that?" asked Lannon, while Jeanine said, "Why?"

"Most European headquarters still use landline telephones, which don't have letters on their keypads. The word 'StoneEdgUS'—that's a vanity number, Lannon—won't be dialed by a customer with a numeric handset, Jeanine, unless he has the patience to spell it out in numbers."

Carly knew that, of course, but she hadn't thought to advise Julian's voice group about it. She'd assumed they'd known too. And she didn't have time to go over hundreds of numbers, anyway, she left that to the order entry people. But clearly, she should not have overlooked this.

She felt herself blush as Tyler went on, evenly, "It's a common mistake." He looked into the camera. She felt the force of his blue gaze even through the grainy medium they traversed. "Carly. Hello. Would you say a simple credit could fix that?"

His face distracted her as she was formulating her answer.

She liked looking at attractive men and she enjoyed the sizzle of doing business with them. But Suze was right: this guy went way beyond sizzle. He was … a work of *art*. Had it not been for his conservatively cut suit, the bruised circles of fatigue under his eyes, and his expression of edgy irritation, all of which gave him a modern appearance, he belonged in an old portrait, hanging in a gallery.

She would have liked to stare.

But she needed to fix her business.

"Hello, Tyler," she said. "Of course, we'll issue the credit. It should show up the month after next." She forced herself to look away from him, to Julian. "I'll let your Milwaukee office know, Julian, since they were the ones who wanted those numbers for you. I should have advised them."

Suze nudged her elbow. "Would you look at his mouth!!!" her note said now. "Bet he's a good kisser."

Carly bit back a giggle. "You're a grandmother. Act your age," she scrawled back, aware of Tyler's eyes on both of them. At least he couldn't read the notes.

"Hi there, I'm Tyler Harding," he said. "Won't you introduce yourself?"

Suze looked at the camera. "Suze Ralston," she told him. "I'm the office manager, and if you're ever in Milwaukee I'll make sure everything goes well for you."

"Thanks." A smile lit his severe features. "Milwaukee. Great beer, right?"

"Great Green Bay Packers," Suze corrected.

"Cheeseheads?" Tyler's laugh lit up the screen. "Is that okay to say?"

"Whatever you say is okay by me," Suze told him. "I am officially in luv," she wrote to Carly before she left.

"Suze is a manic fan," Julian told Tyler. "It's like a disease."

Jeanine and the lads signed off. The conference was Tyler's now, and he turned to Julian. "It's all about the network." They seemed to be taking up an earlier conversation. "Whatever you layer onto it, WI-FI, WAP, L2TP whatever version, it's the backbone that counts."

"You're right, absolutely." Julian began to enumerate StoneEdge's bandwidth requirements in terms of their expansion plans. It was the kind of discussion she'd been wanting to move toward for months with Julian, and she felt a jolt of jealousy that Tyler had so effortlessly engineered this at his first meeting.

Of course she knew Julian was a man's man, skeptical of women's competency, like the majority of men in telecom. And Tyler was sharp, she gave him that: he'd caught the international tollfree thing right away. Easy to be sharp, of course, when you didn't have to sweat every detail and hammer out all the follow-through.

He looked at her suddenly, as if he'd known she was watching him. "Carly, excuse us." He smiled again, projecting a warmth she could tell was deliberate. She met his gaze, hiding the physical reaction he evoked, even with manufactured charm. He must be dynamite in his negotiations with women: she'd bet he never lost a deal.

"Carly doesn't miss anything. You're taking this in, right?" Julian's broad grin appeared "She's a jolly good sport," he told Tyler. "She's put up with all my raving. And she called me at two in the morning, her time, last Saturday! That's commitment."

"Must have been an emergency." Tyler's tone said he knew them all.

"I had to let Julian know about our tech, so he could get into the building. Jack Rigby was terrific in getting someone assigned the morning of the protests."

"Ahmed Rasheed," Julian confirmed. "Good man. Turned up right as rain, in spite of the millions in the streets. Nice job, Carly, thanks for your efforts there."

What luck to have a senior GlobeAll exec hear this from Julian! But she tightened her lips over the smile of surprised relief she felt rising. She wanted to appear as serene as possible in front of these men. "I'm glad it worked out, Julian."

She sat back and surveyed them, deciding to try for an expansion of rapport. "Have things gotten back to normal now, in London?"

As they looked at her onscreen she saw a resemblance between them whose nature eluded her. She could feel their thoughts simultaneously turning away from telecom, and she wondered, suddenly, whether her choice of topic was wise.

"They'll *never* be normal again, not between the U.S. and Europe," Julian said.

Tyler nodded. "I've seen that, this trip."

"And we're bearing the brunt of it in the UK, since we're siding with your man. Ours has made himself a laughing stock. Bloody Pentacostalist."

She needed to narrow this conversational door she'd opened! "Well, Tyler, I hear you were in Paris during the weekend demonstration, was traffic miserable?"

Wrong question: his intense blue stare felt very cold and way too long. Did he think she was out of line, bringing up controversy? He was about four levels above her. He could end her career with one e-mail. She gazed back at him with as much aplomb as she could muster, cursing her subject pick, willing him to drop it.

But he didn't. "Miserable, that describes it, Carly."

He turned away from her, to Julian. "I knew it wasn't just his pro-war stance annoying you all so much," he said. "He's more religious than the average Prime Minister, right, and that goes against the grain here. There's a feeling like that in the States too, that religion is creeping into the political arena. It makes some people feel uncomfortable." He shrugged. "Others are okay with it."

Julian leaned toward Tyler eagerly, seeming to relish the argument, unheard-of in Carly's experience: most non-network conversations with customers stuck strictly to sports, weather, the stock market and genialities about family. Politics was as taboo as religion. But neither man seemed to care; they would have continued, she thought, if not for Dudley's entrance: showing up for his five minutes of fame, as scheduled.

"Julian! Good seeing you again. You know I'd have joined more of your meetings, but Carly doesn't always let me know when they are!" His chuckle was fake enough to stock a laugh track; the men on the screen looked annoyed at the interruption. "Tyler, how're you doing? We've met before, on conference calls. I'm Dudley Miller, branch director in the tri-state area." He always exaggerated in front of new people. He had Wisconsin, period.

As Dudley launched into a canned spiel about the state of the telecom industry, Julian looked pointedly at his watch.

"Goodness, look at the time, past seven. I've promised Tyler a visit to my favorite pub here, and he's probably quite thirsty by now."

"Wish we could join you!" Dudley laughed.

"I've told Carly she must come to London, she's welcome anytime, but Dudley, you have to thumbs-up her travel budget. Legitimate customer business, you know."

Julian's invitations had always seemed like threats, as if he'd lock her in StoneEdge's London basement data center with the other mistake-ridden vendors, his own Bluebeard collection. No thanks.

"For sure, she'd love the shopping, right Carl?" Dudley's little eyes peered at her.

There was a silence.

"*Shopping?*" Tyler said finally, as if it were a foreign word. His and Julian's eyes slid toward each other and then toward Dudley in mutual disdain.

"Shopping for GlobeAll dark fiber, for my best customers," she quipped, lamely. Julian chuckled, and Tyler's raised brow recognized her attempt to make light of Dudley's gaffe.

"Nice commission on that, eh Carly? Really, I'm serious, you must come over. Too bad it's not right now, you could join us at the pub." Something in Julian's look was more than suddenly empathetic because of Dudley's boorishness. He must be happy about the effort she'd made on the upgrade, and on the billing fixes, and on getting Tyler to London. He was regarding her keenly, without his usual sneer. She didn't know if this was a good sign or not.

"One gets the feeling our Carly might be quite a bit of *fun.*" His voice was plummy with speculation. Not a good sign at all. She stared down at the video console, fighting the angry flush she could feel heating her cheeks, wondering what they'd think if she just clicked off, breaking the stream ... oops!

Dudley seemed not to have heard. "Well, it's been good speaking with you both again, but other commitments beckon, gentlemen, I must be on my way."

"Cheerio," Julian told him. "Arrange a visit soon then Carly, there's a good girl, I should *really* like to meet you in person."

Tyler didn't acknowledge Dudley's departure. He was studying Julian. "We don't call account executives 'good girls' in the States," he said pleasantly. "We don't call them 'a bit of fun'."

"No matter how lovely they are?" Julian challenged, unrepentant. IT culture in the UK had never adopted the U.S.' politically correct stances. "Even on video."

Tyler looked at Carly.

She couldn't tell, from his expressionless scrutiny, whether he was sharing Julian's assessment or commiserating with her on Julian's loutishness. Looking into his eyes onscreen took her out of the videoconference, as if they were communicating about something else entirely. After what seemed like too long, she had to look away.

Julian laughed. "Admit it, she's jolly good-looking."

"On that note, I'll call it a wrap," she told them briskly. "Thanks for your time, Julian, and Tyler, thanks for making the trip."

"Oh before you go, Carly, there was one other thing." She braced herself. Julian was notorious for dropping bombshells before a meeting was supposed to adjourn. "Actually perhaps Tyler would address this as well. Better him than Dudley, certainly."

Tyler waited, his face still as he watched Julian. Carly wished she'd thought to warn him of Julian's trait—she was glad she was an ocean away.

"I heard the most peculiar rumor the other day, about GlobeAll," Julian began, dividing his gaze between the man next to him and the woman on his screen. The miracle of telecom, thought Carly irrelevantly, Pure Fucking Magic. She wished she could make Julian magically forget whatever was on his weaselly mind right now. "I heard UTT's considering a lawsuit against your company for passing on high access fees to them, illegally, through Canada."

This was much worse than Julian's usual rants. She had no idea what he was talking about. She was good at improvising, but now she just sat there, sweating, willing a comeback to flow from her mouth. Lucky for her, Tyler was already responding.

"What big ears you have," he told Julian, mildly. "I heard that too. We'll see what develops out of it, but as you know, this kind of mud-slinging goes on all the time amongst rivals. UTT can't stand it that we're more financially stable than they are right now, so they'll level anything they can against us."

"I heard there was some truth to this allegation."

Tyler shrugged. "All telecom carriers try to avoid access fees, through any means. We like to keep costs down for our clients. It could be that our Canadian partnerships provided for some shifting, perhaps, that looked like a vulnerability for UTT to exploit." His body language was relaxed, his smile bland, but Carly saw how he kept his gaze on Julian.

Julian was silent for a moment, eyeing him. Then, "You're good," he said admiringly. "You're quite smooth. What does your FCC have to say about it?"

"They know our network." Tyler's eyes flicked to Carly and he repeated, flat, the buzzwords she'd brought up yesterday. "It's all about *respect*, really, for the network's *integrity*."

145

Julian laughed; actually, he guffawed, Carly thought. He reached over and slapped Tyler on the back. "What you mean is that GlobeAll has the balls to try something like this and get away with it! That takes guts, as you Americans say."

Tyler regarded him with a half-smile that revealed nothing.

"Well, speaking of respect, old man, I say we respect our hostess' time and head off to the pub," Julian said. "We'll carry on exploring our business partnership."

Resentment boiled up in her as Julian and Tyler stood. They'd go swanning around London, bonding with big-boys' talk: she was stuck in Wisconsin with her truculent manager. "Thanks ever so much for setting this up Carly. I'll speak to you at our weekly review on Friday."

Tyler looked at Carly, and she saw one of his eyelids lower with what looked like the barest of winks. What was that supposed to mean? She trusted him even less than Julian after hearing his fluid spin on the alleged UTT rumor. Slickmeister. There were a lot like him in the higher echelon of the corporation. "We'll catch up later, Carly," he told her. "I'll call you on your mobile."

"Have a nice evening," she said faintly. She clicked off the console. She slumped back in her chair, reviewing the last hour, and waited for some of the tension to drain from her. Then she stood, pushing the wheeled chair away from her so violently that it went spinning into the wall. She charged out and headed straight for Dudley's office. She marched in without even knocking.

Twenty-Two

S HE KNEW SHE WASN'T INTERRUPTING; he was reading the newspaper.

"Dudley," she began, "what's with this rumor about UTT suing us over Canadian access fees? Have you heard anything?"

"I saw something, but there's no truth to it, no reason to panic the sales force. What did you hear?"

"Guess who told me about it. Julian!"

"Mmm. You should have called me back in to discuss it with him."

"Tyler Harding did that, so at least Julian's okay for now, but I need to be prepared with a good comeback."

"I'm sure Internal Comm will send out a statement."

"Will you forward it to me?"

"Everyone will get a copy, probably."

"Because I really need to socialize this with the StoneEdge execs."

"As I've told you before, you should let *me* conduct that kind of senior level communication, Carly, we've gone over this."

She glared at him, frustrated beyond courtesy. His answering gaze was blank with dislike. She'd felt his hostility ever since she took over the StoneEdge account from him, when he'd been promoted to management three years ago. She supposed he resented that she'd done so much better than he with StoneEdge, tripling its revenue stream to GlobeAll during her tenure. Probably he thought she was after his job. As if! What a bore, especially in this branch!

StoneEdge was the only company of any size on their list, and she'd about played out all the domestic potential in their telecom spend; that's why now she was going so aggressively after the international. Once that was secured, there'd be nothing left to grow in the account.

Maybe she should try to allay Dudley's suspicions. They needed each other in this company, like it or not: despite lip-service given to equal opportunity, there were few women executives at GlobeAll and even fewer African-Americans. Dudley seemed not to realize this. Perhaps he thought his ethnicity made him immune to the continuous rolling breakers of layoffs tumbling perilously ever closer to shore. If so, he really was as stupid as she'd always suspected.

"You're right, of course, Dudley, and I'll let you use your StoneEdge contacts to broach this subject." Let him fall on his own sword. "I just want to be forewarned. I had no idea there was something like this going on."

"It's probably nothing, Carl," he sighed, as if her query was annoying him. She hated that he called her 'Carl'; she'd never asked him to and she thought it was an obnoxious nickname. "It may be just the usual stuff."

The usual stuff?

Even in these litigious times, your biggest competitor suing you over a fraudulent access-avoidance scam was not usual at all. UTT had never gone after GlobeAll this way, in fact UTT was fairly standoffish when it came to marching in the lawsuit parades that swept with regular fanfare up and down telecom street.

And the alleged fraud was *international*? With the Patriot Act breathing down everyone's neck on security standards? Every foreign dealing was now under severe scrutiny, even with clean, friendly, innocuous Canada. GlobeAll was a major supplier to the U.S. government, including plenty of Defense Department contracts, as one of the 'big three' in telecom. She could just read the headlines now: "GlobeAll compromises U.S. security by passing sensitive traffic through Canada"!

Honestly, Dudley was such an ostrich. "Well, Dudley, if it gets into the trade rags, you may want to get ahold of your StoneEdge folks before they get ahold of us."

"I really don't see that happening, Carl," he drawled. Mountains out of molehills, his tone implied: just go sell something and leave me alone.

She barely restrained herself from slamming his door. Her nice blue suit was now, she knew, sweat-stained inside the armholes; her bra felt unpleasantly damp, her hair was frizzing up. Good thing she didn't have any more customer-facing appointments. In fact, she saw, checking her calendar, she didn't have any further obligations at all today.

She was going to damn well take the rest of the afternoon off. She might just call over to her favorite day spa, in the upscale mall near their building, to see what services were open today. She'd walk over there to let off steam, do the health club workout first, but then she could get a massage, or a body wash, one of those sensual poundings of water that made her feel so relaxed. She'd bloody well earned it, as Julian would say.

"Suze, I'm out of here. Page me if anyone important calls, okay?"

"Okay, hon." Her brown eyes conveyed sympathy. "That video man was a looker. No wedding ring. Pleasant, too." She was always trying to match-make Carly. She'd taken enough of Francisco's calls to know he couldn't be called pleasant, and she objected on principle to liaisons with 'foreigners.' "A smart, normal American."

Oh sure, that was all she needed: some long-distance dalliance with a GlobeAll senior exec, a glamorous New York City slicker who was probably stealing her customer right now as they sniggered in some clubby pub about how hot she'd looked—literally, sweating through her clothes—during the videoconference. Tyler had been gracious, in the meeting, by chiding Julian's ogling of her, but she knew businessmen well enough to know that he probably did plenty of ogling too.

She realized, suddenly, how it was that Julian and Tyler looked alike to her. They both radiated the high gloss of superbly confident alpha males, best of breed, in charge of the world, lording it over everyone else including all women. Fuckers.

Carly stopped herself from a nasty retort. None of this was Suze's fault.

Several hours later she was lying naked on a sort of gurney, in an individual little tile cube, under the rushing waterfalls that poured down from the ceiling in certain places—her back, her shoulders, her legs, her butt—in a rain that varied from gentle to vigorous. It was no more than a glorified carwash, really, but the aromatic candles placed in corners out of the rain, the soft new-age muzak, and the warmth of the water made it perfect therapy.

She turned around, carefully, so as not to slosh into a mouthful of water, to let her front be stimulated and soothed. She'd had an orgasm in here once, from a strategically placed water jet, but had since reminded herself this was supposed to be an elevation, not a base confirmation of physical pleasure. But she wondered now how many other women had just let go. The thought was kind of sexy.

As relaxed as she was feeling, however, she couldn't get the nagging out of her head. She had a low sensation of dread. The UTT lawsuit rumor was just the latest in a mounting accumulation of troubles, from her mom's illness to her twisted Francisco relationship to her precarious situation with Dudley.

She was taking a risk playing hooky like this, she knew; she was just lucky Suze liked her well enough to cover for her. She wriggled onto her front once more and tried to recapture her calm. She let the muzak fill her head and breathed in the scent of eucalyptus.

Her reverie was shattered by the shrill sound of her cell phone, in the alcove area where her clothes were hung. She'd forgotten to turn it off. How annoying!

Well, she didn't have to answer it.

It couldn't be important, anyway, she knew her mom would be napping and that Francisco was at a gallery. Unless Suze had something. Or, she panicked, it might be Tyler Harding. She couldn't miss his call. Dammit!

She rolled off the table and snatched open the cupboard door, clutching the handle to keep from sliding on the wet floor in her haste. Yes, it was a UK number, even though it was past eleven pm in London—the pubs had just closed, but if it was Tyler she'd bet he would be cold sober.

Remembering his face made her take a deep breath and stand up straight.

"Carly Emerald."

"Carly, hello." She was right—he sounded perfectly alert. "Tyler Harding here. I thought you'd want to know how my talk with Julian went."

"Yes. Thanks for calling."

There was a little silence. "Is that—what, does it rain in Milwaukee in February? I thought you were … in the Snowbelt?"

"I'm in an atrium," she lied smoothly. "This client has one of those fake waterfalls, you know, in the lobby? It's right behind me."

"Sounds like you're in a shower." His voice sounded friendly, but his presentiment stiffened her. She wasn't about to share any amusement with him. She was sweating again, dammit, and her grip on her phone was slipping.

"Julian?" she prompted firmly.

"Julian is in a position to give you a lot more Asian business."

Whoa.

He went on, "You'll want to exploit that next time you meet. He's worried about their current vendor, thinks their coverage is too thin, too regional. He's right. I reiterated, as you asked, that we're a more global player. If you need details on our portfolio there I'll have my staff brief you. There's a great engineer I use in Singapore, called BK—"

"That's awesome, Tyler, thank you so much!" She couldn't contain her excitement. She'd only wanted some executive oil on troubled waters—she hadn't thought he could actually find something new for her to sell. "BK's the best! He's already part of my StoneEdge team! I *love* him." Oops. *That sounded stupid.*

But he agreed, "Oh, me *too*," with a hint of humor. "Anyway, I got Julian thinking the four Rs." The four Rs, as they called them at GlobeAll, were Reliable, Robust, Range, and Reach.

"What about ethical?" she wondered. "Does he still believe that?"

"He doesn't need to," he said quietly. "He's on board with our network, and that's all he cares about, because he thinks it'll never go down. He knows our SLAs are the best in the industry." SLAs were service level agreements, hefty compensation given to customers in cases of network failure.

"What do *you* believe?"

The water around her filled the distance between them until he replied.

"I believe we're in for some trouble."

This was also unexpected—usually slickmeister execs like him spun to their last breath—and she exhaled more loudly than she'd planned.

"Sorry," he added, dry. "You asked."

"But you told Julian the network would never go down—"

"I didn't tell him that, it's his assumption, and it's correct. The network will remain even if GlobeAll doesn't."

He meant ... they could get bought.

She wished she could turn off the damn water. "So ... what do you think will happen?"

"The press will carry this in a day or two. Corporate Comm will put out a statement. Legal will freak, but they're good at that, no biggie. Finance will wrangle a way to up dividends, placate shareholders. Government Relations will spend a boatload on lobbyists this month.

It'll blow over, but there'll be some bad casualties. The Canadian deal: gone."

She wondered if he'd be held responsible. "Aren't you in charge of Canada?"

"Our current alliances, yes. But not this original access deal." She listened through a short pause. He continued, coldly, "I would *never* have approved it. What happened was a crime. UTT is right to go after us."

This was scary. "But you think GlobeAll will be okay in the end."

"It'll take time," he said slowly. "We'll project an attitude of business as usual."

As usual! How different this sounded, coming from him, than from Dudley. Aside from her dismay at the implications of the scandal, she was aware of how blasé he seemed, how sophisticated, how much higher up the food chain from her.

She swallowed her intimidation. "Thank you for uncovering this Asia business during your time with Julian. What did he talk about, otherwise?"

She heard him exhale. "Politics, the Iraq invasion, of course. And women."

She didn't know whether to laugh or stay quiet. The other GlobeAll execs she knew were never this frank. "What did you think of him?"

"He's a prick."

Another surprise. "But ... you seemed to like him?"

"I fawned," he said. "That's what you wanted, Carly."

"You're good at it," she blurted, conscious of how she had underestimated him by conflating him with Julian. "I could tell, Julian thought you were sincere."

"It's what I do."

"Well. Thanks very much."

"Julian can make you a lot of money. And he likes you."

She couldn't think of how she could express her apprehension, about the tenuous and sexist nature of Julian's liking, to this guy who'd probably been beyond such concerns for his entire career. He seemed to read her mind anyway.

"He thinks you're a helluva salesperson," he said. "He's a prick, but a good businessman. So no worries, Carly. You'll do well, and their network will be fine."

"Really?"

"Yeah, really." He went on like a good sales coach. "Be upbeat next time you talk, reinforce the billing fix you outlined today, tell him when he'll see his credit for the tollfree. Discuss the Asian solution with BK. I sent you an e-mail with all the details, by the way. Julian won't know what hit him."

"And the UTT lawsuit?"

"Let that boss of yours handle the fallout with StoneEdge local HQ, if he can," he said sharply. "That's why we pay him the big bucks. Another prick! You seem to be surrounded." He laughed. "Excuse my bluntness. It's late. I'm tired."

She was starting to like him.

"Your half hour's up, hon, you're all done in here." The masseuse came in, oblivious to Carly's stance, and proceeded to turn off the water and the muzak, drawling in a broad, loud Wisconsin twang. "Doncha just feel squeaky-clean good all over, Carly? Betcha don't even need a massage now! But we can go ahead anyhow, hon, if you're ready, I got all the oils and aromatherapy on tap."

Carly had the newest-fangled type of GlobeAll cell phone; she hadn't been able to resist its sleek appearance, and its entire flip-top was a giant microphone. She was *busted*. She signaled frantically to the spa lady to leave her alone just for a minute.

"Uh, so, Tyler, thanks a lot."

"Who the hell was that?"

Her silence confirmed that the situation was unorthodox.

"Yeah, *atrium*. Waterfall." She heard a short exhalation of laughter, just half a 'ha.' "I see why Julian likes you. You'd take his call no matter what, no matter where." There was a pause in which she could almost hear his mind shifting gears. "So, you *are* in a shower!"

She remembered how he'd caught her just out of the shower yesterday too. Now she knew what he looked like, her skin was responding to his voice. She wrapped her free arm around herself. "Not really." She kept crisp. "It's just a ... circumstance."

"Interesting *circumstance*, Ms. ... *Emerald*," he said slowly, and there was no mistaking the innuendo in his tone, no mistaking that he was 'big-picturing' her right now, as clearly as if they were once again on video. "Please excuse my ... interruption." He spoke so provocatively that she knew he was mocking her. She could almost envision how devastatingly sexy a real grin would look on his face.

"I saw the UK number," she said, trying to sound casual, unable to prevent a defensive note from escaping. "I didn't want to miss talking to you."

"Hope I was worth it," he said, flip now. "I'll let you get to your massage. I could use one, too. Calling you was my last to-do tonight."

"Thanks for your ... understanding," she managed to choke out. Of course now she saw him lounging on his hotel bed in pajama pants, receiver to his ear under the crisp black waves of his hair, his other bare arm behind his head, smiling as he talked to her, blue eyes vivid with teasing light. "I appreciate your help with Julian."

"Anytime, Carly Emerald." His amusement overflowed into a chuckle. "Thanks for the laugh. I needed one. Make a lot of money from StoneEdge." He was quiet for a moment, before speaking again in a sober voice. "Make it as fast as you can."

Twenty-Three

AFTER HER MASSAGE, Carly walked slowly back to the office. It was dark now; just the streetlamps and occasional passing headlights lit her way on the neat urban sidewalk. The icy wind from Lake Michigan seemed to want to slice right through her but she walked on, not feeling it at first, wrapped in a heavy down coat, thick hat and mittens.

Tyler had called her as his final chore, conscientious, focused. He'd wanted to dutifully report on StoneEdge, in spite of his pub time with Julian, maybe feeling a little looser than usual—but no. He hadn't sounded loose.

She could see him bending tiredly over his hotel laptop, blue eyes shadowed with fatigue, clicking up his notes as he talked to her—but no. He spoke too quickly. Notes wouldn't even register with him.

She imagined him lying on a bed, tossing back a nightcap, flicking the remote, maybe stopping at the sex shows—she knew what those racy European channels featured—but no. High level business travelers really had no time for that.

He'd sounded perfectly professional up until the very end, when her being at the spa had struck him as funny. And intriguing. She had not misunderstood the awareness in his voice as he big-pictured her in the shower.

She'd felt a physical response as soon as she'd seen his face on screen, a reaction compounded by the intimacy of taking his call in the spa. But his candor about GlobeAll, his encouragement of her sales efforts, and his

156

deft, friendly conclusion, to what could have turned awkward, made him more than sexy: it made him likeable.

But so what. He'd called her, end of story, and he'd given her a fantastic lead: backup network in Asia! She knew what StoneEdge had there: about three dozen sites, major bandwidth. Complex, multi-year, lucrative, "sticky" as was said in sales: something she had not penetrated in nearly three years of dealing with Julian Trent.

She should be thinking of pricing out the sites, to present to Julian on Friday. She should be feeling gratitude toward Tyler Harding for his clever probing of StoneEdge's needs. She *should* be feeling mortified by the embarrassing position she'd revealed by taking his call, and calculating, right now, the HR steps she ought to follow so as to ensure her protection from having been exposed thus to a senior exec.

To every "should" in her head his final, intimate laugh heated her from the inside out, in spite of the Wisconsin winter chill, driving practical thought from her head as effectively as he'd driven their conversation to a professional finish.

She frowned. She was no ninny, to be thrown off track by an unknown man at the other end of a telecom connection, no matter how charming.

She tightened her coat around her. She needed to put a game plan together, to ensure her career survival if the lawsuit rumblings threatened GlobeAll's future. Recent business collapses showed that allegations could kill. Once accounting statements were called into question, once shareholder confidence was lost, very little could keep a company solvent. And Tyler said the Canadian scam was a crime.

This was frightening.

She'd felt so lucky that GlobeAll had the benefits, and respect for family, that she could take the time she needed with her mother. She'd been able to see her through diagnostics, take her to chemo, take off days to keep her company as Mom, stunned, began to understand the severity of her illness. It had been just over a year since her lung cancer diagnosis, a year of tumultuous coming-to-terms, for both of them.

If this lawsuit threatened GlobeAll's existence, all bets were off as far as her staying near Mom was concerned, longterm. Carly had enough of a financial cushion so she could stay in Milwaukee without working for at least six months, an eventuality she'd prepared for in case she had to care for her mom intensively. But after that?

Good-paying sales jobs in telecom were limited outside of the biggest cities and corporate headquarters. So many companies had folded; there were something like thirty-five per cent fewer options than there had been in the late nineties. It was possible, with her experience, that she could find something in international business, but she'd paid close attention to the job market ever since the economy had gotten so squirrelly, and she knew very well how slim the pickings were in Milwaukee.

She walked faster, pulling her hat down over her ears. No wonder Tyler Harding's last communication was "make money fast." He was obviously astute enough to have come to his own conclusions about GlobeAll's survival. It was a heads-up of sorts. But someone like him had all the options in the world: smart, goodlooking, sophisticated young men always did. He was probably busy plotting his next career move right now and she wondered, again, why he'd bothered to take the time to be so helpful with StoneEdge, so open about his GlobeAll conclusions, so friendly with her.

Carly knew she was capable of being deluded about men. She was easily drawn to the desirable ones, the handsome ones like Tyler. She'd usually found out too late that sexual chemistry did not signify character integrity and that the best sex wasn't always worth the negative ramifications. She wasn't quite willing yet, for example, to listen to her wisest self about Francisco. She was still more enthralled by the drama of their affair than appalled by its potentially disastrous outcome.

But in her working life, she'd learned to suppress her reactions to sexy men—the very few she ran across—and was now, at GlobeAll, more careful than ever. Telecom was a harsh environment for women, and attitudes like Julian's typified it. It aggravated her to walk the line: manufacturing the requisite charm for sales; while avoiding the appearance of flaunting, and therefore only being judged by, her sexuality. She was as tired of having to hide it as she was of trying, always, to use it to advantage. It was a no-win-for-women game.

Ergo, Francisco. She could be as free with him as she wanted. He reminded her of Mexico, where men wanted her just the way she wanted them—for a night, for a weekend, a delicious throwaway consumable, just because she was an exotic gringa.

Cristal, they'd called her, naming the color of her gray eyes. She'd been able to pick and choose the most beautiful of them, never feeling a pang of conscience as long as she practiced safe sex, never caring what they thought of her afterwards because she was nobody there, passing blithely through, discovering her libertine nature emerging as she matured, without cultural censure, or at least none that impacted her.

"No soy de aquí, ni soy de allá, no tengo edad ni porvenir, y ser feliz es mi color de identidad," the famous song went: I'm not from here or there, I have no age nor fortune, and being happy is the color of my identity. She'd loved that freedom. She missed it deeply.

Back in Milwaukee, employed at GlobeAll, she'd learned to be careful with men.

She recalled, wincing, a particularly uncomfortable episode, shortly after her return from Mexico.

Brian had been a newly hired sales rep, supposedly off limits due to the no-dating-in-the-office rule, but certainly approachable within discreet parameters. He'd been in his early twenties, exuding virility. He'd had the loveliest hazel eyes, framed by long lashes, and a watchful, shy face that for all its youth sported a perpetual five-o'clock shadow that lent him a sultry air. He'd been quiet in a way that suggested deep waters. All the women in the office hovered around him solicitously.

She'd been in a training class with him, during his first month at GlobeAll, held at a lakeside hotel in full summer, in the spend-it heyday of the late nineties. When told by the instructor to pick case study partners, he'd come to her unerringly, probably because the intense stares, the pheromones she was sending his way were irresistible. He *had* to be as drawn to her, she just *knew* it. They'd found a quiet corner in which to prepare their assignment. He'd fixed her with a limpid look, under those lush lashes; the kind of look that in Mexico would have been unmistakable.

"Well, Carly," he'd said, his slow, hushed Midwestern voice seeming about to promise any number of erotic delights, "let's just *annihilate* the other teams."

Maybe that passed for flirtation in business? She truly hadn't known. She'd still been figuring out the immense differences between men in Mexico, where she'd been rewarded for celebrating her sensuality, and men in the States, who seemed so wary of it; at least those in the business world.

That was as personal as Brian had gotten, in any case. He'd gone out for beers with all of them at the hotel happy hour after the class. His languorous gaze had rested on her with what she would have liked to imagine was yearning but which might well just have been near-sightedness. Her attempts to be alone with him had slipped through her fingers like sand.

For all his physical allure, he was an exceptionally straight young man, she would learn; even a religious one. She'd quashed her crush, since nothing came of it.

Sara had been maddeningly philosophical, when Carly had confessed her doomed attraction, over gin and tonic on her back porch. "Win some, lose some, babeh."

"He was winsome all right." Carly had licked wistfully at her lime. "He asked me, at one point, if I'd accepted Jesus as my savior." All the while staring at her as if sharing a deep secret—which, she had to concede, such a question certainly intimated.

"Well, maybe you should have told him you were open to exploring that." Sara raised dry eyebrows. "Christians fall in love like everyone else. They have passionate sex. They get married." Sara was a solid Episcopalian, happy in her faith, puzzled by Carly's agnosticism.

"I know." Carly drained her glass. "But I would have felt like I was corrupting him somehow. Or a cradle-snatcher; he's only twenty three." Carly at that time had been twenty seven. She contemplated her swizzle stick. "Let's face it, I'm just a nympho."

"Don't put yourself down," Sara answered sharply. "You have healthy needs, you're the perfect woman God made you. It's not a crime."

"It is in Milwaukee." This sounded dire, but Carly knew its truth even then.

She had subjugated the sensuous side of herself to the practical: she had to make a living. Her dad had left when Carly was five, and it had always been clear that Emerald women made their own way in life. So she'd pulled good grades in high school, gotten easily into Wisconsin's excellent university system, and finished college as a business major. She'd considered her three post-graduate years in Mexico, a poorly-paid ESL teacher, as extra study—she'd had a Spanish minor—and as an entree to international business. That had paid off with GlobeAll, which viewed extra languages as a plus.

She'd figured she could stay in Milwaukee and expand her career at GlobeAll, once she'd mastered the corporate culture, and go on to HQ in New York eventually. But, after she'd made her way in three years up to the HQ level, her mom's illness had started becoming apparent. Carly no longer had the option to explore positions elsewhere.

Now frozen by the cold and agitated by her thoughts, she reached her office. She'd worked herself into a state of anxiety, she recognized, and wondered if maybe a trip over to Sara's or Francisco's might have better suited her mood. But she was here; she might as well get some work done.

In her cube, she clicked e-mail. One immediately jumped out at her.

From: Harding, Tyler H. She wondered what his middle name was. Henry? Harold? Hotness?

To: Emerald, Catherine L. Hers was Leslie.

Subject: StoneEdge

Date: February 18, 2003, 10:50 pm GMT

> Carly/Catherine,
>
> Thanks for asking me to meet your client. It was good to meet you too.
>
> I had an illuminating discussion w/ Julian Trent about StoneEdge Asia WAN. Good opp'y for you to explore. Investigate backup solution for 40-site managed IPVPN at 512k up to 4M. Find locations on StoneEdge website. You can quote port from existing contract. Get budgetary local access pricing from engineer Boon Kiat Soon, GlobeAll Singapore, tell BK I asked you to find him and that I'll settle up w/ him later.
>
> Pose solution to Trent at next mtg—he'll be even more impressed w/you than he is now.

Best rgds,

Tyler

Tyler H. Harding

Sr Director, International Alliance Management

GlobeAll Communications Inc.

New York City

He'd written this just before calling her. What an efficient communicator: everyone was told to leave a voice-mail after sending an important e-mail but few people were conscientious enough to follow through. She liked that he was conscientious.

It was only a terse message; still, it sounded just like him. She saw him clearly now, slashing at his keyboard with long fingers, smiling as he contemplated what kind of "settling up" he'd do with BK later. She wondered what had crossed his mind when he wrote "even more impressed w/you."

Suddenly the echo of his low laugh seemed to lift off the screen. She wished she could pick up the phone and call him again right now, feel the reassurance he'd emanated during their talk, feel soothed by the comfort of that worldly charm. Hadn't they appreciated each other, somehow? Or was that just, as usual, her own wishful thinking?

She stared at her laptop, not seeing his message anymore, feeling a loneliness like cold settle into her body. There was nobody who could soothe her in the way that she needed, not Sara, whose patience with her whining was growing thin; not Francisco, whose interest in her—since his return from the holidays—was more rapacious than nurturing; not her mom, for whom she had to be the one providing comfort.

She hated these moments of bleak reflection that seemed to visit her more often, with each passing year, whenever she had time alone and was feeling a little vulnerable. She couldn't regret the choices she'd made, namely not to marry and have children by now, but realizing their consequences was harder than she'd known it would be. She suspected that in a larger city, or with a less conservative corporation, she wouldn't feel so confined by her choices; but there was no way she could move now.

She sighed, and stretched, and switched on her desk lamp. No point in brooding. She had forty sites to find and price out, she had to call BK in Singapore, where his work day was half an hour away, and she should reply to Tyler's message in a way that left no room for doubt about her professionalism or their future interactions. If there were any.

Tyler,
I'm very happy to have met you too!

Thanks so much for your wonderful assistance in uncovering the StoneEdge Asia opportunity. I appreciate your time and creativity with Julian and your support of my efforts. I will get in touch with

BK, who's already part of the StoneEdge team. Will keep you posted as to results with Julian.

Best regards,
Carly Emerald
Sr Global Account Executive
GlobeAll Communications Inc
Milwaukee WI

She looked at it for a moment and deleted "I'm very happy" and put in "Good." She deleted "wonderful." She hit SEND.

Then she started composing her e-mail to BK, who was a regular member of their weekly international team calls on StoneEdge and who would, no doubt, be delighted to exploit this new opportunity in Asia when he opened his messages.

Twenty-Four

HOURS LATER Carly was still hunched over her laptop, exhausted, still figuring out whether GlobeAll's portfolio could accommodate all of StoneEdge's Asia requirements. There were certain countries like Thailand and Indonesia where GlobeAll had to use partners instead of its own network, and that was never as elegant a solution to customers who wanted "one throat to choke" as the grim phrase in telecom went.

In the Philippines and Malaysia, where international business had been booming for years, GlobeAll still had limited bandwidth, and only in the capital cities of Manila and Kuala Lumpur. That might be okay for financial services firms but did nothing for manufacturers, like StoneEdge, whose factories or subassembly plants were way out in the boonies where telecom was but a dream.

It was funny, she thought, that companies didn't usually take the telecom infrastructure of a country into account when they picked a place to build or acquire a factory. They seemed to only consider the cost of labor and capital. That was so short-sighted. She'd seen that even in places like Mexico, where there were a gazillion foreign plants, the only way to get mainframe information traffic from A to B was with the quaint old copper wire—long replaced by optical fiber in the States except in the most rural areas—or in desperate circumstances, microwave.

Most developing countries were still so highly regulated that all global carriers were beating at the same door, usually that of the Ministry of Information, which grudgingly doled out licenses in tiny bandwidth amounts to foreign telecom vendors who wanted wireline service for their customers.

Misery of Information, one of Carly's colleagues had moaned, when trying in vain to wrangle coverage for a client's Middle Eastern regional headquarters in Dubai. He'd pronounced it 'D*oob*-yay.'

"You'd think they'd *want* to sell this stuff," he'd exclaimed, sighing after arguing with GlobeAll's international provisioning team for the better part of an hour, about GlobeAll's inability to buy any in-country facilities in the United Arab Emirates. "Wouldn't it be like, a boost to the local economy? What's *wrong* with them?"

Like most American businesspeople Carly knew, he was bemused and impatient when it came to international commerce, not understanding the territoriality with which PTTs jealously guarded their own markets.

Carly could only agree that the industry seemed dauntingly Byzantine. If GlobeAll had more of an international footprint, there would be no limit to what they could sell; demand for bandwidth was that high, even with the flailing world economy. But regulatory restrictions meant that no telecom carrier really had a true worldwide portfolio. Most had to patch their regional offerings together with other carriers, through agreements of the sort she supposed it was Tyler's job to negotiate.

Right now her head was aching. She couldn't imagine how Tyler had so blithely reassured Julian that GlobeAll could handle all those Asian sites. There were at least seven where GlobeAll had no facilities, and how was she supposed to gloss over that?

She could piece together a hodge-podge of GlobeAll's own and partners' networks, she guessed, but it wouldn't be something *she'd* buy. Not when she knew how ugly it would be, trying to fix anything that went wrong. Sure, one throat to choke. Try four. Try getting somebody in your language, in the middle of their night, halfway around the world, when there was an outage on a local network that even GlobeAll's partners had no visibility into. She could just imagine the calls she'd get from Julian if she sold Tyler's recommended solution and it fucked up StoneEdge's Asia network.

She sat back, sighing, and rubbed her lower back. She'd put this aside until tomorrow, look at it again when she was fresh. Besides, BK hadn't responded to her e-mail or her voice-mail. He probably had a million other projects going.

Tyler had just been trying to help, but after all, she guessed, like so many execs, he was out of touch with the realities of sales here in the field. It was a disappointment. He'd seemed like such a superstar.

She tried the Singapore office once again, this time using the main number.

"GlobeAll Singapore," said a perky woman's voice.

Carly identified herself, and asked, "I'm looking for Boon Kiat Soon?"

There was a short pause. "I am sorry, he is not in today."

"When will he be back?"

"I don't know," the woman said slowly. "He is sick."

It was extremely unusual for anyone, but especially engineers, to take off sick days. He must be really ill. But she couldn't worry about that right now, she couldn't wait on this pricing.

"Well, doesn't he have some kind of backup? Who's covering for him?"

"His backup is out today also, at customer site. You can send her e-mail and I can put you in her voice-mail system."

Okay, if that was the best they could do. Carly hung up, frustrated. How was she supposed to price this network out by Friday, with BK and his backup both out? At this rate she wouldn't get any response for another twenty four hours, and she'd have to stay up late to discuss it live with the Singapore engineer tomorrow night.

She wrote out a painstaking e-mail anyway, detailing all the addresses she'd gotten from StoneEdge's website, pleading for a fast turnaround and promising rich rewards if they could assist in the sale. For good measure, she mentioned that this had been Tyler Harding's suggestion. She cc'd him too. Maybe his name would spur alacrity.

She got up and stretched.

She went to use the restroom. Once back, to turn off her laptop, she was astonished to see a reply, to the e-mail she'd just sent, from Tyler. Did the man not sleep? It was, she checked her watch, only six thirty in the morning UK time.

Carly,

If you're still up, call me at the GlobeAll London office to discuss engineering resources in Singapore as re: StoneEdge Asia NW. I'll be in NY office 7 am yr time Friday. Will check final pricing w/you then.

Tyler

He'd listed numbers for his hotel, his mobile and the office. She stared at the e-mail for a moment, wondering if she really should call him. How had the evening flown by without her realizing it? She had talked to him, in the spa, over seven hours ago. He'd think she had no life outside the office, just a drone, a bore, an e-mail slave. She wouldn't call him.

On the other hand, if she waited on the Singapore engineers she wouldn't get her proposal together in time for her Friday meeting with Julian. If Tyler had anything to give her she ought to take advantage of it now, before he was traveling again.

She dialed the office number, standing, coat on, as if that would hasten her departure from this new encounter with him. He'd no doubt slept away his recollection, if he had any, of their last conversation, and she wasn't about to remind him by betraying the nervous flutters she felt inside. She'd be all business.

"Harding." His voice was wide awake. But surly.

"Hi, Tyler? This is Carly Emerald?" Damn! She sounded as tentative as if she wanted to ask him for a date. And she could tell he had her on speakerphone.

"I read the e-mail you copied me on, but I never heard of the person you sent it to. I told you to get BK."

"He wasn't there," she stammered, taken aback by his terseness. "He's sick."

"I'll tell his boss to release the pricing. You should have it tomorrow."

"Was that the expectation you left with Julian? A proposal by Friday?"

There was a pause, during which she heard clacking. He was multitasking, answering e-mail while he talked to her. Typical, but it stung. She was about to ask again, less politely, when he said, sounding annoyed, "No. I never promise what I can't deliver personally."

"Then ... just how *did* you leave things with him?"

"I left him with the goodlooking blonde he picked up, at his famous favorite pub," he said dryly. "I assure you, his Asia network is the last thing on Julian's tiny mind right now. Whereas, Carly Emerald, it is uppermost in yours, even at past midnight your time. You probably spent your evening working on this, right?"

He went on without giving her a chance to respond. "I knew you'd be able to exploit StoneEdge's Asia weakness." She supposed she should take this as a compliment, although she wasn't liking the tone of this conversation. "Julian isn't aware that I extracted these concerns from him. It's up to you to unsettle him further with the information you dig up on his current vendor, and suggest our alternative."

He didn't have to tell her how to sell. But she had to know *what* to sell. "Our alternative is a patchwork, Tyler. We don't have the coverage he needs in Asia."

She heard a buzzing in his background. "I have to take another call, Carly, can you hold on just a moment?"

"Okay." On hold, she barely had time to recognize Steve Earle's gravelly voice before Tyler came back on.

"*Steve Earle?*" she couldn't help blurting. She didn't remember the American folk-rocker doing any telephony songs.

There was a pause, wherein she thought she'd have to explain the whimsy of GlobeAll UK hold music, before she heard his low laugh. "It must be "Telephone Road," Carly, do you know it?" To her surprise he started singing, in a warm smooth bass. Then they both laughed.

"You sound good, Tyler. If your day job doesn't work out …"

"Thanks for the tip." His voice sobered. "Back to StoneEdge—we do have coverage for them, with the agreements I signed in Asia late last year. That's why I knew this would be a good opportunity for you. They're not up for general launch until next quarter, but BK's team can get you pre-launch pricing." He interrupted himself, to repeat thoughtfully, "BK, sick? That's a first in five years of knowing him. He must be really feeling bad. He was fine last week."

"I have to get a proposal in front of Julian on Friday," she reminded him.

"You'll hear from BK's team tomorrow. I'll make sure of that. But, remember, this is only for you, for StoneEdge. Not for the rest of the field sales team. You won't find it in the online product guides. I'll get you a custom arrangement."

She knew she should be grateful, but she'd wasted hours struggling over the sites. "Well, jeez, Tyler, how the heck would I have known this? It's a good thing I copied you on the e-mail!"

He dealt with her annoyance directly. "I wouldn't have let you down. I'd have followed up with you once I got back to New York, to make sure you got what you needed with BK. But you're lucky I read your message right now. Usually I archive what I'm just copied on."

"Then why did you read mine?"

"I was surprised that you're still up working. And I'm curious, now, about the StoneEdge project."

"I'm *always* working," she said. "As you discovered before."

There was a moment wherein, she imagined, they were both recalling their previous interaction. "Yes indeed." His voice contained an undertone of warmth. "An unusual trait, in my experience of Stateside GlobeAll salespeople."

"I'm used to the international side of StoneEdge, where work goes on 24/7." She bit her lip to keep from bragging further. She was no better than Dudley.

But he was laughing. "Anytime, anywhere, even in the shower. The Emerald work ethic. Does your boss appreciate how dedicated you are?"

"He resents me," she surprised herself by confessing.

"That was obvious during our meeting. Does he often get in your way like that?"

"He likes to keep in touch with StoneEdge. It used to be his account."

"Then he should be grateful to you. You've made it a goldmine. Or, should I say, an Emerald mine." He laughed again. "Julian told me you've tapped deep veins."

She wondered just how much he and Julian had talked about her, in the London bar, Julian on the lookout for blondes, maybe Tyler too, who knew? "Don't tell Julian about the shower," she said in a rush. "I mean, if you talk to him again."

"I wouldn't tell anyone, Carly." He sounded surprised. "Consider it forgotten." Then he added, in a lilting tone, "although, I admit, I enjoyed … our moment."

She knew he was kidding, but she was glad he could not see her face flush with the heat that washed through her as he said this.

A sudden silence between them spun out until it made its own point, one that neither might have intended but that now held significance, in their dialogue. The sound of a mobile phone ringing interrupted it on his end.

"Carly? I have to take this. I'll call you Friday morning when I'm back in New York, before your meeting with Julian, to close this project out with you."

"Thanks." She knew he was being extraordinarily helpful, but she was too alert to the vibration that had just hummed between them to be able to elaborate her gratitude.

"Goodbye then."

"Safe travels," she told him, too late. He'd already hung up.

Twenty-Five

A SAD PEARL JAM SONG, "Thumbin' my way Back to Heaven," accompanied Carly's drive from the office. The night was even more frigid, more bleak than on her walk from the spa. Eddie Vedder sang wistfully about rusty but true signs being ignored for shiny but false ones, strumming a poignant acoustic guitar tune. She'd add this one to the list, for sure.

At her mother's behest she'd started downloading a collection of music to be played at Mom's funeral. Mom wanted just about every Grateful Dead song, which would outlast any memorial service yet known, but Mom wasn't thinking "service"—she was thinking "party." Carly hoped she would be strong enough to keep a festive mood going for the length of time it would take for Mom's many friends to run out of the manic agony she could see was already possessing most of them. Mom was fifty-four, barely into middle age, and her lung cancer diagnosis had reverberated as a frightful wake-up call throughout her Baby-Boomer circle.

Carly took a sharp left, away from the route to her own apartment, toward her mom's. She knew that she'd be welcome, however late it was now. For once, she wanted to cry on her mother's shoulder, to pour out her worries and frustrations and fears, to feel the soothing comfort of her mother's touch.

Her mom was still up, she could see from the light in the window of the neat little bungalow on Blue Mound Road that was home for all of Carly's growing up. She used her own key to open the front door. Rebecca

Emerald looked up from her recliner, remote in hand, not surprised to see that it was Carly, who had the only other key.

"Catherine Leslie. I'm just catching up on my planet facts. Did you realize there's new evidence of a galaxy similar to ours, light years away of course, but definitive?" She turned the sound down. "What are you doing here at this hour on a work night?"

"Hi, Mom." Carly walked over to envelope her now-frail mother in as strong a hug as she thought Mom could take.

"Darling, what is it?" Rebecca's tired gray eyes took in Carly's expression. "I was about to have a brandy, why don't you pour us both one."

Mom's supplementary pain relief, self-prescribed, included tea with brandy and plenty of red wine. She had a cornucopia of doctor-prescribed drugs too, but she said they knocked her out too much. She claimed to prefer to stay as lucid as possible, but the grip of pain meant she got half looped most nights.

Because she no longer had the strength to manipulate the corkscrew, she now stocked her liquor cabinet with wines that had screw-top caps, thereby limiting her repertoire to awful vintages. Carly had discovered to her own dismay that Rebecca, an old hippie, actually preferred the taste of swill like Boone's Farm Strawberry.

Carly fetched them each a glass of brandy, along with hot tea. She sat on the floor next to the recliner and leaned her head on her mom's bony knee, feeling as soon as she did a soft hand stroking her hair. They sipped for a moment.

"So what's up?"

"I'm just ... a little worried, I guess."

"How come?"

"GlobeAll's in trouble." She repeated what she'd heard from Tyler Harding. "This guy, this New Yorker in the international sector, made it sound pretty serious."

"This guy was worried about GlobeAll's future?" Mom had the ability, always, to nail a nuance. "And he's in a position to know?"

"Yeah. I think he is." Saying it out loud frightened her even more.

Mom's hand kept stroking her hair. "If you need to, you can move back in here with me, as soon as you can get out of your lease. Use me, honey, you can say I'm in hospice, your landlord has to cave. Use it with GlobeAll, too, so that you can take the time you need to interview with other companies before you're forced out."

"But that's so pessimistic."

"I'm a realist, hon. All I do these days is watch the news shows and Discovery. I see what's happening to the economy. And the solar system too, of course."

"Mom. I can't move back in here with you. I'd crowd you."

"I know Francisco wouldn't like it, but it's time he made up his mind about you anyway."

"It's not about that—"

"Then *you* need to make up your mind about *him.*"

"I'm not worried about him right now, Mom, that's not why I stopped by—"

"You're worried about him all the time."

Carly twisted her head fretfully under her mother's touch. "He's gotten so weird lately, is all. I still love him, I just can't quite see where it's leading." Mom had no idea he might be married. If he was. Whatever he was.

"I don't like the sound of that," her mom said predictably. "Weird means dangerous, sweetie, why do you need that in your life right now?"

"But he's ... interesting."

"Danger always is. But you need to find the courage to push it away." She twisted Carly's corkscrew curls in her thin fingers. "Easier said than done, of course, I know."

"How'd you get so smart?"

"Plenty of stupid mistakes." They shared a laugh.

"So … you really think you could stand to have me back home?"

"You'd be a comfort to me, Carly, you know that. But I wouldn't make you play nursemaid. You'd have your independence."

She thought over the idea. Before this news about GlobeAll she wouldn't have considered it, not before Mom really needed her on a daily basis, but tonight it made sense to act sooner rather than later.

"So who's this New Yorker?"

"What?"

"I heard a certain note in your voice." Mom sipped, watchful.

"Nothing." Carly shifted away. "It doesn't mean *anything*."

"What doesn't?"

"I mean. You know how I always get caught by a pretty face."

Rebecca smiled. "I know."

"So. This guy, that's all it is." She hadn't even had a chance to describe him to Sara, who would certainly have welcomed a change from her obsessing over Francisco. Her mom was raising eager eyebrows, encouraging her to say more, and she indulged herself. What harm was there in a little admiration? "He's not only intelligent, he's *really* good-looking. Blue eyes, black hair, beautiful mouth, sexy laugh."

"Crewcut?" Mom didn't like contemporary men's haircuts. She favored long hair or ponytails. Francisco's hair was the only thing she liked about him.

"No, it's long enough to see a natural wave." She sounded just like Suze! "He's a hottie, Mom, you'd enjoy him." Saying it like that distanced him comfortably.

"How'd you meet?"

"He's helping me with StoneEdge. He went to see Julian in London for me."

"He didn't come to Milwaukee?"

"We met on a videoconference."

"You kids." Rebecca smiled. "How can you get attracted to someone on TV?"

"It's not like that. Exactly. I'm not really attracted." Carly frowned at this lie, but did not correct it. Her reaction to him was too new to be examined further. "I mean, we've talked some, and e-mailed. That's all." She tried to recapture the feeling that she and Tyler were becoming friends. It seemed an elusive concept, held up to verbal expression. "We're just getting to know each other." That was the truth.

"Tell me more about GlobeAll. What exactly did the New Yorker say? What's his name again?"

Carly relayed what little she knew of GlobeAll's situation and of Tyler, feeling as she did a lightening of the burden she'd come in with. Her anxieties seemed to dissipate in the peach-colored walls of her mother's living room, soaking into the deep red sofa, the rust-flowered curtains, sinking into the plush rose carpeting.

Everyone always joked that Rebecca's place was like the stage set of *The Vagina Monologues*. Her mother's house was the most visually engaging place she knew, pulsing with feminine hues that encouraged every kind of expression. Carly had grown up with weeknight gatherings of Druids, battered women, Transcendentalists, divorcees, gardeners and various Book Clubs. She'd been included in every discussion, even when it was well beyond her.

Her mom's profession was interior decorating and she encouraged Carly, from an early age, to appreciate physical beauty and comfort. Rebecca's house looked a little frowsy these days, which probably pained her aesthetic sense.

"It sounds like he's going out of his way to help you with StoneEdge."

"He's been much more helpful than I'd have expected a GlobeAll exec to be." For the first time Carly wondered if Tyler was stalling his return to HQ, biding his time before the UTT news hit the press, not minding taking extra days to see Julian: being close to customers always provided armor during times of corporate crisis. And getting into the details of an Asia network deal might prove a welcome distraction for him, something concrete to focus on rather than the threatening but vague UTT lawsuit fallout.

"So when do you meet in person?"

"Mom." Carly turned to smile at Rebecca. "This isn't some soap opera."

"Even juicier. It's real life." Her answering smile stretched thin on her emaciated face. "At my stage we look for every little thrill. Your New Yorker sounds cool. Hot. Whatever you say, these days." She yawned.

"I'm helping you get to bed."

"Then stay here tonight. It's late for you to be driving home."

"Deal."

It was comforting to nestle under the down duvet of her childhood bed, a nightlight glowing in the corner, knowing her mom was sleeping soundly just down the hall. Maybe she'd work from home tomorrow, to give herself some breathing room to prepare for the storm of controversy that was sure to break when the UTT lawsuit made the news.

For the first time in a long time she did not toss and turn over Francisco. Her last thought before sleep was that Tyler Harding's day was well underway, over there in the GlobeAll London office. She liked that they'd shared their enjoyment of the UK hold songs. *But I bet he doesn't get put on hold very often.*

Twenty-Six

A S SOON AS SHE CHECKED e-mail the next morning, Carly knew working from home was not an option. Dudley had called for an all-hands mandatory in-person meeting. The news of UTT's lawsuit against GlobeAll was on the front page of the *Wall Street Journal*.

After a quick shower and change of clothes at her own apartment, she drove to the office. She felt lucky to have heard the news leaked from Julian, and countered by Tyler. She was even grateful, in retrospect, for the impulse that had sent her to confront Dudley. He'd insisted on handling the issue with StoneEdge. Since they were her only customer, she wouldn't have to face the barrage of questions that would certainly hit her coworkers from all sides.

"Team," Dudley said when they were all assembled in the Wausau Room, the large conference space, "the allegations against us are serious. But Internal Comm has prepared talking points for us to use if customers bring this up."

"Why would customers care?" one of the newer salesmen asked. "It doesn't affect their bottom line or our service to them."

"It impugns our integrity, and makes our financial stability seem suspect. Our accounting statements reflect what's supposed to be the true cost of access." Carly had to give Dudley credit. He projected a calm gravitas, an approach all of them could emulate.

"If our cost looks like it's been artificially manipulated, or somehow illegally avoided, then we look bad," Dave Seymour further explained. "Look at the trouble WorldFon got into over *their* funky accounting practices."

"But it still doesn't affect our network, and that's all my customers care about," insisted the first salesman.

"It might affect our future customer service, if we have to declare bankruptcy the way WorldFon did," said a saleswoman who sat in a cube near Carly's.

Bankruptcy. The word slithered through the room like a snake gliding under water, venomous tail twitching from side to side.

"We're a long way off from having to worry about that," Dudley told them. "But these are valid concerns, and that's why I wanted all of us to get together to discuss this, so we're all on the same page. Let's review the talking points."

Suze switched off the overhead lights to illuminate the presentation.

In the sudden dimness, Carly looked around at her coworkers.

GlobeAll's unspoken preference, for sales, was to hire goodlooking young people who'd played team sports at some time in their lives. The confidence that came from being attractive, athletic and cooperative usually led to success in sales. Telecom knowledge could be created over time, except in the least intelligent, and those were quickly weeded out. GlobeAll had an extensive training program to ensure that its salespeople were as technically sharp as it was possible to make them.

So the faces that Carly looked at were smooth-skinned, their teeth straight, their hair neatly styled. But their expressions were tense.

Everyone knew that the knee-jerk reaction to this kind of scandal, in American publicly-held companies, was to deny, deny, deny—and then downsize the workforce. Everyone in telecom knew someone who'd worked for WorldFon before its implosion, or Direxx, or Global Borders; or one of the unremembered fly-by-night ISPs or dotcoms; or one of the cable-laying consortium holding companies like TyRoll and Onron. Everyone knew someone who was still looking for work.

To a generation that had come of professional age in the United States nineties, when the sky seemed to be the limit and the growth never-ending, the seismic economic shift of the twenty-first century—the zeroes, they all called them, bitterly—was a cold shock. People who'd been used to thinking more, bigger, better, were stuck in costly investments—huge new houses, fancy SUVs, timeshares in exotic locales, memberships in haughty clubs—which had been so easy to acquire, on limitless credit, and which now were so hard to get rid of. The obligations and losses were staggering.

Carly supposed she should consider herself lucky, given her mom's offer last night to move back home— she had no economic commitments, no dependents, no loans to repay. She'd been thinking she'd stay with Rebecca when she got worse, anyway. She'd also been refusing to recognize how much worse her Mom already was.

In fact, if Carly could bring herself to admit it, she knew Mom might soon need hospice more than she needed her daughter's company. Carly hadn't focused on it during her visit last night, but she recalled, now, how frail her mother looked, how even the smallest action sapped her energy, how wine was the only thing keeping pain at bay. She'd seen Mom's stiffness as she moved to the hospital bed.

She'd heard her gasping in the night. Carly'd gotten up to help her use the bathroom—a bedpan might soon be necessary— and to take some pain meds. Daily visits from friends weren't going to see her through the hard times to come, and Carly wasn't equipped to be a fulltime nurse. She'd been putting off looking into hospice. But it was probably time.

The loneliness clutching her late last night, dissipated by the warmth of Tyler's encouragement and the comfort of her mother's presence, dug in deeply now as she watched her colleagues.

In spite of having no major financial commitments, she didn't feel lucky. She'd trade places with the married ones, just then, to have someone to share the love and pain of caring for Mom and the anxiety of this UTT lawsuit crisis. The worst aspect of her attachment to Francisco, although he understood so well her anxiety over Rebecca, was her inability to count on him for longterm or even public support.

She had to force herself to listen to Dudley.

"In the worst-case scenario, we might be barred from doing new business with the government," he was saying gravely. "But that would only happen if it appeared we'd routed government traffic through Canada too, along with the commercial traffic we diverted up there." Just as she'd feared! "Since most of our government contracts are for domestic traffic, it's very unlikely. In any case, that kind of prohibition would be just a temporary measure, until the accounting's straightened out."

"Don't we have a lot of government contracts up for bid right now? Losing that would really hurt us," said one of the older reps.

"The ban, if it's imposed, would only be temporary, as I said, and only for new business. We'd keep current traffic, of course." Dudley's smile was an attempt at reassurance. "And I can't tell you with any certainty we'll lose government contracts. It certainly isn't necessary for you to share that scenario with any of our customers, you understand. Our spin is that this misunderstanding is most likely due to accounting errors. That's all *you* need to say to any of your clients, if they bring it up. Of course we'll say, consider the source of the rumors. You all know the FUD on UTT."

FUD was an acronym standing for the Fear, Uncertainty and Doubt that GlobeAll's marketing spinmasters created about competitors. The standard FUD on UTT was that it was too big, too unwieldy to be flexible, that its salespeople were unwilling to think out of the box, that since it was a former monopoly the company was out of touch with current customers' requirements. More recent FUD was that UTT was in financial trouble, since the spin-off of its cable and wireless divisions. International FUD was that UTT had no solid global partnerships.

One voice rose from the back of the room.

"How much Department of Defense traffic does this branch carry?"

They all turned to look at the speaker. He was standing in a clump of SEs, Systems Engineers, and he looked to Carly as if he was about eighteen. He was obviously a new hire—he wore a Tshirt/flannel shirt combo, a glamorous blond ponytail and a golden hoop in one ear.

It was a look that might have been okay on engineers at GlobeAll for a couple of minutes back in the late nineties, just as it had been okay for salespeople to wear cute corporate logo shirts with their pressed khakis, but it had been all suits, all the time for sales, since 9/11; and even engineers had gotten more tailored. Carly was surprised that nobody had yet told him to straighten up, to lose the hair and earring and invest in some work pants and polo shirts.

"Our federal contracts are out of the Washington D.C. office," Dudley said.

"Lionel, why are you asking?" Dave Seymour's customary courtesy sounded chill.

"Just wondering," answered Lionel, "about the accounts that are government contractors. Like StoneEdge, for instance."

Dave glanced at Carly. "If you have a professional need to know, that kind of proprietary information can be made available to you," he told Lionel, frowning.

Lionel returned Dave's look, leaning casually into the wall.

Carly remembered Julian's dour comment about the certain wartime need for StoneEdge's Stoney Fighting Machine. She saw a convoy of the bulky beige armored vehicles clanking their way across the Iraqi desert. StoneEdge built tons of weaponry for the U.S.

government. They'd amply outfitted every U.S. war campaign for more than a hundred years. StoneEdge execs asserted their footprint mirrored NATO's.

Of course StoneEdge would need telecom transport to Iraq, she realized with a jolt, if only to coordinate shipments with the in-country logistics people. And their contract with GlobeAll was almost exclusive, for international traffic.

The looming invasion presented as much opportunity for GlobeAll as it did for StoneEdge. It made her feel queasy.

However, would the possible ban on GlobeAll's doing business with the government extend to its *customers* who had such contracts? Dudley hadn't mentioned this, but she was sure Corporate had to consider it. She could let Dudley take the heat with StoneEdge about the lawsuit, since he'd insisted on that yesterday, but if there were going to be some kind of moratorium on even customers' government-related traffic she might lose the potential Asian business. A number of StoneEdge's key Asia sites, she knew, were devoted to Department of Defense networking, at military bases there.

She studied Lionel. As people left the room he lingered behind, looking down, deflecting those stray curious glances that landed on him. Dudley's and Dave's cursory looks hardly seemed to touch him. She approached him just as he was leaving.

"Lionel, I'm Carly Emerald. I'm the StoneEdge account manager."

"Carly, hi. You're the person I'm here to help. Dudley doesn't even know it yet, but I've just been assigned to the StoneEdge network." This was not the coincidence it might have seemed—new System Engineers, recruited out of college and trained intensively, were routinely given complex accounts to cut their techie teeth on, under more experienced supervision. "That's why I asked that question."

"You're thinking they'll need transport for their defense business."

"Well, yeah. They've already got GlobeAll running their international private lines for DOD in Afghanistan," he said, as if she should have known this. But it was news to her. "Kuwait's next."

"Really. Where was that contract signed?"

"Wholesale. The Government Services side." She'd heard GlobeAll's Wholesale Division had a piece of StoneEdge's government subcontracts. The reality of how StoneEdge made its money had never seemed so stark to her as it did today, after watching a weekend of worldwide antiwar demonstrations. As she looked at Lionel her expression must have reflected her dismay. "You mean you—didn't know that?" he asked, his brow wrinkling.

"Wholesale, yes, I knew they had some StoneEdge business. I didn't think about—Afghanistan. Kuwait. Iraq, of course, if the President gets his way."

She did not know what induced her to say what she did next. She blamed it, later, on his silly earring, as if because of his alternative look he could be trusted with the subversive thought that she hadn't, yet, even fully expressed to herself. "I guess I'm just wondering how I feel about the DOD traffic, since I really don't agree with the invasion."

A silent moment froze them in place, there in the Wausau Room, the sun streaming in through the windows that Suze had opened the blinds to, following Dudley's presentation. There was snow gleaming outside on the immaculately tended grounds in front of the corporate park complex, lending a bucolic Christmassy ambiance, with its artful little pond iced over: its resident decorative geese had flown south months ago. Carly, aware that she'd just uttered heresy, felt a shiver race up her back as cold as the scene out the window. What the hell was she thinking, talking like this at work? She stared at Lionel.

He stared back. "Then let's talk fast. As soon as the FCC moratorium comes into effect, this branch will have to manage StoneEdge's government-related network. I

185

need to know all about that, before you leave." His mouth curled up, as if reluctantly, into a grin that revealed a badly crooked tooth. How had he gotten past GlobeAll's ordinary-good-look-o-meter? "That is, if you're serious about splitting."

"Won't a moratorium affect our StoneEdge government-related traffic?"

"The FCC won't interrupt vital national-interest transport. They'll uphold a ban on GlobeAll publicly, sure, they'll slap some kind of sanction on the Wholesale division that handles government, which is why this business is now *yours* to manage, since technically you're in Retail, but they'll let mission-critical traffic through. Quietly. The lawyers will have engineered that." He wasn't as young as he looked.

"You've thought this out."

"Yeah," he replied, and his tone said, *duh, you haven't?*

"The ramifications of this lawsuit are just now sinking in, for me."

"I'd advise you to get up to speed, if you're keeping the account. This is gonna come down quicker'n any of them think." He jerked his head in the direction of the now-deserted hallway.

"The FCC action."

"Iraq," he corrected. "We don't call it an invasion, by the way, Carly, if you're gonna stick around you should know that. We call it liberation. GlobeAll should have designed StoneEdge's Kuwait in-country network yesterday, to support their Iraq shipments."

She took an involuntary step back.

"Uh huh." That crooked smile again. "I just came from a training stint at the IT department of the Army War College. We learned all about the paths to the hot zones. That's why they assigned me to StoneEdge." And he looked like such a hippie! He could have been one of the million street protesters she'd watched on TV last weekend.

"So ... that's what you were asking about."

"Yeah. I wondered if any other local company, maybe some other manufacturer or one of StoneEdge's suppliers, would be interested in going in on a short-cut spur, to the international gateway in New York, y'know, get some highspeed bandwidth to go direct."

He walked over to the window and looked out as Carly had done, but like almost everyone who stood there, he wasn't taking in the placid landscape. He traced a map in the air with his forefinger. "We can hop the traffic on a private line over through Europe, to the network DOD's set up in Turkey for intra-unit comms. TAT-14's good for a buncha Gigs."

TAT-14 was the newest transatlantic subsea cable, capable of transmitting, Carly heard, more than a million phone calls at a time. Its was capacity 640 Gigabytes. "Or, we could go through the domestic DOD network that's been engineered through Houston, and just satellite to Turkey. It's private, of course, but StoneEdge's got clearance up the wazoo." He looked over. "Which way y'think they're gonna go?"

She wanted to slow him down, to give herself a chance to think about what she'd blurted earlier, to let her mixed-up feelings settle. She drew in a deep breath against her confusion.

"I'd want to talk it over with them." She looked pointedly at her watch. "I can still catch my StoneEdge contact in London, he's the decision-maker for their global networks." Hopefully Julian wasn't too hungover from his booze and blonde. She moved to the door. "I'll get back to you this afternoon."

"Nobody in London's making these decisions. Those international IT people shouldn't even know about this. It has to come from StoneEdge Corporate, right here in Milwaukee."

She stood still.

"If you think you can't stand the heat, Carly, I recommend you get out of the kitchen. This network's gonna get built whether you like it or not." His voice was quiet, at odds with his terse message and the impatient drumming his fingers conducted on the window ledge. He watched her for a few seconds, and then walked around the room to stand beside her. His air of expectancy was so demanding, she had to look at him.

"Well? Which way are you going?" His eyes were the brown of bitter chocolate, half hidden behind tiny black-wire-rimmed glasses.

"Can you give me … a moment?"

"I can get what I need from the Wholesale folks, but your relationships, your management of the account would make this easier. UTT's got their eyes on government contracts, y'know, just waiting for GlobeAll to slip up so they can shut it down completely and take over that business. You better be smart."

"I asked for a moment."

His eyes narrowed, slightly, but he turned back into the room. "I'll wait."

Twenty-Seven

INSTEAD OF GOING BACK to her cube Carly took the stairs outside. Frigid air cut through her suit and clung to her skin in an unwanted gelid embrace. She crossed quickly to her car, where she blasted on the heat.

She punched on the CD button to hear her current favorite song, Coldplay's "Clocks," but its contemplative melody was too distant for her right now. The lush waterfall of music sounded as chill as the view from the parking lot, a stretch of abandoned railway trestle bridge.

The office park designers must have thought the trestle was picturesque, a reminder of the region's history of commerce and transportation, for it was not landscaped over. It looked lonesome. It reminded her of the John Hyatt song about the girl who killed herself on the Monon line. She held her arms tight around herself.

Can't stand the heat?

As if. It was the *cold* she wasn't standing—the cold knowledge of too much reality crashing in. Worst, of course, was that her mother was dying. She forced the thought quiet, as if God might hear her and take a closer look at the sweet, funny woman in the neat little bungalow on Blue Mound Road, take a closer look and decide to hasten the inevitable. She didn't even believe in God. She hushed that thought too.

She wanted to crawl away from the truth, curl up, hide. She had been closing her eyes to it for too long, but she closed them again now, against the sting that welled too easily. Her throat ached with the effort of caging tears.

She switched to radio, her favorite Chicago station WXRT, who were playing White Stripes, "Seven Nation Army," infusing her with enough steel to count her troubles and wonder, after a brief bleak litany—Mom/Francisco/StoneEdge/Dudley—whether quitting her job would bring any kind of relief or satisfaction.

Would it alter the course of history one iota, if a suddenly gun-shy sales rep from Wisconsin were to flinch from selling some private lines to StoneEdge? They'd buy them anyway, from somewhere, Lionel was right. Besides, StoneEdge didn't single-handedly create the wars it equipped.

She knew that government and industry—specifically, the Department of Defense and the telecom industry—were inextricably interdependent. Many telecom ideas were born in the military, and many of GlobeAll's best engineers had gotten their start in the armed services. The government funded the most cutting-edge R&D. DARPAnet, the old Defense Department electronic bulletin-board, had birthed the Internet. Telecom companies commercialized military applications and then sold them back to the military. No surprises there.

Would she feel happier selling to some retailer, or banking company, or to schools? Everything was intertwined, anyway, the world's economies and politics; she'd explored that concept many an evening at Rebecca's little salons and more recently with Francisco. If she were to pose this dilemma to either of them there would be an instantaneous vehement response. Of course she should quit, they would declare, caught up in the antiwar fever that was energizing a new generation to the fervor of the sixties movements.

Rebecca had watched the news coverage of the demonstrations approvingly, last Sunday night, and had pointed out to Carly several straggly people holding up a wavy-written long poster: "Workers Don't Kill Workers."

"Look, honey, there are just enough Wobblies left to hold up a sign." She'd sounded nostalgic. "Wonder what rock they've been hiding under for the past thirty years.

They look like they haven't even changed their clothes." She'd leaned forward to look more closely at the screen. "They sure haven't cut their hair."

"Wobblies?"

"International Workers of the World. Like Communists." She'd laughed. "I guess everything does come back into style, if you wait long enough."

Francisco, too, had been enthralled by the sight of the demos, and had wanted to go out to the Milwaukee protest contingent gathering to brave the cold. But in the end he stayed away, afraid of risking his visa status by getting arrested.

Sure, they'd support her if she quit, but theirs were not the opinions that counted, and any other working option would eventually lead to the same kind of inexorable conclusion. Even Rebecca's old back-to-the-land commune-dweller friend Wander had known it. "There's no escaping the military-industrial complex," he would usually declare sadly, as the joint was passed round. "Can't get away from it, not even by leaving the country." Globalization had ensured that.

The thing was, she *liked* her industry. It was fun, building networks, figuring how to get traffic where it needed to go, working with engineers to design the right solution of bandwidth and equipment and protocol. It was a puzzle that she loved solving every day. She'd even thought she was helping to contribute, in some small way, toward economic development in the countries where GlobeAll connected StoneEdge's traffic. Workers of the world, indeed.

It was the most enjoyable job she'd ever had, not to mention the most lucrative. She got along with everyone she worked with, except for Dudley, and she respected GlobeAll's rigorous standards and good reputation. This Canadian access thing seemed an anomaly, some mole's notion of a good idea, not something any stand-up executive would create and defend.

Even Julian, when he wasn't making her miserable, provided entertainment and novelty. She could just imagine what he'd make of her out-of-the-blue pang of conscience. She wasn't even politically attuned, most of the time!

"Pull my other leg, it's got bells on," she heard him saying, in the witty sneer that just bordered on nastiness. "Bit late to get queasy on StoneEdge now. You've had the account three years already, what the bloody hell did you think we were making? Gollywogs?" He'd sounded fairly bitter about StoneEdge's wartime sales potential, when they'd spoken on Valentine's Day, but also resigned. He'd think she was a fool to contemplate quitting. "Just as well wait until they fire you all, anyroad, over this dirty Canadian business," he'd snort.

What would Tyler Harding say? His face as she'd first seen it came to her mind's eye; his solemnity evoking an old-fashioned photographic portrait, from the age when it was considered unseemly to smile as one's countenance was being preserved for posterity. From that glimpse, she'd deduced his normal expression was one of guarded watchfulness. His exhaustion suited him as naturally as his sober clothing.

She recalled how he'd studied her, alert, when she'd mentioned the antiwar demos choking Paris and London. She recalled how he'd avoided responding, instead turning the talk to the PM's politics. There'd been more tension behind those deep blue eyes, she thought now, than just a keen awareness of current GlobeAll and world events. He appeared, for all his corporate glibness, to be a thoughtful man.

But did her musings and misgivings even matter?

The old railway trestle beyond the parking lot was sinking, pitted and rusting, into the unwelcoming earth, which pushed it away with spiky nettles and spearlike fronds of tough weeds. The earth would prevail, the weeds crawl over it, a kind of canceling-out. If she sat here long enough she could almost watch it happen.

She was in no position to leave GlobeAll right now.

She turned off the radio. For another minute she looked at the view. Then she hauled herself out of the car and walked back into the office.

Twenty-Eight

L IONEL WAS STILL in the Wausau Room, seated at the conference table, hands folded, expression patient. He looked up when she came in.

"So, which route you think StoneEdge would prefer?"

"They always want the fastest routes, but the most secure. They're very paranoid about who we peer with."

"They should be." Lionel nodded. "We'll do the private thing, through Houston, I think." He jerked his head in the direction of Dudley's office. "Your boss was looking for you."

Dudley quickly confirmed for Carly that she was indeed now responsible for all of StoneEdge's government-contract traffic, and that Iraq was indeed on the StoneEdge radar screen for an immediate private line buildout.

"Perfect timing for you, Carly," he told her hurriedly. He seemed too distracted to be jealous. "Wholesale won't get this business and the traffic path will be a first for GlobeAll too. You'll get the credit *and* the new route commission."

With that terse statement her workload quadrupled. She had no time to re-consider whether she was comfortable with her new responsibility. She barely had time to breathe.

She and Lionel holed up in the Wausau Room with a commandeered speakerphone, studying network diagrams, conducting conference calls with the Washington D.C. Wholesale teams who'd been handling the traffic, and tallying up the existing and planned globe-spanning configurations that StoneEdge routinely depended on. They got the highest-level GlobeAll people they could scare up to order bandwidth allocation throughout Europe and into Turkey.

"No time for site surveys in Iraq," Lionel said cheerfully. "We'll wing it. Figure DOD's got that covered."

Carly wasn't sure. If the U.S. government couldn't even verify whether the UN weapons inspectors' findings in Iraq were accurate, how were they supposed to have scoped out the in-country terrain to the degree usually necessary for even the most rudimentary telecom schematic?

"Microwave, or a mobile earth station on the back of a truck," Lionel shrugged. "No big, Carly, StoneEdge's used to this, right, they're selling to the world's mercenaries. Nobody's gonna stand around doing a survey, they're gonna get the hell outta the way in case the next convoy coming down the road's full of bad guys."

It was a new world, and she was obliged to plunge in as gamely as she could, sweeping her doubts aside with a mental shove.

Suze brought in a pizza for them around lunchtime. She gave them status on the shock waves rattling the rest of the office as the salespeople dealt with their accounts' reactions to the lawsuit. In the fickle whimsy that was Wall Street scheming, GlobeAll's stock shot up when the story broke: fund managers figured the company would soon be up for grabs, sold to the highest bidder. Everyone was making frantic, furtive calls to their brokers, Suze reported, in between fielding the onslaught of customer inquiry.

"Dudley's got me polishing up his resume." Suze grinned, sitting down comfortably, snagging a slice of pizza. "He's on the phone to his mortgage company. It's a madhouse out there, kids, you're better off just locking this door."

Lionel swallowed half of his piece in one gulp. "I'm not scared. I don't own any GlobeAll stock, don't owe any money, and I'm a renter."

"You planning on staying here at GobeAll?" Suze yanked gently on his ponytail.

"I'm getting it cut. We have to design this network first."

"I'll leave you to it." Suze stood, and raised her eyebrows at Carly. "That TelMex rep's been calling for you. I told him you're in an all-day meeting."

"Thanks Suze." Francisco was suddenly the least of her worries.

"We need the Turkish PTT for this one leg," Lionel was saying. He stabbed a fretful finger at the Atlas spread out in front of them. "This local loop, at the hub, we need more access right away to get these installs on track." He frowned at Carly. "Who's in charge of the PTT relationships around here?"

"It's a guy I know." Carly glanced at her watch. "He's on a plane right now, coming back to New York. He'll be calling me tomorrow morning," she remembered. "He's met the UK StoneEdge team. We're putting an Asia bid together for them."

"Let's call his backups. We can't wait for this."

They called the number Tyler had given Carly and spoke to one of his staff, who found Aziza Bahrami, the Near East manager.

"It's after hours now in Istanbul, of course," she told them in lightly accented English. "But we can schedule a call with our partners first thing tomorrow morning. Is six a.m. central time too early for you?" She sounded unflustered by their hasty demand and, presumably, by the chaos at Headquarters. "They're about ten hours ahead of Wisconsin time."

"It's fine," Lionel answered for both of them. "We use our own people there?"

"We don't have a node in Turkey. It's a highly regulated market, and we're not allowed to place wholly owned facilities in-country. So we use a partner to deliver service."

"So you're saying these aren't GlobeAll people, we'll be talking to?"

"We use partners there," she repeated patiently. "So, no, they aren't GlobeAll people."

Lionel muted the phone and looked at Carly. "Clearance," he said, although it took her a moment to realize what he meant.

She unmuted. "We might want to re-think the call until we can verify their confidentiality," she told Aziza. "Do they have non-disclosures with us?"

"Of course. PTTs always do."

"We're just talking access." Carly went on, "no transport's needed, Turkey is just a pass-through."

"Of course, they'll be more accommodating of your urgency if there's decent business for them," Aziza said delicately. "Can I ask, who is the client? What's the application? How much bandwidth are they needing? What's their timeframe for install?"

Lionel muted again and looked at Carly. "She a GlobeAll employee?"

Carly nodded. She used Aziza for all her Middle and Near East stuff.

"She a foreigner?"

Carly shook her head, but then clarified, when Lionel kept staring at her, "she's Iranian, originally." To her surprise Lionel twisted up one side of his mouth in what looked like disdain. "But she's been here since she was a kid!"

"Yeah, right," he muttered, before unmuting again. "Listen, Ms. Bereni—"

"Bahrami," Aziza corrected quietly.

"We don't need a technical discussion. We just want to make sure enough access is available in country to get this traffic through. It needs to be dedicated." He suddenly ruffled through a file folder. "Doesn't GlobeAll have dark fiber in Turkey?"

When Aziza didn't answer Carly wondered if the phone was still muted, but its little green light shone unblinking. Lionel looked at it then too. Funny how objects took on meaning, as did the silence that halted their conversation.

"I am not sure how you heard that," Aziza said finally, stiffly. "You must be mistaken."

Lionel's brows twisted up into his forehead in a parody of disbelief. "No, Ms Bahrami. *You* must be kidding."

Carly moved her gaze slowly from the phone to the top page of Lionel's open file folder. Reading upside-down was a skill learned quickly by salespeople, who were as paranoid as they were optimistic. It looked like an International Capacity Statement, a report on global network availability. She could just make out, upside-down, who the author was: Harding, Tyler H. She wondered how Lionel, a newbie SE, had gotten that kind of highly proprietary information.

"I've been assured at the very highest levels that we have the capacity for this project," Lionel was telling Aziza in a pedantic tone. As he leaned forward toward the phone to emphasize his point, speaking loudly now as inexperienced Americans always did with "foreigners," his ponytail slid forward and his earring gleamed. Aziza could have no notion what he looked like. Carly wondered suddenly who the hell he really was. "GlobeAll *has* the fiber."

"I'll have to defer to my boss on that." Aziza was colder than Carly had ever heard her.

"And he is?" Of course Lionel assumed it was a he.

"Tyler Harding. He's not due back in our office until tomorrow. He's traveling."

Lionel glanced at his folder. "Yeah, okay, have him call me as soon as he gets in. Tell him this is absolutely top priority." He rattled off his mobile number and then leaned back, as if defeated, when Aziza hung up. "We're fucked for today, excuse my language, I cannot get the goddamn elephant to dance on this right now."

Could *she* get the goddamn elephant to dance, now that she'd taken on this onerous project? Tyler'd said he wasn't Provisioning; he was just Alliances. "Maybe I can talk to International Network Ops."

"Yeah but the dark fiber is a partnership thing."

"Network will know about it."

"Now you're talking," Lionel said with approval. "Call em up."

Carly's Network Ops buddy answered right away. "Ed Olson, hi Carly Emerald." She'd used this speakerphone so many times to call him he recognized the caller ID.

"Yo Ed, we want some dark fiber in Turkey. Whatcha got?"

"*Tur*-key," Ed said, drawing out the word dubiously. "For StoneEdge, we got fiber, but it's gonna cost em. *And* you."

"Like what?"

"Approval from our Alliance group. This is definitely a special arrangement. Fact is nobody's supposed to know about this yet." He waited a beat. "How do *you* know?"

Carly raised eyebrows at Lionel. "StoneEdge has … unique clearance," she guessed.

"This is unique, all right." Ed's tone grew suddenly sharp. "Can we get something straight up front? No discussions of this on cell phones, okay?"

"Okay," she agreed, bewildered.

"Cause you and I both know the business StoneEdge's in, and I can guess why they need this fiber and what route it's gonna take."

Lionel reached over to punch the mute button. "This guy's in the Atlanta NOC?" Network Operations Center.

She nodded.

"Is it an elephant cage?" She didn't know the term. Lionel seemed to have a thing for elephants. "Airtight data box?" She shrugged.

"Hey Ed," Lionel said, unmuting, "I'm Lionel Burke, a new SE for GlobeAll. I'm here with Carly, helping on this deal. Are you in a secure location?"

"Of course."

"I'm glad we both understand the sensitivity of this project. We just talked to the New York office, where the Alliance group is, and got nowhere. Frankly I'm not convinced of their confidentiality. I'd rather deal with your team directly."

There was a pause. Then Ed said, carefully, "I can vouch for them. We defer to the Alliance organization for approval of offshore dark fiber use. We have to. They're the only ones who know exactly where it's been commercially promised, to which other carriers or retail customers."

"But you do the implementation."

"Based on Alliance forecasts, and Sales' reports."

"But you could just groom off some excess for StoneEdge, right, light it up quietly, we don't have to get a lot of corporate committees overseeing this."

There was an even longer pause. "How long have you been with GlobeAll?" Ed asked.

Lionel raised his hands, obviously exasperated. "Never mind, Ed, it's cool, I get that you can't do this for me."

Ed's voice sounded detached, when he finally answered. "We have a set order entry process. Carly can coach you on how things work here."

"Or how they don't work, you mean," Lionel muttered.

"Carly? We can't just go out of the box here, you know that," Ed said. "Who did you talk to over at Alliance Management?"

"Aziza."

"I can get Tyler Harding's okay pretty quickly on this, but I know he's traveling."

"You mean *no-one else* in the entire company can make this kind of decision for us right now?" Carly felt irritated by the very concept, by the seeming ubiquity of all-international-roads-lead-to-Tyler Harding. She was also, she knew, irritated by Lionel's pushiness.

But most bothersome was the growing uneasiness, insistently physical, spreading throughout her body, prickling across her skin as her awareness deepened: she had *chosen* to be a conscious cog in this grinding machinery.

"I'm not going above Tyler until I talk to him first, if that's what you mean," Ed countered. "His VP won't know the details of the deals he's been doing in Europe, anyway, and I'm not assigning fiber to anyone who hasn't been sized yet. Who hasn't been qualified."

Lionel rolled his eyes.

"Especially not in Turkey," Ed concluded firmly. "There are some real snaky characters in telecom over there right now. Look how they screwed MotorOptics." There had been recent reports of significant fraud perpetrated on that company by a crooked Turkish consortium.

"They're an ally, Ed," Lionel broke in. "We're gonna need their cooperation, so we should hustle with giving them some business."

"An ally? Those Turkish crooks?"

"Their government, Ed. We *need* them."

"GlobeAll's solid with Turkish Tel, we don't need anyone in the Info Ministry."

"Not GlobeAll. The United States. *We* need Turkey."

Enough, thought Carly. Lionel was the worst business negotiator she'd ever heard. "Never mind, Ed, we'll wait for Tyler. Another day won't make that much difference."

She clicked off the call. Lionel looked at her. She'd thought of brown eyes as warm-looking, before seeing his, and she'd thought of Systems Engineers as fairly affable, and certainly diffident toward Global Account Executives, before meeting him.

"I'm not here to waste time. If I have to ruffle some feathers so be it."

"How about if I talk to your management, Lionel, explain the situation…"

"I'm on independent contract. Once I get this StoneEdge deal done I'm outta here."

She'd begun to suspect as much. "Independent contract—for who?"

"If I told ya I'd hafta kill ya," he drawled, teasing, but his smile didn't reach his eyes. "You can't talk to my management."

Certainty settled as she looked at him. She had friends in GlobeAll's Government Service Division; she knew that sometimes Defense Department contractors haunted their dealings when critical DOD traffic was involved. Lionel must be one of them. She supposed the threat of a government boycott necessitated their shadowing the regular sales force; still, it was surprising how quickly he'd materialized here, the very morning the UTT lawsuit story broke. The government usually moved much more slowly.

"Last I heard, GlobeAll is still a private sector company," she drawled back, keeping her gaze bland. "Your role is only to facilitate things, as far as I understand it, not push them to the degree it makes people suspicious."

"Nobody's suspicious."

"Everybody's suspicious, that you've talked to this morning." She tried to speak tactfully. "Your approach worried Aziza and Ed. That makes my job harder. And you need me."

"Not as much as you might think. I do respect your relationship with the account, but my involvement with you is … just a courtesy to StoneEdge execs."

"Then be courteous," she said simply. "Let me do my job, okay, Lionel? Try not to alienate people I'll have to keep working with long after you're … vaporware."

His eyes dropped and his mouth crumpled into a sheepish smirk. "Okay."

Twenty-Nine

WHEN CARLY FINALLY LEFT the office the parking lot was twice as frigid, the scene twice as lonely as when she'd come out in the morning. She couldn't think of a time when she'd been more tired. Lionel was chugging along beside her in an unlikely sheepskin jacket. He must have thought his hippie getup would somehow blend in here in the Midwest hinterlands. Winterlands. Splinterlands. Christ she was exhausted.

"So, Carly, let's get some dinner." His breath puffed out, visible.

"I'm worn out. And I need to go see my mom."

"I could come along. I'm good with moms." His genial grin attempted to affirm this.

"No. Sorry."

But he kept following, and stood next to her as she opened her car door. "Look, the thing is, I need a ride. I took a cab here straight from the airport to catch Dudley's meeting. Didn't have time to get a rental. I'd appreciate a lift to where I'm staying." He fumbled in the jacket pocket for a wallet. "I'll pay."

She eyed him. *Our tax dollars at work.* "That's okay." She climbed into her car and motioned for him to get in next to her. "Where are you headed?"

"I'm at a motel, wait a minute, yeah. Here's the address." As he peered at a scrap of paper in the waning dusk, Carly saw another vehicle spin into the lot behind her, a vehicle made familiar by its squealing tires, the insistent glare of its high beams in her rearview, the slam of its passenger door and the aggressive bulk of its driver advancing toward her car.

Just what she needed.

"Hold on Lionel."

She got out to meet Francisco in the beam of his headlights.

"You don't take my calls today, or yesterday, or any this week?"

"I got caught up in a fire drill, did you hear any business news today? UTT's suing us—"

"If you don't want to see me, Catty, you have to tell me—"

"It's not about you!"

"I know you're not happy that my other novia is coming." The headlights picked out stray ends of his hair flying around his head in wild streams that curled back into one another in the wind. She let her eyes follow the strands for a moment instead of looking into his face.

"Catty. It means only that we don't meet for a short time, just some weeks." He moved close and reached around her. His strong fingers threaded through her hair, finding the tension at the back of her neck, easing the muscles there.

She wanted to close her eyes, lean on him, let him wrap himself around her like the thickest quivering fur until she melted completely, shape-shifted with him into one being, all troubles forgotten. She could hear Mana singing "Who's gonna cover you with kisses? Only me."

She wanted to shove him onto the old train trestle as if a ghost line could mow him flat, maybe a vintage Canadian National screaming down from the north, accompanied by a couple bandits crouching on the top of the car, or better yet old-fashioned savage Red Indians— tomahawks held high, ready to slice off those tempting, twisting, living locks.

"She leaves in April," he murmured into her ear. His warm breath made her shiver.

She didn't know how she summoned the strength to pull out of his embrace. "That's not going to work for me."

His smile told her how uncertain she sounded. He reached for her again but she moved back. "No," she told him, more firmly. "It won't work. It's not good for me."

"Maybe I can come to you, sometimes, I tell her I have something to do."

She shook her head. The wind found its icy way into her ears. She covered them with her hands. "It's no good, Franco."

He stepped close. "Is too cold to talk here. Come with me, we can discuss—"

Lionel chose that moment to get out. He planted himself equidistant from them, looking from one to the other. "Everything okay, Carly?"

Francisco snared Lionel, then dismissed him, in one sweep of his narrowed black artist's eyes. "We speak later, Catty, call me." He strode back to his car, got in, and roared away.

A frustrated exhalation escaped her and her hand half lifted toward his receding taillights before sinking into her pocket.

"That your boyfriend?"

She turned to Lionel, lounging now against the side of the car as if in midsummer with all the time in the world. He only needed a long weedy straw in his mouth to perfect his laconic hayseed act.

"Obviously he's not a boy," she retorted before she could stop herself. She got back in and slammed her door. "Not much of a friend anymore either," she finished to herself in a disconsolate mutter.

Lionel slid into the passenger seat. "He an Arab?"

She bit back a "what the hell?" and drove out of the lot.

She remembered, then, a story that seemed to inform his question about Francisco. Days after 9/11, State troopers on the East Coast had stopped a truckload of migrant workers at a highway checkpoint, thinking that by their dark looks they must be Middle Eastern terrorists. The police had not understood that the workers were speaking Spanish. They'd been thrown in jail to languish, in the let-God-sort-it-out mentality that was gripping jittery law enforcement entities, until some public defender took pity on them and enlightened the local media.

Lionel watched her, waiting. She sighed. "He's Mexican."

"Looks like an Arab. Sounds like one too."

She pressed her lips together to keep from snapping at him. She got onto the highway without thinking, her normal route toward home. "So then, Lionel, where to?"

"Let me buy you dinner. Least I can do for you."

"Not hungry."

"A drink, then, c'mon Carly. Looks like you could use one."

"No, thanks," she gritted. "I need an early night."

"You seem to me like a Cosmopolitan kind of girl," he went on, relentless. "Or maybe a margarita? To go with your Mexican?"

She turned on the radio to drown out her irritation. "Where am I taking you?"

"I don't know," he said, slouching, lolling his head toward her. "Where *are* you taking me?" Inappropriately, 'Let's Spend the Night Together' came on. He chuckled.

The scrap of paper he'd been looking at was curled in the cup holder. She snatched it and, between arc lamps, read an address not far from her mom's house. "We'll be right there."

"So tell me about your boyfriend. Seemed like you two were having a fight."

She took the exit leading to her mom's neighborhood. A few snowflakes began to dot the windshield and she flicked on the wipers and turned down the music.

"What were you arguing about?"

She kept her voice pleasant. "This doesn't really interest you."

"It might. Depends who he is and what he knows."

This was unbelievable. His paranoia was worse than Dave Seymour's but, she realized just in time to stop from snarling at him, that's probably what he was paid for.

"He's an artist, from Mexico, we've known each other about six months," she said evenly. "He has zero interest in my work or in StoneEdge." Of course she wouldn't mention how politically radical he was. "I think he might be married," she added, glancing to see if that would shut Lionel up. "That's why I just broke up with him."

This statement resonated with a finality that sounded like relief.

Relief felt good. She sat up a little straighter.

"That what you did?" he asked quietly. "Didn't seem he got that message."

"He tends to hear what he wants to hear."

"He the type to hang on?"

"I doubt it." She wouldn't let any sadness from that conclusion alter her relief, not yet, not until she was alone. If Lionel would leave her alone.

"Mind if I check him out?"

"You don't need to. He's not—he isn't anyone, to you."

"What's his name?"

"None of your business!"

"How do you know he's Mexican?"

"He speaks Spanish, all right? We met at a Mexican band concert."

"I'll just run a quick query. He won't have to know about it."

"He's from Vera Cruz!"

"And that makes him clean."

"Well, Lionel, it *does*." She'd lost her patience with him so much earlier in the day that a kind of exhausted calm was starting to creep in. "Trust me on this. He's not worth investigating."

"I like to come to my own conclusions about people, these days." In the darkness of the car his expression was impossible to read, but the hayseed was certainly gone now, replaced by a calculating analyst with a chill dry voice.

She pulled over in front of his motel. "Here we are."

When he didn't get out she glanced at him. His stare was frankly unfriendly now as he asked, "Were you serious this morning, about quitting this account?"

A Strokes song came on and filled the silence with weary amusement until he turned the radio off and answered his own question. "I know you weren't kidding. It makes you uncomfortable to support the Iraq liberation, doesn't it?"

She stared at the snow accumulating in the corners of the windshield. "Yes," she said finally. "I don't believe in it."

"But you decided to keep the StoneEdge account anyway. You went out and came back. Where'd you go?"

"I wanted to think things over."

"You weren't calling somebody? Your boyfriend?"

"No!"

"Do the StoneEdge people know how you feel? Does Dudley?"

"Nobody talks about politics at work."

"Did you go to the protests here, last weekend?"

She shook her head, not in denial but in termination, enough her mother's daughter to remember, belatedly, that he had no right to ask her anything. She shook her head again, more vigorously, as if released from a spell.

"Good night."

"Yeah," he said softly. "Okay." He got out. She didn't drive away until she saw him talking to a clerk at the front desk.

Then she went home.

She didn't want to infect her mom with the nastiness of her life right now. For the first time ever, she swallowed a sleeping pill, from a bottle Mom had left behind once, before climbing into the shower to wash away the day.

Thirty

HER MOBILE SHRILLED HER AWAKE at six in the darkness of the next morning, and she groped for its lighted face. She clicked on when she saw the French country code. Jack Rigby again?

"Carly Emerald," she croaked.

"Carly, this is Tyler Harding. I know it's early, but I told you I'd get back to you this morning by seven, New York time."

She sat up, confused, and looked at the number again. "You're ... in France?"

"I had to come back to Paris for a few days."

"Oh. How come?"

"Long story, you don't have time for it."

"Sure I do," she said, still groggy.

"You don't have time," he repeated firmly. "Did my team get you the Asia pricing you were looking for?"

Asia pricing. She tried to remember if she'd seen any messages on that, during the few chances she'd had to look at e-mails yesterday.

"Carly?" He sounded rushed and impatient.

"Uh." She rubbed the bridge of her nose with her left forefinger and thumb. "I don't know."

"You don't *know?*"

"They might have sent it, but, Tyler, all hell broke loose yesterday. I have to handle all of StoneEdge's traffic now, not just the commercial, but their government stuff too." She was starting to wake up now. "It's a good thing you called. I need your approval for some dark fiber in

Turkey. Maybe Aziza already told you? Or Ed, from Network Ops?"

"No."

No, he wouldn't approve it or no, they hadn't told him? "What do you mean?"

"They don't know where I am."

What difference did that make? E-mail and voice-mail went everywhere. "So?"

"I'm taking a couple of days off. I just called you because I told you I'd follow up today with the Asia network. I can prod Singapore if you need me to do that."

"But you have to ... approve the fiber ... " If he was taking a break from GlobeAll then its writing was on the wall, clear as the nightlight shining out in her little hallway. "Tyler, your name was on the Capacity Statement Lionel had."

"Who?"

"The engineer who's helping me with the Turkey ... design." She suddenly remembered Bob said not to mention StoneEdge and Turkey on a cell phone.

"I didn't authorize any dissemination of my report," Tyler said slowly. "Those Statements are highly proprietary, even internally."

"Well, this guy's in a position to get information from all over the company."

He was quiet, no doubt absorbing that bit of intelligence. Then he said, "You need the fiber for StoneEdge."

"I don't want to talk about it on my mobile."

She thought she heard a short exhalation. "Okay." He suddenly sounded older. "How soon can you get to your office?"

"About half an hour."

"Let's set up a seven a.m. call, your time, on the secure bridge." GlobeAll had a 'hacker-proof' conference calling service used for most international audio meetings.

"But you don't have to, Tyler, I mean, if you're on vacation? Maybe you can just tell Aziza that you approve the fiber use?"

"My break's over. I knew this was coming."

"I have to let Lionel attend our call."

"Sure, have him join us."

"He's very pushy," she warned. "You might find him a bit rude."

"Thanks for the heads up." He was obviously unbothered by the prospect of anyone being rude to him. His tone signified their conversation was over.

She staggered out of bed on shaky legs. Her head was throbbing and her mouth felt stuffed with cotton. This would teach her to take sleeping pills! Still, the oblivion had been welcome. She would have been up all night otherwise, going over the horrid twists and turns of yesterday, making herself more anxious.

She could try practicing what she had made up as a joke one day with co-workers —a phony 'old Japanese time-management skill' known as 'just-in-time worrying.'

"Why worry until you absolutely have to?" she'd laughed then. "Use that worry judiciously. Don't waste it ahead of time."

She couldn't now recall what crisis du jour had prompted the creation of the joke, but it paled in comparison to what she was facing now. She laughed, but her humor felt as weak as her body, wobbling on the edge of collapse.

Francisco would carry her back to bed and rub her all over, with his sure firm palms, rub away the tension until she was vibrating in anticipation of his more intimate touches. He'd talk her into calling in sick or pretending to have some appointment or "working from home;" that vague pajama-clad euphemism. They'd spend the day in bed or at least until he had to go. *He* never called in sick, she realized, *he* never missed an appointment. Not for her.

She made a pot of strong coffee and sat at her kitchen table to drink some as soon as it brewed. It felt good to have her tongue stung by the first sip, good to feel the discomfort of heat on her fingers clutching the mug. Physical pain trumped emotional, no contest. If it hadn't been so early she'd have called Mom to say hello.

She filled her largest to-go cup, bundled up, and was already halfway to the office before it occurred to her that Lionel wouldn't have the means to get a rental car this early, and that if he was going to make their secure call she'd probably have to pick him up.

Dammit. She didn't even want to see him again, let alone drive him to work. She wondered how paranoid it would make him, if he were to be left out of the discussion with Tyler. Pretty paranoid, no doubt. Reluctantly, she called him on her cell.

"Burke." He sounded as sleepy as she still felt.

"Lionel, it's Carly. I talked to Tyler Harding this morning. We've set up a secure bridge for seven, in the office. I suppose you'll need a ride?"

"Yeah, that'd be good."

"I'll come right over."

"I'll be ready. I'll wait outside for you."

He must have taken the world's fastest shower, she thought sourly as she watched him climb in some ten minutes later. His hair shone, he smelled good, his grin was fresh.

"Hey there, Carly, how're you doin this mornin?" Hayseed was back. "Thanks a lot for the ride. I'll get over to a rental place later today and stop being a nuisance to you."

Not enough time had passed between them for her to feel cordial. She sipped her coffee and kept driving. He opened a file folder and flipped through until they reached the office.

By the time she opened the call she was jittery with caffeine. She folded her hands together to keep them from fidgeting.

"Harding." Tyler announced his attendance on the speakerphone.

"Tyler, Lionel Burke. I'm the engineer assigned to StoneEdge. I think Carly filled you in, right, we need some dark fiber from you, for StoneEdge. Turkish." The way he said it made it suddenly sound like some kind of exotic hashish, and this a clandestine deal. She hid her smile.

"I didn't see that request coming through the Special Arrangements group," Tyler said, referring to GlobeAll's custom channel.

"Because we're not using them," Lionel told him easily. "We're using you."

"I don't know what else is in queue unless they vet it for me first. I don't track it."

As yesterday, Lionel muted the phone and fixed Carly with an imperious stare. "What's this guy, some kind of bureaucrat? I thought he was the ultimate decision-maker?" Without waiting for her to react he unmuted. "Tyler, I was led to believe you're the go-to guy on this. But if you can't help me I'll go beyond you."

There was a short laugh. "Go ahead."

Lionel stared at the speakerphone. Carly was pleased to note his discomfiture even though she wondered what it might mean for Tyler. "You're being ... uncooperative?"

Tyler laughed again. "If you want to call it that, Mr. Burke. I can't authorize this request without a feasibility study, at least, to see what our capacity situation is. We don't promise what we can't deliver here at GlobeAll."

"How about if I go outside of GlobeAll?" Lionel asked impatiently. "Who else has dark fiber there? You got any contacts in the Turkish mafia?"

Tyler's voice, when he finally answered, was cold. "This is GlobeAll's call, Mr. Burke. It's not ethical for you to ask that, or for me to disclose it to you."

"Stop calling me Mr. Burke." Lionel plunged a hand through his hair, rumpling its neat flow. "What the hell did you think we were going to talk about?"

"This is your official request on StoneEdge's behalf?"

"You betcha. This is as official as it gets, because I don't have time to fuck around."

"Request denied," Tyler said promptly, crisp and unpleasant as burnt toast.

"You have got to be kidding me."

"Anything else I can help you with today?" Tyler continued cheerfully. "Carly Emerald, anything you need?"

She found her voice. "You do know why StoneEdge wants the fiber in Turkey?"

"I'm sure I can guess," Tyler said.

"Are you in New York?" Lionel demanded. "I'm gonna have my management pay you a visit."

"Have them pay me a visit in France, that's where I am today. Carly has my mobile number. If they call, I'll tell them how to find me."

"*France!*" Lionel made it sound like an insult. "Maybe that explains your attitude."

The light went red. Tyler had hung up.

"Who's his boss?"

"Philippe Nouri," Carly said, feeling a near-hysterical giggle rise in her throat, knowing how Lionel would react. "He's a VP, runs our international division."

"New-ree? What kind of a name is that?" He glared at her. "Indian?"

"Lebanese."

"God damn it. Why aren't there any Americans in global telecom, for Christ's sake."

She covered her mouth and let the laughter out, quietly, into her palm. It was too early. Too stressful. She'd had too much coffee.

"This amuses you?" As frosty as he was, she could not help laughing harder, and wiped a stray tear of mirth from one eye. He leaned forward and studied her as if memorizing every feature. "I guess you would find this funny," he concluded quietly, but as soon as he said this it wasn't funny at all to her anymore. "Give me Harding's mobile number. And, excuse me, I need to talk to him alone."

She scribbled a number, passed it to him, and left the room.

Thirty-One

SHE CLOSED THE WAUSAU ROOM door quietly, so he wouldn't think she was slamming it. She ran down the hallway to her cube. It was the first time she'd actually *run* here, but she was too anxious to enjoy the unique sensation. She landed on her wheeled chair so hard that she smacked shut the lower drawer where her keyboard rested.

She snatched her phone and dialed Tyler's mobile number with frantic fingers. Even though she'd made the 7 look like a 1 on Lionel's pad, as she'd pretended to scrawl the correct number, it wouldn't take him long to find the right digits. Answer, Tyler, she willed.

"Harding."

"You've got to know the risk you're taking by not giving him the approval."

"Hello again, Ms. Emerald."

"I'm serious," she hissed. "He's scary. He'll get us fired. Maybe even arrested."

His laugh was short but comfortable. "Nah. Don't be scared."

"If we don't give him this business it's a reason for us not to get *any* government business. It's another reason for UTT to take it all away."

"He's not that powerful, Carly, he's just a DOD rep doing his job." He paused. "He *is* DOD, right, that's what I assumed?"

"I've heard these guys know how to make waves."

"This is *one* private line for one client. No matter how important StoneEdge is to the government, it's still just another circuit to us. We're in the middle of the biggest scandal in company history. Upper management won't give a flying f— they won't even notice."

"I'm afraid he'll cause trouble for me."

"No."

"He'll complain to Dudley."

"That ass? He'll be too busy worrying about his own future to bother with yours. Managers are a lot more vulnerable right now than individual salespeople."

She twisted the phone cord. She twisted it so regularly that its coil was snarled into a slick ball that slid now though her fingers. She had looked at this cord too often, during some of the most anxious moments of her life. Ugly object to focus on! Maybe she wouldn't be so anxious if she dolled up her cube a little, put some flowered plants or soothing photographs, a child's drawing? But she didn't know any children.

"Carly." How could he, who'd been a stranger until three days ago, sound so reassuring? "You're a good salesperson. You can work for any company, anywhere."

"I can't—leave here." A sob broke, embarrassing her, as she blurted this—why was she telling him?

"You must have a good reason to stay." His voice was kind.

"It's my mom. She's … she's really sick."

"She's in Milwaukee."

"Uh-huh."

"So … it's good you can be there. Take the time you need with her, that's what's important," he said quietly. "This will blow over for GlobeAll, at your level. The job should be yours as long as you want it."

"What should I do about StoneEdge's Turkish fiber?"

"My refusal isn't your problem. Nothing to do with you."

"Why won't you approve it?"

He didn't answer right away. Then he said, slowly, "Their requirement doesn't take precedence over what's already been promised for another deployment."

"Another customer?"

"Just tell the overeager Mr. Burke that you did the best you could."

"Lionel wants to take this to Nouri."

He laughed, sharply.

"Won't Nouri overturn your decision?"

"Doubtful. He's a little distracted right now. Exercising his stock options. Negotiating his exit package." He laughed again, but not amused. "Looking for someone to blame."

"Then they'll go to UTT for this," she warned again.

"Let em."

"You're not worried about your job?"

She heard his long exhalation. "The truth, Carly, I'm probably leaving GlobeAll."

Executives jumping ship—this confirmed her worst fears. She squeezed the balled-up cord tightly. "Because of the lawsuit?"

"That's part of it."

"I knew it." She pulled at the knotted cord and began to stretch it out. "I was afraid this would start happening. So where will you go?"

"I don't know yet. I haven't made up my mind."

She threaded her little finger through the cord, untwisting it. She didn't want to end their conversation. "If you could do anything else, what would you do?"

"Any other job, you mean? Outside the industry?"

"Yeah."

"Guide rafters down the Colorado River," he said, and his voice echoed the amused surprise she felt, hearing his choice. They both laughed. "But I'm still hooked on global telecom. I've always been fascinated by the subsea cable companies. I might go with one of them."

"Like FLAG." "Fiber Link Around the Globe," as the name indicated, was the most aggressive of the deepwater cable-laying companies. Its much-admired recent venture had spanned every ocean, circumnavigating the world, in a swashbuckling project whose progress had been jealously followed by everyone in the industry. "Sounds like fun. They hiring?"

"You interested, Carly?"

"Milwaukee's port is open to the St. Lawrence Seaway nine months of the year." She joked, "No reason they couldn't make a landing station here."

"I'm thinking about FLAG," he said. "Maybe I'll sail by some day and throw you a router or two."

"I'm a good catch."

"I'm sure you are, Carly Emerald." He let a pause underscore the warmth in his voice. "So, what would *you* do, if you could?"

She thought for a moment as she continued to untangle the cord. "I like this industry too." She glanced down the empty hallway and took a chance, feeling the impending pressure of Lionel, testing the fledgling trust between them. "But I don't like feeling that I'm contributing to … the invasion."

His reception was matter-of-fact. "By supporting StoneEdge, you mean."

"I know all our industries are twined together, that if I don't tie up just this one little stitch it won't make any difference to the whole tapestry." She let herself follow the analogy. "The master weavers will go on and finish what they started. But I don't have to *choose* to be such an active participant. Even though I am, already, by investigating this Turkish dark fiber for them."

"You're free to drop this … one little stitch, you know."

"StoneEdge will pick up the thread whether I hold it out to them or not, right, they'll find another carrier."

"They will."

"But I thought I made up my mind about this yesterday, when Lionel … erupted."

His chuckle relaxed her. "You can still work StoneEdge without this particular project."

"So, then, this Turkish fiber really doesn't matter," she finished, feeling her urgency unwind with the phone cord. "In fact, it's *all* irrelevant."

"Think it over," he cautioned. "Don't talk yourself out of a job until you have a decent replacement."

Good advice. Was he following it? She pondered in silence for another stretch of the coil.

"I mean, do you have a solid support structure there while you're staying near your mother? Funds, friends, some kind of backup plan?"

"I just dumped my boyfriend," she confided.

There was a short silence. Maybe she'd startled him by getting more personal. Then, "You don't sound too broken-hearted," he said, tentative.

"I'm better off." But maybe it hadn't sunk in yet? Maybe she hadn't had a chance to properly grieve? Maybe a massive breakdown was awaiting her, as soon as she had the breathing room to indulge it? "That's what I'm telling myself, anyway."

"I had a … similar experience recently," he said quietly. "It isn't easy."

"It took awhile to realize he wasn't really good for me."

"Then you're smart to have acted, Carly." He let another small pause go by, and his voice was crisp again when he resumed speaking. "You can have the job as long as you want it, I'm sure, StoneEdge or not. You know whoever buys the GlobeAll network will keep the good people."

"But it'd be boring working here without the excitement of StoneEdge," she admitted. "It's the only account with an international network. I'd miss that challenge."

"I could tell you liked the global side of the house. When you're free to leave Milwaukee, I can get you some job leads, if you want. And Julian'd hire you in a heartbeat, for the instruments division, not weapons, your choice I'm sure. You'd have to put up with him, for awhile, but you'd live in London. It's a good global launching pad."

"Down in the StoneEdge data dungeon? It's still the same company, Tyler, frying pan into the fire. I don't think even Julian likes it."

"So you guessed he's having second thoughts."

"Something he said about the body count."

She felt, as much as heard, his deep sigh. "Yeah. Jesus."

"It was the first time he ever got political on me."

"He was struggling when I saw him. He was … *obsessed*. We talked of nothing else, after I got the Asia intelligence out of him, at least until he got plastered and started hitting on women. Not a happy man."

"You're right," she said slowly. "That's why he's been such a pain to deal with."

"My guess is he'll leave StoneEdge. But he'd put in a good word for you with wherever he goes next."

"I don't think so. But thanks so much for thinking of it." She heard a phone ring in his background. "I'll let you go."

"Yeah, I need to take this call, but Carly, let's keep in touch."

"Okay, Tyler. Watch out for Lionel. He wants a piece of you."

"He can get in line." His ironic laugh stayed in her head after he hung up.

Thirty-Two

SHE SAT AT HER DESK, looking at her cube as if for the first time. She'd been working at GlobeAll since she was twenty-six years old, at this very cube, yet there was not a scrap of a personal touch: nothing that indicated she lived here. Her workspace was as clean and orderly as she felt her life was not.

Six years in this same beige space. What did she have to show for it? Some money saved up, the memory of a few unusual network configurations, an assortment of contacts, a good-looking resume. The tally felt less substantial than a dream.

If she walked out right now who would follow?

Of course it was still so early that she and Lionel were alone in the office, but otherwise, even if the space were filled with GlobeAll salespeople, who would notice? Suze would stay in touch, but she'd become a friend. Dave might call once, and she'd blow him off, and he wouldn't call back. Dudley would be annoyed at StoneEdge's being left in the lurch. Lionel would probably ... she didn't know what Lionel would do. But he was too new a problem to matter. She felt the adrenalin that had powered her the last week drain away as she straightened the few files on her desktop.

"Carly!" Lionel was calling from the Wausau Room.

"Yeah." She didn't bother to get up or raise her voice.

"I couldn't get ahold of that guy in France." His voice got louder as he approached her from the hallway. "Who's his boss again?" He stood just outside her cube.

Her skin shrank against his accelerated breathing. She didn't turn to look at him.

"Philippe Nouri. I'm sure he's in our online directory."

He stood there still. She pretended to be checking her e-mail.

"Who's e-mailing you at this time of the morning?"

"Global salespeople have to be on twenty-four seven. I never sleep."

"What's that do to your, you know, circadian rhythm?"

"Takes a lickin, keeps on tickin."

"What do you hear from your Asian teams? Anyone sick out there?"

She twisted in her chair to face him, thinking of BK. "Sick?"

"There's some kind of virus just starting to spread. Like asthma. I just got word on it. Pretty ugly, I've heard." He leaned forward as if to peer at her screen. "You hear about that yet?"

"One of our engineers in Singapore is sick," she told him, not bothering to try to hide his view. She knew her screensaver was on, an undulating sand-dune motif whose mesmerizing waves she'd stared at during many a mind-numbing conference call, its scene evoking some Arabian desert where from behind each dune, depending on the decade, romantic Bedouins or armed terrorists might, mirage-like, emerge. Lionel, predictably, frowned at it.

"So Carly—how'm I supposed to get this Turkish fiber?"

"I've done all I can until my manager gets here. Dudley Miller, you met him yesterday? He usually comes in around nine. He might be able to escalate this for us." She bent down to pick up her purse. "But right now, Lionel, I'm going out for some coffee. Maybe breakfast. I'm tired and hungry—"

"You're blowing smoke."

She looked up at him.

His expression was hidden by a glint of light off his little glasses.

"You're blowing smoke at me," he repeated, moving closer so that now she could see how angry he was, mouth a thin line and dark eyes flat as his voice.

"I can't escalate this any further."

"You mean, you won't. You don't want to."

"I will, when Dudley gets here—"

"He can't do anything about this and you know it. You're the global account manager, right, you can make things happen on the international side if you want to."

"I'm not in charge of assigning dark fiber in some weird country!"

"Don't play dumb." He surveyed her, eyes narrowing. "You were all over this yesterday, what happened?"

She spread her hands out, wide. "Hey, yesterday I thought this would work. But we ran into a brick wall, okay? I didn't expect the Alliance group to be so finicky."

"You broke up with your boyfriend and you changed your mind," he concluded. He took in her pristine cube. "Looks like you've already cleaned out your desk. You don't want to help StoneEdge in the war effort, you're thinking the hell with it, you'll quit and go someplace else so you can forget about all this."

"I was the one who got Harding on the call this morning," she reminded him. "I've more than demonstrated my commitment here."

"Don't be thinking you'll get a good reference," he warned her.

Don't be thinking you're in any position to influence that, she told him silently, returning his stare.

He stepped back, finally, giving her a once-over that somehow felt creepier than any of his other observations. "Later then, when Dudley gets in."

"Later." She waited, until he'd retreated down the hallway, to get up and put her coat on. She checked her watch: just after eight. HR ought to be in by now. She could stop by their office on the second floor on her way out, pick up the Family Medical Leave forms she'd need to start the process of taking her official leave of absence. She didn't even need to come back to this building, if she didn't feel like it. She could mail them to Suze to get Dudley's signature. She looked at her screen. One last e-mail review.

To: Emerald, Catherine L.
From: Harding, Tyler H.
Subject: next steps

Carly, here's my home number in New York. I should be there in a couple of days, probably not at the office. Let's stay in touch.
Best,
Tyler

He didn't, she noted, use his corporate signature, and in someone so careful it seemed like a deliberate omission. Was he already thinking himself unaffiliated? More likely, she thought, reflecting on their ever-more-comfortable conversations, he was indicating that, to her, he was a friend. That made her smile.

To: Harding, Tyler H.
From: Emerald, Catherine H.
Subject: Re: next steps

Tyler. Thanks for your message. I'll be taking leave after today to look after my mother. I'll still have my laptop so we can keep in touch via email. I appreciate your

She hesitated. Your what? Friendship? Concern? Interest?

I appreciate your friendship. Carly

She hit send, then deleted the exchange so Lionel's prying eyes could not easily connect Tyler with her, or find his home number; although certainly Lionel had other resources to unearth whatever information he needed. But at least he wouldn't get any more out of her.

She logged off and left her cube.

PART THREE

Thirty-Three

Manhattan

TYLER HEAVED HIS CASE inside, shoving aside piles of mail he'd arranged to have the doorman deliver.

His apartment was a mess—even more bereft than when he'd left it last month. The windows were lit with wan streaks, illuminating the dusty bare floor, the couch and chair, the tall speakers begging to reverberate with musical life. The place—he couldn't think of it as home—gave off the stench of abandonment. It made him want to turn around and go back to the airport.

But he pushed his suitcase further inside and slammed the door behind him with one kick. He went to the window and craned his head sideways toward the river, glinting a beauteous pink in the sunrise, many stories below and blocks away.

Four thousand dollars a month let him perform this neck-wrenching ritual and call it a view.

Programmed by the sight of dawn, he turned to the little galley kitchen to make coffee, but stopped himself mid-fill at the faucet. It was, he figured, about two in the afternoon by his internal clock. Fuck coffee. He'd been drinking on the Air France flight; he might as well stay with alcohol.

He opened the little refrigerator to see if he'd remembered to store any beer. No. The shelves gleamed empty white, reproaching him to buy groceries. Okay, he'd have a Scotch.

He ran a finger across his CDs and loaded up Phish, Strokes, White Stripes, Coldplay, Hives, U2. He clicked to Phish's "Taste" and cranked up the volume. The song reminded him of telecom, with its phrase "I can see through the lines"—hearing it, he always saw fiber optic lines with their bursts of light at each end.

He toed off his shoes, shrugged off his suit jacket and sank into the armchair. He drank deep and yanked off his tie. Flying Business Class, the last perk GlobeAll allowed on long transatlantic routes, he always dressed the part, never knowing whom he might meet. This flight it'd been a Brit from Cable & Wireless Marine. Wasn't everyone in telecom, after all? They'd spent a very enjoyable time talking subsea cables.

The guy, Mark Regan, early-forties, sun-bronzed, blue eyes bloodshot and blond hair bleached white with too much south Asia, had called himself "cable trash." He had not worn a suit. He dressed like a wintertime Jimmy Buffet.

Over a number of excellent free Business Class drinks he'd regaled Tyler with tales of cable-laying in exotic locales but cut himself off, mid-story, to make an urgent call to one of his ships in Penang harbor, using the seatback phone that cost at that distance rate, Tyler knew, more than eight dollars a minute. Highway robbery, in telecom terms. Captive audience.

"Wish I had my satellite phone," Regan had muttered. "They took it away at check-in, fucking security—"

"How much does one of those sat phones cost, anyway?" Tyler had wondered.

"Who gives a shit?" Regan had flashed a piratical grin before delivering an obscenity-laced tongue-thrashing to his minions in Malaysia.

They'd exchanged cards as they were landing, Regan distracted by mandatory Immigration forms. He told Tyler to get in touch. There were openings in the Marine division for more cable trash: experts who traveled the globe, physically burying endless long ropes of fiber into the oceans from massive slow-moving barges.

Tyler sat now, stunned with fatigue, letting the music wash over him and the fresh injection of alcohol infuse his system with false energy. He had to quickly line up and explore his options. He could afford a short break, maybe a couple of months, but then he'd need income. He'd figured it all out; during the polite silence of his driving Delphine back to Paris, he'd planned a neat to-do list.

But he'd gotten fucked up since then.

As soon as he'd dropped off Delphine at her apartment he'd had agonies of second and third doubts about letting her go. Her only real fault had been in withholding what she knew about GlobeAll; and he should be grateful that she'd finally given him a heads-up, he'd known that. But his pride wouldn't let him admit it to her right away.

He'd turned in the rental car, alerted his VP to the impending lawsuit, checked in at the Paris office and booked his flight to London as soon as Jack told him a key GlobeAll client wanted some attention.

Anything to keep moving, to keep from thinking too deeply.

Carly Emerald and Julian Trent had captured his interest very effectively until his conscience caught up with him in London, as he was making his plans to fly back to New York. He'd found the courage to confront Delphine again.

Julian, unwitting, had proved critical to that courage. Julian had been so genuinely dashed by the disparity between his personal feelings about Iraq and his company's prerogative that he'd gotten rip-roaring drunk, that evening in London.

"Normally the business never bothers me. Twenty years with StoneEdge. The Iran-Iraq war. Afghanistan One. Somalia. Gulf War One. Bosnia. Chechnya. Afghanistan Two. Every little skirmish in between, every little soldier. Never blinked." He'd taken another long gulp of ale. "This is different. This feels like opening the doors to bloody hell: all the Muslims of the world will be rushing out, knives in their teeth, ready for revenge. And for what? For what?" He'd stared at Tyler with real pain in his eyes. It was a rhetorical question, Tyler knew, for which there was no answer. "For *fuck*-all." Julian drained his glass and ordered another.

His sincerity had impressed Tyler, in part because it was so unlike the formality of American business exchanges, where small talk kept to sports, food, travel, or vague general-interest news. After a few more gloomy observations, Julian had finally flogged off with a fetching flaxen-haired barfly.

Tyler had stayed at the bar, head ringing with the sober truth of Julian's drunken enlightenment.

First he brooded on how many industries stood to profit from the upcoming war. The list was so long he had to keep drinking.

Then he'd started to examine, again, his unease about GlobeAll's Canadian traffic diversion and his depressing suspicion that Nick had somehow, for some "fuck-all" reason, engineered it. Although Tyler had seen less of him in recent years, since rising beyond him in the company, he remembered Nick as having been so strong. It was impossible to believe he could act out of weakness.

Tyler had imagined that Delphine would have listened with sympathy to his misgivings. But since he'd severed their tie, tactfully, on the way back from Fontainbleau, he could not possibly call her to commiserate.

He'd gone back to his hotel that night to answer endless e-mails and deliver his StoneEdge verdict to the poised, silver-eyed U.S. account manager he'd met on video: the intriguing Carly Emerald. She'd been in some kind of spa, of all places, when he'd called her to report on Julian, but sharp as if at a conference table. That snagged, like a cold gust of air, his attention and amusement.

He liked the edgy energy she exuded. He was always on the lookout for salespeople to recommend for promotion. They seemed, in GlobeAll U.S. offices, to be few when it came to real knowledge of the global arena.

Carly was a natural. She was quick enough to grasp, immediately, the significance of the Asia business he'd sussed out of Julian, and tenacious enough to stay up for hours designing a GlobeAll solution for it. He'd looked up her online bio and was even more impressed—she was a language major, fluent in Spanish. He'd wondered why she'd buried herself in Wisconsin instead of coming to HQ to work for the Americas team. He'd wondered, briefly, whether she ever smiled.

As the rest of that day dawned in London, after his finalization of the Asia StoneEdge information for Carly, startled into awareness of how easy it was to talk to her, he'd found himself for once without any desire to keep working.

The implosion he'd known was coming for GlobeAll, and all its professional ramifications, sapped his interest in immediate deals, once he'd dealt with StoneEdge. There'd been plenty of room, then, for Delphine to fill his mind.

He'd flown to Paris that afternoon, on his own nickel, to apologize in person.

"Why you are here now, asking to see me, is beyond reason."

Once again they were at the coffee shop in her building, clinical as a bus stop; well, a bus stop in France, where even the vending machines sold fresh gourmet cuisine. She did not smile, did not take his offered hand. She was fully armored in stiff corporate dress and makeup. Remorsefully, he recalled her relaxed erotic open-ness at the cottage. He'd never get that back.

"I had to tell you how sorry I am."

"Sorry that your company is failing."

"Sorry that I reacted badly."

"Sorry that your stock portfolio will benefit from my advance warning?"

Stock portfolio! He hadn't even thought of that. "I'm sorry that I blamed the messenger, Delphine. You were right to tell me the truth then. Fuck the stock. Fuck the company."

"You're so quick with swear words, just like Guy. I am sure you already made your trades. I would expect nothing less. Probably you are even richer now."

"Delphine." He couldn't even look into her eyes for more than a moment. He wished he had the fluency of a Frenchman, who would ease his way around stressful topics to comment on the passing traffic or the cunning arrangement of her scarf or the dubious quality of the sugar.

He stirred his bitter little espresso, wondering briefly how love and business was conducted in the days before coffee, staring into its steaming shallows as if he could divine some better future beyond this painful meeting.

"Delphine, I only came to tell you, face to face, how much I regret the way things between us ended."

Her head drooped. "Thank you, for that, at least. I regret too." Her sigh was deep and tired. "I chose a wrong time to tell you about GlobeAll. You don't have to blame yourself completely."

Her exoneration didn't register then. "I shouldn't have acted the way I did."

"You were shocked. You are young." She'd shrugged. Hearing an opening, he'd reached for her hands. She'd drawn them back, abruptly. "Tyler. Leave us some dignity."

At the time he hadn't really been able to understand that; hell, he still didn't. Why couldn't he have made things right between them by apologizing? Their chemistry was still strong; he could tell by the flush in her cheeks. He'd wanted to reach over, unwind that scarf and mess up her hair, rise up from the booth's confinement and grab her, stroke her, kiss her senseless, to remind her how good it had been—

When she'd been the one to get up she'd confirmed for him, by the fixed way she looked at him, that the remnant of their idyll resonated in her without requiring any reminder. But the finality of her dark look silenced him then as it had silenced him since.

"Goodbye Tyler. I appreciate, that you came back to see me."

With a twirl of elegant fabric she was gone, the lingering scent of her perfume his only certainty that she'd been there at all; that and the bill presented by a discreet yet prompt clerk who had doubtless observed the interaction and wanted every last score settled.

It had cost him twenty five Euros to be blown off by the woman who'd brought him back to sensual life. Not a bad price, he thought now in his chair in the New York morning, to be reminded of what he'd been missing.

He'd be missing her for a long time.

There was no point in pursuing her. Of course things between them couldn't have worked out, anyway: their competitive stance, the distance, Guillaume, her estranged husband, the lawsuit. He poured himself another shot from the bottle beside him on the floor, sipped, slid deeper in the chair and rested his head back, eyes closed.

Far worse than the scene with Delphine had been his discussion with Nouri, who'd arranged to stop and see Tyler in the GlobeAll Paris office on his way back from Hungary.

Thirty-Four

"STATUS ME, HARDING," Nouri had said, closing the door on them in the conference room. His cool tone hadn't concerned Tyler at first, as they'd never been particularly friendly—both had reputations, at GlobeAll, as men who kept their distance from others.

Nouri was as polished an executive as Tyler had ever known.

Tyler studied his boss keenly whenever they met in person, noting his poise, his measured diction, the way he used silence, his careful body language, his fashion-plated European dress sense; absorbing him like a lesson he might one day use. He'd even studied Nouri's e-mail style.

But after nearly three years of reporting to Nouri, without getting to know him well, Tyler had still not decided how much of the man he *wanted* to emulate.

"I need your final authorization on the agreements I signed this trip," he'd told him once they sat down. "You were at the Matav deal, so you know that's complete. Telia's also signed, GTS is signed, DT's been put off for awhile, and of course, as you know, we lost FF." Although it hurt to say this last, he kept his tone as even as his boss'.

"As I well know." Nouri's tone was dry. "What about this urgent request for Turkish dark fiber, for the government division?" He glanced down at his notes. "I received a call from a ... rather irate young man from the U.S. DOD."

"That one can wait until I check with Ops."

Nouri's dark gaze had stayed on him, then, longer than felt comfortable, but Tyler didn't flinch, not until Nouri leaned suddenly forward, clasping his fingers into a sharp-looking knot pointed directly at Tyler. "Tell me about the Canadian renewal deadline you missed. The one that's generating this lawsuit."

Tyler took a breath. "TeleOne. I was uncomfortable about re-signing it. The financials looked fishy to me. Access didn't add up."

"Yet you know who structured it." Nouri did not speak the way the Americans at GlobeAll did: although he had no discernible accent, he distinguished himself by hardly ever raising his voice, speaking almost without inflection, as if he were a bloodless scholar instead of a titan of industry. Most American GlobeAll-ists thought he was too aloof, too un-"salesey." He was trusted less than ever now, as an "old"-European.

Tyler watched him, wondering where this was going, not liking the feeling of suspicion creeping up his spine.

"You and Fournier were always close, weren't you Harding?" Schooled in the UK, Nouri used everyone's last name or "Miss": another reason Tyler figured he was disliked. American workers embraced informality even in executives; it was part of their beloved classless delusion.

"We were, yes. But I didn't supervise Nick. I didn't keep track of his agreements."

"I'm sure you were aware of the details of *this* arrangement. This was … special."

Tyler froze.

"I understand your reluctance to sign again. You knew that this time your friend's deception would be uncovered. Tell me, what was his motivation?"

"I didn't know about it." Tyler's voice was almost a whisper, unrecognizable to him.

"He was ready to retire. Perhaps there was some kind of payoff. Surely you can explain it? You must have taken part in the TeleOne discussions in 2001; you were advising all the country managers then. That would have included him."

Tyler's head cleared.

The TeleOne puzzle he'd been trying *not* to solve, so he wouldn't have to question Nick's reputation, unraveled before him.

An illegal access-avoidance scam couldn't put money in an individual country manager's pocket—but it could make a lot of money for the corporation behind it; for the business unit that managed profit and loss for such arrangements. And, in particular, the executive with signatory responsibility: he would receive a handsome bonus for reducing costs. Cheap lemons and sugar water made profitable lemonade. Cheap access, interexchange and fiber made profitable telecom.

Tyler found his voice. "I didn't know anything about this," he repeated, firmly. "But *you* must have approved it, Nouri. You were the Director then."

Nouri surveyed him as if from across a great divide.

"*You* knew." Tyler sat forward now too. "You knew then! Nick might have arranged it, sure, maybe he judged poorly—but *you* had to sign off then, just like I'm having to sign off now. And if it doesn't add up to me, it wouldn't have added up to you. Except for maybe the bonus you'd get."

Tyler went on, figuring it out as he spoke, "and Carmody gave you final approval. Was he in on it? Of course, he didn't need any bonus, he could just sell GlobeAll short." Andrew Carmody, their former International VP, had cashed in options early in 2002 and left the company. "And you're sitting there trying to pin this on Nick? Or on *me?*"

"You're released from signing off on anything further, for the time being."

Tyler pushed his rolling chair away from the table with arms that felt suddenly shaky. He stood up anyway, rigidly, rocked by anger. "Are you *firing* me?" He clenched his hands to stop them from reaching out to throttle Nouri.

"Of course not. You're a valuable team player, and your skills are very much needed here." He didn't know how Nouri could continue to gaze at him in that bland, detached way, his black orb-like eyes motionless in their sockets. The guy's a fucking alien, Tyler thought savagely, consumed by unfamiliar rage, surprised by its power. "I'm sure this whole issue will be clarified soon. We'll conduct an … investigation as we prepare our defense against UTT."

"You'd better hope your tracks are well covered," Tyler told him tightly.

Nouri raised faint eyebrows. He steepled thin fingers.

"I advise you to take a short hiatus, Harding. Paid, of course. We'll be in touch."

Tyler replayed the conversation in his head, still slumped in his chair, still drinking. "Theme from the Bottom" came on and he sang along in a whispery undertone, Brilliant song. But he'd never identified with the bottom-feeder narrator until just now, remembering Nouri's contempt. The singer wondered about seeing something worth trying for, even if forced to swim up.

With Delphine, why, he'd seen, he'd tried, and if it hadn't worked out, well, what was the expression? "Better to have loved and lost?"

But he was a bad loser.

He didn't know *how* to lose.

In fact, he'd never lost before, not like this. Right now loss was crashing in like massive waves, tossing him helpless as in "Theme from the Bottom." Trust in GlobeAll. Nouri: although they hadn't enjoyed any real relationship, he'd assumed Nouri respected him and would treat him fairly. Nick, twice now. Delphine. Time; it felt like ten years down the drain, although he had to hope that would be a temporary feeling.

He needed a major project of some sort to distract himself, but he didn't have the energy, yet, to fully contemplate next career steps. He listened to the rest of the song, about tossing away un-needed stuff and knowing who was a friend. He wondered if he had any

237

real friends. He finished his drink, set the glass on the floor, and closed his eyes.

He must have dozed off, for when he opened his eyes it was early afternoon, judging by the light. Phish were still chuckling to themselves on repeat in the corner speakers.

Tyler surveyed his forlorn apartment. In his mind's eye he contrasted it with the vibrancy of Delphine's and Juliette's Parisian flat. If he was going to have any kind of life now, he'd need a suitable place in which to conduct it—or, if he wasn't staying here, he'd need to make it into a decent sublet. Making a home out of it would require movement, at least.

He stripped off his suit, put on jeans and Tshirt, clicked to the next disc, White Stripes, and began the process of putting the place to rights. It was satisfying to discard most of the mail, wash away the grime, and sort out his laundry.

He dug out the last of the boxes Julee had packed in the closet. It was past time he started using fun stuff in the kitchen. He took extra blankets out of the oven, which he'd only used as storage space, and stacked them by the door to give away.

After a couple of hours his kitchen looked efficient enough to cook in, his few furnishings gleamed, and he'd exhausted himself so that he knew he'd be able to sleep that night. He was going to stay up as long as he could—his anti-jetlag technique—so he dumped his trash and went out to drop off his dry cleaning.

Energized by his progress and the crisp outside air, he sprinted over to a shopping area nearby where there was a Pottery Barn, Starbucks and Whole Foods carved into a rehabbed highrise. He appreciated the enterprising nature of the U.S. retail industry even though he'd never had time to be much of a consumer: it was the first time in his life he'd been inside a Pottery Barn. He bought bright red cushions for his couch, a brilliant red-patterned rug and shades, a red comforter; stuffed into two huge carrier bags which he lugged to the Whole Foods next door and jammed into a shopping cart.

He bought several days' worth of real food, even a slim container of milk: God knew when he'd last bought milk! He piled everything into a taxi and chatted with the driver, Obama Oudad, originally from Nigeria but now enough of a New Yorker to complain about the Knicks' lousy season.

He hung his new shades, made dinner: steak, baked potato, salad. He toasted himself with a big glass of red as he sat at his miniscule table.

"You can do this. You're doing fine! Keep it up."

Tomorrow he'd go out for an early run. Then he'd sort through the queries that had come to him via headhunters, erstwhile competitors and alliance partners from all over the world since the story broke. He was lucky, he knew, luckier than a whole lot of GlobeAll people were going to be. His reputation, built up by years of relationships, couldn't be sullied by anything Nouri might say. He'd have his pick of next jobs when he felt capable of caring about work again.

And he was going to get his dog, schedule be damned. He could practically see that happy grin, smell wet fur from winter runs, hear that lapping tongue.

Once he'd washed his dishes there was nothing else for him to do.

He refused to unpack his laptop or un-forward his landline phone or recharge his mobile tonight, so he could get a real break, although not hooking up gave him a disoriented feeling. If nobody could reach him, if nobody was allowed to demand his attention, then who was he, really? What defined him other than his work?

He stood by the window again, finishing the wine, listening to Phish, watching the wonder of lights come on in the buildings all around him. He didn't own a television set, so this was his evening entertainment. It was beautiful.

And comforting. He was surrounded by millions of other people who, if they were alone in their apartments and as fatigued as he, were probably also asking themselves who the hell they were and what the hell it was all about besides watching TV and feeding the cat. The thought made him smile. At least they had a cat. But watching the city go about its evening routine made him feel less lonely. The music seemed to coax and then orchestrate the lights display, so much that he knew he was more than a little drunk and probably overdue a month's worth of sleep.

He went into his tiny bedroom, rolled up in his soft new red comforter, let the years-long tidal wave of exhaustion wash over him. He pushed immediately into the welcome depths of slumber.

Thirty-Five

H E WOKE MUCH TOO EARLY with a terrible hangover. He staggered into the bathroom to pee for what felt like an hour, then swallowed some aspirin with two long glasses of water. He drank standing by the window. The glass loomed close and he rested his forehead on it. Forty stories down, traffic was shifting to and fro on the city streets, making him dizzy. He turned from the sight and stumbled back to bed.

When next he awoke, he made coffee and took it to his chair.

He was about to close his eyes again, just to rest them, when his doorbell buzzed. Fuck. Who knew he was back in the city?

He pressed the intercom warily.

"Ty? It's Gerard. Let me up."

With a sense of resignation, he buzzed in his big brother. Gerard nosed out sibling nuance, like a hunting dog, keenly aware when certain movements were in the air. His attention to Tyler was rare but accurate. He'd shown up when Tyler had broken his leg skiing, for instance, and again as soon as Tyler had told him about Julee.

He went to the door to let Ger in. The brothers' coloring was similar but Ger was taller, more muscular, with a much broader smile. Their family constellation had been fixed long ago, so that when they were together Tyler still thought of Ger as 'the goodlooking one' and of himself as 'the quiet one.' He *was* quiet when his brother was around. Ger was more gregarious, although he'd gotten less trusting and more shrewd as his skills as a white-collar-crime prosecutor had sharpened; finely honed on plenty of corporate disgrace. No wonder he was here: the GlobeAll scandal was plastered all over the business press.

Tyler sank into his chair and watched Ger peel off his overcoat and sprawl on the couch. Fresh air seemed to sweep in with him, threatening the calm Tyler had built. Ger surveyed the apartment, slowly taking in the new touches of color, and then his brother.

"How'd you find out, G?"

"Saw the news. Called your office."

"What'd they say?"

"You're in France."

"Why'd you think I wasn't?"

"Called Jack Rigby over there. He said I shouldn't let on that you came back."

Tyler'd made a few phone calls in Paris to make sure the engineer's job was safe.

"But nobody told me you'd *quit*. Or did you get laid off?"

"Neither."

"So ... they don't know you're here. In hiding." Ger's blunt, gravelly voice was heavy with disapproval.

"Taking some time off, is all."

"Because ..." Ger raised his brows, waited.

Tyler tried to shut him up with a cold stare.

"Until when?"

Tyler raised his hands. He just wanted to finish one goddamn cup of coffee.

"You can't roll over and play dead. You've got to attack this head on, you know, or they'll think you're hiding because the Canada thing's your fault." Ger hitched forward and leaned earnest forearms on his knees. "Get back out there and combat the suspicion."

They exchanged another long look.

"What's that boss of yours have to say about it, anyway?" Ger asked abruptly. "He's got to come out with some kind of statement shielding GlobeAll, or it's all over, you *know* that."

"I know."

"So what're you gonna do about it?"

Tyler shrugged. He looked at his new rug.

"What the fuck, man, you're letting this bullshit get you down? You're sitting here in your pajamas at noon on a Wednesday?" Ger stood. There was barely room for his frustration in the small apartment. "You can't let this happen!"

"I didn't *let* it happen," Tyler snapped.

Ger started to pace. "Who connived the switching?"

"It doesn't really matter, does it?"

"Yeah it does, you have to make sure you're not associated with it. Some fuckheads decide to mess with your access arrangements to save a buck or two, and because it's Canada everyone assumes they must be international fuckheads. Ergo, *you* look guilty."

Ger's accusing tone stirred his apathy to anger. He stared at his brother, unable to find a way to tell the truth without smearing Nick's name. "What if it was just ... somebody's poor judgment?"

"This kind of thing is never just "somebody" in a corporation like GlobeAll. It's gotta be at least a couple suits and an engineering team who can divert routing tables." Ger knew telecom from many discussions with Tyler. He looked down, frowning, and Tyler could see that, beyond his customary lust to find the culprit, there was a deep concern for his little "bro."

"Tyler, where's your outrage?" he exclaimed suddenly. "They *betrayed* you!" He emphasized this with a sternly jabbing finger.

Gerard always managed to nail things.

"That is, actually, how I'm feeling right now," Tyler agreed. Admitting this seemed to allow new air to expand into his body. He sat up.

Ger sat down again, studied him. "You look like hell."

"I'm jet lagged. Westbound is worst."

"You eating okay? Sleeping?"

"Oh yeah."

"Natalie told me to bring you back with me to Greenwich tonight."

"Not necessary."

"I called Mom and Pop." Ger reached behind him to pick up his coat. "But you should call them too. Maybe go out there for a few days." He stood.

"I need to stay here and find a new job."

Ger laughed. "Let the old one go first."

"I'm trying to."

"Then *do* it! It's called "handing in your resignation," Ty, not "sitting in your pajamas on a Wednesday." You send em an e-mail. Or call em up. How's your HR situation?"

Tyler shook his head. "My stock's fucked like everyone's, but I have some money stashed away. Enough for awhile, anyway."

"Huh," Ger said. "I'm thinking severance. Big time. Wrongful termination."

A little of G's litigious relentlessness went a long way. Tyler told him patiently, "I'm not terminated. Yet." Oops. He hadn't meant to let the last word slip out, but Ger rounded on him, scenting blood.

"Tell me what the fuck is going on, T. *Tell* me you're not just sitting here waiting to get the ax like some stupid patient lemming."

A jolt of pain stabbed through him as Ger said this. He slumped forward, elbows on knees, and he squeezed his eyes shut.

"Tell me." Ger spoke gently now, putting his large hand on Tyler's shoulder.

So he did. He related the whole sad, too-common tale, starting with his early misgivings about the TeleOne agreement and ending with his confrontation with Nouri just two days ago.

Ger's broad smile appeared for the first time. "We're going to *kill* that weaselly little fucker."

Tyler, warmed that Ger said "we," let out a shaky laugh. But he shook his head. "We can't. I don't want

Nick's name getting into this, and Nouri will blame him if I'm not in the line of fire."

"Stop being so fucking noble! If you don't fight this you're screwed! Just as screwed as UTT was by this, as screwed as GlobeAll's gonna be!"

"Nick gave me the chance of a lifetime with GlobeAll. He believed in me even though I'd never had a corporate job. I owe him my loyalty."

Ger squatted in front of him and grabbed the chair arms as if he'd launch himself right into Tyler's lap. "Listen to me. You had great creds even then, and you'd have used them well no matter where you got a job. You had plenty of other interviews, remember, you were a hot property. He did *himself* a favor by recruiting you.

"And Ty, I know it's still a sensitive subject with you, but you couldn't have stopped him from going into Tower Two that day, even though I know you keep blaming yourself. He was doing his job."

The stab of pain Tyler had felt intensified into a path, widening as it spread in him, forcing more air into his lungs, clearing his head.

"We'll keep Nick out of it." Ger stood up, started striding around, working up his case. "You're forced to resign to avoid the appearance of any personal impropriety. You'd nobly hang on, captain of the sinking ship, et cetera, but it would be committing professional hara kiri. You can't, in all conscience, allow your stellar record to be besmirched by the taint of scandal."

Ger stopped pacing, grinned widely. "So on the advice of your longtime counsel, but in the spirit of fairness—to avoid more disgrace to GlobeAll—you'll allow them to settle with you out of court. *If* they keep this quiet, that is. Otherwise you're obliged to tell all about Nouri, and anyone else we dig up, to protect the ever-unraveling integrity of shareholder value."

Tyler felt a bubble of laughter rise.

"Ha. I knew I'd get you."

"You're good, G."

"The best," Ger corrected. "And for you, a onetime *special* offer, just for today—free! We'll make this stick." He hooked his coat on his shoulder. "Why didn't you want to tell me?"

"I ... knew this would make Nick look bad." It was suddenly easy to add, "I loved my job. I was proud of GlobeAll. I don't want to seem like some fuckup."

Ger's gaze was steady. "You can still be proud. Canada was a lousy choice, not yours, not GlobeAll's overall policy. You have no reason to feel bad."

Now Tyler knew why Ger was considered the best victims' advocate in his rarified field.

"Let's settle our strategy soon." Ger checked his palm pilot. "We'll have lunch tomorrow at the firm and review your options. You can decide how you want it to go."

"Thanks."

"At least you're not watching daytime TV," Ger snorted. "But call Pop, okay, I told them I'd make sure you weren't going to dive out your window."

Tyler stared. Did his brief disappearance seem that dire?

"Rigby said you seemed really down." Ger went on, "something about a woman?" He waited, expression inquiring, but when Tyler said nothing he nodded. "Okay, little bro, all in good time." He walked to the door. "Come this weekend, okay? Jerry wants to see you. Nat too. You were gone a long time, this trip."

Thinking of Jerry's eager grin made Tyler smile. "He wants to know what I brought him."

"Sure he does," Ger agreed. "He thinks you have nothing else to do in Paris but shop for more of his Rai CDs at FNAC. Hey, he's been IM'ing that boy you put in touch with him. Guillaume. They're already plotting some Phish-head odyssey this summer. I'm gonna have to veto that unless I go along. Nat's orders."

Tyler hadn't expected to think of Guy. Regret suddenly tightened his throat.

"What? *You* want to go with em instead, see Phish live?" Ger frowned. "Or is it the French kid? I thought it was some woman had you twisted up, Ty, not a teenage boy." He wiggled insinuating eyebrows. "Kinky."

Tyler shoved him. "Shut up."

His brother nodded in his infuriating know-it-all way. "In time, bro, in time."

Thirty-Six

Milwaukee

CARLY STOOD IN HER LIVING ROOM, looking around at the order she'd made out of chaos. She wasn't a very neat person at home, unlike at work, so her place had always been a cozy, jumbled haven where her favorite things were tossed about. She wasn't slovenly, just casual—she sorted things out on weekends, usually.

So it gave her a chill to see how sterile everything looked now that she was ready to move in with her mom. She'd never been very good with sudden change, and she'd arranged all of this pretty quickly, in less than two weeks.

She wasn't resigning from GlobeAll. She was taking a leave of absence, having completed all the paperwork and gotten Dudley's grudging approval. She wondered now for the first time, surveying her empty apartment, whether she might not suffer some kind of culture shock from not working, not putting on business clothes and makeup, not going out every day to competently deal with all of StoneEdge's network demands.

How would it feel to give up her autonomy? Mother and daughter had both agreed it would be a good interim step, a help to Rebecca and a safety net for Carly. She loved her mom's house, the house of her childhood, but wasn't it a kind of regression to childhood to move back in there?

Neither she nor Rebecca had the nerve to discuss how long this interim might last. She could admit, in the mood of realism that descended on her during her last confrontation with Lionel, that it frightened her to care for her mom. She didn't feel nearly as capable as the job required.

The window showed an expanse of ethereal blue, studded with pink-tinged flat clouds which flung themselves across the sky like waves of sand. Gold lined their edges. She stood watching for a moment, drinking in the purity of color, letting the last tote fall limp at her side.

The ringing doorbell jolted her out of her reverie. Probably the landlord; they'd arranged a key transfer and the return of her security deposit. She dropped her bag and opened the door. For the first time, as if she were no longer a tenant, she didn't check the peephole.

Francisco stood there. A bottle of white wine, no, Champagne, dangled from his left hand; his right was in his pocket. The expression on his strong face was sweeter than she'd seen in months. The smile in his eyes made her forget why she'd forgotten him.

She stepped back.

"Munequita mia," he murmured, moving forward. My little doll. *"Eres mas bella que nunca."* You're more beautiful than ever.

He didn't try to embrace her. He strode into the empty living room and sank onto the white carpet, long olive raincoat billowing around him. He set the bottle down and fixed her with a knowing stare, under his long eyelashes.

"How is Rebecca?"

"Not good. I'm going to take care of her."

"Is good. Is the right thing to do, Catty." He leaned back on his palms and stretched out his long jeaned legs. His luxuriant hair tumbled down in a froth of curls as he tilted his face to her. "I come to say goodbye to you."

The sunset gilded his hair, sparkled on the gold foil bottle top, and in his eyes. He unwrapped the foil, untwisted the wire holding the cork in place, eased the cork out of the bottle so smoothly it didn't make a sound.

He held the bottle up to her, smiling again, so beguiling that he hardly resembled the man she'd recently known. He seemed like the one she'd met last summer, the one who'd gazed longingly and listened patiently and loved so thoroughly that it still made her wet to recall, so that as she looked at him now she felt herself moisten.

He raised his eyebrows slightly and held the bottle a little higher.

Carly swallowed the water gathering in her mouth as she looked at him.

Well, why not? Even condemned-to-death prisoners were granted a last meal of everything they wanted. Maybe they should say goodbye as they'd said hello: air between them liquid with desire. She walked toward him slowly, feeling as if she were wading through a heavy swell of living waves. She sank down cross-legged beside him and accepted a drink. The long slide of cold Champagne hit with a delicious shiver.

"*Cara*," he whispered close to her ear just before he took his turn sipping, so that she felt the movement of his lips and heard his swallow. He kept on talking to her in Spanish, words of seduction, a steady flow of soft endearments. How enticing, she thought before her fourth sip, if he'd been like this all along I might not have minded about his other mujer—his *mujer*!

She yanked herself away from him and took another long swig. She wasn't going to be taken in by all this sweet talk, no sir. He could project that lovely limpid gaze as long as he liked, she wasn't going to fall for it. No way. She drank again and handed him the bottle with an unsteady thrust.

"You can stop looking at me that way."

"What way, *linda mia*?" He touched her then, the lightest of fingertip to temple stroking, finding as always the very nerve ending of tension in her. "I am looking with love, for adios."

"You want to leave with the upper hand," she sputtered. "You want the last goddamn word. I'm not fucking you again, so you can just cut it out."

"We don't fucking, no," he answered, wistful as the last hot pink gleam around the clouds out the window. "We only loving." He put the bottle to his lips, swallowed, licked the rim while staring at her with half-lidded eyes, and then put it to her mouth.

God. She took another swig.

Then she sat up straight. *I want to be the one making this decision,* she thought, *I want this to be my choice.* She fixed him with a stern glare as she gestured with the bottle, waving it in his direction.

"Francisco. I can't let you be a part of my life anymore."

"I know that, Catty. I assept." He dropped his gaze for a fraction of a second and then lifted again to her, with a wicked half smile. "I only want to say goodbye."

"Okay," she returned, "goodbye then."

His answer was to reach out a tight arm and pull her down next to him as he sank onto the carpet.

She lay on her back next to him. She sensed his rapt focus on the ceiling, knowing he was scanning the luminous colors reflected there like a camera, as surely as she felt his firm embrace and the tickle of his sprightly curls against her cheek. She could gauge, to the second, how long it took his artist's eyes to absorb the shifting patterns of sunset. She'd observed him that closely before.

Then he brought his mouth to hers. His warm tongue met hers. She rolled toward him and hugged him closer as their familiar kiss deepened. It was just goodbye, she told herself as his hands slid over and up her legs, as he continued gliding with sure fingers under her sweatshirt. A goodbye was not a lapse in judgment. It was "closure."

Francisco rearranged her clothes. He moved slowly, stroking, teasing, nibbling with his mouth, prickling her sensitized skin with his long hair. It had been so long since he'd concentrated on her like this that she had almost forgotten how to relax into it. She finally closed her eyes and let her body hum with the vibration of pleasure.

"*Quien te va a banar en besos?*" he sang softly, lips grazing, strong fingers moving inside. Who's going to bathe you in kisses? He intensified his focus and skillfully brought her over. He'd learned her so well.

Her sweet dissolution was short-lived. Maybe nobody else would ever know her so well, she realized, wrenching herself away from him. She might never feel this good with a man again. Or this bad, a little voice whispered, not Francisco's.

He turned her around to face him. "*Dulce,*" he murmured, his eyes gleaming with satisfaction. He reached out to catch the trickle of tear from her cheek.

She wrapped an arm, folded a leg against her nakedness, trying to look at him evenly. "Is this your goodbye, then, Franco."

He planted a kiss on her lips as if planting a flag. "It's goodbye to make you think of me. *Que me querras siempre.*" He said it like a curse: you will always want me. He strode to the door, looked back at her just once. "Adios."

Which left her half wondering if she'd imagined the whole thing.

Pondering this was definitely Latin American.

She unpacked a Mana CD. Her portable player and a few CDs were the only things left in her apartment. She buttoned her coat and propped herself against the wall, finishing the Champagne, listening to Mana, wondering about reality and about Francisco, as he had surely intended.

Thirty-Seven

S HE TURNED OFF THE TV when it was apparent that the only break from "Shock and Awe" daytime coverage was the toddlers' channel. The invasion was too upsetting to Rebecca, who alternately cursed and wept at the ubiquitous wallpaper of explosions.

"They make it look like fireworks, like it's the fourth of July," she gasped. "It's *pornography*. Worse than pornography. Those people are *dying*." She bent over in a paroxysm of coughing.

"Mom. I turned it off."

"That doesn't mean it's not still happening." Tears streamed down Rebecca's cheeks. "Carly, promise me one thing."

"Of course."

"Promise me." Rebecca was crying harder now. "Promise me you won't lead a life that's sustained on the backs of poor people."

"Mom, no, I won't," she began, her own eyes watering.

"Because you know it's always the poor people, the uneducated people, who sacrifice the most for wars." She broke off to cough again, a deep hacking that left her gasping. "They're so obedient, so patient. They believe all they see."

"I know, you told me that." Carly impatiently swiped away her tears. "But please, try not to think about it for a minute, just so you can catch your breath."

"It's all I can think about." It was as if she thought her crying would somehow cleanse her of sorrow. Carly suddenly felt enraged by her mom's convictions, which so twisted her up when she should be easing, mellowing, relaxing; so that her illness would be less painful. "We are already guilty, you know, just being white and in this country." Rebecca's face was a grimace of agony.

Carly grabbed a Kleenex from the box she always kept nearby. She wiped Rebecca's face with it, gently, and then dabbed another over her own eyes to stop their leaking. "I'm here right now, Mom, and I'm *damned* if I'm going to spend time with you in sorrow instead of in joy."

Rebecca ground her fists into her eyes and took a shaky breath. "Only for you, babe. When Wander comes around tonight I'm going to bawl to my heart's content."

Wander was her old *Ramparts* op-ed buddy, the back-to-the-land guy who was so pessimistic about globalization when Carly got into it with him. "Oh great. You can expire in his arms instead of in mine."

Rebecca managed a weak chuckle. "I'd rather, tell you the truth."

"I suppose he was one of your lovers too," Carly muttered. She'd heard many a confessional story the last weeks, a perk of being witness to Rebecca's passing.

"Only for a short time."

"Weren't they all?"

"Don't be bitchy. Some were true loves, like your Dad."

Carly wasn't going to argue about anything Rebecca said, as long as she wasn't crying. She was reminded of the Mana song "No para de llover" which described the narrator's eyes' inability to stop weeping. Of course almost everybody in Mana's songs was always crying, over love. But there were a few, like Rebecca, who wept over injustice and oppression.

Rebecca's objections to television covered not only the current news but other shows that Carly had vainly flipped to, other days, in an attempt to brighten Rebecca's pre-invasion mood: reality TV whose dramas scorned and quickly eliminated the underdog; human interest and women's programs with their hopeless, Rebecca insisted, emphasis on self-actualization: "There's no such thing as self-actualization when the state has us all by the balls!" She even hated crime mysteries: "They want us absorbed in this crap so we don't focus on the *real* criminals! It's all bullshit!"

"Let's hear some music instead." She saw, by the way Rebecca settled back in her La-Z-Boy, a replacement of the too-sterile hospital bed, that this was the right choice. She stacked up the Grateful Dead, of course, and an assortment of Mom's current favorites, whose CDs were lined up next to the sound system. She didn't recognize most of them.

"Who *are* these guys?"

Rebecca's head was moving back and forth in time to the music. "Hives. Turn it up." She opened her eyes and smiled at her daughter. "Listen to something other than the Top 40 and there's no telling what you might discover."

Carly only had time to listen to music in her car.

Of course, now she had more time, more than she could ever remember having, but more little pesky chores to fill it up with too.

Rebecca gave into her illness with relief once Carly moved in, so there were umpteen household tasks. Phone calls to the insurance company. Updates delivered to Rebecca's many friends who showed up almost every evening to hang out. Even though they always brought food and drink, and provided much-needed laughter, their visits often left Carly exhausted and, she suspected, Rebecca too.

Carly was grateful for Sara, who came over every couple of days so she could nap; and for Rebecca's friend Emma who came to stay every weekend.

There were fewer trips than she would have expected to the oncologist, Dr. "It's just a matter of time" Klein. He seemed to have lost interest in Rebecca once declaring her inoperable after the last failed round of chemo. His utility to them was full strength pain meds. Rebecca took them all now without complaint.

Carly hadn't slept a full night since she'd moved in. She was crispy with fatigue but unwilling to give in to it, unwilling to miss a moment of Mom's lucid life. She got by on lots of coffee and alcohol. It made for a dramatic kind of mood roller coaster which in its own way provided distraction from having to notice, more closely, how quickly Rebecca was deteriorating.

Her range of movement had narrowed to the La-Z-Boy and the little first floor bathroom. She needed help now to shuffle from one spot to the other, and help getting onto the toilet and into the shower. It was time to talk hospice. But Carly dreaded bringing it up. She didn't think she had the heart, or nerve, or whatever personal steel, to discuss this out loud. She didn't want to name Death as their ever-nearing third party.

She turned up the music now, a dutiful daughter. Hives. Hmm. Not bad.

"Listen to this one song, Carly, it's about our current political leadership." Rebecca sang, wispy, "see the idiot walk," before interrupting herself to cough. "You should have heard me sing when I was young, honey, you wouldn't believe how good I was."

"I believe it."

"I was on that one Steely Dan album, I forget what it was called."

"*Can't Buy a Thrill.* It was huge, Mom. You were awesome." Rebecca still got small residual checks from her days as a backup singer. Steely Dan was still a strong seller. Carly had gotten her nickname from the time Rebecca sang with Carly Simon; they'd both been pregnant then and had bonded. Carly thought it was cruel that illness had robbed Rebecca not only of her voice but of its memory; she'd forgotten so much about her past since cancer and pain meds.

"Darling. Listen to me." Rebecca reached for Carly's chin, to bring her closer. Her blue eyes were faded and blurry, her hair was reduced to thin strands, her skin was grey. But her expression was intent and her voice as strong as it could be. "It's time for us to talk about what happens next."

Carly shrank back, wondering if she'd somehow transmitted her fretful thoughts about hospice, shoulders hunching in denial.

"Yes, hon. Let's talk it over while I'm still awake."

"I don't want you to be ... care-taken."

"I don't want *you* to be the only care-taker," Rebecca said. "It's unfair."

"It's not." Her throat ached too much to say more.

"I need you to be strong about a lot of things right now, Carly, and this is one of them. Even Em thinks it's too much for you."

The ever-helpful Emma was Rebecca's oldest friend, frequent visitor, biggest support to Carly. It stung now to imagine her as Mom's co-conspirator.

"I want to stay with you alone." Even to herself she sounded like a six-year-old. "We haven't done everything on our list." They'd spent hours watching videos, going through photo albums, listening to favorite music and talking, talking, talking—as much as Rebecca was able.

"We've done plenty, Carly, all but Black Bear Lake."

Black Bear Lake was five hours' drive north on crappy county roads. Most of the cabin motels were closed October through May. Maybe they could make it up there in the spring? If she rented, say, a comfortable mini van instead of her hard-riding little Honda?

"We'll go, Mom, there'll be time."

"Remember how we played Monopoly all week last time?"

"We could play here."

"We forgot to put board games on our list."

"You used to like doing puzzles up there, I'll get you some new ones."

But Rebecca's head twisted fretfully on the seatback now. "Can you change it?" she asked, short, with a tone that Carly had learned meant the pain meds were running out of gas. She checked her watch. It was still an hour away from the next scheduled dose, but what the hell.

She'd been cutting it shorter and shorter these last few days. Mom was going through a really bad spell right now, but the hours when she was okay were bright, warm, filled with the leisure to laugh as they had not had time for in many years.

"What do you want to hear, Metallica?" Rebecca hated them. Carly winked at her and stood. "I'll get your meds."

"It's still an hour away," Rebecca answered sharply. "Don't try fooling me. Put on Mana."

Carly felt doubly rebuked, but she put on the CD that Francisco had given Mom last Christmas. It was their unplugged set, humid with poignant ballads and chiming minor-key harmonies. Although it was only three thirty in the afternoon, Carly poured herself a glass of white wine in the kitchen when she went to check on the meds. If she listened to this music sober she'd be bawling as much as Rebecca had over the stupid war. She drank half the glass standing right next to the refrigerator and filled it up again.

"Por eso aun estoy en el lugar de siempre," one of the irresistibly lively songs on the CD came salsa-ing into the kitchen, making her take a few dance steps, wine slopping high in the glass. "This is why I'm still in the same place as always," they sang, sounding suddenly prophetic and even mocking.

To shut them out, she went into the little room that had been hers since childhood, closed the door, and turned on her laptop. Although she was on official leave she dialed in every few days just to see what was happening.

Most messages she skipped over or deleted quickly, not quite admitting to herself that, after their last conversation nearly a month ago, she was looking for ones from Tyler. There were several scathing memos from Lionel to which she did not respond, a frantic-sounding one from Dudley about Lionel's displeasure, and a placating one marked CONFIDENTIAL from Suze regarding the others:

Don't get yr undies in a bunch over messages from Dudley and Lionel, it's a tempest in a teapot caused by that sexy-looking New Yorker and his boss quitting last week. Lot of bla over Canadian access & Turkish fiber. Sounds nuts to me. See ya tonight.
xo Suze

So Tyler had quit! The scandal must have reached directly into his group. Word on Wall Street was that GlobeAll would settle out of court with UTT. Apparently—although it was news to her and to the other colleagues she stayed in touch with—access switching was a fairly common practice amongst telcos.

She wondered if he was en route to Colorado to join a rafting outfit.

She could call him, but what would she say, now that they didn't have GlobeAll in common? Now that she was no longer a hotshot account exec? Her reluctance rose, she knew, from the diminished space she felt herself inhabiting. She wasn't sure she would hold his interest anymore.

Oh well. It would be a hoot to see Suze tonight and catch up on GlobeAll gossip. She figured Suze and Wander would get along like a house afire. She would tell Suze to bring more wine, since she was starting early, and check on munchies in case anyone else showed up. She went out to the living room.

Mana sang on and Mom rested, eyes closed, in her La-Z-Boy. Carly went into the kitchen, refilled her glass, made a short grocery list. She then shook out Mom's meds. She took them into the living room with a glass of tepid tap water, no ice, the only way Mom could tolerate it.

"Mom, wake up, meds." If she didn't wake her on time, Carly had learned, there would be agony later. Mom usually fell right back to sleep.

Mom was sleeping very deeply. So deeply that she did not stir, not even when Carly moved her shoulder, gently. But the shoulder felt odd under her hand.

NO.

She could *not* have passed over.

With Mana guiding her through.

While Carly was checking e-mail.

She could *not* have. It wasn't supposed to happen like this.

The water glass slipped from Carly's hand and fell splashing onto the rug.

Thirty-Eight

"SHOCK AND AWE" blazed onto the huge flat screen TV like a twisted mirror-planet reprise of the worldwide Year 2000 celebrations that Tyler had watched in this same place, Ger's and Nat's den.

He frowned as neon green flares illuminated the low palm-studded skyline of riverfront Baghdad, illuminated its changing face as orange explosions boomed and resounded and smoke billowed into its night sky. He thought of all the Muslims he knew, around the world, who'd be watching this right now.

Then he stood, bottle in hand.

"Get me another too," Gerard said, eyes fixed on the screen.

"I'm not coming back in."

Ger shot him a keen look. "I'm tallying every million-dollar bomb, bro. I need to know just exactly where the fuck my tax money's going."

"Me too," Natalie declared, sitting forward, staring furrowed-forehead at the display. "This is happening in our name, like it or not."

Tyler didn't have the stomach, though he knew it was wiser to comprehend the extent of things than shy from them. But there were times when the extent of things could not be faced because their reality was too annihilating.

He thought suddenly of his mother's father, dead five years now. Ouri was an Egyptian Jew who'd made a torturous escape from Alexandria at the outbreak of

261

World War Two. Alone in the States, trying his energetic hand at real estate, he'd married a California girl who converted to Judaism at his request. Tyler thought of their unlikely union as a triumph of the proverbial melting pot.

Their bright daughter had been the light of their lives. It had been a gentle irony when she, raised in freedom from oppression, had come of age in the turbulent sixties and renounced organized religion. She'd married a blond, blue-eyed, self-proclaimed Buddhist geology student at Berkeley. Tyler's parents were well matched: they both loved the Rockies' rocks and they both needed solitude.

Tyler had a recollection of grandfather Ouri, in his garden in La Jolla; sipping sweet green tea, teaching him to count in Hebrew and Arabic—the numbers so similar Tyler got them mixed up at first. Ouri's dark eyes had twinkled as he'd stroked Tyler's head and proclaimed him a natural linguist.

What would Ouri, with his experience of Rommel and his friendships with so many Egyptian Muslims, have made of "Shock and Awe"?

Tyler took his beer outside, to the back porch, and sat on the steps. Ger and Nat lived in what felt to him like country. The night sky here was clear, filled with stars whose abstract beauty negated the allegedly precise decimation occurring on earth right now. He could almost imagine some Martian peering at a screen and remarking, "the barbarians are at it again."

He remembered feeling the same way as a grad student during the first Gulf War. Although he'd been proud of the American ferocity with which the topic had been debated in Congress, he'd turned away then, as now, from the coverage of the actual attack: it felt like bad luck to witness. *Guess I'm just not cut out to be a soldier.* Maybe the only battles he was good for were in commerce, and maybe not even in that.

It was a bad time to be looking for work in global telecom. The leads he'd thought would pan into lucrative jobs ended up being offers for more work at less pay than he'd been accustomed to at GlobeAll. A pay cut was unacceptable. He could not afford to accept less; no one would take him seriously otherwise. He was in the prime of his earning years.

The immediate options were grim. Ger had not convinced him to sue GlobeAll, a move which would have black-balled him in the industry. But just the threat of action, to Nouri, had been enough to shut Nouri up, about Nick and Tyler both. Nouri resigned just before Tyler. Tyler's telecom friends swore that his own integrity was intact in spite of the scandal, that everyone knew he was an honest broker, but their reassurances hadn't been accompanied by solid job offers.

He'd counted on the Bahrain privatization meetings turning up some international leads, but that meeting was postponed indefinitely because of the Iraq war. Bahrain's Ministry of Information had announced that it would wait for the outcome of the invasion before going ahead with its deregulation. Another casualty.

His dwindling choices left two emerging paths: being a consultant or joining a cable company. Consulting gigs were a decent if unexciting short-term option; plenty of his cohorts had made out pretty well that way. Some had landed permanent positions with the big research firms like Yankee Group or Forrester, outfits whose opinions were highly respected and whose judgments could make or break a carrier's reputation.

The cable route was one he had not given enough serious thought, beyond just liking the idea of getting away from it all on a cable-laying ship. Warm water, long sunsets, pristine beaches where the trenches were dug for landing wire. He had a feeling there was probably more to it than that, more than he wanted to know. Mark Regan had left him a couple of messages urging him to call. He supposed he might do that soon.

He'd given himself a deadline, the end of March, to come to a decision about subletting his apartment. He enjoyed the feeling of home he'd made for himself, but he could not afford four thousand a month just to look at

Manhattan going to bed every night. His funds were running low. April and May were the big moving times in the city, so he couldn't wait.

He leaned back on the stairs, bottle dangling, and stared up. Every constellation shone in perfect relief against its black velvet background. He picked out a satellite, crossing like a beacon: SAT-9. He knew the trajectories as well as he knew subsea cables. He waved, knowing the gesture was silly, enjoying the lift of spirits it gave him.

He remembered the last time he'd really looked into the night sky: with Delphine, at Versailles.

He was about to stand when he heard the back door close. He turned just as Jerry sank onto the top step above him.

"Nice out here, Uncle Ty." Jerry shook a cigarette out of a pack in his shirt pocket, lit it.

"New vice, Jerry?"

"Don't say anything."

"Oh like they can't smell it on you?"

"Don't ask, don't tell." Jerry's grin was squinted through smoke. "We have a non-disclosure agreement in our house."

Tyler had to smile at that.

"Don't you wanna see the first installment of "Shock and Awe"?"

Tyler shook his head.

"It's a special two-hour edition."

"I saw the original. This one's a lousy remake."

"Mom says you're depressed."

"Because I don't want to watch the war?"

"Dad says you need a kick in the ass."

Sounded like G. Tyler slumped back on his elbows, closed his eyes.

"You know how Guillaume and I've been IM-ing? He says his mom's moping around too. She's raggin on him and his cousin all the time to clean stuff up. She's all like, mad and shit, cause I guess his dad's not coming back."

His cigarette hit the bottom of Tyler's beer bottle with a little sizzle. Tyler opened his eyes.

"Guy says that about his mother?"

"Yeah. He's coming here this summer, he's sick of it over there."

For one distracted, amused moment Tyler thought about anti-globalist Guy coming to the U.S., the great Satan, belly of the beast. "What's the attraction here?"

"Phish tour, *duh*," said Jerry. "He says hi to you, by the way, he thinks you're cool, but he asks why your e-mail was returned."

"I don't have e-mail anymore, Jerry, you know that, I only had it on my work laptop." He'd been tethered to GlobeAll for so long he'd never bothered to get his own personal computer, or his own cell phone. He should be feeling free as a bird, poised to fly out of the nest, instead of teetering on the edge, afraid to plunge forward or fall back.

"So *are* you depressed?"

He looked at the boy. Jerry had his mother's blond curls, wild instead of tamed, and his father's blue eyes, soft instead of piercing. The sweetness of his face would have been pretty but for the wicked black spike threading through his right eyebrow. Nat had a fit when he came defiantly home with it; Ger told her it was temporary camouflage and they should pick their battles. Jerry's eyes were fixed on him now, full of puzzled concern, as if he saw a stranger.

"I don't know. Maybe."

"The job thing's a drag, and you're probably freaking about money, so I get why you're not smiling anymore." Jerry leaned forward to stare closely. "But Guillaume thinks you and his mom had it goin on. Even though she's at least, like, Jeez, forty."

Tyler dropped his gaze. "Huh."

"So, you know, if that's why you're depressed, you don't have to be anymore. I mean, she's like, available now."

As if it were that easy! "Thanks for the news flash."

Jerry didn't seem put off by his dry tone. He stood up with the air of someone whose duty was done and hunched his shoulders into his jean jacket. "Getting cold out here, Uncle Ty, whyn'cha come back inside."

Tyler picked up the bottle. He'd have another, watch Jerry play some video game, listen to his latest CDs. The week here would pass. Saturday he'd get on a plane heading west. He could stay out in Colorado for awhile. He could mull this news about Delphine. Not that it really made much difference. Did it?

Jerry was still talking as they went back into the kitchen. "She's okay, didn't you think? I mean, for a fifteen-year-old kid."

"What?"

"Monique. She e-mailed me her photo," Jerry said patiently. "Lil hottie."

Tyler had learned enough about the use of reverse psychology on teenagers to let Jerry's remark pass without voicing the dismayed rebuttal that sprang to his mind. "I ... don't recall."

"But Guillaume says her mom would never let her come visit alone."

Juliette was no fool, thought Tyler.

"Ty?" Natalie called him from the front hallway. "Phone's for you."

Thirty-Nine

TYLER TOOK THE CORDLESS phone into Ger's little study and closed the door. He'd given out Ger's home number to only a couple people, for use only in dire emergency.

"Harding," he said cautiously.

"*Ahlan, ya* Tyler," said a male voice that he did not recognize, in Arabic.

"*Ahlan. Wa enta min* …?" and you're from?

"It's Youssef Hamzi, you don't remember me?"

"Youssef, *keef halek.*" How are you. He'd practically forgotten the kid in the wake of GlobeAll's scandal. He wanted to ask how he'd gotten this number.

"*Alhamdulillah.* I hope they blow that bastard Saddam into the hell where he put other people all these years." Many Kuwaitis were enthusiastic members of the "coalition of the willing."

"I'm sorry we won't be seeing each other in Bahrain, Youssef."

"And I'm sorry to bother you at home. Your assistant Aziza gave me the number. She was reluctant, but I insisted."

"Yes?" What the hell time was it in Paris, anyway, four a.m.? "Where are you calling from?"

"I'm calling from Istanbul." Tyler counted ahead, force of habit. It was eight in the morning, Turkish time.

"We're ready to light the fiber here."

"Oh, right."

"I signed off on the purchase order forms and e-mailed them to your office. I just confirmed the sale with your assistant."

"I don't work for GlobeAll any more."

"I realize, I heard that, but I wanted to let you know anyway, that you did us a very great favor and we don't forget. We know how much demand there is in Turkey right now. Our customer needs this fiber to support the water consortium. You know, that new pipeline construction."

He'd assumed as much, when Hamzi asked for the fiber during the meeting where Delphine appeared. Six European and Near Eastern companies were collaborating on a pan-Caucasus water project. It had been a no-brainer to honor his first promise to Hamzi rather than give in to Lionel Burke's unpleasant brokerage of StoneEdge's demands. But now he wondered why this simple transaction warranted a personal call.

Youssef went on, "Usually, I know, a salesperson gets a commission on this kind of deal. It would be a good commission. GlobeAll's making a lot of money out of us."

"And ..."

"And we think you deserve the commission."

"That's GlobeAll's responsibility, not FranceFon's." Not that he would ever see another commission penny from GlobeAll. His resignation hadn't been taken easily, in spite of Nouri's threatened investigation.

"I know. But it's something the group decided on here. We appreciate all the effort you put into the alliance work."

"I didn't get us an agreement," Tyler reminded him wryly.

"Not that time, no, but you know there's another opening now that GlobeAll isn't declaring bankruptcy." This was true. Telecom companies' attention span appeared to be as deep as the average toddler's: in spite of the bitter rivalries that plagued the industry, everyone was

PRIVATE LINES

quick to forget past transgressions, once resolved, in favor of new partnerships.

"Tyler, we know what happened wasn't your fault. In fact we were wondering if you'd ever consider coming to work here."

"For FranceFon."

"Yes."

The world's a funny place, he thought, not for the first time. "Sure, Youssef, I'll send you my resume, but you already have a North American alliance broker."

"Delphine de la Plante? She's moving into another position."

"What's she doing now?"

"She's going to be with the Foundation. It suits her background better."

"Huh."

"So anyway, where should I send this check?"

"It's really not necessary."

"It's already budgeted. Would you prefer a wire transfer?"

"Tell you whu-ut," he said slowly, thinking, lapsing unconsciously into an old Westernism, "why'ncha make it out to the salesperson who really gave up this fiber."

"That's ... not you?"

"Her name's Catherine Emerald. She's on an account that wanted this right after I gave it to you, so I wouldn't approve it for her to sell. I'm not sure of her address but send her check to me, in dollars, please. I can get it to her."

"You're sure?"

Tyler thought about their last conversation: Carly's mom was too sick for her to leave Milwaukee. The job situation couldn't be good, not with those assholes Miller and Burke breathing down her neck about this fiber deal they wanted for StoneEdge. *Stone Age, really, solving political problems with arms instead of diplomacy.* He'd told her not to worry, but he could imagine, as tight as things were even for someone with his creds, how limited the choices would be for Carly when she came back from her leave.

269

He figured the check would be at least fifteen thousand; the deal had been worth over a million. "Yeah. Send it."

"Done. Shoot me your resume. I'm in New York next month, let's talk."

"*Shukran, ya* Youssef."

"*Shukran aleiki.*" Thanks to you.

There was a strange unsought symmetry to things sometimes.

He called Aziza at the office to leave her a quick voice-mail. He was surprised when she picked up.

"Hey, Aziza. What are you still doing there?"

"Tyler, hello, how nice to hear your voice," she said sweetly. "I had some things to finish up." He felt, belatedly, guilty. The workload had probably doubled with his absence. At least she might get a promotion out of it. If GlobeAll management was smart they'd name her right away.

"I hope all's well with your family?" He remembered that her ancestral home was not far from the Iraqi border.

"Thank you for thinking of them. Everyone is nervous, but we have to trust, don't we, the bombers know where the targets are."

"You mean who, this time," he said. It was no secret: Iranians expected to be next.

"I would like to think you called just to wish me well," she said lightly, with a hint of the laughter that he'd enjoyed getting glimpses of sometimes.

"Of course, I did, but I also just got off the phone with Youssef Hamzi."

"I am sorry he disturbed you at home. He was very adamant," she began.

"It's cool, you did the right thing. I just wanted to make sure his order was complete."

"Turkish Tel promises they'll get the local circuit delivered next week. Of course, you know them. They'll use what's happening right now as an excuse to take their time."

He laughed, tickled to be caught up once more in PTT-bashing. "I remember."

"But no worries for FF, their line will be installed on time. Youssef's office should have been notified by Global Implementation already."

"I'm actually calling to ask you a favor, look up GlobeAll in Wisconsin for me."

"Of course."

Within seconds he had written down the Milwaukee sales office address. "Thanks again, Aziza. I'll let you go, it's late, but tell me when they name you Director, okay? And you know you've got my support if you need a reference."

"Okay, Tyler." She sounded hesitant. "I wonder, do you think, would you be able to have dinner with me some night when you're in town?"

This was not entirely unexpected.

He'd sensed some hero-worship in her, toward him, from the beginning when he'd first hired her. He'd mentored her into a fairly important position. He'd known she'd go far at GlobeAll if given the opportunity and he'd been happy to promote her. She was bright, easy-going, and politically astute. She was pure pleasure to look at: liquid dark eyes, glossy hair, that beguiling shy laugh that lit her features. He'd scrupulously avoided eliciting her lovely laugh on purpose, or returning any of her warm glances.

He was accustomed to speculative interest from women. He'd learned, at work, to lower his gaze, and be terse, unless he was making a deal. But sometimes he forgot to be guarded, forgot to check if someone was really listening and catching on or if they were making eye contact to send some other signal which he, caught up in the idea under discussion, excitedly staring back, might not correctly interpret. He wondered if he'd inadvertently done that with Aziza. He took a careful breath.

"Great idea! In fact, I told Youssef that we could all get together next month when he'll be in town. It'll give you the chance to revive the alliance talks with him before the Global Traffic Meeting in May, when you'll meet the rest of their team."

He waited through a pause, hoping she was sophisticated enough to appreciate that he was opening one door for her while keeping another firmly shut.

"Yes, that would be … useful. Thank you." She sounded a little disappointed, but aware. Good. Unless she had some fabulous job offer for him, in which case he was now a major asshole.

"Aziza?" he backpedaled, soft. "Thanks for asking. I want to stay in touch."

"There's something else. I meant to tell you in a letter."

"Mmm?"

"It's bad news, Tyler, I'd prefer to say this to you in person."

He sat up straight. "What is it? I like to hear bad news right away."

"It's BK."

He felt cold.

He'd forgotten about BK, stricken with some strange pneumonia.

Since quitting GlobeAll, he hadn't thought about anyone but himself, really, moping in misery as if his was the world's only. He knew what she was going to say. Everyone knew about SARS now. The latest scourge, among so many sudden ones, for the erstwhile unafraid international businessperson.

"Don't tell me," he said abruptly. "I don't want bad news after all tonight."

Silence.

"Give me his family's address."

"I knew this would upset you." There was a short pause. "When you're in the city again, tell me, and we'll have a little gathering for BK. A remembrance. Anyway we've been wanting to see you, all of us."

Hot shame chased through the cold massing inside him around BK. He'd fled his group, each of whom he'd hand-picked and mentored, without a backward glance. He'd been their touchstone and he'd let them down. "Of course, Aziza. I'll come in on Thursday. Will that be enough time to get the gang together? We can meet for lunch, or drinks, or whatever you think. On me."

"Drinks. I'll tell everyone."

"Done. I'll see you at the usual place." He hung up.

Their conclusion did nothing to alleviate the heaviness of BK's death; choking his throat like salt filling a shaker. BK's wife was expecting their first child. He'd need to collect a donation of some sort. He stared at the wall.

A few minutes later Ger came in and found him there, heard his news, put another beer in his hand and sent him to Jerry's room.

"You need to be around the next gen, bro, absorb the positive vibe." He leaned down and stared at Tyler. "Imagine your friend's energy around you both."

For once his brother's glibness did not irritate him. He went to find Jerry.

Forty

AFTER FOUR DAYS, the mostly female crowd on Blue Mound Road was grieved out. The garbage was taken away, kitchen scrubbed, dishes washed, cupboards replenished, refrigerator filled. The three small bedrooms were completely cleaned, sheets changed. The errant pipe-burned and wine-spilled spots in the living room were strategically covered by re-arranging the furniture. The rug was vacuum-tracked.

Rebecca's wish list of willed possessions was given out to every giftee in a last-night "closing ceremony" no less punctuated in equal measure, by laughter and tears, than the funeral had been. The CD and LP collection was thinned after the give-aways; the remainder was dusted and alphabetized. Flowers were taken to the local hospital along with the wheeled oxygen tank, its long plastic lifeline drooping sadly, ineffective, over the handle. The driveway emptied.

"You need a kitten," Emma stated, looking around the spotless space after the last of the tribute-payers had left. She stood with Carly in the living room.

"No."

Emma looked at her. "You *do*," she repeated.

Carly sat down. Exhaustion whomped her like a rogue wave. "Nah. I'm a lousy caretaker." As soon as she said this her eyes filled with tears again, how could she still have any left? She bent her head and let them roll down unchecked.

"Hon." Emma sat beside her and rubbed her shoulders briskly.

"I sh-sh-should have gotten hospice—"

"I'm putting you to bed." Emma pulled her up and walked with her, hugging tight, to the room Carly had repossessed on her return.

"You know I'm right."

"Stop."

Carly tumbled headfirst into the pillow as if diving into that awful rogue wave, and felt Emma's strong hands tucking the eyelet bedspread around her. She gave in.

"See you in the morning." Emma gave her a final pat.

She awoke with the stain of dawn blushing across the white counterpane. They'd taken every curtain to the drycleaner or to the garbage. The windows sparkled. It was unnatural but nice. Rebecca would have loved the re-do, would have given pointers from her La-Z-Boy.

Carly should have been here more often, this last year, to keep things up and keep Mom company. She should have ... but her mind ran out of shoulds and the familiar tears did not prickle. She was wrung dry. She stared at the ceiling and began to take stock.

She had the house, and it was a sturdy little house in a decent neighborhood. Almost paid off. Relatively low taxes: Wisconsin had an excellent educational system but did not dun its homeowners unnecessarily. She could afford to stay here if she went back to work soon.

Her position at GlobeAll was guaranteed by the Family Medical Leave Act— thank you, Bill Clinton. But she wouldn't go back to the StoneEdge account. Her replacement was doing fine with it, she'd heard, was mining the base with the guy who'd taken Julian's position at StoneEdge UK after he'd quit. Apparently they'd found a way around the Turkish fiber issue.

She could take a regular sales job at the office here, keep working for Dudley. She'd get her suits out of storage and make one of the bedrooms into an office. It could be a comfortable life. She had friends, and she could meet men again, once she was over this blue period and her sexual attachment to Francisco. He'd come to the funeral, sober in black, no jewelry for once, and even in her anguish for Rebecca she'd felt a sting of yearning when he folded her close for a brief consoling embrace. She'd get over it.

She could concentrate on work. She'd have accounts whose requirements would be mostly domestic. OC12s here and there, lots of lower-level bandwidth, wireless, local where GlobeAll was local. It would be complex enough to be somewhat interesting. She could imagine the IT departments she'd work with, the CIOs she'd have to cajole, the internal Finance hurdles she'd have to leap to get the clients what they wanted.

Selling domestic might even feel kind of exotic for awhile. Spokane to St. Louis. San Francisco to Savannah. It was a huge country, after all, plenty of interesting local access and capacity challenges. Terrestrial challenges. Landlocked. She'd miss the transoceanic ones.

Transoceanic subsea cables were the mainstay of global telecom. She could picture the ropy lengths swaying gently on the sea beds of the planet, buried wherever possible, weighted down where not, undisturbed but for the occasional curious sea animal—at the lowest depths they would be nearly transparent, brief veins of color showing through their bodies like lava-lamp trails—or a hungry shark attracted to the gummy oil-based covering which protected the copper skin wrapped around the thin optical fiber.

Miles of this encircled the globe multiple times; competition ensured many diverse routes were available. The cables were heavy with electrical repeaters which pushed the light signals through the fiber at precise intervals throughout their length. The cables were laid by subcontractors of conglomerates of consortiums of a mish-mash of hugely profitable global holding companies It all boiled down to a relatively small number of ships and people. There were perhaps six hundred active individuals laying cables right now, she supposed.

What had become fascinating to her, while working the international side of StoneEdge, was this vision of mundane telecom traffic plunging into the romantic unknown, traversing the mysterious depths of the subsea system, where science and wizardry coexisted to enable a marvelous amalgam of service delivery, to the most boring office spaces imaginable on either end. It was rote yet miraculous. It was taken for granted and yet there was triumphant if unheralded power in every transaction. PFM: she believed it *was* magic. Domestic just didn't have that same pull for her.

She missed her global account team conference calls. She'd usually held them at six a.m. central U.S. time, clutching her first cup of joe, huddled on her couch with her land line, while the European team sat properly in their mid-day cubes, and the Asians hung in their only private space at home, usually the bathroom, except for the Australians who would invariably be at some late-night bar. She tried to keep her calls short and to the point, but over the three years' of her StoneEdge account management they'd all become friends and shared bits from their personal lives. Occasional videoconferencing and two annual meetings, with their StoneEdge counterparts, had increased this sense of camaraderie.

She knew Fiona in London, Edwin in Amsterdam, Yakov in Tel Aviv, BK in Singapore, Karima in Cairo, Nisit in Mumbai and George in Melbourne as well as she knew Suze in Milwaukee. Weekly updates kept them current with StoneEdge and with each other. She suddenly wondered if she should maybe call in to check that all was well.

Was it Wednesday? That was when she held her calls, and she'd insisted that her replacement keep the same time on everyone's calendars and the same call-in information so nobody could use her absence as an excuse to miss a meeting. StoneEdge expected their network to run as uneventfully and as powerfully as the tides. GlobeAll had to make it seem like a natural phenomenon.

277

She saw that it was early enough, certainly, to get in on the call if she wanted to. But of course it made no sense for her to join; she was no longer their global account team lead. She'd given that up the moment she'd left her office, after that final confrontation with Lionel.

She turned restlessly in bed, feeling the empty cleanliness of the post-funeral house surround her, feeling the emptiness of her life beginning to nibble unkindly at the edges of her awareness. She wished she'd been able to sleep longer. Was this what waking up would feel like from now on?

She got up, dressed in sweats, and quietly left the house.

As she strode around the neighborhood she forced ideas of renewal, rebirth, and renaissance into her head.

It didn't work.

What started to work, slowly, was the movement of huge puffy clouds against the dawn—alligators, cartoon figures, a map of England complete with banners flying and then dissolving, insubstantial wisps, into the blueing and pinking sky.

Clouds were a staple in telecom chalk-talk presentations; engineers and salespeople were always drawing them hastily and pointing to all kinds of lines that went into and out of "the cloud" by which they meant the network.

The magnificent show above her now was so gorgeous that she found herself smiling, thinking of how Rebecca, uplifted there, would enjoy their formations. She'd be sailing, no doubt, on some Swan Lake-type config, surrounded by devoted attendants, snowflakes floating around, half-cupping her hand in a royal wave.

Carly pictured a celestial configuration as clearly as she'd drawn many a network diagram: dedicated private lines from her to her mother in the cloud, with separate dotted lines linking Rebecca to other connections, friends, critical-mass memories. Hubs and spokes. Any-to-any. Multi-cast. Like all great unconditional loves.

She sagged against a bench. She wished she'd brought a portable CD player. She suddenly wanted to hear one of her favorite walking songs, Phish's "Taste." She liked it because it reminded her of telecom fiber optics, seeing through the lines, but right now it seemed to indicate how closely tied she was to her mother, how their mutual regard would permeate time and space into whatever Carly made of her future: home, career, marriage, children—or none. Thirty-two felt young to lose a mother but fifty-four was *way* too young to lose a life.

She wondered again, for the hundredth time in hundreds of days, whether if she'd convinced Mom to give up smoking it might have made a difference. Eked out a few more 'quality' months or years. Prolonged the wasting-away. In the next thought she repeated to herself what made so much sense when said by Emma or Wander or Sara: "She was too sick to live. It was her time to go."

She raised her head. The wind had eased. The sky had quit its psychedelic contortions. She stood, and walked slowly back toward Blue Mound Road.

Forty-One

EMMA WAS POURING A CUP of coffee when Carly came through the back door. She looked up, smiling, and poured another. The scent of baking filled the small kitchen and a steaming platter sat in the middle of the table.

"I made blueberry muffins," Emma said. She sat at the table, indicating the place opposite her for Carly.

Carly sipped and nibbled gratefully.

"Good run?" Emma's tone was casual but her eyes surveyed Carly closely.

"Mmm," Carly mumbled, mouth full of warm muffin.

"I'm leaving, but you know I'm nearby whenever you need me." Emma lived in Appleton, a picturesque town a couple of hours north, a paper-mill community which time seemed to forget, flourishing in every economic season.

"I'll be okay, Emma, you don't need to worry about me. I'll call you right away if I get to feeling too blue." She said this because she knew Emma expected to hear it, but also because she hoped it would be true.

"Okay." Emma's smile relaxed.

Half an hour later Carly stood in the driveway, waving as Emma's Volvo purred off down the street. It was mild for the end of March; the air heady with a hint of spring, the trees' swaying softened by the fuzz which greened their limbs.

She nodded to the mail carrier who came puffing up the porch stairs to hand Carly a rubber-banded stack of mail. She took it inside and sorted through over another cup of coffee. There were so many sympathy cards she'd have to devote an entire day to respond. She'd have to notify those few clients who still corresponded with proposed decorating projects. There were magazines whose subscriptions she'd have to cancel, although it would give her a pang to coldly dismiss *Mother Jones* and *Ramparts*. She wouldn't tell Wander.

There was a large envelope of mail from her office, which she sliced open without curiosity, out of a sense of duty. One piece was hand-addressed to her and bore the GlobeAll New York headquarters return. She looked at it for a moment, wondering if news of her mother's death had reached HQ and a corporate HR drone was sending some boilerplate condolence card.

Dear Carly,

this is yours, for the sale of that Turkish fiber, which would have gone to StoneEdge if I hadn't given it to FranceFon first. I hope all's well with you and that you're able to spend some quality time with your mother. Give me a call if you feel like it. I always enjoy our talks. By the time you get this I'll be in Colorado so use this number.

Best regards, Tyler Harding

His handwriting was just like him, black bold slashing. There was a check folded inside the envelope, she saw, a FranceFon check for seventeen thousand five hundred dollars. She held it, reading the amount over until it became meaningless, knowing it would safely cushion her so that she could take her time deciding what to do next, knowing it but not really believing.

She reached blindly for the phone and dialed the number he'd penned. Colorado! So he was really going to be a tour guide. She thought of life vests, rubber boats, red rock canyons.

"Harding." But it was an older voice than Tyler's, and she hesitated.

"Yes?" It was an impatient demand.

"Hi, sir, I'm looking for Tyler Harding?"

The handset was dropped with the usual negligent clatter that made everyone in telephony wince. "Tyler!" The older voice sounded a faint yodel, already fading, already having lost interest in the caller.

"H'lo." This was Tyler's voice, but slower, lower, lackadaisical.

"Tyler, hello, it's Carly Emerald."

There was a pause as if he was trying to remember who she was. "*Carly*," he said then, in the same mellow tone. "Hey."

"I got this ... check?" She looked at it again, on Rebecca's gold-lozenge-flecked, chrome-banded Formica table that one of the friends had insisted would make a bundle on eBay and which was why Rebecca had kept it. "You sent me a check," she repeated.

"You earned it, am I right? With that DOD spook, what was his name, Lionel? What a creep." He sounded amused. "Least I could do." His exhalation gusted toward a laugh. "Carly Emerald. How the heck're you?" She pictured him in worn jeans and a faded blue work shirt, tilting back a chair, putting up booted feet, nudging with a long forefinger some huge-brimmed hat from his black hair, settling in for a long chat, somewhere in Colorado.

"I don't know how I am. My mom ... she died last week." No matter how often she'd had to say this, it didn't get easier. She still didn't know how to say it without shivering as if it were sacrilege, the worst bad luck. Step on a crack. But if the crack was already crossed, too late.

"*Carly*." His voice, urgent as she'd first heard it with Julian Trent, was loud now in her ear. She pictured his chair jolted upright, boots planted, hat forgotten on the floor as he hunched over the phone. "I am sorry to hear that."

She closed her eyes, listened to his voice as if he were next to her.

"And I'm sorry you have to tell me on the phone. That must be so hard." She heard him sigh. "I'm sure it's not something you can ever get used to saying."

"No."

"What do you need most right now?" he surprised her by saying.

"Talk to me," she surprised herself by saying.

"Yeah. Okay." The cowboy re-appeared. "I've spent the last two weeks hiking with my Dad. He does geological surveys, so there's a lot of tramping around and stumbling over rocks. Studying geodes. And getting blisters."

Her laugh sounded unfamiliar to her.

"But it's beautiful. I'm glad to be here." His tone changed. "Tell me about your mother."

Because his chatter had succeeded in relaxing her, she was able to talk about how her week had been. She was even able to recount, for him, some of the funnier aspects of the Rebecca-fest that had occupied the little house.

"Sounds like she would have enjoyed every minute."

"Mmm." She hoped this was true.

"So what's next for you now, Carly? Or is it too soon to ask?"

"I need to think about it, but your check makes it easier to take my time. Thank you."

"*Your* dues earned it, not mine," he said, sounding for a moment as brusque as the first Tyler she'd met. "What kind of options are you looking at?"

She enumerated: stay in the house and work for GlobeAll, stay in the house and work somewhere else in Milwaukee, sell the house and take some other kind of chance.

"You want some global contacts?"

Global contacts. Did she have the strength to muster a confident face in front of potential international telecom employers?

"Doesn't have to be connected to Shock and Awe, either, Carly, I remember how you feel about that. Plenty of PTTs are looking to expand in the States right now, you know, since U.S.-based telecoms aren't attractive anymore to rest-of-world clients. I could put in a word."

"I'm not in the mood to be very impressive right now, Tyler, I don't know if I'd do your word credit."

After a pause he said, "Sorry. I asked too soon."

"No, I'm thinking along these lines, I'm just not at specifics yet, so when I got this check I thought, wow, now I can put off this decision a while longer. So I called you." She let herself slide down in her chair, reached to sip her coffee.

"I'm glad you did. I wondered how you were doing."

"So, what about you? Are you on vacation with your parents out there? Looking for tour guide gigs?"

He laughed. "They live here. I'm visiting for awhile."

"I thought you'd be roughing it on the rapids by now, saving tourists and collecting tips."

"I could, if I really wanted to."

He sounded very sure of this. She concluded, "You visit often, then?"

"I grew up here."

"I thought you were a city slicker!"

"I put on a good act."

"I remember! So what news do you hear of GlobeAll?"

"Same thing you do, probably. The company will come back clean as a whistle."

"Everything forgotten?"

"And forgiven. Bankruptcy. It's better than Confession, for business in The Zeroes." His wry tone was, again, like the man's she'd first met. "Or "the uh-oh's", that's a new one I just heard from some GlobeAll-ists."

They shared a laugh. "You don't sound sorry to be away from it."

"No. This break's been really good for me. I feel like I'm thinking clearly for the first time in years. Clearly enough to plan my next steps carefully."

"That's wonderful, Tyler."

"You should come out here," he said, surprising her. "Come for a week and get some fresh air. Take some walks. See the stars."

She imagined walking side by side on some moonlit mountaintop with him. She saw, anew, his captivating face, and felt herself blushing, hot as if she were actually in the room with him. He was probably even better looking in person, in his well-worn Rocky Mountain cowboy clothes, hair tousled, grin easy. She was amazed to be feeling this flash of embarrassed lust, in this otherwise low-key conversation, in the midst of her mourning—what was *wrong* with her! They'd been talking so casually, like longtime friends, that she'd forgotten the fierce attraction to him she'd felt initially.

When she didn't respond he said, "Hey. Carly ..." he laughed a little, sounding embarrassed too. "I just had the thought that, you know, maybe you could use a change of scenery. But it's probably too soon for you. And you probably have other family, friends you need to see."

She found her voice. "I think I need to hang out here for awhile. But thanks for thinking of me. Maybe a little later." Maybe never. She wasn't sure she could trust herself to be friends with him in person, if she was going to have this strong a reaction to what was just his simple gesture of hospitality. She finished brightly, "It sounds like a great idea for summer."

"You're welcome anytime. Just let me know and I'll tell my folks." He sounded friendly, still, but a little distant now. I blew it, she thought.

"So, what else have you been doing?" She kept it light.

"Looking for work, finding a tenant for my condo, reconnecting with my family."

"Tell me about them."

"I've been here a couple weeks, first extended time in years, seeing my parents. They're both in geology, but Mom's into gemstones and crystals and Dad's into the hard science. They love to argue." His affectionate chuckle made her feel lonesome for that kind of connection. "You'd like them, Carly," he went on, warming her with his easy inclusion. "My brother Ger lives in Greenwich, so I spent some time with him earlier this month. Caught up on new music with my nephew, Jerry. He turned me onto the Hives."

"Funny, so did ... my mom." She tightened her grip on the handset, remembering Rebecca asking her to change the Hives CD. That had been almost the last thing her mother had said. The gold lozenges on the table were blurring. Her throat closed.

"Tell you whu-ut," Tyler said in her ear, slow and amiable, "when you're ready? I don't mean right now but sometime, you'll probably know when, go put on her favorite music, maybe light a couple candles, have a glass of wine, and listen to her music like she's there with you. When you're ready. Maybe with a friend nearby."

He sounded just like Wander! "How do you know?"

"I'm just guessing. Trying to put myself in your shoes."

"Thanks for understanding." She put his distracting face out of her mind, and declared, "Tyler, I'm glad we met."

"So am I, Carly. It's been awhile since I had time to make a new friend." The hint of sadness in his voice sounded like sympathy to her.

"Me too. Our jobs don't make it easy, or I should say, they didn't."

"I've been thinking about that. I didn't make time for a lot of important things, because I was too busy chasing. I let my work be my life." He sounded as if this were still surprising to him.

"What do you think you left out?"

There was a pause as if he were really considering the question for the first time. But his answer was so calculatedly humorous that she knew he wanted to make light of it, at least for now. "I never got a dog."

She could not help laughing. "A dog! Not a family!"

"Is that what you want?"

"I do. I'd make a good mother." As she said that word the lozenges started blurring again.

He let a moment pass before answering, "And meanwhile, Carly, you've birthed all these great global networks for StoneEdge." He laughed. "Think of it that way. Telecom midwifery."

She sniffed, watching the lozenges solidify, listening.

"I'd like to have a family too someday," he went on. "But all my creativity, so far, was for GlobeAll. I had a hell of a ride! I don't regret it, really, except for the dog—not a minute of it. I hope you don't?"

"No. I loved the challenge of figuring out all the aspects. It was like a game I played every day, trying to get the pieces aligned. I miss it."

His warm answering laughter vibrated down the phone line. She envisioned its traversing the local Central Office in, where was he? Boulder? It wasn't a Denver exchange, she would have recognized the 303; switching at the Local Exchange Carrier, probably GlobeAll's since Tyler as an employee would have gotten a discount; winding back down into her local SBC loop in Milwaukee.

"Where are you, exactly?" she couldn't help asking.

"My folks' house, just north of Telluride."

"Where the ... ?" she laughed. "PFM, Tyler, you know what that means?"

"It means I can call you from some of the country's highest mountains and get good reception. How many COs you think we're crossing? What kinda lines?" Just like a phone person, she thought, hearing the amusement in his voice.

"Must be some of ours. GlobeAll's got a pretty decent domestic footprint."

"We're on Sprint right now. Theirs is more robust out here."

"Sprint!" The horror, using a competitor's network.

"My parents' house, okay, not my decision."

"Didn't they show any family loyalty?"

"Tried that. GlobeAll was too expensive for them. They said."

"Ouch."

"But what the hey, I'm not bleeding for GlobeAll anymore."

He was tilting on the back chair legs again now, she was sure, grinning into the phone with a glint in those deep blue eyes. She added silver studs to chambray shirt in her vision, and fine tooling to his boots. Irresistible. She recalled his saying he'd just broken up with someone about the same time as she had with Francisco. She wondered if he had a new girlfriend yet. Should she ask him?

But suddenly he morphed into the sober slickmeister again. "Carly. Are you using the same GlobeAll e-mail address while you're on leave? I can get these global contacts to you, when you're ready."

"Yes, I'm still using it."

"I'm wondering, d'you think you'd like working for the subsea division of Cable & Wireless Marine? I met a guy wants to hire somebody fast, for a marketing job. It'd be a short stint, but interesting. Pays well."

Had he read her mind? "I don't know anything about sailing," she hedged, joking.

"He needs someone who knows the business end of transport. Someone who knows global networking. He wants a salesy observer of a cable lay to do some promo."

"What about you? I thought you were interested in FLAG?"

"The industry fascinates me, but I don't want a marketing job."

"So where are they laying the fiber?"

"Next dedicated landing's in Newfoundland."

"Brrr."

"In July. Right now they're still mid-Atlantic."

"Pretty slow-going."

"Gotta make sure it's all weighed down, you know how they have to track every centimeter. And they've got a layover in Iceland coming up next month. Switching point. That's where he needs someone to board."

"Sounds like you're the one who needs to go, Tyler, I can hear the wanderlust in your voice."

His laugh rippled in Rebecca's little kitchen. She still couldn't think of it as hers. "I am finally learning to slow down some, and although it would be a kick, certainly, to sail on a cable ship, I need at least another month here to chill. And this guy needs someone now. His name's Mark Regan. So, if you feel ready, I'll tell him about you."

She looked around at the silent, clean kitchen, the square little yard out the window, the humble garage. She envisioned the familiar streets beyond, emptied of meaning by Rebecca's absence. She thought of Dudley and Dave, the corporate park, her old twisted phone cord. She remembered Lionel.

"Sure, give him my name. What have I got to lose?"

"What have you got to gain? Maybe some fun."

"You think?"

"I'll be sailing along with you, vicariously, and your Mom will be too." The smile in his voice buoyed his words, beyond encouragement, into conviction.

"You'll be tromping around the Rocky mountains."

"Thinking of you dodging icebergs."

Was he flirting? She felt bold enough to ask, "When will we meet?"

"Come here before you sail. We'll tromp around together."

She didn't think he was flirting, she realized with some disappointment, he was being friendly. But friendly was good. "I'd like to meet you, Tyler."

"We'll meet. If now isn't convenient then some other time. Meanwhile you can think about a change in direction, if you're ready."

"What makes you think I have what he's looking for?"

"I'm a pretty good judge of professional character."

"What makes you so sure he'd hire me?"

"I'll recommend you. Highly. If you want."

"But I'm a woman."

"Well, yeah," he said slowly. "I certainly noticed that." *Was* he flirting?

"There aren't too many in cable-laying."

"Don't tell me that intimidates a strong person like you? Someone who faced down Julian Trent on a daily basis? Nah. I don't believe it."

289

She pictured herself the lone female, on some hulking barge in mid-ocean, surrounded by menacing waves and horny foreign men and immense coils of steel-coated cable. Of course, that about described any job in global telecom: substitute office cube for barge, anxiety waves for those of water, add a few intrepid women. The cable, unchanged, was always there, as were the horny men. None of the rest of it would be there otherwise, she supposed.

"You think they'd expect me to cook?"

He just laughed.

"What if I don't want to be beholden to you?"

There was another short pause.

"We—ell, Carly," he said finally, old sage to young upstart, "sometimes career advancement is about knowing, and promoting, effective people. So how could *you* be beholden to *me*? It's the other way round. You make a great candidate, so you make me look good for recommending you."

She could not argue with this logic.

"*And someday, maybe, who knows, baby, I'll come and be cryin to you,*" he crooned suddenly, melodic as Rebecca had been; the line was not an easy one to sing.

"I know that song. Bob Dylan."

"You may be able to do me a favor some day, is all I'm saying."

She studied the golden lozenges. "I'll be glad to do you a favor, Tyler."

"I'll talk to him, and send you his details, and you can take it from there."

Forty-Two
Washington D.C.

S TRANGE TO BE SOLO at the annual Washington D.C. Global Traffic Meeting, for the first time in ten years without GlobeAll's protective coloring, without any affiliation. Tyler had to pay for his own ticket and a pricey suite at the conference hotel. It was worth it, for the interview he'd set up with one of the attending companies. His badge read GUEST which meant NOBODY.

It was like being at a party where everyone recognized him but nobody remembered his name. Their gazes took him in, stopped for a moment and then, as if recalling the UTT lawsuit or just that he was unemployed and probably job-hunting, slid over and past him.

The bolder ones, and ones he'd worked with most closely, weren't as standoffish, but they all wanted to know what he was doing now. Meaning, had he found something or was he still looking, was he important to them and worth engaging in conversation, or could they pat him on the back, wish him luck and then ignore him so as to find more meaningful contacts?

He didn't blame them. He'd have behaved the same way. Nobody had time to waste on nonentities. There was capacity to be planned, fiber to be haggled, funding to be secured for cable buildouts, a million crucial deals to be made in only four days and nights. And with the hysteria of war, and its related disruptions and opportunities, this meeting had an urgency to it unlike any he'd felt before.

All the mobile carriers were frantically schmoozing the few DOD reps standing around, lobbying at the eleventh hour, trying to position themselves for the Request for Proposal being let shortly to construct a mobile network in Iraq. Rumor had it the bulk of the project would go to MSI, soon to emerge clean from recent scandals, propped up by government guarantees. The other carriers were bitter, full of venom but hiding it well, scrubbing their contact rosters to see who they knew at MSI and what subcontracting arrangements they could make.

It felt strange, but he was okay with it. He wasn't tired anymore. His weeks back home had been so restorative that he figured nothing could shake him. Indoors, he'd cooked with his mom, been a sounding board for his dad. Outdoors, he'd had time to hike endlessly and reflect deeply and plan well.

He looked around the grand ballroom, wondering if in the crush of hundreds he'd be able to single out those with whom he might share an enjoyable chat. He sipped his vodka—first time he'd bought his own drink at the first-night hospitality reception—and surveyed the crowd.

His distance from the hullabaloo allowed him to notice what he might have otherwise missed: the fewer carriers this year; the cheaper array of hors d'oeurves; the preponderance of white men, even as PTT reps, whereas before there had been, he was sure, more diversity and more women.

All were clear signs of the dismal economy, scandals and bankruptcies, heightened security in Washington D.C., and the decreasing affinity that worldwide telecom companies held toward the United States. There had been talk, he knew, of holding a European-carriers-only GTM in future. Like the flailing WTO, many erstwhile internationally-focused, multilateral industry and trade organizations were splitting off into regional blocs, eyeing former co-members with disaffection. All the more reason to carry out the plan he'd come up with during his mountain meditation.

A hand touched his shoulder and he turned to see Youssef Hamzi's grin.

"*Ahlan, ya* Tyler," he said.

"*Keefik, ya* Youssef!" He gave Hamzi a brief hug. "It's good to see you."

"You too." Youssef's dark eyes narrowed on him. "You look much better than when I saw you in New York. What did you do? A new kind of diet?"

"I finally got some sleep," Tyler answered. "How's life at FF these days?"

"The government's holding up its end of the IPO agreement, so everyone's still working, hopefully until the end of the year. No more strikes. *Alhamdulillah.*"

"And your Alliances group?"

"We're all here! Everyone will want to say hello to you."

"Did you hire a North American broker yet?"

"We would have hired *you*, Tyler. But it's okay. I respect your decision."

"It just wouldn't be right for me."

"Thanks for sending Aziza Bahrami our way. I'll be meeting her here for an interview tomorrow."

"I can vouch that she'd be a good fit for the job. I don't know anything about her personal situation, though, whether she'd be interested in relocating to Paris."

"I'll find out." Youssef's eyes wandered beyond Tyler, looking, he knew, to see if there was another conversation he should be joining nearby. "So, what else is new with you, Tyler?"

"*Zefir.*" Tyler smiled. Nothing.

Youssef frowned at him slightly. Having nothing new probably sounded terrible to him, like old age, or retirement, or some other kind of career death. Only losers would admit to having nothing new. "What are your plans, then?"

"I've researched where I want to be. I'll be talking to some people here."

Youssef looked him over, curious, before giving his arm a farewell pat. "Let me know if there's anything I can do for you, Tyler, I owe you for that Turkish fiber."

"You don't owe me anything."

He watched Youssef join a group of other twenty-somethings. They were probably making plans to split this boring scene and go out on the town. He remembered those nights, so many of them, but the memory evoked no nostalgia. He would never miss that frantic networking, jockeying, calculated flirting, competitive drinking and too little sleep. Let the kids have it. Who needed the anxiety?

"Tyler?" A soft, lightly accented, familiar voice, one that had a monopoly on haunting his dreams, was right next to him.

He turned. She was more beautiful than ever, in a stunning black velvet suit that molded her curves yet conveyed severe dignity. As usual, her makeup was perfect, her hair gleaming, her cream satin scarf expertly tied.

"Delphine."

She studied him with a leisure he would have found presumptuous, had they not once been intimate. Her dark eyes, lively with that little spark, roamed over every inch of him and her full red lips pursed in a twitch of pleasure that grew as she surveyed him.

"You're looking … very well," she said, low.

"You too." Her scrutiny felt so provocative that he was afraid to shake her hand, afraid he wouldn't be able to restrain himself from reaching for all of her.

She didn't hold out her hand, sparing him the awkwardness. Her smile sobered as he didn't return it. He felt a wave of dizziness and had to drop his gaze. He thought to offer artlessly, "Can I get you something from the bar?"

"That would be nice."

"What would you like?"

"What would I like?" she repeated. She laughed outright, her gorgeous body-shaking laugh, and then pulled her lips together enough to say, "Champagne, of course, is what I will drink. Thank you."

He blundered toward the bar, which was, now, as irritatingly thronged with drinkers as it had been empty before. He had to push past people, like the kind of jerk he disliked, to fight his way to one of the harried Hispanic bartenders and demand a glass of their best Champagne.

"We got only one kind open right now, mister," said the weary white-jacketed youth, eyeing Tyler with suspicion. "Otherwise you got to buy the bottle."

If it was Andre he'd tell her they didn't have any.

"We got Korbel."

Well, that was sort of acceptable. He glanced behind him to see that she had maneuvered herself to stand close enough to hear what he might say. He had a moment's indecision. Would a Frenchwoman think Korbel was good enough? The guy was holding up the bottle, waiting, one sleek eyebrow raised as if to condemn Tyler forever to asshole-hood in front of the entire GTM audience.

Inspiration struck. *"Que piensa senor, a ella le va a gustar?"* he asked, nodding briefly to Delphine. What do you think, would she like it?

A slow smile appeared on the bartender's face as he glanced behind Tyler to look at Delphine. *"Por ella, serra la Veuve. La Madam."* He reached below the bar and brought out a sealed bottle of Veuve Cliquot, its surface misted with cold. *"Le va a costar, mano."* It's gonna cost you. *"Cien dolares."*

Jesus! Oh, what the hell. Tyler peeled off a hundred, added twenty for a tip, and slid it toward him. *"Muchas gracias, senor, me agradesco su avicio."* Thanks, I appreciate your advice.

"Que le vaya muy bien con la dama." Hope it works out for you with her. He handed over the bottle and two flutes.

"Is there any language you don't speak, Tyler?" She was smiling, pressing close enough to his arm that he could feel the contour of her breast underneath the soft velvet.

"Let's find a quiet corner to drink this, hmm?"

"Is there one here?" She laughed.

He looked into her eyes. She was sending all the right signals. "Would you rather come to my suite?"

But she glanced away from him toward the entrance, as if looking for someone. "Well, I am not sure if—"

Okay, she wanted to flirt a little more first. "Let's just find a table, hmm?"

She led the way across the ballroom, expansive and devoid of atmosphere as a concrete sports stadium. He followed the sway of her black velvet hips.

He could make short work of this bottle. She'd looked at him as if she liked what she saw, as if their last awkward meeting was forgotten. He knew exactly how to remind her of how good they'd been together. And his suite was so well suited to seduction. There was a fine view of the Capitol, there was a Jacuzzi in the huge tub, there was a great big bed they could roll all over.

He managed to recall how to behave just in time to pull her chair out at one of the round tables set up near the corner of the giant ballroom. It was a deal-making table, not built for romance; but he knew how to improvise. He used his smoothest smile as he opened the bottle. He poured a long slide into a flute and handed it to her.

"Thank you, Tyler." She sipped delicately, eyelashes lowered. Her pink tongue slid out to lick an errant golden drop from her red lower lip.

Those lips.

He stood undone, unable even to pour himself a glass.

"It looks as though we are just in time!" Suddenly Novoa and Terrell were there, magically materializing out of the crowd to hover at Tyler's elbow, looking expectantly at the Veuve Cliquot, holding out glasses.

"Allo!" Delphine greeted them with a warm smile. "Sit down, gentlemen, join us. Tyler was just opening the wine."

He had no choice but to carry on, smiling genially, sitting to chat as if they were all still in their stuffy conference room back in Paris, like the morning he'd met her. Didier Terrell took out a pack of Gaulloise and lit one surreptitiously, glancing over his shoulder as if the tobacco police would storm over and snatch it from his mouth.

"No worries." Tyler roused from his lust stupor to tell Didier, "they know their clientele for this meeting. They relax the no smoking rules for the GTM."

"Merci." Didier shot him a grateful glance.

"Tyler, tell us all about yourself now. We heard that you were a martyr to the GlobeAll cause, sacrificing yourself for the good of the company." Novoa grinned and gulped. Tyler was obliged to pour more for him.

"Yes, Tyler, tell us," Delphine added, tilting her elegant head to one side.

He took a deep breath. "It wasn't like that, friends, sorry to diminish the drama, it was my choice to leave. I'd been thinking about it for awhile."

Their eyes fixed on him brightly, disbelieving, wanting more.

"It was time, you know, time to move on to something new? I was there ten years! Way too long." Novoa and Terrell looked away as if disappointed. Only Delphine still stared at him. He looked back at her for a moment.

"What is your something new, then, Tyler?" she asked.

"Yes, what will you do, because we heard you don't want to join us," Novoa said. "Delphine isn't pleased about that."

She dropped her eyes from Tyler's and shrugged. "I can't really move into the Foundation work until we find my replacement."

"Her husband isn't pleased either," Didier commented, tapping a long ash into his empty glass. "He told me just last night, Delphine, he still doesn't see you any more than when he was traveling. He came to the GTM this time to keep *you* company!"

He laughed, and Novoa chimed in, and Delphine smiled. Tyler was aware of the steel chair holding him upright. He reached for his flute, found it dry since he hadn't served himself, and poured in the last of the bottle. He remembered to sip, not drain.

"It's hard to be the husband of a working woman," Novoa declared. "I could never do it."

"My wife works, but only part time," added Terrell. "Tyler, you're not married, I recall?"

"No." He reached for composure, lowered his shoulders consciously, looked at her directly. "Guy must be very glad to have his father home."

"He is, yes, but he still wants to come to visit your nephew this summer. Jerry and Guy have become such close friends. I thought I will take the opportunity to call your brother or even take a quick trip to see him while I am here." She had the nerve to smile at him warmly. "Perhaps, Tyler, you would be so kind as to accompany me?"

"Surely your husband would rather go with you. My brother and his wife will be happy to host you both." He was glad he'd never admitted to G his involvement with her.

"He will be going back to France after the GTM. That's when I would visit your brother's family."

"I won't have the time," he gritted politely.

"What will you be doing? Everyone is curious to know about you." Novoa leaned forward eagerly.

Tyler spared him a glance. "I'll let you know when I get there," he said, and he managed to stand up without wobbling. "Great seeing you all again! Give my best to Nguyen!"

He made his way out of the ballroom. He remembered how to get to the elevators, what floor he was on, and which suit pocket his keycard was in. Once inside he headed to the minibar to take out another vodka but stopped himself, suddenly, remembering his interview in the morning. Thinking of that interview, the first in what he hoped would be his next adventure, he hung his suit neatly instead of flinging it onto the floor.

But he flung himself, carelessly, onto the wide bed, throwing his arms up over his head and staring at the ceiling.

Don't be such an American, he told himself. She has the right to do whatever the hell she wants, in or out of her marriage. So you still look good to her, as good as she looks to you, so what. You can just smile and move on. No harm, no foul.

He frowned.

He was seeing again the river, the snaky Colorado, which had eaten its patient way through bleeding bedrock into the heart of the canyon. He'd studied it so closely last month it was etched deep as a neuronet. Something about the persistence of that simple water had captured his stare until it was burned into him.

One other sight had struck him at home, regularly.

He watched the way crows would gather in a row, like sentries, facing in one direction on their branches as if waiting for a command. Always, two or three crows did not fall in line, did not even alight, but kept on wheeling and cawing above their brethren, choosing not to join the crowd. Something about their independence amazed him. They were blunt-brained birds like the rest, but they chose to behave differently, and the fact of their choice was baffling. They knew, somehow, they were free.

He'd mentioned his observations to his mother.

"Telluride is special, T, go with it," she'd told him. "It's a vortex, hon, stronger than Sedona. It's exerting its power on you at last. Drink it in. Enjoy. Learn."

When she talked like this, Gerard and Tyler usually scoffed.

A storm front had been moving in and the snow clouds gathered, luminous and heavy, on the mountainside behind the sprawling log structure that had been home since before he was born. He was slicing pieces of beef for stew, his mother chopping carrots.

"You think there's *meaning* in this ... vision?"

She glanced at him, steady, between slides of the big knife. She had her father Ouri's bright black eyes, his sure hands, his quick wit. "Of course, Tyler, this is why I raised you here." She only called him Tyler when she had something serious to say; usually it was T; so he knew he'd better listen up. "Pay attention," she told him sternly.

"So I can figure out how these sights relate to me? Why they're bugging me?"

"So you can stop trying to figure everything out."

Well, that was just it, she always had these Zen-like pronouncements about what most bothered him. She'd infuriated him as a teenager, amused him as a young adult. Now he found her more insightful than amusing, but her advice still puzzled him.

He was no philosopher. He didn't know how the timeless water or the autonomous crows connected to who he was becoming or all that had altered him in the past few months. He only knew that being home in the mountains seemed to be showing him it was time, in his life, to be quiet rather than loud, to watch rather than move, and to lead only when he was absolutely sure of where he'd be heading.

He let that conclusion sink into him anew, lying on his hotel bed high above the hubbub of the GTM reception still roiling in the ballroom. He let it lift the vision of Delphine and her husband away until they were mist. He let it infuse his limbs with heavy peace, a peace he knew he'd earned.

Forty-Three

"EMERALD! PHONE!"

The singsong reverberated down the dank corridor into the head where Carly had just finished vomiting. She rinsed her mouth and splashed cold water on her face from the tiny coldwater sink. There was no mirror, probably a good thing, if she had to see how nauseated she looked it might upheave her stomach again. She slapped her hands on her jeans to dry them.

She lurched toward Comms, the room whose equipment was the pulse of the barge, on shaky legs, hands splayed to the walls to keep her balance, and staggered into the makeshift booth used for crew satellite calls. The heavy handset nearly slipped through her clammy fingers.

"Emerald," she croaked, unconsciously using the moniker she was called on board the *Emperor.*

"Hey, Carly." His slow warm voice settled her. She closed her eyes, to savor it, but had to open them immediately to stop the spinning.

"Oh Tyler."

"Still seasick, huh?"

"I'm caving, Ty, I'm going to take the pills." She hadn't been willing to, before, since she'd heard they were soporifics that sapped concentration, but she couldn't concentrate like this anyway. "D'you think that makes me a wuss?"

"Nothing could make you a wuss! Do what you have to. Just don't let yourself get dehydrated. Crew still being nice?"

"They think I'm hilarious, I can tell, but they're kind."

"How's the lay going?"

"It's pretty awesome," she said, sitting up. "It's so simple, but so precise. For the first time I wish I'd studied engineering. But I'm getting a lot from the guys."

"How would you compare it with the landing?"

She thought about it. "The landing was more like a fixed process, you know? Everyone knew exactly what was supposed to happen. Feed the cable through the beach manhole, secure it inside the landing station, bolt it to the grid in the wall. Pure function. Whereas the laying—" she glanced around at the massive and minute equipment lining the walls of the Comms room— "it *should* be a science, but conditions make it an art."

"What kind of art?"

"Jocko calls it a black art." They shared a laugh. She'd told him about her Australian crewmate Jocko, enjoying his fourteenth cable lay this voyage. "It takes a lot of experience to know how the ocean floor shifts, how the wave patterns affect the ship's position, how the cable payout rate calibration depends on slack." She laughed again. "You would not *believe* how intense the discussions get about slack!"

"Gives a whole new meaning to telecom, huh."

"Remind me to *never* take it for granted."

"I don't think you ever did." His voice lowered slightly. "How're you feeling otherwise, Carly?"

She nodded as if he could see her. "This was the right move. I'm sick as a dog, of course, but I love it. It's an adventure every day out here. I can imagine Mom getting a kick out of it. I think she'd approve."

"That's good to hear."

"How about you, Ty, how's the Radium search going?"

"I've got the final interview next month."

"Which you will *ace.*"

"If you tell me more about the flaws in C&W Marine cable slack, maybe ..."

They both laughed again. "No way! I'm not helping you get a job with the competition. Even though I'm grateful you got me this one."

"I don't see it as competition, exactly. More just an ... alternative."

"Hey Ty, wouldn't it be wild if you could go on one of *their* vehicles the way I get to go on this one?"

"Just show me where to sign. I'd love it."

"You'd have to pay a lot more for these calls."

"Who says *I'm* paying?" he asked, sly. "My GlobeAll calling card was never de-activated, but I don't get the invoices. Billing error, no doubt."

"Hacker!"

"Entrepreneur, please," he corrected smoothly. "Expensive minutes on the network, hey, what's not to like? I'm still a GlobeAll shareholder, after all."

Carly's hilarity was interrupted by a friendly jab on the shoulder. Bill, one of the British engineers, was indicating that her time was up. "Second call today, Emerald, quit talking to your boyfriends and pay attention to the clock." A little lo-tech alarm clock was glued onto the table where the sat phone was affixed, reminding users not to spend more than three minutes per call. She pushed Bill away.

Tyler was laughing in her ear. "Quit talking to your boyfriends, Emerald," he repeated. "Take your pills and feel better. I'll call you again in a couple of days."

"He's not my boyfriend anymore. I told you I dumped him—"

"What?" His laughter turned into confusion. "I'm just kidding, Carly, talk to whoever you want."

What she wanted was to make this perfectly clear to him. "The guy who called me earlier this afternoon? I broke up with him in February. He wasn't convinced that I was over him, but he got the message loud and clear from me today."

"I remember," he said, careful now, "the one who wasn't ... good for you."

303

"Right. When I told you, you said you'd had a similar experience."

There was a little Tyleresque pause, the one she'd gotten used to whenever the conversation touched on his personal history. But she'd noticed the pauses were getting fewer and fewer. "So ... why wasn't he good for you?"

"He was getting strange. Sexually." A month's close quarters with twenty crewmen had made her blunt. Tyler maintained an alert silence: she could imagine his curiosity about what "strange" might mean to her; he was a guy, after all. "And I suspect he might have been married."

"Huh," he said at last. "So's the woman I was involved with."

Yet another thing they had in common! "Sucked, didn't it."

"I realized that yeah, eventually, it really would have."

"So ... I guess we just go on and learn from these mistakes, eh Tyler."

"I guess we do."

Bill poked her again, less friendly. "Time, Emerald." She made a face at him.

"Talk to you soon, Carly," said Tyler. "Drink lots of water."

Cheered, as always, by their chat, she elbowed Bill aside and went up to keep her vigil on the cable laying. The engines' churning vibration, their constant noise, their fuel stench made her more nauseous than the slow movement of the barge through the North Atlantic, but she spent most of her time on deck anyway, drawn by the hypnotic repetition of the lay. It was not only what she'd been hired to record, so as to create FUD to combat the other subsea cable companies' claims; it was what mesmerized her. She knew it powered the world's telecommunications: Pure Frickin Magic revealed.

In the center of the barge was an enormous tank where the cable was spooled. During laying, which on this voyage was almost continuous, the thickly coated cable was brought up from the tank with steady winches. Its track ran up and down, in a uniform steel design on top of the barge, so as to maintain the integrity of the cable's minimum radius of curvature. Any untoward bend or nudge could violate that, so utmost care was taken. The cable was fed, meticulously, onto the top of the injector unit.

The injector was a huge steel cleaver rigged to the side of the barge. It slid directly into the seabed: at certain geographies more than eight thousand meters down. It forced powerful streams of pressurized water downward, drilling a path for the cable, such that it could rest easily on the fluidized ocean floor.

The delicate balance between the speed of belaying out the cable and its settling was calibrated by a concise estimation of tension maintained on the cable being lowered—the famous 'slack'—as it contrasted with the speed of the ship, its position, and historic and satellitic geological mapping of the seabed.

Transoceanic cables had been in use since 1858. The PFM, Carly thought, consisted of the fine-tuning calibration performed by the wizards in Comms, who studied not only the GPS data onscreen, but that also conveyed by the two South African divers who, fearless, plunged the depths when needed to confirm, or to estimate anew, seabed geometry. She felt more respect for them than for any other workers she'd known.

Watching the slow, measured, even ponderous rolling of the cable lay, Carly could not contain a grin that erupted into an amazed laugh. There was joy in witnessing the elemental, powerful toil of human beings toward perfection, such joy that she had to swipe a few tears from her sun-scoured cheeks. As the only female on board, she could get away with this kind of sentimentality. She took shameless advantage.

Forty-Four

THE WAVES ROSE UP against the side of the ship, tilting it like a toy boat in a bathtub, rocking it to and fro as easily as if it were part of the water. Flemish Cap seas averaged about thirty feet, making the crossing one of the Atlantic's more alert for most ship captains and unbearable for any non-seaworthy passengers or cargo.

The tightly lashed coils of cable in the center tank did not move on board this particular ship, but it was obvious that belaying the cable down into the tightly calibrated pathway designated for its rest on the ocean floor presented a significant challenge. The ship was simply not able to orchestrate its movements with the precision required because it could not stand still; notwithstanding its powerful Harbormaster thruster engines, positioned at each end, which throbbed mightily to keep it steady.

In heavy seas, there was always a real danger that the anchor line, dropped at check points to stabilize the ship, would interfere: six percent of cable lay faults in the deep Atlantic were due to ship and anchor activity; a dry statistic that was in actual experience wet, chaotic, sometimes life-threatening and always expensive.

Given that submarine cable systems ran easily a billion dollars plus between hemispheres, every little hitch added up quickly and could break a subcontractor before the captain even had time to relay the bad news to the ship owner.

It was an enterprise dared only by the brave and well-funded. It was a business fraught with potential for imponderables like weather, fish bites, and fishermen who carelessly snagged fragile fiber-optic cables in their wide-net trawlers.

Repairs cost upwards of $30,000 a day, and could take weeks, as had been the case of a link between France and North Africa last summer when an earthquake hit Algiers. The regulatory environment in many emerging market countries like Algeria resulted in the existence of only one in-country provider, making cable repair even more crucial since that was usually the sole fiber link. The funders of the Algeria-France cable, FranceFon, had lost millions when frantic users had turned to their mobile phones, whose backup network ran on satellite systems.

"That's why satellite makes so much more sense," Tyler told his small audience, clicking off the video of the rocking cable ship and replacing it with a Radium clip. Now the screen showed the elegant trajectory of a long-limbed satellite, wings spread wide, moving against star-studded black space in a choreographed ballet, its path fixed, its obstacles nonexistent.

"See how clean?" he said, after they'd had a little time to appreciate the sight. "No service interruptions. No regulatory restrictions. No disturbance of ocean ecology. No weather. No bloody fishermen."

They laughed. He smiled.

"What about solar flares?" asked one.

"Minimal impact. Average measured delay less than ten minutes a year, and almost impossible to pin down to the satellite transmission itself. Even the most stringent Service Level Agreements can stand up to that."

"What about the 89 blackout in Quebec? Or Sweden, earlier this year?"

"Sun activity can't be blamed on Radium. We've engineered our birds to interact completely separately from electric grids on Earth. We've also deployed non-GPS navigation so sunstorms don't disorient us."

"What about latency?" asked another.

"What about it? We don't have any. Uplink, downlink is shorter than the average laptop log-on time. Let the end user worry about latency on their devices."

"And the regulatory issues …" began a third.

"Again, they're the end users' concern. But three months' time spent doing the required earth station feasibility and licensing in emerging markets sure beats thirty thousand dollars a day when a cable goes down. Ask any large investor. And the right in-country people can minimize that time."

"But don't all those in-country people want bribes, aren't they slow on purpose just to grease more foreign hands at Americans' expense?" complained a fourth.

"That's old-world thinking," Tyler stated. "Good IT people in emerging markets are as sharp as Americans, and a lot hungrier. And they know the Ministries! They have a shortcut to the approval process. It's in their interest to get the best service in the least amount of time. That's what builds customer loyalty and they know it."

"So how would *you* propose to use those in-country people?"

"I'd sell their expert advice as a package, call it professional services, with a separate one-time charge that could be extended for the life of the contract, like a maintenance plan. Or, to sweeten big government tenders, an in-kind contribution."

He looked around the room. "Any more questions?"

There weren't.

He let them murmur as he clicked out of his presentation, switched off his laptop and unplugged the datashow. He wound the cords neatly and packed up the case. The admin who'd hefted it into this conference room would appreciate his care, and he knew that in these lean-resource times top execs were unusually close to their admins. They all talked. This one might mention how helpful he'd been.

He quickly realized that kind of mention wasn't going to be needed. The chief negotiator and CEO, Austin

Leopold, came up and patted Tyler lightly on the shoulder.

"We all like your entrepreneurial spirit," he said. "I'm making you the offer. VP, Business Development. Reporting to me."

YES!

"Thanks for your confidence in me, Austin."

"But I'm only interested in results, you know, not quotidian details," Austin added. It meant Tyler would be almost like a general manager.

"How many direct reports?"

"Seven." Austin nodded to the group behind him, who had just watched Tyler present. "Them."

His final panel of interviewers, besides Austin, were the directors of the satellite consortium, from seven world areas, bright and vigorous and adventuresome. Tyler didn't let himself smile yet. Some newly named VPs would fight to build their own teams, but he knew this multinational bunch was the best in the business and he'd feel privileged to lead them. But he wasn't obliged to let Austin know that right away.

"How much?"

"We thought we could start you at four hundred base, variable commission."

"*Variable?*"

Austin laughed. "You drive a hard bargain."

"I'm a sales guy." Tyler grinned now.

"Variable based on performance of the regions."

"Not aggregated. Individual." He knew the risks in emerging markets, in spite of his glossy speech. He could take a hit on the separate buckets, but he didn't want his total numbers to sink or swim depending on some volatile region's shaky political, economic and regulatory future.

Austin looked at him. "Individual, okay, but it's up to you to make the regions pay out for us as a whole."

"Based on ..."

"Based on carrier acquisitions."

309

EMMA GATES

Tyler nodded. That shouldn't be a problem. Carriers were desperate for reliable backup networks, and satellite provided a cost-effective alternative.

Austin held out his hand and Tyler shook it. It was a firm but not tight grip, signifying that Austin would indeed leave him alone to do the job but be supportive when needed. "Deal. We'll have you come out to Houston next week, get paperwork signed, have you meet the rest of the crew. We'll want you to visit Chandler, too, as soon as possible, so that you can see the business from the physical layer up."

"I've been there before," Tyler reminded him. He'd met Austin years ago on the plant floor in Chandler, Arizona, when he'd been a global business grad student on a Thunderbird field trip. That afternoon had been one of the most memorable of his education, viewing rockets and satellites being built, seeing the flags from the many countries involved in the project. They'd been taken to a viewing room where old videos from the sixties space race had been shown, along with a live showing of a Russian satellite launch on behalf of the Radium consortium. Former enemies coming together to build for the future had been a heady lesson for the group to learn. Everyone had cheered when the Russian launch was successful.

"That's right, you mentioned that in our initial interview." Austin studied him. "I don't remember you from then, of course, there were so many students."

Tyler recalled Austin as a harried engineer on the glassed-off clean-room plant floor, oblivious to the awed students, striding around checking screens and clipboards in his white coat and goggles like a hi-tech doctor while his observers watched wide-eyed from behind the security-controlled viewing area. He'd muttered a brief hello to the group when he exited, and Tyler had noted his name and title for future reference. Nick Fournier had recruited Tyler to join GlobeAll before he'd had a chance to look into Radium further, and he hadn't regretted his choice.

310

Radium's initial launch was of a heavy, expensive satellite phone, usable only in mid-ocean or on a mountaintop, functional only when unobstructed by buildings. It was a flop. There was no mass market. It was bought by elitist travelers, who complained about service, and by oceanographic or archeological organizations, mostly non-profits with no money, who begged for freebies. The multinational satellite project went bust in the later nineties. The internet became the darling of the telecom industry, and a giddy boom of subsea cable systems its happy offspring. For a time.

Cable systems proliferated until their numbers drove down prices below sustainable levels. Balky governments refused right of landing, forcing cable layers to go far out of their logical geographic way. Sharks chewed the cables' gummy covering. Fishermen snagged lines. Earthquakes shattered entire systems. Repair costs surfaced, far grimmer than the most daunting heavy seas. The dotcom bubble burst and demand plunged, briefly, deeper than the deepest ocean trench. Forced to diversify, telecom investors looked for other transmission mediums. And the satellite industry revived.

Radium, re-invented with a fresh crew of diverse global participants, was a key beneficiary of the new interest in sat systems, and Tyler had researched its origins, funding and business plans. He liked the prospects for sat growth worldwide. He respected the technology behind the marketing hype. He relished the idea of starting with an entirely new venture where he could take a lead in shaping the company's future. He could use his old contacts to make new deals in an environment where the problems were less complex than with terrestrial or subsea transport.

He'd looked at FLAG too, since he was still intrigued by the massive physical undertaking that was the subsea cable industry, but FLAG's work was completed and their only current activity was maintenance. He called Carly every few days, to hear her Cable & Wireless Marine adventure unfold, and her report of the daily travails on board helped convince him to look elsewhere. He'd thought of her as he edited the video of the cable ship, glad that her current journey wasn't as rocky as the one he'd chosen to depict. She'd been through enough heavy seas this year.

With Radium, he wouldn't have to travel as extensively as with GlobeAll; he'd have his in-region people in close touch with their markets and with him. What a relief not to feel as if he were the only one who knew enough! With a team as bright as those behind him, whose test questions he'd just fielded, he could comfortably delegate.

And he'd be free to live where he wanted, which he thought would probably be a split between New York and Colorado; he hadn't given up his condo after all, but he wanted to ensure plenty of spirit-restoring mountain time.

Radium's HQ was in Houston, since its long history with NASA made that a logical proximity, but Austin saw the company as virtual and wanted all the non-lab employees to work in the environment that made them most creative.

"And that ain't grey cubes in some industrial park," he'd told Tyler at their first interview, at the GTM in DC last month.

"Wait'll you see my workspace in Telluride," Tyler had answered then. He meant the cliffside where he watched the river continue its relentless drive downward and the different-drummer crows exercise their freedom. Water and birds: subsea cables and satellites. He'd since made that elegant connection.

"I remember *you*," he told Austin now in the conference room. "That visit to Chandler made an indelible impression."

"What grabbed you most?"

"The room where the old maps are kept, showing the location of every Cold War Russian missile silo, and the guide telling us about the room he'd seen in Radium's

Moscow office with a map of sixties silos in the United States."

Austin's smile brightened his lean, lined face. "Yeah. That's a mind-bender. We keep that map up for Chandler visitors, and the Russians get such a charge out of it."

"And the one in Moscow?"

"Ask Yuri," said Austin, tilting his head toward the Russian director, still standing with the rest on the other side of the room. "Or you can see for yourself when you take his Moscow tour."

Tyler nodded. He and Austin looked at each other for a moment longer. "Thank you," Tyler repeated.

"We have liftoff," Austin replied, grinning.

Forty-Five

CARLY HADN'T EXPECTED land to sway as wildly as the ship had swayed when she first boarded. But after two months at sea, the solidity under her feet was as alien as the ceaseless motion of water had been in the beginning. She grabbed the railing with her free hand as she made her way down the gangplank, and hefted her backpack to try to redistribute its weight with that of the duffle she dragged beside her.

"Steady on," said Jocko beside her. "You'll need time to get your land legs."

Jocko had befriended her the first day on board, when she'd barely kept her feet long enough to stop from caroming into the cable tank. He'd shown her every rope there was and how to tie them into knots. She now knew so much about the business that Mark Regan, who'd hired her for this stint, wanted her to join Cable & Wireless Marine permanently. The job would be based in New York City. She wasn't sure she was ready.

"Thanks for all your help, buddy."

"No worries. Anytime you want to join the cabletrash, mate, I've got yer back." He swung her suddenly into a tight embrace and smacked a wet kiss on her cheek. "Is he meeting you, then, I hope?"

"I think so," she told him, looking at the groups of people milling behind the security walls on the huge dock. She shaded her eyes with her hand but still could not see clearly. "I told him when we'd arrive."

"Keep in touch then Carly." Jocko bounded ahead, fleet-footed, his lanky frame overtaking the other straggling crew members.

Watching her feet, she fielded other farewells and good wishes.

"Still hungover Carly?" joked Bill. "Looking a little wobbly there." They'd had a party last night, ostensibly to say goodbye but also to drink as much as they could of the last of the booze. She'd been too wound up to drink much, however.

"Stay cool," she told him.

"No problem doing that here. It's fucking freezing."

The chill wind that greeted their docking got stronger as they disembarked onto the wide concrete pier platform. They straggled past the security barriers to the Port Authority enclave. Carly ducked her head down to toss her hair aside, but caught a mouthful of curls that obscured her view.

"Catherine Carly Emerald." A warm hand gently peeled the strands from her cheek. She looked up, startled. Tyler was right in front of her.

"I—I didn't know if you'd come." She'd hoped he would, so she could see him at last right away; and she'd hoped he wouldn't, so she could properly prepare to meet him at some designated civilized spot later.

"I wouldn't let you arrive alone." He took a step back and looked at her, half smiling, taking her in. He was bigger than she'd imagined, like a figure leaping, larger than life, from the pages of a well known book. But he didn't look somber or tired anymore. His longer hair flew around in the wind, a whipping black storm, and his blue eyes glittered as if reflecting the waves she'd been living on. He wore a bulky sweater and jeans just like her. He looked as if he'd never worn a suit in his life.

She didn't want to look away from him, but a snaking line around her ankles forced her to glance down. A mottled black-and-white animal wriggled at the end of the leash Tyler held.

315

"Oh, Ty!" She caressed its bent ear. "You finally got your dog!"

"Rocket the shelter mutt. I share him with my nephew Jerry, when I travel."

His expression told her he was also comparing what he'd learned of her during their long correspondence with how she appeared. She hoped she looked okay to him, but with little privacy or time on board she'd had to pretty much forego any beauty routine. She wasn't even wearing makeup! She squared her shoulders and smiled back.

"Thanks for being here, Tyler." She patted Rocket again.

"Welcome home."

She was younger-looking than he'd imagined. She'd lost her slick sophistication from their video meeting, but her silver-grey eyes shone out of her high-cheeked, sun-browned face with the same determination he'd seen in her then. She had freckles, he noticed, smattered across her nose and cheeks, lending friendliness to her angular features. Her hair was unbound now—long and wild. Her slow smile, the first he'd seen, erased the illusion of innocence as it shot into him.

She dropped her bags, stepped forward, and gave him a strong hug.

He was surprised, but he hugged her back, and patted her head. Her mass of hair was softer than it looked and he found his fingers threading in to feel the springy life in her curls. He felt his arm tightening around her shoulders, enjoying the way she felt, warm and vital, pressed close. Heat seized him. Then he pulled back a little, because he hadn't expected her—his good buddy Carly—to strike him this way in person. But when she kept holding tight to him, he realized that he might, perhaps, have been lacking imagination where she was concerned.

Seriously lacking imagination.

"It's so good to meet you," she mumbled into his chest, like an idiot. He laughed. When she finally let go of him, and looked up at his face, his eyes looked even brighter and his grin more familiar. She grinned too, watching him laugh for the first time.

"It's good to meet *you*. At last." He reached for her duffle. "Is this it?"

"Yep, can you believe it? I just wore the same stuff day in and day out."

"I believe it. Like camping."

"I always hated camping, before." She knew already that her life was now divided into before and after. She would never underestimate herself in the world of men again. "But after this experience I think I could land anyplace in the world and survive."

"So it was good."

"It was … a fantastic adventure. I'm so glad you pointed me toward this."

"I knew you'd be up to it." His glance struck sparks in her like a match to flint. "You look strong."

Their long strides matched as they maneuvered together, with Rocket, out of the crowds and into the parking structures across the street. The wind picked up and she shivered. "Jeez, Tyler, is it always this cold in New York in September?"

He wrapped his free arm around her, shooting electricity through her again.

"This is a cold front. But the car's right here." He stopped at a small Corolla and opened the door for her. "I'll drop you and Rocket at my place and then return this."

"You didn't have to rent a car just to pick me up. That's so nice of you."

"I didn't know how much stuff you'd have."

Their chatter did not diminish her awareness of him—submerged by the easiness they'd found in each other over the months of becoming friends—roaring to life the moment he'd touched her cheek, to peel her hair away, on the pier.

Keep cool, she warned herself, he doesn't have to know how you feel.

He drove through a landscape that was ugly, in its concrete bulk, to her eyes so used to seeing only the moving seascape. The highrises looked like toys to her, a fake Disney-esque backdrop, the way they always did when she came to New York. She wondered how it would have felt arriving here alone, navigating this overwhelming city. No more overwhelming, perhaps, than the ocean she'd just left; still, she was very glad he'd met her ship. And Rocket, panting in the back seat, was the perfect welcoming accompaniment.

"Are you sure it's okay for me to stay with you?" He'd made the offer weeks ago, casually, and she'd accepted without thinking twice. Now she wondered how she was going to be able to live with him for a week. Two month's proximity to a shipful of men had not prepared her for even a moment's proximity to this one. He was now one of her best friends—they'd spoken or e-mailed regularly since March—but he looked like an enticing stranger. Much too enticing to treat like some ordinary buddy.

"I'm sure." He looked over at her. "Are you?"

When she quickly looked out the window, away from him, he knew. He shouldn't have been surprised. She was as lively physically as she was virtually. And they'd shared serious stories and stupid laughs, were enthralled by the same things in their industry and worried by the same things in the world. And they'd flirted, a little, the way men and women who like each other do, and it had been easy between them. No, he shouldn't be surprised. But the rush of arousal he felt, looking at her, seeing her corresponding, was a shocking pleasure. He liked surprises like this.

"I liked hearing how it was going for you on board," he told her, keeping his tone casual and his eyes on the road.

"I liked seeing the satellite world through your eyes."

"Did you get your final report done?"

"No, we lost reception just as I was finishing, wouldn't you know."

"Lousy cable connection?" He had to tease her a little.

"It was Inmarsat," she teased back. Inmarsat was a satellite ship-to-shore service used by the cable barges.

"If it had been Radium ..."

"We'd have been paying for it for the next five years!"

They both laughed, the same laugh they'd shared before, yet with such a different texture, now that they were next to each other, they didn't know how to gracefully conclude. They laughed again then, perhaps with relief, when Rocket barked in response to their mirth.

"So, Carly, did you decide to accept their offer?"

She looked out the window again at the darkening city. "I told Regan I'm taking a little time off. I still need to figure out the house thing, you know, to sell or keep renting it out. And I don't know if I really want to live here in Manhattan."

"You're welcome to stay awhile and get the feel of it."

"But you're going to Houston again next week, Tyler, you don't want some stranger staying in your place."

"You're not a stranger." He pulled up in front of a highrise. They all looked alike to her, soaring structures like Chicago's which were so tall their tops could not be seen, but unlike Chicago they were thickly forested, making canyons of the streets. Their lights were all coming on. He put the car in park and came around to open her door.

He hoisted her duffle and tossed the keys to a uniformed doorman. *"German, gracias por guardar el coche unos minutos."*

"Your Spanish is pretty good. But I thought you had to return the *coche*."

"Later," he said. "I want to go up with you now."

Rocket climbed out and loped after as he led her through heavy glass doors to a marble lobby and a bank of brass elevators. "Nice place, Tyler," she chattered, keeping her excited mind off the implication of going up to his apartment with him. "You must be selling a lot of those sat phones."

When the doors enclosed them they fell silent, studying each other in the mirror, assessing what their suddenly enhanced friendship looked like, glancing down at Rocket, who looked back at each of them, unhelpful, tongue lolling.

"This is like meeting an internet date." Shut up, Carly, she told herself.

"How does that work?" His gaze was steady.

"It's usually kind of awkward."

"Meeting you doesn't feel awkward," he said. "Feels great." He grinned, unmistakably provocative, as he moved closer.

His warmth told her he was fully aware of the new vibe between them, so she could smile more easily, and follow him into the home he'd told her he made.

He didn't turn on the lights.

"Just look, Carly."

"Oh!"

He could see, in the illumination from the buildings, the way her face lit up in delight, erasing the faint signs of weary shyness he'd glimpsed on the dock and during their drive into the city. She clapped her hands together. "It's *beautiful!*"

"This is why I wanted to come up with you—to see how you liked it."

"I'm definitely re-thinking Manhattan!"

"I'm definitely re-thinking *you*, Carly," he told her, and even though he hadn't known he was going to say that it felt just right, as right as the way she turned to him, her smile a smashing mixture of allure and sass.

"It's about time, Tyler."

They moved in unison to stand side by side and look at the lights.

Author's Note

Private Lines grew out of a discussion I had in late 2002 with women friends, one of whom asked the group if, given the choice, we would come back in another life as a woman or as a man. Most of us, including me, said of course we'd rather be women since 'we're so much more flexible, more able to multi-task, more in touch with our emotions,' et cetera (we were mostly career-driven working mothers and feeling pretty self-important about our do-it-all stellar abilities in those days). However, one woman said she'd come back as a man—but only as a young, goodlooking, healthy, successful, 'mainstream' American man—because she'd like to see how it felt to be a 'master of the universe.' This was said somewhat tongue-in-cheek since at that time we'd also been discussing the nature of America's newly revived warrior status, prior to our invasion of Iraq in early 2003. The discussion got me thinking. I'd just completed *Praying for Rain* and was ready for the next idea.

A popular exercise has writers imagining a character very different from us: one we might not like. I always write stories I want to read, and I'd never seen one on global telecom or even, credibly, international trade. I decided to take on the challenge of writing about a seemingly cold American who's at the top of his game in global business.

Of course as soon as I envisioned my 'master of the universe' he was beset by problems, and I found myself getting a kick out of him, and following his and his cohorts' adventures and dilemmas with keen interest. I am sure that for all their trials, Tyler and Carly will have a 'HEA' as is said in the romance-writing biz (happily-ever-after).

Acknowledgements

My thanks to: My mother who gifted me with rich, deep, strange stories. My sister whose lively imagination peopled our childhood with fabulous characters and whose love of reading inspired mine. My husband who always encouraged me and who has fascinating stories of his own. My children who allowed my writing to eclipse any notion of home cooking (apologies to my hungry eldest son who always wants me to add scenes of people eating barbecue). My writing collective—Julia Buckley, Elizabeth Diskin, Cynthia Quam—who shepherded my work from the beginning, who are the best editors, publicists and critique partners any novelist could hope for, and without whom I would never have finished a manuscript. Wells Street Press, for getting me from manuscript to publication. Other writers and artists whose generosity has moved me: Karen Osborne, Sam Reaves, Kathi Baron, Jennifer Stevenson, Marilyn Brant, Erica O'Rourke (the latter three from the august ChicagoNorth Romance Writers of America). Colombia College Chicago for Story Workshop. The Oak Park Fabulous Women who had the discussion that was the genesis, for me, of PRIVATE LINES. A certain telecom company from whom I learned so much and wherein I made pals around the world. The courageous people of New York City. Mana. Cherished friends: aDOORables, NapaGals, YaYas, and Ann L to whom I declared my first novel 'finished' years ago after writing THE END and running to her house all aglow. Snaps to Mary H with whom I cooked up the idea to get serious about writing on a napkin in Canada. The Oak Park community, including The Lowell Society, whose care has nourished my family and me during my illness, especially Mary, Fran, Beth, Elizabeth, Kathy and Kathryn. Pulmonologist Benjamin Margolis and Sherrie Majdic, and oncologist Philip Bonomi and Irene Haapoja, whose care granted me time. Special thanks and love to Sue.

Playlist

I often listen to music while I write. Sometimes I choose from the era I'm writing about, from my own collection, but sometimes my favorite radio station provides inspiration which can creep in to inform the story ambiance (shout-out: WXRT Chicago).

Thanks to my sister whose great suggestions augmented the list! Thanks to my brother, who always shared the best music, and to my children who gave me the very great compliment of saying how much they liked my musical taste. Thanks to the artists whose brilliance so greatly illuminates my life.

MUSIC ON HOLD for GlobeAll London office (expanded list available on request to Wells Street Press):

I Wanna Hypnotize you Baby on the Telephone – White Stripes

Operator – Grateful Dead

Wichita Lineman – Glenn Campbell

Never There – Cake

Hanging on the Telephone – Blondie

Call Me – Blondie

Telephone Road – Steve Earle

867-5309 – Tommy Tutone

London Calling – The Clash

Hello Goodbye – The Beatles

I Just Called to say I Love You – Stevie Wonder

So Far Away from Me – Dire Straights

PRIVATE LINES Playlist:

I'm so Tired – The Beatles

Road to Joy – Bright Eyes

No Soy de Aqui – Facundo Cabral

Clocks – Coldplay

American Idiot – Green Day

See the Idiot Walk – Hives

Vivir Sin Aire – Mana

Rayando El Sol – Mana

De Pies a Cabeza – Mana

Se Me Olvido Otra Vez – Mana

Thumbin my Way back to Heaven – Pearl Jam

Taste – Phish

Theme from the Bottom – Phish

Daysleeper – REM

Seven Nation Army – White Stripes

About the Author

Award-winning writer Emma Gates was born in New York. She earned a BA in Spanish/Latin American Studies from Indiana University Bloomington, and an MBA with concentration in Arabic/Middle East Studies from Thunderbird. She worked for three years in Mexico and five in Saudi Arabia. She is an international business and telecoms specialist currently living near Chicago with her family and two inscrutable cats.

www.ingramcontent.com/pod-product-compliance
Lightning Source LLC
Chambersburg PA
CBHW030642260626
47157CB00007B/2450